Guts for Garters

Linda Regan

Published by Accent Press Ltd 2015

ISBN 9781783752683

This book is dedicated to my husband, Brian,
who will always be my hero.

Acknowledgements

Thank you so much to all at Accent Press, who have been sooo lovely to work with.

A million thank yous, and a few sweeping salutes, to my brilliant editor, Greg Rees, who with the eye of an eagle has helped make this book better.

Also to every single Metropolitan Police detective and C019 officer whose ear I have bent with a million questions. You have helped me keep my technical and procedural descriptions accurate, and I am so grateful for your precious time.

Finally – to all the gang members who spoke to me, and all the residents on high rises, and all the street girls who told me how it was. You made this book spring to life. THANK YOU.

One

The blade of the machete was sharp, and Alysha's aim was practiced and precise. It sliced into the skin between the inch-high letters – SLR – that adorned Burak Kaya's muscular forearm.

Kaya drew a sharp intake of breath as the pain hit. Dark blood erupted and snaked downward, onto and over his wrist, onto the dirt and grime of the concrete floor. He was tied up in a derelict garage, Alysha's three lieutenants standing guard. This was the Aviary Estate in South London, where killing came easy but respect was a lot harder to come by.

Alysha Achter had earned that respect. Fifteen years old, she was a queen, the leading light of the Alley Cats, the all-girl gang that owned this territory. She made the rules and no one was going to fuck with her or the residents of the Aviary any more. Those days were over. All the top Alley Cat soldiers had grown up on the estate, been abused as children, become under-age prostitutes or thieves or muggers. All had been users of hard drugs to get them through. Some had been young'uns and firearm-holders for the drug barons who fed their habits. Some had ended up in institutions, others in foster homes, where they were abused again.

Now things were going to be very different.

The Alley Cats ran the Aviary now. They made the 'corn', the money, on the estate. All drugs, weapons, and street trade around the estate belonged to them, and they had big plans for how the profits would be spent. They didn't want violence and fear; they wanted families, kids of their own, but they wanted a better life for them first. They wanted them to have opportunities, opportunities which weren't limited to selling drugs, prostitution, thieving, or prison. Right now there was nowhere for kids to be kids. The estate playgrounds were vandalised and burnt, the community hall closed down, the

1

shops boarded up. The council had refused grants to improve the estate, so the Alley Cats were doing it their way. They had recruited nearly forty soldiers and these girls now policed the estate. They sold drugs only to existing users, no kids, and they pimped their girls fairly and gave them good protection on the streets.

Despite the endemic problems it was a large and thriving estate, so a lot of nearby gangs were targeting it. The Alley Cats knew this; they also knew if they were to keep their territory safe so the residents could walk around without fear of being mugged, or worse, then they had to send the message that this was their territory. Anyone that dissed them, who broke their rules, had to pay.

Kaya squeezed his face taut and threw his head back as he waited for the agonizing pain to subside. When Tink and Lox had tied him up they'd used rope to bind his upper torso to the back of the chair, then secured each of his legs to a chair leg, leaving his groin accessible so that the girls could get a good aim if they decided to stamp his balls in. They had also stripped him of his sweatshirt, and snapped his silver chain, breaking its symbolic SLR charm into pieces and dropping them on the floor in front of him.

Leaving his torso bare for the punishment it would endure. Kaya was well known to the Alley Cats. He was a top lieutenant for Harisha Celik, his cousin, the leader of the South London Rulers gang from a neighbouring estate. The Alley Cats had recently discovered that Celik had taken over this garage on the Aviary. He had first had the owners' car stolen. It had belonged to a couple of pensioners from the Raven block, and Celik knew if he took their old Nissan, then they wouldn't bother using their lock-up. He had broken in, changed the lock, and now used the space to store an assignment of weapons smuggled in from Europe.

To add insult to injury, he hadn't even given the pensioners any corn for nicking their car.

Celik needed to learn a lesson, and the perfect opportunity arose when they caught Burak Kaya red-handed on their territory, together with Celik's girlfriend, Melek Yismaz. The two of them were sneaking into the lock-up with two cases of machetes and handguns.

The Alley Cats had pounced on the pair and had taken them hostage. Kaya was tied to the chair. They had tied Melek to the inside of the door to the lock-up to watch. It wasn't Alley Cat policy to hurt, or start a fight, with another girl, even if the girl was in an enemy gang, or a rival's baby mother. But heaven help any girl that picked a fight with an Alley Cat. A screwdriver, a cricket ball, even a knife in the gut: if that's what it took to protect their territory – and one another – they'd do it. All the girls had learned to fight well; they'd had to, to survive on the estate. All were prepared to fight to the death for the other girls, and the estate kids, and anyone else who was vulnerable or bullied on their territory. They saw it as their job. And today was a working day.

Melek was tall, leggy, and olive-skinned. Her long dark hair hung down her back, reaching way past her shapely bottom. The Alley Cats had tied her hands to the garage door handle, allowing her a good view of the torture they were bestowing on Kaya, knowing she would report it all back to Celik. Melek shivered as she watched. Cried her pretty dark eyes out.

None of this had been planned beforehand, it ,was just a lucky catch. Panther and Tink had been on Alley Cat business around the estate when they stumbled across Kaya and Melek sneaking into the lock-up. The girls had been photographing the estate playground. The ground was covered in dog shit, and huge rats scurried around, feasting on mouldering fast food containers that had been left to rot. The playground had been set fire to so many times that the estate kids had to look elsewhere for recreation, and the council did nothing to help.

The girls had their own plans for the neighbourhood. Panther was going to give self-defence lessons to the estate women as soon as the community hall was repaired and open. She'd already taught Lox how to fight properly, how to use her teeth or stiletto while locating her weapon – shank, broken bottle, or the .38 that top ACs now carried when they needed to. Lox wanted to make records, or be a DJ or an accountant, she hadn't fully decided yet. She'd gone to a top school and was good with numbers. She did all the book-keeping for the ACs and was in charge of the rebuilding plans the girls were making.

So Harisha Celik trespassing on the Aviary, taking a garage from pensioners, and using it to store weapons – and drugs which he intended to sell to children – had more than insulted Alysha. She had been waiting patiently for this opportunity and, now she had it, she was burning with anger. She dug the edge of the machete into the open skin on Kaya's arm. He screamed in pain.

'And he calls us pussies,' Panther laughed sarcastically, raising her eyes to heaven.

Panther bore many scars from past scraps. She was capable of taking anyone on and coming out on top. She was tall – over six feet though only sixteen – Jamaican, and angry. Her mother had died when she was four, and she and her older brother had been in and out of care until her uncle took her in when she was eight. He regularly abused Panther, and prostituted her to make money. When she was fourteen the brother she'd never really known died of gunshot wounds and her uncle had a stroke which confined him to a chair. It was left to Panther to look after him and to make enough money to provide for them both, which she had dutifully done by continuing to work as a prostitute, for Alysha's pimp. That was how they'd met. When Panther's uncle died a few months later, she moved into Alysha's top floor flat on Sparrow block of the Aviary and became an Alley Cat lieutenant. Her job in the gang was pimping the street girls, looking out for them and protecting them from vicious punters.

Alysha handed the machete to Lox, whose street name came from her waist-length hair – and her aptitude for picking any lock in record time.

Lox had run away from her alcoholic mother and a father who had sexually abused her from an early age. She started

4

working the streets, alone, to make enough corn to buy drugs, which was how Alysha had met her. The local pimp had found Lox on his territory, trying to get punters, and started to beat her for trespassing on his patch. Fourteen-year-old Alysha had been chosen as his 'mistress' a year earlier. He was a violent pervert, and Alysha hated him, but had chosen him over being alone, over screwing up to twelve punters a day for him. Alysha intervened on Lox's behalf and persuaded the pimp to take her on as one of his whores. Lox looked young for her age, so was hired out to well-paying and sadistic punters who liked hurting underage girls. But Lox was angry and always hurt back when they abused her. The pimp regularly beat her because she bit or kicked the punters when they burned her. Alysha liked her spirit, saw gang potential in her. When Alysha, single-handedly, took on the pimp and took over his territory, she immediately offered Lox a way out of prostitution. Alysha taught Lox about surviving on the Aviary, got her off drugs, and invited her to live in the Sparrow block flat. Lox did so well that Alysha made her a lieutenant in the Alley Cats. Lox repaid Alysha with fierce loyalty and Alysha adored her; they would lay down their lives for one another.

Lox took the machete from Alysha and brought it down across Burak Kaya's upper arm. Fresh blood erupted, and Kaya let out a huge wail in pain.

Panther was holding a large roll of black gaffer tape. She pulled a piece about six inches in length from the roll, bit it free, then moved to secure it across his mouth with her large hands, white and floral plastic nails digging into his skin. Kaya jerked his head away, puffed out his cheeks, and spat a mouthful of sticky phlegm at her. It landed on the dark brown skin of Panther's cleavage and the edge of her leopard-print T-shirt.

No sooner had it landed than Tink retaliated. She swiftly planted her pink Doc Martens boot hard into Burak Kaya's balls.

Tink, too, had grown up on the Aviary. Her mother was an

5

addict and Tink had no idea who her father was. As kids, Alysha and Tink were close friends, living from hand to mouth. Alysha's mother had died when she was less than a year old and she'd grown up with an alcoholic father who was never around. She and Tink used to stand together outside the fried chicken shop and beg for scraps. One day a dealer approached them and offered them money to run errands for him. They were about six years old and happily agreed to deliver drugs and hide guns for him when the feds were around. Eventually both girls went on the game, and then Alysha was taken in, at the age of thirteen, by the pimp, to be used for his sadistic pleasures alone. Once Alysha had taken control of the territory she took Tink, like Lox, out of the misery of prostitution. Tink had lived on Sparrow block on the Aviary, same as Alysha, but in the flat one floor down. Now, like Panther and Lox, she had moved in to Alysha's place. Officially, Alysha lived there with her father, but her father rarely came home. When he did Alysha gave him a wad of money, and he went off to drink himself stupid until the money ran out.

Melek Yismaz rattled the garage door she was tied to and shrieked as Tink kicked Kaya in the balls. 'No, please!' she screamed out. 'That's enough. No more.'

'Gag her,' Alysha told Panther without even glancing in Melek's direction, 'she's doing my head in.' Alysha then followed Tink and kicked Kaya in the balls, hard. As he grunted in pain, she leaned in towards him until her face was just inches from his. 'A message for your prick of a leader. Remind him this is Alley Cat territory. Tell 'im, if he thinks he can steal from my residents, an' do our kids with drugs, then this is just a taster. Got it?'

He didn't answer.

She kicked again.

'I said, 'ave ya got it?'

Kaya's dark eyebrows had lifted and his lips were squeezed together in pain. He still said nothing.

'Yes or no?' Alysha withdrew her boot and then kicked hard

6

several times.

He screwed up his face in pain but stayed silent.

'He's got a death wish,' Panther said. She was attempting to tape Melek's mouth. Melek was pulling her head away like a horse refusing a bit. 'Please don't, please!' she pleaded. 'I'll keep quiet, and I'll take your message to Harisha.'

'Fine,' Alysha said, barely turning her head more than a few inches to acknowledge her. 'You do that.' She leaned in to Burak again. 'See, your cunt of a leader thinks he can take this lock-up, and sell his gear round 'ere, so until you agree to tell him that we said no, then you are gonna keep getting hurt.'

He spat at her.

Lightning-quick, Alysha grabbed him by the hair and pulled his head back. She lifted her leg and dug the dirty stiletto heel of her boot into the cut on his forearm.

As he screamed out in pain, she twisted her heel further in.

'The SLR owe money to two old dears on my estate,' she told him. 'You tell 'im to pay, or face the consequences.'

Rivulets of perspiration were breaking out over his forehead, but Kaya stayed silent.

She took the machete from Lox and held it in the air. 'I'm waiting for an answer.'

He didn't move.

Alysha turned to Melek. 'You might wish your mouth was plastered up, 'cos your so-called lieutenant here's gonna keep getting hurt until he nods his fucking head.' She brought the machete swiftly down across of Kaya's hand. 'Oh dear, no wanking for you for a bit,' she said, as more blood flowed and he screamed in pain.

'Burak!' Melek half-screamed and half- pleaded. 'Nod your head, and let's leave Harisha to sort it.'

Burak shook his head. 'Not to these pussies,' he whispered in agony.

Tink stubbed her cigarette out angrily on his other hand. 'Just in case he's left-handed. Wanking's not nice, see.'

His face had turned red and perspiration was running down his temples. Tears also ran from the sides of both his eyes.

7

Melek was watched in horror.

'See, the thing here is,' Alysha said calmly lifting his head up again by his hair, and watching the tears spill from the side of his eyes and roll down his blood-stained neck as she kicked him continuously in the shin, 'that you ain't going nowhere until you nod your fucker of a head to say you'll take the message back to your poxy leader. Message is: you can't trespass on the Aviary, disrespect us, and get away with it. Got it?' She watched him for a second before raising her voice and shouting into his face, continuing to kick his shin, 'No one rips off our pensioners, you piece of shit. He pays them, in full, for the car he nicked, and a year's rent on this lock-up. All these weapons now belong to us.' She moved her face away from his. 'That's the message.' She raised her voice. 'Got it?'

'Yeah, he's got it.' Melek's voice, high-pitched and desperate.

Alysha didn't turn around. 'I'm talking to him,' she said, still kicking Kaya with her boot. 'An' 'e's *really* pissing me off.' She raised her voice and the machete. 'If you don't nod your head, this time it's your eye. An' you know I mean it!'

He nodded his head.

'Finally,' Alysha said turning to her girls, 'We are getting somewhere. She turned back to Kaya. 'First clever fing you done today.'

He was trying to keep his eyes on her, but he was slowly slipping into unconsciousness.

'He's said we agree,' Melek pleaded again. 'Now let him go.'

'We want your contact for these machetes and firearms, the one in Europe,' Alysha said. 'Give me that, and then I'll let you go.'

Nothing.

'Tell us, and you can go,' Panther said to him.

Kaya was silent.

Alysha shook her head and turned to the other girls. 'He's not answering again, how rude's that?' She stood up and pulled a small, but very sharp, knife from her boot. ''Fraid you 'ave to learn,' she said. 'It's fingers this time.'

'No. Don't! Stop!' Melek shrieked wiggling desperately trying to release herself from the door-handle she was tied to. 'He doesn't know who the contact is in Europe. Neither do I, or I'd definitely tell you. But if you let him go, I'll give you my word that I'll find out, from Harisha, and I'll tell you.'

'What, you think we was born yesterday?' Panther said to her. 'You think we're gonna believe that you'll do just that, fuck Harisha's brains out believing he'll tell you, and then you'll come running and tell us.'

'I swear I will.'

Alysha turned to her. 'Listen, darling, you're more stupid than I thought. Harisha ain't gonna tell you nothing; he ain't even faithful to you. If his lieutenant,' she kicked Kaya's boot, 'really don't know, then Harisha ain't gonna tell no one, 'specially not a skank he's honking. Which, incidentally, is all you are. Once 'e's got you up the duff, he'll cast you aside. That's the way it is with him.'

'I know where he keeps his other weapons,' Melek said after a beat.

Alysha and the girls looked at each other. Alysha turned to Burak Kaya. He had gone a very pale colour. She turned back to Melek.

'Tell, now. You need to take him away and look after him.'

'You'll let us go if I tell you?' Melek asked.

Alysha clicked her tongue against her teeth angrily. 'I just said, didn't I?'

'They're in the old war tunnel,' Melek said, turning to look at Burak. He showed no reaction.

'Where's the war tunnel?' Lox asked her.

'It's near Lambeth Bridge, in Keepers Street,' Melek continued. 'There's a big manhole by the steps to the river. Just by that is another drain, a bigger one. It's at the base of the steps. He keeps a padlock on it. If you can undo the padlock, there's a rope just inside the grille, on the left, it's fixed to the inside of the tunnel. You tie that around yourself and then you have to lower yourself down and into the tunnel. It's narrow and it's a long drop, but there are firearms and crates of machetes and drugs there. He sells from there. It's safe, but hard to get in and out of.'

'Where is the key to the padlock?' Alysha asked her.

'Harisha has it. He keeps it in his flat somewhere.'

'I can pick it,' Lox said.

Alysha nodded. 'Yeah, you can pick anything, mate.'

'Except a decent bloke,' Tink teased.

'Let him loose,' Alysha said to Panther.

She turned back to Melek and looked at her. 'Your fella is the lowest of the low, don't you know that? He's robbing old pensioners, and filling eight-year-olds with crack.'

'And you are so much better, I suppose,' Melek spat back. 'If I don't get Burak to hospital, he's gonna die.'

'We ain't cut any arteries,' Alysha told her. 'An' we only sell drugs to addicts, not to kids. An' we look after the elderly on this estate, and help the addicts when they want it. So don't you give me all your fucking lip.' She held Melek's angry eyes, then she said evenly, 'Lower than your man ain't born, you must know that. If you get fed up being pushed about, and want proper loyalty, we're recruiting soldiers. But you'd have to pass a lot of tests, cos you're well fucked up with that lot, an' you're the loser, believe me. So, till we're sure of a soldier, they stay the enemy, got it?'

'Fuck off.'

'Get them out of here,' Alysha said to Panther.

Albert Wilkins was standing at the side of the window watching the goings on the estate grounds below his first floor flat. He was a nervy man in his early seventies, thin and small, with fine, thinning hair and astute, but frightened, blue eyes. He was holding back the frayed pink and yellow floral-patterned curtain that covered their lounge window. His fingers, nails bitten down to the quick, twitched nervously as he watched Melek Yismaz with Burak Kaya's arm draped around her shoulders, practically dragging him across the estate grounds.

'Someone out there looks as if he's half dead,' he shouted to his wife. 'He's bleeding like a pig in an abattoir. There's a girl with him. Come and look, Vera! It looks as if she's dragging him.'

'None of our business,' came the reply. 'Less we see, less we know.' Vera walked into the room and saw Albert looking out of the window. 'Get away from there before you're seen! Get away, d'you hear? If someone's dead, we don't want to get involved.'

'They can't see me.'

'They can, and they know who lives here.' She raised her voice yet again. 'Let the curtain go and move away from the window, will you, or they'll come after us again.'

Albert ignored her. He pulled glasses from the pocket of his home-knitted cardigan, and pushed them on and moved in closer to the window.

'I've seen them before. I know who that boy is.'

Vera hurried back into the kitchen.

'It's one of them Turkish boys,' he shouted to her. 'I don't know which one, but it's one of the ones that broke all your eggs when they tripped you up and you tore all your tights and grazed your legs. You know, when they stole your pension money and your keys.'

'For Christ's sake, Al! Less we know, the better. Who knows what any of them are capable of now? The police never sort anything and we can't stand up for ourselves.' Her voice cracked. 'Al, please, leave the curtain be. They've got the car, just leave it be.'

'He's being dragged, or half carried, by that dark girl. And that's blood, or I'm an elephant. It's leaking all over the ground.'

There was a rattle of china teacups, but Vera didn't answer.

Two

14:00 Monday

Georgia Johnson enjoyed the challenges of being a DI in South London. The murder department especially was always busy. In this area of London, gang warfare was fast accelerating, and shootings and stabbings over territory were becoming everyday occurrences. When a gang leader was sent down by the police, or taken out by a rival, another gang usually emerged, and the turf, the territory, was taken over. Often, some of the previous gang would reunite and fight for their old turf, which usually resulted in a lot of bloodshed.

Being black as well as female, in a force like the Met, still meant you had to work harder to prove your worth, despite all the race and gender equality pamphlets that were handed out at regular intervals within the department. Georgia ignored the jokes and remarks made at her expense, despite knowing she could pull any of those responsible into a disciplinary, but she chose to let the discrimination wash over her head. She'd joined the force to catch criminals, and she was doing well. She was quite young, at just over thirty, to have made DI, but her sights were set much higher. Murder investigations were all-consuming and usually exhausting, but the feeling of euphoria when her team had tracked and caught a killer, and she stood in court watching the families of the victims seeing justice done for their loved ones, knowing their own lives could move on because of it, was worth everything she had been through to catch that killer.

Georgia was strong and independent. Her Caribbean mother and her Indian father were both doctors, and her four siblings had followed suit; only her sister had also moved a little towards the world of crime, becoming a forensic biologist. Georgia was the youngest of the children. At one time she'd aspired to be a physiotherapist, but had changed her mind at fifteen, after the winter's night when she walked home, at nine o'clock, across Clapham Common, disobeying her parents' rule to never walk there alone in the dark. That fateful night changed her life.

The man that raped her could still be alive and free. Georgia had no idea who he was, although she would never forget his voice, or the words he spoke after he brutally stole her virginity. She had been too afraid of the consequences to ever tell anyone what had happened that night. Even all these years later she never spoke of it. There was no point, she thought. No evidence now. But the mental scars had never healed; and even all these years later, if she closed her eyes, she could still hear that voice, and feel her heart beating in terror as the memory of her knickers being torn from her young body jumped back into her brain. Then the reek of stale tobacco mixed with garlic would engulf her nostrils and the ghastly sensation of his foul tongue pushing into her mouth and his penis into her virgin body, as he grunted and bounced like a wild animal, clamping his hand over her mouth while his sweaty unshaven cheek rubbed back and forth over her breast. After he was done, his heavy fingers pinched into her cheeks and he spoke those words that were implanted in her mind: *I will kill you, if you tell. I will know, and I will come after you, and then I will really hurt you.*

He took her white knickers as a souvenir, pulling what was left of them from between her bare, bruised, and bleeding thighs and pushing them into his pocket, leaving her to get up from the filthy ground and limp home, bruised and terrified. Even now, if a prisoner had grubby nails, or a heavy buckle on the belt of his jeans, or smelled of stale tobacco, she had to go to the loo and wash her hands continually until the memory once again left her mind. Often just the sight of dust or dirt would start her hand-washing ritual. Working in the murder division meant she was constantly called out to dirty locations, derelict murder sites or the crime-ridden high-rise estates where gang stabbings and shootings were far too frequent. She had learned to deal with it. She kept disinfectant hand gel with her mobile phone, and never went out without either.

Having to constantly wash her hands she felt was a small price to pay for keeping people safe and London rid of criminals. Sometimes she resented being born a woman. But if she was a man, could she really do more? She didn't think so, even if there were some in her department who would disagree. She trained constantly and kept herself in top condition, and could outrun any of the men in her squad. And she was afraid of no one. If someone broke the law, she went after them, and if their crime involved rape, then she was like a greyhound after the hare: on their trail, chasing hard. She'd never let up, not until the perpetrator was caught and charged.

Despite the terrifying ordeal of the rape, Georgia hadn't shut herself off from sexual relationships. For her, intercourse was like a good massage, It helped her to focus, and unwind, particularly on demanding and difficult cases, but it could only happen in her own bed; she would never sleep in anyone else's. And she chose her partners very carefully, never allowing any of them to get too close, though she kept the same ones. Currently there were three in her life, all very good friends as well as lovers, and chosen because she knew they wouldn't get clingy or emotionally needy.

Sergeant Stephanie Green, Georgia's close friend and confidante, always said Georgia didn't get laid often enough, but then Stephanie had to bed at least one new man every week. Stephanie collected sexual conquests, she wanted as many as she could have, but then she tired of them, often after one date. Georgia teased her about it, telling her there was Italian blood in her genes. Nothing could be further from the truth; both of Stephanie's parents were from Stepney in the East End, part of long-established families. Their daughter's name was a way of keeping in touch with their roots when they moved south of the river and started a family.

Stephanie's nickname in the incident room was 'the tube', as it was a well-known fact that Stepney Green tube station was easily accessible to most of London. Stephanie thought the nickname both funny and complimentary; nothing like that bothered her, she was very much one of the lads, even though she had been intimate with most of them. For Stephanie, once a conquest was bedded she was bored and off looking for her next, although she always kept them as friends – something Georgia found of great value, as Stephanie had bedded at least one man from each of the many departments in the Met, from technical investigation through to pathology and the firearms unit. If Georgia needed help on any enquiry, then Stephanie usually had a special friend somewhere who could be persuaded to assist or get a job done quicker.

Georgia put Stephanie's appetites down to the suffocating marriage she had freed herself from. She had married young, to a man she referred to as her 'waste of space', though he had given her two beautiful children. Her daughter Lucy was planning to join the Met after university; she had already done work experience there and a job was waiting for her, providing she got a good degree. Stephanie was thrilled and flattered that her daughter was following her into the force. Georgia was, too; secretly, she'd always wanted a daughter, and had become close to Lucy. Stephanie's son, Ben, had just turned seventeen and was almost always out, leaving Stephanie free to run her own life and invite who she wanted into her bed.

Georgia was going from one case to another, and more often than not two or three murders at the same time these days. As far as a DI's job went, once on a case, you worked on it until it was solved. You worked flat out for results. That didn't bother Georgia, she was a workaholic. What did bother her though, bothered her quite a lot, was the fact that Detective Inspector Alison Grainger was moving back into the murder department.

Alison Grainger had been away on compassionate leave after a close friend and work associate had been killed on duty. When she first came back to work, she had taken a position in the Sapphire Unit – the South London rape unit – where she had been for a while. Recently, she'd put in for a transfer back to murder, saying she was ready, and now wanted to work in her old department again.

Georgia knew Alison, but not well. She had bumped into her

a few days ago, on Alison's first day back in the murder department, and thought her withdrawn, nervy, and very pale-looking. Georgia wasn't convinced she was ready to come back and track down murderers but had kept those thoughts to herself. It wasn't her place to make judgements, and it was also difficult inasmuch as DI Alison Grainger was the girlfriend of the chief, DCI Paul Banham. Everything that was said and done on cases and within the department, when Alison was involved, would now go straight back to Banham. Most things did anyway, work-wise, but Georgia had always been careful to keep Stephanie Green's private life away from his ears, feeling that it was in the sergeant's best interests. Georgia didn't want the DCI thinking that one of his sergeants spent too much time indulging her enormous sexual appetite or distracting any of the team from their work. The truth was, there was no better detective than Sergeant Green in the whole of the department. Stephanie had a nose for it, she was streetwise, uncannily sharp, and highly intelligent. The only reason she hadn't gone further up the career ladder was by choice: she'd wanted to share her time between her children and her job.

Georgia trusted Stephanie with her life. She was also very aware that Stephanie needed protecting from herself at times, so Georgia always played down the rumours about her, feeling it was in the best interests of the department. However, with Alison Grainger back, and in the DCI's pocket, things could get complicated. Or, worse still, difficult.

Today, Georgia had told herself, she wasn't going to think about work. She was having a much-needed day off. She was officially on HAT duty, the Met's term for being on standby, just in case a murder happened on their patch that couldn't be covered by a team on duty; if so, she would be called out. But with Alison Grainger newly back, and obviously raring to go, Georgia was confident that her day was her own.

She had chosen to stay at home and clean her flat, *really* clean her flat. She had a large bucket of sugar-soap mixed with warm water next to her where she stood, on the top step of a high ladder. Soapy water was running down her arms and into her black plastic household gloves as she manoeuvred a mop sponge on the end of the long wooden handle. A flowered plastic shower cap covered her wiry black hair. She glanced up at her work. The ceiling looked like a zig-zagged pedestrian crossing; from the angle she was working there were certain areas the mop wouldn't reach. She made her way hastily down the ladder, re-positioning it, so the unwashed part of the ceiling was within her reach. She climbed the ladder again, positioned the mop, and started to clean frantically, just as the pocket of her denim dungarees started vibrating, followed by a loud rendition of 'Onward, Christian Soldiers'. Her phone was telling her the HAT team had found a body and her presence was required urgently.

Stephanie Green was also on HAT standby, but had taken herself off on a mechanics' course – another step towards fulfilling her secret dream to build her own motorbike.

She was leaning over the engine of a car. Her voluptuous size sixteen bottom had wiggled its way to the front of the mainly male group taking the one-day course. She more than knew her way around the engine of a car, and the tutor had assigned her the task of tracking down the cause of the engine's failure to start. She had got as far as the cellanoid. She had taken it out from the steering column, shown the other participants what she was doing, and was about to take it to pieces, when her phone burst into a rendition of the Bee Gees' 'Stayin' Alive' – the tune she had uploaded to alert her when the HAT team were calling.

As her grease-covered hands speedily pulled her phone from her pocket she caught sight of her face in the wing mirror. Engine grease streaked her nose, cheeks, and chin. Her lank, mousy copper-streaked hair had also absorbed some and, to add insult to injury, she reeked of engine oil. But the HAT team were calling and she had to go; there was no time to go home and change. Not a fitting scenario for a sergeant who was trying to bed her DCI. She made her apologies and hurried out of the garage where the course had been taking place.

As she hurried to her car and settled behind the wheel, she pulled her hair back from her face, securing it with a rubber band and leaving yet more greasy marks. She backed her car out of the car park, congratulating herself on having handed her personal card to her tutor over lunch, and not waited until the end of the day. He was very eligible, and she wanted the opportunity to bed him too.

Max Pettifer wasn't a popular man. His greying hair was combed into a whiff of a quiff on top of his head, in a failed attempt to hide the fact that he was both balding and coming up to retirement age. He had grey eyes, a reddish tinge around his nose, and a black sense of humour. Pettifer was still head of Forensics, but only working part-time these days as he fast headed towards his pension. Today he was working, covering for the pretty and popular Phoebe Aston, who was now away for the second time on maternity leave.

Georgia took a deep breath when she saw him. Working as a pathologist one could excuse dark jokes at the expense of the victim, but Max's cynicism and the dull drollery with which he delivered his so-called funnies was never enough to bag a smile from any of the murder team. It was difficult to know who disliked him the most, Georgia or DCI Banham – both had good reason. He was the sort of man who went to all lengths to be unhelpful. He never made any assumption or speculation, and would never even give them a hint of what they might expect to hear about how the victim was murdered, until confirmation from the over-worked and always behind schedule forensic laboratory was official.

Georgia often felt the killer could have gone to the other side of the world, had a dozen plastic surgery operations, even undertaken a complete sex change by the time Max got around to delivering any helpful information. The only thing Georgia could think of to be thankful for, in the case of Max Pettifer, was that Stephanie Green had never fancied jumping his bones.

The cadaver was curled in a foetal position over a pool of congealed blood. His arms were covered in stab wounds. The wall behind him was patterned in blood. It looked as if the boy had leaned against the wall and then slid down as he tried, and failed, to stem the blood from his many cuts.

'A stabbing?' Georgia asked, lifting her white forensic mouth mask to allow herself the freedom to speak, and tentatively moving as near to the scene as she dared without hindering the blue-overalled forensic officers who were busily working around scene.

Max shrugged in his usual non-committal way. Already he was an irritant. Georgia could only hope that Phoebe Aston wouldn't get too content with motherhood; the murder department missed her.

She turned to the exhibits officer. 'Any footprints?'

The exhibit officer, holding a video camera on a lead around his neck, shook his head. 'Nothing at all, ma'am,' he said. 'Not that I can see.'

Georgia looked up to see Stephanie hurrying along the estate path, pulling the bluebell-coloured Forensics suit up and around her large body as she hurried. Her hair was already half out of the obligatory plastic cap detectives had to wear at the scene of a crime, and the white mouth-mask was hanging around her neck.

'Glad I've had lunch,' she said looking down at the pool of blood, then flicking a piss-taking smile at Max, and adding, 'And I wasn't referring to you, darling.' She stretched one side of her mouth downward, and winked at Georgia to share her disappointment at seeing Max at the scene. Georgia was staring at the streaks of black grease jotted over Stephanie's face, but decided not to comment. She discreetly tapped her pocket, checking, yet again, that she had her hand-gel with her.

'I guess we half expected this, didn't we?' Stephanie said letting out a noisy sigh. 'Gang battles for custody of the Aviary Estate territory. No one actually runs it right now that we know of.'

'This isn't quite Aviary territory though,' Georgia reminded her. 'It's just on the edge.'

'Battles starting over the territory control then,' Stephanie suggested.

'South London Rulers?' Georgia said, leaning in and pointing to the blood-stained 'SLR' tattooed on his forearm. 'And he certainly looks Turkish.' She then lowered her voice to Stephanie, 'My informant lives on the Aviary. Let's pay her a visit.'

Stephanie leaned over the cadaver, examining it carefully. 'His finger has a very deep cut and there are cigarette-shaped burns on the back of his hands.'

'Not what killed him,' Max said abruptly.

'He was tortured then,' Stephanie said.

'Or a punishment,' Georgia added.

'Do we have any identification? She asked the forensic officer who had been kneeling at the back of the body.

'Nothing in any pockets,' he replied.

'And robbed too,' Georgia said. She was about to tell them to take DNA and run it through the file, when she heard Banham calling to her. He was at the cordon signing the book. It was common knowledge that Banham wasn't good around corpses, especially bloodied ones. He'd been known to throw up at many a murder scene, giving Max Pettifer fuel for his 'jokes'. Banham was with Alison Grainger, both were dressed in the bluebell forensic suits as they headed down the path. Georgia noticed Stephanie's expression.

'I think you've missed your chance with the DCI,' Georgia whispered to her. 'Looks like DI Grainger will be shadowing us on this one.'

Alison Grainger was tall and skinny with extremely long legs. With her pale skin and reddish-brown hair there was possibly Celtic blood in her genes, and her reputed fiery temper would back that up. Right now her hair was furled into a blue plastic cap, accentuating her wide-set, grey-green eyes, which currently bore an apprehensive gaze.

'You all know DI Grainger,' Banham said as he approached. 'I'm delighted to say she's back with us in Murder after her time in Sapphire Unit.'

Max Pettifer looked up. 'I heard you hadn't the belly for this

21

lark anymore,' he said, catching Banham's angry glare but ignoring it. 'Well it's not a bad'un for your first one back. No maggots or decay, it's fresh and doesn't stink the place out.'

'How specific can you be for time of death?' Georgia asked him, quickly changing the subject. 'What would you say, about three hours ago?'

Max shrugged. 'Perhaps.'

'Someone must have seen something,' Stephanie said looking up and around at the tower blocks that surrounded them. As was usual around the estate when someone was murdered, all the residents had crowded onto their balconies for a good look, but if questioned by the police, no one ever claimed to know or have seen anything.

'Who phoned it in?' Banham asked.

'Anonymous, of course,' the exhibits officer told him.

'It's only three o'clock now,' Georgia said looking up at the residents who were leaning over their walkways looking down at the proceedings. 'Lots of people would have been coming and going, this is one of the main entrances to the whole estate.'

'I'll instruct uniform to start the door-to-door,' Stephanie said hurrying off to find the police sergeant in charge.

'I'll come with you,' Banham said hurrying after her.

Georgia looked at Alison. Both knew he was going round the corner to throw up. Neither said a word.

Banham was back within minutes, wiping his mouth with his handkerchief. He had told Georgia once, in confidence, about the murder of his first wife, how he had come home and found her and their eleven-month-old baby axed to death. Georgia had her own skeletons. She more than understood his.

Banham stood next to Georgia and lowered his voice. 'I'm putting Alison with you on this one,' he said to her. 'You're all right with that, aren't you?'

'Yes, guv, totally,' she said. 'I still get Sergeant Green though, don't I?'

'Of course.' He turned to check that Alison wasn't in hearing distance. She wasn't, she was talking to some of the forensic team a little way away from where they stood. 'She's been away a while, and she'll need a close eye kept on her. I'd like you to report all back to me.'

Georgia didn't answer.

'She'll need to be updated on all that's happened around this area,' he said. 'You have strong contacts down here, and a good informant, so I'm putting all this in your hands.'

'That's fine, guv.'

'I'll want to be kept in the loop with everything.'

'Guv.'

'We have to remember she lost one of her closest friends in the line of duty, and it'll be a case now of taking everything one step at a time.'

'With respect, sir, I'm a detective, not a nanny.'

Banham's blue eyes bored into her. 'You've been a very good influence on that Alysha Achter. You've done a lot to get her back on her feet and that hasn't gone unnoticed,' he said. 'Some might say that would be a social worker's job. Alysha was a criminal, Alison is one of us.'

Georgia swallowed her anger. 'Alysha Achter is my informant,' she said evenly. 'She became a criminal out of desperation. I helped her because she was alone and underage, and now she pays us back by giving us information that leads to the prosecution of criminals.'

'She gives nothing. We pay her well for it,' Banham reminded Georgia.

'This estate has the highest crime figures in the whole of Greater London. It took work to get Alysha on side. In case you hadn't noticed, no one else around here gives us the time of day.'

'I have noticed,' he said curtly. 'And again I say, all credit to you.' He kept his eyes on her for a silent moment then he said. 'Please keep a close eye on DI Grainger and report everything back to me, I'll consider it a favour. I'll see you at the briefing. Don't be late.'

As he turned to go, she quickly asked, 'Sir? I am Senior Investigating Officer on this case, I presume?'

It took a few seconds before he answered. 'No. Alison

Grainger is the more experienced officer out of the two of you, but you have the contacts and knowledge of this estate, so I'm making you joint SIOs.' Again his eyes bored into her.

She knew arguing the point was futile. The man was in love with DI Grainger, so she nodded. 'Guv.'

Banham turned and walked away.

Max Pettifer looked up from his place of kneeling beside the cadaver. 'You can understand why people want to kill sometimes, can't you?' he said with a chuckle.

Three

Nearly seventy South London Rulers were standing in a run-down garage. It was situated on their territory, but within yards of the Aviary. Harisha Celik had put out the call and all had obeyed.

A lot of the gang members were Turkish, many of them related. Trent and Bilaboo, two of the gang's high-ranking lieutenants, were also first cousins of Harisha, as Burak Kaya had been; all sharing the same olive skin, black hair, dark, angry eyes, and fiery tempers. There were also a dozen Chinese boys in the gang, a few Pakistanis, a few mixed-race boys, and many white soldiers. Harisha Celik's ruthless reputation went before him. He was known to make big money, smuggling drugs and arms from Europe, and everyone wanted to be part of that powerful empire.

He had slyly teamed up with the Chinese boys, the ones with strong European contacts, for the sole purpose of furthering his connections with machete and samurai dealers in Europe, deciding it was cleverer to work with the Chinese, rather than against them, for now. The Chinese were tough fighters, they knew how to use samurai swords and machetes and could teach his soldiers a lot. Harisha wanted that knowledge, and their contacts. Up until recently the SLR had survived by using knives and guns, but since they had machetes at their disposal their street cred had upped. Harisha saw the interest from other street gangs and wanted to be the one to make money from importing them. He knew the Chinese had the connections, but not the nous, so he befriended them; he intended to drop the bastards when he had got all he could from them. The Chinese and Vietnamese were also experts at growing cannabis. Harisha intended building a supply of cannabis factories, so he had no intention of falling out with them, yet. Cheap grass was a good way of pulling in youngsters and setting them on the road to heroin addiction, the brown or the food as it was known on the streets, which made him big money.

He had drawn the young Chinese boys into his gang by telling them they were now family to him. Their own families were all busy working twenty hours a day serving pork balls in tiny takeaway joints, so the boys had nothing to do but hang around the streets. Harisha offered them protection around the south of London, told them there was more to life, that his gang would show them how to make big money. When their usefulness ran out, they'd end up at the bottom of the Thames, but for now he welcomed them. In truth he didn't give a shit for any of his gang, except his blood cousins Bilaboo and Trent, and Burak Kaya, who he had just been told had been found murdered.

He stood in the lock-up, facing his crew, looking his usual cool self in dark glasses and a black leather jacket opened to display a white T-shirt tucked into tight jeans. The jeans were decorated with a glittering imitation diamond-studded belt to match the diamond he wore in his left ear. His face, like his body, was thin. He wore two thick gold chains around his neck and a large diamond signet ring on his little finger.

Melek Yismaz stood at his side, shivering with shock and crying loudly. Her noise was annoying Harisha, who up until now had found her highly desirable. Her perfect figure, long legs, and long dark hair, peroxide intermittently streaked through it, drove him mad with lust. In the past he had shared his girls with his cousins, to keep the interest going for himself, but not Melek, he was jealous and possessive with her, and after her gang-bang initiation into the SLR he had allowed no one near her. Right now, though, as she stood by his side wailing, his attraction was fading fast.

Every time he asked her to tell the crew exactly what had happened that morning, what had led to Burak being shanked and murdered, she was unable to answer through her wailing. This was embarrassing him. The girl should show him respect.

If he told her to do something she should fucking do it. Enough was enough. He curled his ring-embellished fingers into a fist and quickly punched her, hard, three times, on the side of the head.

Her head hit the concrete wall behind her, and she immediately went silent. It had done the trick. He snaked his arm around her neck and pulled her into him and kissed her gently on the cheek.

'Good girl,' he said. 'Stop crying.'

He turned back to his gang. 'Burak is murdered. Murdered by those skanky Alley Cat Crew bitches,' he shouted angrily. 'They have started a war, and we are going to make them wish they never had. Death is too good for what they have done to our lieutenant.' He raised his voice. 'If they think they can steal our machetes.' He looked at the Chinese boys, who were holding their long sharp knives up in support. 'Our boys risked everything to bring in them in from Europe. They've been stolen along with thousands of pounds of brown.' He became louder and angrier. 'Those filthy whores have killed Burak, and taken our weapons and drugs.'

All the crew were now waving weapons and verbalising their agreement and anger. Harisha went even louder.

'And now those bitches think they can deal, on my patch, and say it is theirs!'

Melek started sobbing again. He glanced quickly and irritably at Melek and then brought his attention back to addressing his gang. 'I want those whores brought here to me, alive. We will roast them on a spit like the pigs they are, slowly. They will burn, for revenge for our Burak.'

As his crew cheered, he snaked his arm around Melek's neck, and pulled her in to him and stroked her hair.

'Why you cry so much, my darling,' he said to her. 'You are safe now, my angel.' He kissed the top of her head softly, and whispered through gritted teeth, 'Shut up.'

Melek looked at him, her make-up had run down her cheeks and stained her face. 'I thought they were going to hurt me too,' she told him. 'I begged them to stop, but they didn't. I tried to

27

get him away and back here, but he died in my arms. I had to leave him when I ran to find you,' she cried again.

He lifted his sunglasses and stared at her. Up until now he had been mesmerised by her mean eyes, her long legs, and the long flowing hair that tumbled down her back to her arse. He liked that she would do everything he asked her to, sexually.

He pulled his arm away from her neck and turned her chin so she faced him. When he saw the fear in her wet and frightened eyes he felt his cock harden and wanted to fuck her right there and then.

'You are my woman, no one would dare hurt you,' he said to her. 'I will look after you.' She sniffed, and fluttered her wet lashes.

He turned back to his soldiers. 'Fucking pussies,' he spat. 'They have terrified my woman and killed my lieutenant.' He took an angry breath. 'One by one they will die, a slow and painful death.'

The soldiers raised knives and weapons. Some pulled their dark blue SLR bandanas up over their faces as they cheered in agreement.

Harisha opened the box behind him and took a large block of cocaine from it, holding it up so all could see it. 'And rewards for whoever brings them in.' He turned back to Melek. 'Did they use names to each other?'

She looked a little muddled, as she tried to think.

'Describe them. How many?' he pushed.

'Four.'

'One was Alysha Achter, Alley Cat cunt herself, right?

'Right,' she nodded.

'And the others?'

As Melek described the tall, brown-skinned, clumsy, loud-mouthed lieutenant, one of the soldiers shouted, '*Panther!*' Then '*Tink!*' as she talked about the skinny runt with the pink hair and heavy pink boots. 'Long brown hair with green streaks and a green nose stud and matching nails': '*Lox!*'.

Harisha put the coke back in its box and lifted his own perfectly manicured hands, placing them against the air in front

28

of him as a sign of a fait accomplice. 'Burak will be avenged,' he said. 'Next bit of business is the feds. There's a tent been put up where Burak died. It is guarded by feds. They've taken Burak's body, and they'll be belling his family.' He looked all around at his gang, taking them all in, but his eyes rested on the Chinese boys. 'They will be bothering us soon. No one says nothing. You say you've never heard of him.' He turned to Bilaboo and Trent. 'Except us. We say he was family, but we never hung out much with him, we don't know nothing of his tribe.'

The cousins nodded.

Harisha then turned to Melek. 'I'm gonna buy you a nice big diamond for those pretty hands of yours, 'cos you are going to do just fine when those feds catch up with you, aren't you?'

She nodded, and then sniffed.

'No matter what they say, and how much they push you, you never saw no one, you don't know nothing, and that's all you say, ain't it, my angel?'

Melek lifted her pretty hands and wiped the snot from her running nose. 'Yeah,' she assured him. 'I'll say that. I won't say nothing else.'

He smiled and raised his voice, his mean dark eyes narrowing. 'Cos we are going to do the punishing, ain't we?' he said to his soldiers. 'We are gonna tear their pussy-arsed heads from their bodies and cut them into slivers of pig food. We are going to do that for Burak.'

The noise of the gang high-fiving their retaliation for their fellow soldier's death rung around the garage. One by one blue bandanas and hoods were pulled up as they turned to leave.

'I want them dragged in here,' Harisha shouted as they were all leaving. 'No one kills them, right? They'll learn who runs the fucking turf on the Aviary Estate, and that no one messes wiv us.'

Hooded heads were nodding their agreement as they made their way from their hideout.

'And watch out!' he shouted after them. 'The feds are sniffing.'

When all the crew had left Harisha moved to Melek. He had a hard-on that he had no intention of suppressing. He removed his sunglasses and stared into her frightened eyes. She was watching him back.

His body was now only inches from hers, and the wall was behind her. He could feel the fear in her breath. That was making him harder. He stroked her tiny waist and then moved his hand and tugged down the zip of her jeans. As he felt her body tense he knew he had to get inside her, he could hardly contain himself. He stroked her hair and then her face, very tenderly, and then he tugged her jeans down to her ankles.

'Step,' he commanded. His fingers now under her white lace G-string

She obeyed.

'Turn round and get on your knees,' he told her.

He allowed himself one second to stare at her perfect bottom with the white lace snaking between her buttocks.

'Open your legs,' he commanded, pulling her G-string across to one side as he unzipped his throbbing cock. He pulled his jeans swiftly down, stepped out of them, and entered her from behind. Within seconds his cock felt better.

'He's definitely dead.'

Three of the girls were curled up on the large, fluffy animal print rug, in the living room of Alysha's thirteenth-floor flat. Alysha was sitting on the uneven sofa talking to them. 'That tent in the grounds says there's a stiff in there, and they're knocking on doors, and asking who saw what.'

'No one will squeal,' Tink said. 'We know that.'

'Nothing to squeal,' Lox said. 'We was in the lock-up. No one saw nothing.'

'We didn't cut him that much,' Panther said. 'He might of needed stitching, and he was bleeding from all that, but we didn't know the weak fucker was going to go and die.'

'Well, he has,' Alysha said. 'One less bastard to do wrong on our patch. So for that I'm glad he's dead, but I don't want us to go down for it. We never meant to kill him and if we go down who's gonna fix the playground and rebuild the community centres, and keep them South London Rulers from selling drugs to our tinies? We can't take a lump, we vowed to help our residents and make this a safe place to live.'

'What we gonna say then, when the feds knock? Lox asked.

'It'll be the black fed, Georgia Johnson,' Alysha told her. 'Cos she'll want information. We'll give her info and charge her as usual, but it's what we tell 'er, that's what we gotta decide.'

Panther had an afro comb in her hand. She was bent over, dragging the afro through her wild, unruly mass of badly dyed thick orange hair. 'We need a plan,' she said from her upside-down position.

'An' you need your hair sorting,' Tink said to her. 'I'm gonna put it right for you. She was sitting against the ancient upright wooden dining chair, her pale face worried as she watched Panther. 'Let me do that, mate,' she said stretching her arm out for Panther's comb. 'You are making such a mess of yourself.'

Panther handed her the comb. 'Ta, babe,' she said, sitting the right way up. 'What they got on us?' she asked Alysha as Tink combed through the orange knots. 'Nothing, cos we never killed 'im. Ain't our fault the fucker couldn't take a bit of a shanking. We're saying we know nothing, ain't we?'

'Yeah, course,' Alysha said as confidently as she could manage. 'We tell Georgia Johnson that SLRs was running this patch, and they've got a beef with them old Wilkinses, cos SLR stole their car and then stole the lock-up.'

'We ain't gonna get the Wilkinses involved, they've got enough beef as it is,' Lox interrupted. 'They're just a sweet, frightened old couple.'

'We're gonna help them,' Alysha assured her, leaning in and stroking her cheek. 'ACs are about a new tomorrow for the Aviary. Safety for our old residents. We'll keep standing up to them bastard SLRs, and anyone else who tries it on wiv our pensioners or kids. They'll all learn if they mess with ACs, they'll pay.'

'As long as 'e don't kill them,' Lox said. 'They're on our patch, we look after them, ain't that right?'

'Course,' Alysha said leaning over and stroking her face. 'This is 'bout protection, and a new tomorrow for the Aviary. Don't matter what it takes, we ain't gonna let anyone take our territory. We'll clean it up, and if that scum Burak Kaya is dead, then that's what it takes to get the Wilkinses what they deserve. We'll keep standing up to them SLRs until they learn they can't mess wiv our people.'

'You think we can make enough to rebuild the play area and start on the burnt down community halls this year?' Panther asked, lifting her bushy eyebrows, and nodding her thank you as Tink passed the comb back.

Alysha nodded. 'We're gonna try. Lox is in charge of money,' she turned to Lox.

'The street trade's making us good corn,' Lox said. 'All the girls pay up, and they all earn well, and we'll get corn from the feds for informing on Burak. We got the regular corn coming in from dealing to the addicts, and how's about we tell the feds that if we help them find their killer, then they have to agree to get the council to rebuild the kid's playground.'

'Good idea,' Alysha nodded. 'But we gotta tell them something or they won't agree nothing.'

'What do we say then?' Panther asked.

'That the SLRs are selling on this patch, and putting the frighteners out on some of the residents.'

'So someone must have killed Burak Kaya cos of that?'

Alysha nodded. 'We'll say other gangs are trying to move in on the area and the SLR are fighting anyone that tries. That Burak Kaya is cousin to Harisha and so they done him to warn SLRs off the patch.'

'And that'll keep the feds off our case, you reckon?' Panther said.

'I reckon it will,' Alysha said. 'No one saw us shank him, if they did, no one around here will squeal.'

'Wilkinses won't say nothing to the feds nor no one else,' Lox said. 'Bless them, they are shit scared of everyone.'

'Except us,' Alysha said. 'We'll do whatever it takes to keep this estate under our rule. Not SLR scum, not no one's gonna take our estate from us. We'll fight till death for it, and we're gonna turn it round and make it a better place for all who live on it, with protection if you need it, and opportunities for the kids so they get a better deal than we did. We'll keep doing the selling round here, but only to users. The profits will get a youth centre up and running, and Tink's hair and make-up school going. Look how good Tink is at hair and beauty stuff, an' that's before she's been to college.'

'Yeah,' Tink brightened, looking at Panther's orange afro locks proudly. 'We're gonna build the studio site back up too, so the kids can make music and do dance classes again. Lox could produce girl bands, she'll be the next Simon Cowell, as well as doing the accounts, and Panther can teach self-defence.'

'After I've killed them South London Rulers,' Panther said.

'And all the other gangs that get in our way,' Lox agreed.

'We only kill if we 'ave to,' Alysha said sharply. 'Cos otherwise we'll get locked up, and too many people round here need us, and need what we're gonna build them.'

'We gotta frame Harisha Celik, then,' Panther said.

'Let's lead the feds to the lock-up,' Tink suggested, 'and give them the machetes, that'll include the one we used to punish Burak. It's all clean now, there's nothing in there says we've been there. I bleached everything. We tell the feds the lock-up has been taken by Celik, anything in there is his, and he will go down for all those weapons for sure.'

'No, that ain't smart,' Panther argued. 'The SLRs would come after us then, and the feds would have taken all the weapons, so they'd slaughter us.'

'The SLRs are gonna come after us anyway,' Alysha told them. 'That Turkish bitch will have grassed us up to them by now.'

'So we need them weapons to fight,' Panther argued. 'They got heavy weapons, mate. They are gonna try and slaughter us.'

Alysha shook her head. 'No, Tink is right. It is a good idea. Remember that the Turkish bitch told us about the tunnel in

Keepers Street. There's gonna be loads of weapons down there already. So let's go and steal them, and when we got them, then we'll give up the lock-up to the feds, and then when Celik gets arrested his soldiers can't come after us cos all their weapons will be gone from the tunnel.'

Tink nodded her agreement. 'And the feds will be on side wiv us.'

'We'll need them if them SLRs have got other weapons,' Panther said. 'Cos if we grass Celik up, they ain't gonna let that go, not never.'

'They gotta know that it was us who grassed 'im up,' Lox said. 'Feds won't tell 'im it was us, so how will they know?'

'What you think of Melek?' Alysha asked the girls. 'D'you think she'd screw Harisha up if we made it worth her while?'

'I think she would,' Tink said nodding at Alysha. 'She knows we're a better bet. Harisha hurts her. She ain't happy with him. She'll see the light. I'll lay money on it.'

Lox picked up a joint. 'Shall I light this for us?'

Alysha caught Panther's eye. Panther had her bushy eyebrows raised in disappointment.

'If you must,' Alysha said with a shrug. 'But you know you can only 'ave one a week now.' She registered the disappointment on Lox's face. 'You're doing real good. You've been clean for six months. One joint every week, and then after this year, none ever again, that's the deal.'

Lox high-fived Alysha, and then the other two, then put the joint in her mouth and struck a match to light it. Then she hesitated and suddenly took the joint from her mouth.

'I can do without,' she said.

15:00

The investigation room was filling up. The team had been picked and the first meeting for Operation Aviary was starting.

The dead boy had been identified as Burak Kaya by detectives who recognised the tattoo, the lizard with 'SLR' graven between its eyes, from previous arrests. They were waiting now on DNA confirmation, as neither of his parents could be found at this time. Two uniformed officers were outside their house waiting for them to return home and break the news, and ask them to go to the morgue and identify their son.

Another team of uniformed officers, along with Trainee Detective Constable Hank Peacock, were out searching the surrounding area of the Aviary for anything that might help with their enquiries. There were sniffer dogs working too, following the blood trail as far as they could. So far they had all drawn a blank.

Georgia was sticking photos on the whiteboard with Blu-Tac. Alison Grainger had perched on the nearest desk. She was sifting through the pictures that the exhibits officer had printed out, and was choosing which ones to pass to Georgia to put up.

'How are you feeling?' Georgia asked her. 'I imagine you must be slightly apprehensive after your long break.'

'No, I'm ready to get back to this work,' Alison said.

Georgia held her gaze for a brief second. Alison looked tired. Her pale, slightly freckled face was devoid of make-up, and her long wavy hair was pulled into an untidy ponytail. Georgia would have liked to give it a good brush. Georgia always wore make-up, and if she tied her hair back, which she often did, she also used gel so it stayed in place. Alison wore Levis with a chunky navy jumper over them. Her long body was very slim. Georgia remembered DCI Banham raving about this woman on many occasions, telling Georgia how beautiful she was. Georgia wasn't convinced; she thought she had a pleasant face, but that was it; the DCI was clearly besotted. She would have to tread carefully. Georgia knew he would have all his attention focused on Alison, and she'd half thought that would leave her and Stephanie with more freedom to get on with the job. That now seemed less likely, given that he had given breathtakingly beautiful and ultra-sensitive DI Grainger the position of joint senior investigating officer on this enquiry. All fine, she thought, as long as Alison held her own. Georgia had already made it quite clear that she was no nursemaid, and if Alison proved to be a problem, or held the case back, then, lover to the DCI or not, Georgia would take her to task, and in front of the DCI if necessary. A killer was at large and she intended to find them.

The murder team were coming into the room, in ones and twos, coffee and sandwiches in hand, a hint that the briefing was minutes away.

'You may not have heard of Burak Kaya,' Georgia said to Alison. 'Or indeed the SLRs?'

Alison looked blank. 'South London Rulers,' Georgia said. 'They're a growing gang, and are causing havoc in this part of South London.'

Alison shook her head. 'It was the Buzzards running that territory when I was last around,' she said. 'Which seems like an age ago; you think this is a gang retribution killing?'

'I think it's too soon to tell, but it's looking that way. There've been a few takeovers since the Buzzards, and currently there's a lot of gang feuding in that particular area. Various postcode gangs are dealing, running prostitution and protection rackets, and laying claim to the Aviary Estate and its surrounds. It was run by a gang called Brotherhood up until a year or so back, but no more. According to my informant no one has sole claim to it as yet, so many are vying for the territory.'

'So this is just the tip of the iceberg, we're expecting a lot more violence, is that what you're saying?'

Georgia sensed DI Grainger was a little tentative, and wondered if she was ready for this case. Everyone knew gang retribution could turn very nasty, and the body count could mount quickly. Why, then, had Banham thrown her in at the deep end? The woman wasn't even clued up on the gangs around this area and it was a tough call to handle as a joint SIO.

'We know there was a delivery of Mac 10 machine guns, which came in from Jamaica, about a month back,' Georgia told her. 'They were intercepted at Dover, and as far as we know no more have hit the streets. If those Macs had got onto the South London streets there would have been a massacre. And here's the gem: we think that the information we had on the Mac 10s came from one of the gangs fighting to takeover of that part of South London.'

'So this could well be a retaliation killing?'

Georgia nodded. 'I intend to find out. I have an informant on that estate.'

Most of the team had now arrived and were standing or sitting with a good view of the video screen and the whiteboard. Others were eating their sandwiches as they walked up to the whiteboard and inspected the pictures of the murdered boy at close quarters.

'We believe his name is Burak Kaya,' Georgia told them. 'He was a lieutenant in the SLR gang.'

'One down,' one of the detectives mumbled with a grin.

'Not our business to pass judgement,' Alison Grainger told him sternly.

The room became silent.

'I'm sure most of you will know DI Alison Grainger,' Georgia said cutting into the atmosphere that had suddenly sharpened. 'DI Grainger and I will be heading this investigation. You all have been briefed. We know no more than a boy, who we believe is Burak Kaya, an SLR lieutenant, and a cousin to Harisha Celik, leader of the same gang, was stabbed to death just inside the borders of the Aviary Estate this morning. No witnesses, of course. We need everyone out there. Get hold of any bit of CCTV you can lay your hands on. There isn't much working on that estate, but try the roads around it. Chase up the buses that pass through. We haven't got time of death, but we know it was only a few hours ago, so get the bus depot to hand over all their CCTV for that area. And, keep on with the door to door.'

'So nothing at all, no weapon, ma'am?' Bill Perry, an older DC, asked her.

'Not as yet,' she told them. 'But I have an informant who lives with her father on Sparrow block. Sergeant Green and I will pay her a visit.'

Stephanie Green was sitting next to Georgia scribbling in her notebook and munching on a carrot. She stood up with her notebook in one hand and her carrot in the other. 'Ma'am,' she said joining Georgia at the front of the room.

'I would like to go too,' Alison said to her.

'Probably not a good idea,' Georgia told her. 'This girl is young and vulnerable. She knows and trusts Sergeant Green and myself. I would expect her to clam up in front of a stranger.'

Alison stared at Georgia.

'Why don't you oversee the house to house,' Georgia suggested before turning back to the team. 'Sergeant Green will give you all your jobs,' she said to them. 'So let's get going.'

'Shouldn't we be waiting for DCI Banham?' Alison said to her. 'He said he was coming to the briefing.'

'Then he should be here on time,' Georgia said as politely as she could muster. 'This is golden hour, we can't waste it. He might have got held up, so we'll get on.'

'He told me he was coming,' Alison persisted.

'Do you think he meant he was coming to the meeting, or just coming?' Stephanie whispered to Georgia.

Georgia fought a smile. Stephanie always amused her.

'Sorry I'm late,' Banham's voice boomed from the back of the room at exactly that second. 'I got held up in a budgeting meeting. What have I missed?'

Alison speedily told him.

'Right.' Georgia handed Alison a book. 'I will leave you to familiarise yourself with this book on the gangs in this area. It is kept up to date by Trainee DC Peacock. Everything is in it, the names of their leaders and lieutenants, and where everyone hangs out. Sergeant Green and I will pay our informant a visit. We won't be long,' she turned again to the team. 'Get your tasks off Sergeant Green and let's get out there. Someone around that estate must have seen something; let's find that person or persons.'

'DI Grainger will go with you,' Banham said to Georgia.

Georgia looked at Alison and then she turned back to Banham. 'Sir, with respect, it would be better that I went with Sergeant Green alone. Alysha Achter knows her. She doesn't know DI Grainger. A strange face will make her nervous, I don't want her to clam up.'

She noticed Banham's expression harden.

'This is the Aviary Estate,' she further argued, 'where no one talks to us except Alysha and her friends.'

He kept his eyes boring into hers.

'Sir, we're desperate for a lead,' she persisted. 'Alysha Achter knows everything that goes on down on that estate, she could give us vital information.'

'I would also like DI Grainger to be hands-on. She needs to re-familiarise herself with the location.'

Stephanie and Georgia flicked a glance at each other. Both knew better than to argue.

'Guv,' Georgia nodded obediently, then remembering what Banham had said about Alison being the worst driver in the word, she added, 'We'll take my car, shall we, and I'll drive?'

'Very good idea,' Banham said, his eyes twinkling, but his face saying nothing.

40

Four

15:00

Everyone knew Zana Ghaziani was a looker. Her perfect heart-shaped face, striking dark eyes framed with heavy brows, and pert Bardot mouth with a tiny beauty spot adorning its edge made her face stand out in a crowd. Seventeen and from a strict Muslim family, she was allowed little freedom. Living in South London and attending a school where other pupils enjoyed nights out with others of their age, Zana had become rebellious. She had taken to sneaking out when her family were working in their dry cleaners. She would slip off her hijab, smoke cigarettes, and hang out and have fun with the friends she had made around the streets, just a bus ride away. She had a secret boyfriend and loved the attention she got from him and his friends. Her brother Wajdi was always on her case and a few times had caught her hanging out with her boyfriend. The beatings she had endured from him and the threats were all worth it, though, for the fun she was having. She was confident Wajdi wouldn't tell her parents because the punishment they would dish out to her, she knew, was worse than anything he would inflict.

Today the wind was cold and fierce, and her long black hair was blowing freely around her face and body, which felt really good. She loved combing her fingers through it, something she watched other girls at school doing, aware that hers was covered and inside its prison. Sometimes she dreamed of having her hair cut short, in a bob, and dressed in trendy layers, feathered in towards her well-defined cheekbones, but she was too afraid of her parents' reaction to actually do it.

Today, as soon as she was out of sight of the dry cleaners, she had stood in a shop doorway and removed the claustrophobic hijab, then defined her eyes with black liner and glossed her mouth with nude lipstick. In her pocket she carried a packet of tissues and a tube of E45 cream, along with the packet of condoms, so she would have time to wipe every scrap of evidence away before hurrying back home. She knew she probably had two hours until her brother would be out combing the streets and well on her case, and she had a date to keep.

She hurried along the pavement, a few yards from the Aviary Estate, turning into the familiar alleyway and huddling her back into the uneven fence that camouflaged it. It was the agreed meeting place, in the dip of the fence, by the over-hanging branches of the large tree, just inside the alley. The wind had picked up again, and a branch from the overhanging tree caught at some of her wind-blown hair. Zana turned to pull her hair free and as she did so, heard footsteps behind her. In the moment it took to finish freeing her hair from the branch, the figure was upon her. She saw nothing, but felt an agonising pain in the back of her head from the hammer that hit her. As the next blow came, her knees gave way. The third blow again hit the back of her head and now she was on the damp paving stones, unable to move, her face lying beside a pile of rotting dog's mess.

On the ground near her lay a poster. It had obviously been torn from the fence. She wasn't conscious enough to read the wording: *This is our territory, not yours, enter it at your own risk. We don't make threats that we don't keep.*

Zana was barely conscious, but she smelt the pungent paraffin and heard the clicking of the lighter. Dazed, she had no idea that her hair was the target. She lay, nearly unconscious, next to the stinking faeces, as the flame took its perilous hold.

16:00

Georgia and Stephanie were used to the lift on Sparrow block of the Aviary Estate not being in working use. Even when it was in order, Georgia still preferred to use the stairs. The lift was often used as a lavatory or a depository for used nappies, and she couldn't abide the smell, no matter how many stairs it meant climbing.

As the three detectives approached the lift, even before Alison Grainger could read the *Out of Order* notice, Georgia had shaken her head and was heading towards the stairs.

'How many floors up, surely not thirteen?' Alison asked as they made their way up the filthy concrete stairway at the back of Sparrow block.

'It'll do us good,' Georgia said with an amused smile. 'Some people spend a whole day behind a desk and have to forfeit their lunch hour to work out in the gym.'

'We don't get a lunch hour,' Stephanie reminded her. 'And if we did I'd spend it shagging. 'That works off more calories, and keeps me smiling.'

Alison gave her a disapproving look, then started taking two steps at a time. Georgia flicked an amused glance in Stephanie's direction.

After the first six flights were conquered,' Stephanie said, 'I'm having a burger and chips for lunch. I'll have earned it after doing these stairs.'

'If you just had a salad, and still did the stairs, you might lose some of the weight you're always on about shifting,' Georgia told her, pausing to read the graffiti on the concrete stairwell. *Feds are Dead* was written in bright red paint next to the sixth-floor lift doors, which also displayed an *Out of Order* sign.

'I fancy a burger too,' Alison said, glancing at the graffiti and then carrying on, two steps at a time. 'And double chips, and tomato sauce, and lots of pickles.'

'I'd rather eat the polystyrene packet,' Georgia said. 'How do you stay stick-thin if you eat chips and burgers all the time?'

'Must be the stress of the job because I don't diet these days,' Alison said.

'You've got your man, you don't need to,' Stephanie was now puffing like a marathon runner at the end of a race. 'Mind you, if you ever get bored, just let me know. I'm happy to give him back after a short loan.'

They were finally turning onto the thirteenth floor walkway

that led to Alysha Achter's flat. Again Alison threw her a disapproving look.

'Only joking,' Stephanie said as Alison marched ahead to the flat.

There was no answer when they knocked. There were a few girls at the corner of the walkway watching them. One had bright pink hair and wore a tartan kilt with black leggings and heels that were almost as high as the Sparrow block itself. She was talking to a tall black girl whose hair was a rusty shade of orange from over-use of peroxide, and wild, an overgrown bush. The second girl wore a denim jacket over a baggy beige jumper that stretched down to her knees, jeans, and black Doc Martens. The girl had a phone to her ear and was talking ten to the dozen. The pink-haired girl, beside her, was watching the detectives' every move. Georgia recognised them both, they were close friends of Alysha Achter and had, up until quite recently, been street girls working near the front of the estate. A few other girls had now come from the fire exit and joined them. Georgia also recognised these girls, they still worked the streets at the front of the estate. They were grouping around the black girl and the girl with the pink hair, all watching the three detectives. Georgia smiled, 'Hello,' she said. The girls nodded to her, but looked apprehensive. Georgia was aware that Alison's presence was making them uneasy.

Stephanie walked towards them. 'Do you happen to know where Alysha Achter is?' she asked in a friendly tone.

The girl with the orange hair stopped playing with her phone and slipped it into the top pocket of her denim jacket. 'Yeah, I do, as it happens,' she said in a disinterested fashion.

'So where she is?' Stephanie persevered in a friendly tone.

'Who wants to know?'

Stephanie didn't produce her identification card, she merely smiled, keeping her tone friendly.

'Oh, come on, don't pretend you don't know who we are.'

Before Orange Hair had time to answer, Stephanie added quickly, 'It's a social call. Will you tell her Stephanie and

Georgia popped round, with a present for her. We know she had a birthday recently.'

'Who's the third?' the pink-haired girl asked, eyeing Alison.

'Alison,' Stephanie told her, looking to Alison and then back to the girl. 'She's a friend as well.'

'Not round 'ere she ain't,' Pink Hair told her.

'She don't trust strangers,' Orange Hair said, nodding towards Pink Hair.

Just as Stephanie was about to argue the toss, Alysha turned the corner from the stairs on the walkway. She was carrying a bag of groceries, dressed in jeans and a leather jacket, and looking nervous. Georgia knew immediately that she had been on the other end of the phone to the girls, having already been tipped off that 'the feds' were there.

'Perfect timing,' Orange Hair told her. 'Someone's askin' for you. Friends of yours, apparently.'

'Yeah, s'alright,' Alysha said, nodding and smiling at Stephanie and Georgia. Then she noticed Alison. Her expression grew cold. 'Who's she?' she asked Georgia, eyeing Alison suspiciously.

'This is Alison Grainger,' Georgia told her, fighting with herself not to tell Alysha that she knew the girls were playing games, that they had seen them coming and tipped Alysha off, giving her just enough time to go to the supermarket, which was just outside the estate. Georgia suspected that Alysha might be back on the game; she certainly had something to hide. She had a soft spot for the girl, and had hopes that the money she paid her for informing would keep her off the streets. She certainly hadn't heard any reports from patrolling uniformed officers confirming that Alysha was working as a hooker, and she had asked to be kept informed.

'Can we talk to you?' Georgia said, indicating with her head to Alysha's flat.

'If you can talk, then you can talk to her,' Pink Hair said rudely.

'In private,' Georgia said to Alysha before turning to Pink Hair and glaring at her.

'We've got you a late birthday present,' Stephanie told Alysha, 'and we'd all love to come in out of this bitter wind and have a cup of tea. Can we do that?'

'Yeah, course you can,' Alysha said looking to Orange and Pink Hair, and then turning back to the detectives. 'My dad's out, so you can come into the flat.'

'When is he ever in?' Georgia couldn't resist.

'He works a lot at night, and then he sleeps a lot during the day,' she said.

'It's day now,' Georgia said following Alysha into the flat. 'So presumably he's not working, so why is he not sleeping?'

'Not sure,' Alysha said with a shrug. 'He's out, that's all I know. Tea or coffee?'

'Tea, and I'll help you,' Georgia said, following her into the kitchen which was in its usual squalor. The smell of rotting food threatened Georgia's stomach. Cardboard cartons of half-eaten fried chicken, empty pizza boxes, and remnants of tinned food filled the overflowing bin. Georgia wished she could bring out her forensic gloves and scrub the mugs and dishes that stood stacked in dirty piles by the side of the sink. The last thing she wanted was to have to sip tea out of one of these mugs, but Alysha was her informant and around the Aviary an informant was even rarer than a clean cup in this kitchen.

Alysha pulled three mugs from the cupboard, and as Georgia took them and started to re-wash them in hot soapy water, Stephanie and Alison walked in and Stephanie handed Alysha a tablet computer that they had bought on the way over.

'Nice,' Alysha said, merely glancing at it and throwing it on the side where the unwashed plates were. She turned to Georgia. 'If you want info from me, I want to have corn, from now on.' She noticed the look of bewilderment that came over Alison's face. 'Cash,' she told her, rubbing her forefinger against her thumb. She looked at Georgia and jerked her head at Alison. 'Why's she here anyway?'

'She's been away for a bit,' Georgia told her. 'She's trustworthy, though, and that's all you need to be concerned about.' She threw teabags in the clean mugs and took milk from the fridge. She passed it to Stephanie. 'I'm sure you know why I'm here,' she said to Alysha.

'You want info on the boy that was killed in the grounds of the estate by the old garages this morning,' Alysha answered. She picked up the tablet and turned it in her hands. 'Is this my payment for the last bit of info I give you 'bout South London Rulers trying to bring in Mac 10s from Europe?'

Georgia nodded. 'Yes.'

'See thing is, if anyone from SLR knows or finds out that I grassed on them, I'm dead, you gotta understand that.'

'No one will ever know where anything you tell us came from,' Georgia assured her. 'You, must know that by now.'

'It's just a present, you had a birthday recently,' Stephanie told her. 'So it's a birthday gift for you.'

Alysha looked up and met Stephanie's eyes. 'My birthday was six months ago, but thanks. So I'm still owed corn then, for that info.' Before Georgia could answer she carried on, 'That was a big coup for you, them Mac 10s would have caused a bloodbath in South London, so gotta be worth a lot of corn.' She looked at Georgia. 'Much more than an MP3 player.'

Georgia squeezed her lips. 'Alysha, I'm here over a boy that was murdered. I need information.'

'See, everyone round here knows you're feds,' Alysha said. 'And has seen you visiting me. So now I really have to watch my back.'

'We are watching it for you, too,' Georgia said.

'You said you're gonna help me.'

'And I have. What do you know about the murdered boy?' Georgia pushed her.

'I need some corn first. See, you said you'd help us an you'd talk to the man at the council bout doing up that kids' playground. Ain't heard nothing, an' nothing's been done. Kids on this estate got nowhere to play. They'll get bored and they'll start thieving. So if you want to talk to me 'bout that boy got killed, then I wanna you to talk to the council about rebuilding our kids' area.'

'I have spoken to them, three times in all,' Georgia told her.

'It's not down to me if they haven't done anything.' She opened her purse and took out a twenty-pound note.

'You told me you're trying to go to hairdressing school. Is that still happening?'

Alysha nodded. 'Yeah, me and some mates, we wanna open a hair and beauty salon in them boarded-up shops down below. Need the corn first, though.'

'You're fifteen now, you could get work,' Stephanie told her.

'I'm sixteen, actually. And wouldn't that be sweet. Any idea how hard it is to get anything like a job, if you come from this estate?'

Stephanie sniffed the milk and then started pouring it into the mugs of tea.

Georgia placed the twenty by the kettle. 'So what can you tell me about the boy that was murdered?' she asked her.

'Only that he was seen, dead, in the grounds.'

'By who?'

'Not important. The people that saw him will say they didn't,' Alysha said, holding Georgia's gaze. 'That was 'bout eleven this morning. 'I heard he'd been shanked, 'cos he was bleeding. Rumour has it he was a member of South London Rulers and he fell out with his own gang.'

'So South London Rulers stabbed him?' Georgia pushed.

'That's what I heard,' Alysha said.

'Do you know anything about a consignment of machetes that have been brought into this country and are heading for this area?' Georgia then asked her.

Alysha took the milk from Stephanie and bent to put it back in the fridge. 'I did get to hear some things about that, as it happens,' she said straightening up. She looked at Alison, then back to Georgia. 'Are you sure I can trust her?'

'Yes,' Georgia assured her, silently cursing Banham for making her informant so insecure after she'd worked so hard to do the opposite.

'Only I'm here on my own, a lot of the time,' Alysha said, 'and if it was suspected that I'm a grass …'

'Take my mobile number, and ring if you need me, no matter what the time,' Georgia said, trying to hide the concern she felt for Alysha. The girl was very vulnerable; by managing to change her date of birth on a few official forms, and pull off being sixteen when Georgia knew full well she was fifteen, she had left herself wide open. Social Services wouldn't come to her aid if she needed help, so there was no one, only Georgia, to look out for her. Secretly, Georgia felt that if her own life had been different, and she'd been able to have children, then maybe her daughter would have looked like Alysha. Alysha, like Georgia, was a mixture of African, Indian, and English genes, and a tough survivor.

'Any time you're afraid,' she told her, 'just pick up the phone and ring me.'

'You were going to tell us about the consignment of machetes that's rumoured to be heading for this area?' Alison said to Alysha.

'Was I?' Alysha answered.

Georgia and Stephanie, in unison, threw Alison warning glances. Alison had specifically been instructed to keep it buttoned during this visit. It had taken them two years to win this girl's trust. They had helped her out numerous times when she was in trouble, and kept her out of court when she'd been picked up soliciting or shoplifting. She had become *their* informant, and they had worked hard very hard to gain that trust. Nobody on this high rise gave the police the time of day; this girl was like gold dust. And here was the DCI's mistress, on her first day back after months away, throwing her bloody weight about, and a possible spanner into a murder enquiry at the same time.

Alysha turned to Georgia.

'I need more than twenty,' she said.

Georgia opened her purse and gave her another clean, crisp twenty-pound note.

Alysha looked at it, obviously weighing up the situation. After a few seconds she said, 'I heard that Harisha Celik had fallen out with the murdered bloke. His name was Burak Kaya.

He was one of the SLRs. They run the territory over near the Random, and are muscling around on this estate. Burak had upset Harisha. That's what the word is round here.' She flicked her eyes at Alison and then back to Georgia. 'And them machetes are definitely down to Harisha Celik, that's what I heard.' She rubbed her fingers against her thumb again, as a sign she wanted more money.

'Who's running this patch, around the Aviary Estate?' Georgia asked her, placing another twenty next to the kettle.

Alysha picked it up and pushed it into her pocket immediately. 'Ah, now that's the problem,' she said. 'SLRs are moving on the patch, but another gang's keeping them off. Could have been led by Burak Kaya, then,' she suggested. 'See, no one knows for sure. Couple of gangs from north the river are facing up with SLRs, maybe Burak was leading them. The EIBs, East Is Best, doing a lot of grass sales over here. They're Chinese, they're at war wiv the SLRs over the patch. So lots are trying to own it, but no one owns it, yet, far as I know. But I'll keep my ear to the ground,' she said.

Stephanie's phone broke into a rendition of 'Stayin' Alive', at that very moment, and a second later 'Onward, Christian Soldiers' rang out from the top pocket of Georgia's black leather jacket and a brass band boomed from Alison's pocket. All three turned to each other. There was no doubt: three phones ringing in unison meant another body had been found.

As soon as Alysha had closed the door behind the detectives, she pulled her pink and silver-covered iPhone from her pocket and furiously started texting. *Have sent the feds after SLR n EIB. Seems theres another murder round ere. If u aint killed someone else find out what u can n get up ere asap.* She then pressed *Send* to Panther, Tink, and Lox.

Alysha put her phone back in her pocket, and her hand automatically went to her mouth. 'Killed someone else'. *Shit!* Had she dropped her girls in it? They hadn't meant him to die. Now if they got found out they would go down for years, and if that happened who would be there to keep the dealers away from the estate kids, and build the estate into a better place so those kids had chances? No one. The council didn't understand or care. The feds said they cared, but they didn't understand what surviving on a high-rise was like. The ACs had big plans, and they weren't going to let a lowlife like Burak Kaya dying get in their way.

Alysha sighed. She wondered what it was like to be famous, be someone like Rihanna, and have everything you wanted in life.

Five

It was a driver in a passing car who first noticed the smoke coming from the alleyway. She was a local and used to kids setting fire to bins around the estate, but the alleyway where the smoke was coming from was directly next to children's play area; although the area was derelict, she decided to stop the car and check it out, just on the off-chance that there were young kids around.

She wasn't expecting to find what she did.

Her name was Charlene Lewis. When Georgia, Stephanie and Alison arrived she was wrapped in an aluminium blanket, shivering with shock, sitting at the rear of the ambulance and needing help to hold the cup of sweet tea that a nearby resident had brought her. The Forensics team, kitted out in their usual bluebell attire, with their white masks covering their mouths were already busy.

Georgia and Stephanie made their usual disappointed eye contact as they clocked Max Pettifer for the second time that day. He was squatting in the alleyway, studying the charred body, which wasn't an easy sight.

Stephanie jerked her head, very subtly, in Alison's direction.

Georgia took the hint and moved to beside Alison. Lowering her voice, she said, 'No need for you to put yourself through this, it might not even be connected to our case. Why don't I deal with it, and make some notes for you?'

Alison stared at her.

Georgia continued. 'I really don't recommend that you examine this body with us, not just newly back after what happened to your friend.'

Stephanie, who was standing beside Georgia, quickly added, 'Someone needs to talk to the witness and take her statement, why don't you do that? You can phone it straight through to the DCI. We know he's waiting to hear if there could be a connection with the boy this morning, as this is the edge of the SLR's patch.'

Alison turned to Stephanie. 'Have you forgotten your rank? You address me as ma'am, and you don't tell me how to run my investigation, Sergeant Green.'

'She's merely pointing out that a statement will have to be taken from the witness,' Georgia said, jumping to Stephanie's defence. 'She's also as concerned for your welfare as I am.' She double-checked that no one was in hearing distance before adding sympathetically, 'Don't try and build Rome in a day, that's all we're saying. No one will judge you, certainly not me or Sergeant Green.'

'Don't patronise me,' Alison said to her. 'We are both senior investigating officers on this case, but having been a DI longer than you, that makes me the more senior. I also know myself a lot better than you do, so *I* will decide what's best for me. She turned and started walking towards the corpse. 'Shall we get on?'

'Sorry I spoke,' Georgia said catching Stephanie's eye. 'But, just to remind you,' she raised her voice as Alison had walked off, 'this body may be nothing to do with our case, so you'll be putting yourself through all that for nothing.' She paused, trying to choose her words carefully. It was like treading on bloody eggshells working with Alison, and every bit of shell she cracked would get reported straight back to Banham. How wrong had she been to think she would have an easier time with the DCI when Alison returned? Now there were two of them watching her every move.

Alison turned and walked back to her.

'I'm not patronising you either,' Georgia said with a small smile. 'Just keeping you up to date. Gang warfare around here has accelerated in the last few months. The force are fighting a losing battle, so the corpse may have nothing at all to do with our case. It may well be a completely different scenario, or another gang killing. So, we were thinking of you, we didn't want you to put yourself through what might by a ghastly *deja vu*.' She waited for Alison to answer. When she didn't Georgia added, 'But, of course, you make the decision.'

'Thank you for your concern, but I am fine,' Alison said curtly. She turned and walked towards the alley, but hovered at the wooden posts that marked its presence. She stood reading the sign that lay on the ground by the police cordons. It read, *Trespassers enter at own risk.*

'She's so fucking defensive,' Georgia said, shaking her head to Stephanie.

'Want some advice?' Stephanie asked.

'You'll give it anyway?' Georgia laughed.

'Yes, I will,' Stephanie grinned, nodded and then shook her head. 'Just let her muddle through, and if she can't hack it, let the DCI be the one to tell her.'

'Good morning, ladies. Not such a pleasant sight,'

The sound of Max Pettifer's voice, and the smile that extended far beyond his ill-fitting false teeth, was always enough to set Georgia's head pounding. She pushed Alison to the back of her mind and focused on the job. Someone had just been burned to death and finding out why was what mattered now.

'What have we got?' she shouted as she climbed into a blue plastic forensic suit at the cordon.

Max was poking a long instrument into the pink skin that looked like undercooked meat. Georgia could just see the woman's head as she stared up the alleyway. It was mostly a pink, blistered mass, but she could still see the terrified eyes in the middle of the scorched and swollen face.

'Can't tell you anything at the moment,' Max told her. 'A lot to be done first.' He slowly pushed himself up to standing. He was holding his mouth mask around his wrist. 'So before you tire yourselves out questioning me, I can tell you nothing.' He had that over-large smile across his face again. Georgia would have put money on the fact that his own teeth had been punched down his throat by someone he had upset. He definitely had the knack of rubbing everyone up the wrong way. Add the overgrown and pointed brows that framed his cold eyes, and it was easy to see why he had earned the nickname Max the Monster.

'Now why did I know you'd say that,' Georgia said, pulling on the plastic shoe covers that made her feel off-balance as she walked. She did up the zip on the overall, signed their names in the book that was handed to her by a member of the forensic team, and made her way over to the corpse, taking in large breaths of air as she moved. The body was still smoking and the air around smelt as if a summer barbecue had been in full swing. The cold and biting wind that blew sharply around them did little to clear the overbearing smell.

She looked down at the nearly indistinguishable face; some of the cheekbones had come through the blistered skin. Georgia took a breath and blew it out. Stephanie had just arrived beside her and was looking somewhat queasy, which went to show just how bad this one was. Stephanie Green was the one officer in the whole team who could cope with any corpse, in any condition, and still manage lunch after. It wasn't that she didn't care; quite the opposite, she cared very much. She just never thought of herself, only what she could do to help, and those thoughts easily distanced her from what she faced on a regular basis. Today, for the first time, Georgia thought she was a little shaken.

'OK?' Georgia mouthed, quietly hoping that Alison would stay where she was, talking to a forensic officer at the end of the alley-way.

Stephanie nodded, and then pointed to the handbag that lay about a foot away, and was being photographed by one of the forensic team. 'Not a robbery then?' she said to Georgia.

They were both wearing the blue forensic gloves and both moved over to the exhibits officer.

'When you've finished,' Georgia said to him, studying the sticky mess of black plastic that was still warm and probably contained vital information to this girl's life.

The exhibits officer immediately handed the bag over. 'I'll need it back when you're done,' he told them.'

Georgia carefully opened the bag and looked inside. She

lifted out a condom.

'Just one,' Stephanie said, her notebook open and making notes. 'She wasn't a hooker then, or she would have had a supply of them.' She smiled and looked up from her pad, 'Unless business had been particularly good today.'

'Then she would have had more money in her purse,' Georgia said.

'She could have had it about her person,' Stephanie offered. 'It could have been burned with her body.'

'Possibility, but I doubt it.'

'Me too.'

Georgia picked up the half-melted phone and after testing it didn't work, handed it to Stephanie. 'Get that over to your ex-lover in TIU,' she told her. 'Ask for a list of everything they can get from it, and asap. Call history, texts, address book, all messages, everything that's saveable.'

'Will do,' Stephanie nodded. As she pulled a see-through evidence bag from her pocket to wrap it in a loud thud drew their attention. They both turned around to see Alison Grainger lying face down on the ground by the cadaver.

'Jesus, I expect she'll find a way to blame us for this, too,' Georgia muttered as Stephanie shook her head and threw her eyes northward.

Georgia moved speedily to the end of the alleyway. 'Paramedics over here,' she shouted across to the ambulance attendants by the van. Joining Stephanie again she said quietly, 'I'll leave you to do the mothering and assure her she hasn't shown herself up.' They both fought back a small smirk. Then she noticed Max Pettifer had his phone in his hand and was about to film Alison, lying face down, with the paramedics who had just arrived at her side.

'No way,' she told him. 'Just get on with your job, and let the paramedics do theirs. We need the result urgently.'

'Just a bit of fun, for the office Christmas party,' he said with a shake of his head and a chuckle.

'Sick bastard,' Georgia muttered as she made her way back down the alley and over to the witness.

Charlene Lewis was mid-thirties, dyed black hair, pale white skin, and she wore thick glasses. She looked up as Georgia approached with her ID card in hand.

Georgia perched on the end of the ambulance beside her after checking that she felt OK to talk.

'In your own words, tell me what happened.'

'I was going to pick up some shopping and then get my son. He's been doing karate practice.' The woman's words were tumbling out. Georgia had seen and heard this high-pitched gabble many times with witnesses who had gone into shock.

'I thought there was a bin on fire in the alleyway, so I stopped to check. I was in two minds whether to stop or not,' She fiddled with the arm of her large glasses, lifting them back up her nose and then bringing them forward and repeating the same. 'There wasn't that much smoke, but I could see flames, further down the alley. It's next to a kids' play area,' she said.

'Take a deep breath and slow down,' Georgia told her. 'Did you see anybody running, or hurrying near the scene?'

Charlene shook her head. 'No, but I wasn't really looking. I had been changing the music in the sound system when I spotted the fire. I literally caught the smoke at the side of my eyeline.' She was still gabbling. 'As I said, I wasn't going to stop, but because there was a derelict play area next door, I thought I'd best make sure all was OK. God, did someone set someone on fire? They did, didn't they?

Tears tumbled from her eyes; the young female paramedic next to her moved in nearer with an outstretched hand bearing another hot cup of sweet tea. Charlene lifted a hand in refusal.

'Tell me exactly what you saw when you got to the alley?' Georgia pushed.

She frowned fearfully, then spoke as if she had something stuck in her throat. 'I saw a body on fire.' Her eyes were like saucers through her large glasses as she looked at Georgia. 'I started screaming for help.' She was crying again, wiping away the tumbling tears with the back of her hand, but still talking in the gabbled tone. 'I got my phone out and dialled 999. I was screaming, '*Fire*.' She seemed to be gasping to get her breath now.

'Take a deep breath,' Georgia said, embarrassment creeping over her.

'The girl was burning.' Charlene sobbed. 'I knew she was dead, but her body was still burning.' She let out a heartfelt sob.

The young female paramedic offered her the cup again. Charlene sipped from it, and then handed it back. 'I didn't know what to do. I phoned 999.' She turned to Georgia. 'Can I go now? I need to pick up my son.'

'Very soon,' Georgia said. 'Thank you. You did really well. I'll need you to give your details to my sergeant. And, I will need to speak to you again and take a statement.'

'But you need to call someone,' the paramedic interrupted, looking at Georgia. 'I'm afraid I can't let you drive on your own, you're in shock.'

'And you are sure you don't remember seeing anyone around?' Georgia asked again.

Charlene Lewis shook her head. 'No.'

By the time Georgia got back to the crime scene, Alison had been seated on another put-up chair.

'Anything I can do to help?' Georgia asked as sympathetically as she could muster.

'You could stop sniggering,' Alison said.

'I hadn't realised I was.'

'DCI Banham's on his way,' Stephanie said to Georgia.

'Jolly good,' Georgia nodded. 'Then let's leave this to him. We're on the border of the SLR turf and the Aviary Estate. We now know there is no ruling gang on the Aviary at the moment, but there are on-going battles for it, and SLR are in that equation. We also know Burak Kaya was a lieutenant in the SLR, for what that is worth, but he could have been running with another gang. This death could be connected or not. We need to try and find out if this girl was involved in any way with any of the gangs around here. Do you agree?' she asked Alison.

'Yes,' Alison nodded.

'We have this girl's bag, we have her phone; presuming we can trace her identity, we can proceed and talk to her family. Nothing we can do here until we know more?' Georgia lifted her eyebrows questioningly at Alison.

'No,' Alison said.

'How are you feeling?' Georgia asked her.

'I'll be OK in a little while.'

'Good,' Georgia nodded. 'Right, well, I'm going back to base. I'll try and put some of this together before we present our findings to DCI Banham. Are you coming, or are staying to wait for the DCI?'

'I'll wait for Banham,' Alison told her, 'I'll see you back at the station.'

'Are you sure?' Stephanie asked her.

Alison didn't answer. Stephanie got the message, and turned and followed Georgia.

17:00

The murder room was half empty; it was still 'golden hour' in the Burak Kaya murder and most of the team were out making the most of those first twenty-four hours, which were known to be the most productive. Georgia's brief was to follow all avenues with the female victim, to see if her killing held any connection to the earlier murder. There was a strong possibility that retaliation was on the cards and gang warfare could be brewing, and that would need to be stopped before it turned to rioting. Georgia knew she would be relying heavily on her informant Alysha Achter for information. Alysha had already suggested Harisha Celik could be behind his own lieutenant's murder, so that was where she intended to start, after she had found out all she could about the murdered woman.

She wrote *Zana Ghaziani* on the board. Any identification that was still readable in the bag found at the scene of crime had that name on it. A call to the home phone number on her identification had confirmed that the girl was not at home, had been expected an hour since.

'This is all we have so far,' Georgia told the detectives that had turned up for the meeting. 'The body was found on the borders of the SLR patch, by Broad Oak Street and Kennington Hill, which we know, also borders the Aviary Estate. That is as much as I have at the moment. Could all be incidental, but we need to find out more about this girl, and asap. So I need everyone working flat out, we'll need door-to-door around Broad Oak Street, door to door around where the girl lived.' She paused then said, 'But that is on hold until we get confirmation that this was Zana Ghaziani.'

'Parents are on their way to the morgue, with the brother,' Peacock told her.'

Georgia nodded. 'They can identify the handbag and maybe remnants of clothes. Sadly, the body is nearly unrecognisable, we'll probably need DNA to confirm, unless we get lucky,' she added.'

Stephanie was eating her second bacon sandwich of the day. She had made Georgia stop at a café on the way back to the station, telling Georgia she needed a bacon sandwich dripping in tomato sauce to calm her after what they had seen. Lunch wasn't on Georgia's agenda today, after the sight she had witnessed, but she admired Stephanie's ability to take it all in a day's work. She had stopped at the café and while Stephanie was piling the tomato sauce in her sandwich, Georgia had bought two bottles of fizzy water to calm her own queasy stomach.

'There were remnants from her clothes stuck to the skin,' Stephanie told them.

'That might help, although the parents have said they didn't know what she was wearing, but might recognise it,' added Peacock.

'Unless she changed,' Georgia said. 'And I'll bet they didn't know she had a condom in her bag along with her hijab.'

'TIU have got the phone, and Forensics have got her brace,' Stephanie told the team. 'TIU say tomorrow at the latest, then we'll have a good idea of what was going on in the girl's life. If she is Zana Ghaziani, then she's seventeen years old, so using that condom was legal. And the parents confirmed she wore a brace. So it's looking likely we have Zana in the morgue.'

'Uniform have a photo of the bag, and some of its contents to show to the family, including her hijab and one of the shoes she wore. Once the family identify those, then we waste no more time as we have been given the go ahead on this case. And a warning, the press will be all over us with this one.'

Verbal agreement ran around the room.

'What interests me most,' Georgia said, a little tentatively, 'is that if this is Zana Ghaziani, and she comes from a strict Muslim home …'

'She had a condom in her bag,' Stephanie finished the sentence. 'So she was having sex.'

'Who with?' Georgia said. 'Who was she planning to meet and have sex with, when she was killed?'

'That must have caused friction in the household,' Stephanie said, looking at Andrew Ubdali, a DC from a Pakistani background.

He nodded. 'Maybe that's behind it, and it was nothing to do with gang retribution. We don't know, as yet, if there was any connection to her being there.'

'Wrong place, wrong time,' Hank Peacock nodded confidently.

'We have information,' Georgia said, changing the subject. 'That the consignment of machetes that have come in from Europe, like the Mac 10s that we intercepted last month at Dover, were heading to Harisha Celik, and to the South London Rulers gang.'

She turned to the board and pointed to the picture of the murdered Burak Kaya. 'Burak Kaya was a lieutenant to the gang. So, another possibility: could this girl be involved with a rival gang? We know that several gangs are vying for that turf and already dealing on the patch where she was found. And there was a notice on it saying trespassers beware.'

'We should talk to all the small-time dealers too, if we can,' Stephanie suggested, making notes in her pad with the hand that wasn't holding the remains of the bacon butty.

'Do we know which dealers have been active on the Aviary, apart from the South London Rulers?' asked Grahame, the tall DC. He was puffing on a plastic nicotine replacement cigarette, and everyone had agreed he was hell to work with since giving up his forty-a-day habit. 'There's a lot of small-time dealers out there. We could always set up a couple of us to try it, see who moves in on us?'

'My informant tells us that the Chinese EIB gang is moving this way,' Georgia told him. 'And that would tie up with the consignment of machetes, their favourite weapon.' She looked at Stephanie. 'Call Serious Crime unit in the East End,' she said, 'and find out what you can.' She turned back to Grahame. 'I'll give undercover some thought. We'd have to run it past the DCI, but at the moment we need all our manpower to find out who killed these teenagers, and if gang feuding is brewing.' She turned to Stephanie, who was now crunching into an apple. 'We'll be visiting our informant again tonight, is that all right?'

'Yes, ma'am,' Stephanie nodded.

'I'm hoping my informant may have known Zana, and be able to tell us who she hung out with. As soon as we hear that the parents have identified her and we have confirmation, then Stephanie and I will talk to them.'

Georgia was aware of the looks that passed between some of the detectives. 'DI Grainger is busy elsewhere today,' she said, deciding to personally spare Alison the embarrassment of the team knowing she'd fainted at a crime scene. They would find out soon enough. Max Pettifer wasn't one for discretion.

'Keep on collecting CCTV,' Stephanie told them, changing the subject again. 'Buses around Kennington Hill and Broad Oak Street around the time of the incident, especially. The culprit went somewhere. Someone might be on CCTV carrying an empty container, so keep trying.'

'It's been a long hard day today,' Georgia added. 'You've all done really well. Let's keep up the hard work, and hope that tomorrow we can find something to link all this to the SLR leader, Harisha Celik, and lock him up where we know he belongs.'

Harisha Celik was back with his gang in their lock-up. Melek Yismaz was by his side, her dark eyes still red and swollen.

At least forty SLR soldiers were standing facing them. Most of them wore the uniform low-slung jeans with inches of their boxers or pants showing, trainers or heavy boots on their feet. All held weapons, bats or knives or guns; some had all three.

'This is fucking *war*,' Celik shouted at them. He was wearing more hair gel than usual, so his black hair stood up from his thin head like a cockerel's crest. The narrow scar down the side of his neck, from a flick-knife slicing into his skin, was pulsating as his veins protruded with anger. Normally he covered it so it was barely noticeable, but today, he was too angry to take the time. As soon as the news of Zana's death had reached him he called the meeting.

'Zana's death will be avenged,' he shouted. 'She was Burak's girl.' He took breath, then spat on the ground before continuing. 'Burak was murdered this morning by those filthy Alley Cat skanks. I want them brought to me.' He looked at Melek. 'Tink, Panther, Lox, and Alysha Achter.'

Melek nodded.

'If they killed Burak, then they would kill Zana, too?' he asked her.

Melek nodded again. 'They'll stop at *nothing*. They scared the hell out of me.'

Harisha nodded. 'Reward has just gone up for whoever brings one, or all of them, to me. You'll be promoted to lieutenant in the SLR. Don't matter how many of you, you will get a present from me,' he assured his gang with a nod of his head. 'We are gonna make them scream for mercy, and then slowly, and painfully, they will die. So, remember, whoever brings them in here is gonna have their respect upped no end. But work together, because together, we are many and mighty, and we'll use that, and they'll pay for what they've done. There will be as many lieutenants in the SLR as can earn it.'

Tinny, one of the white boys in the gang, raised his voice, 'What I heard was that Wajdi Ghaziani was out to get Burak, innit.'

'Who d'ya hear that from?' Celik asked him.

'Burak was saying.'

'What exactly was he saying?' Celik pushed.

'That her family had found out about him, and she and him was told by Wajdi that they wasn't to be seeing each other no more. So maybe we should be paying Wajdi a visit, see what he has to say about all this, what you think on that?'

'Let's do just that,' Celik nodded to him, then addressing all the gang in front of him, he said, 'I still want them skanky Alley Cats brought in. We know, for sure, that they killed Burak. Torture them all, till we know what really went down, And when we do, we are gonna even that score, no matter how many we have to fucking kill. No one touches SLR family and don't get evened out for it. Right, brothers?'

All lifted their weapons and cheered.

Celik lifted his knife and raised his voice. 'This, brothers, is war, and we are gonna win. Remember, there ain't no rules in wars, don't matter what, or how, we get them, only rule is we get them and make them pay. Then we are gonna take their territory and make a lot of paper for us.' He rubbed his thumb firmly against his forefinger. Loud cheers of agreement echoed around the lock-up as he did.

Six

Early evening

Alysha was wearing a black tracksuit with a brown imitation fur gilet over it to keep out the cold. The silver trainers she wore were flashing an intermittent row of pink lights around her feet. She was standing by the side of Sparrow block on the Aviary with Panther, Tink, and Lox. They were talking to a large group of their street girls, who were also Alley Cat soldiers.

Alysha had called the street girls to a meeting after she had taken that recent call from DI Georgia Johnson. Georgia had told her that she was coming round with Stephanie Green again. They wanted Alysha to find out all she could about the girl who was burned in the alley near the estate earlier today. All the street girls had gathered in answer to Alysha's call, but none knew who the girl was. The street girls were nervous and afraid that a psychopath, or a new gang out to take the ACs' territory, was on the prowl, and their lives were in danger.

'You don't need to be nervous,' Panther assured them. 'I'm watching your back. You know you're OK working with us. You said things have changed for the better since we been pimping you.'

'Yeah,' Jacinda nodded. 'For the first time in ever, we ain't afraid of the weirdo punters, an' we know we won't get beaten no more.'

Panther nodded. 'We're gonna look out for you all, an' I'll fight for you if anyone threatens any of you, you know I will,' she told them.

'She fights better than any bloke,' Tink said. 'So you don't have to worry 'bout nothing.'

'So if anyone threatens you, or something worries you, just call Panther,' Alysha told them. 'We take a good cut of the corn you earn, but that money goes back into building this estate into a better place for our kids, an' most of you 'ave got kids. So, just keep asking around 'bout that girl that got burned, and don't worry 'bout nothing, just remember we're all gonna be OK, as long as no one breaks the rules.'

Alley Cats rules allowed the girls to rob, blackmail, sell drugs to a punter, or hand a punter over to the feds, if it meant making money for their cause. The punters, they felt, were worthless pieces of shit, who were happy to use the girls for warped or weird sex, so the girls saw it fair to use them back; in the end the money was all that mattered. It was a reinvestment, a life for all the kids without parents around the estate who, like them, had to fend for themselves. No more would low-life dealers get away with feeding drugs and alcohol to kids as young as eight, and turn them into addicts, just to line their pockets. If the kids had already started on the road to drug use then the Alley Cats intended helping them get clean, and for that they needed money. They also needed to give the kids something else, an interest, which was why they had to rebuild the youth centres and rebuild the play area.

There was a lot needed. A youth club was planned, in the run-down halls at the side of the estate. There would be a studio too, for the kids to sing and dance, or DJ, or do sound engineering, whatever they dreamed of. The youth club would have instruments so the kids could learn, and join bands, and they wanted a recording studio to record them. One estate kid, who Alysha knew well, had already made something of himself. He had come out of the slammer and moved on, and was now working as a professional street dancer. He had said that he would come back and give the kids lessons when it was all up and running. Firstly they were concentrating on opening one of the boarded-up shops as a hair and nail salon. Tink would be in charge of all that. Alysha wanted Tink to invest her time in a training course, and then she could teach others on the estate.

There were plans too for a sports area, and enough space in the halls for a computer room and a pensioner's club for card games and bingo. They knew they needed lots of money for all this, but Alysha and the Alley Cats were determined, and they were survivors.

The ACs had few other rules. Alysha insisted no one who took drugs could rise above the role of a soldier in the gang, although smoking weed occasionally was allowed. Tink and Lox had both overcome drug problems. After defeating her pimp Alysha had spent all the money she'd made as a child prostitute to pay the extortionate price the clinic charged to get Tink clean. But it had worked. They'd done the same for Lox. Alysha allowed both girls a little grass, but only now and then. She, herself, never touched it, not after what had happened to her sister.

'The girl that got burnt weren't a tom,' Panther was assuring them, 'cos none of us know who she is, and it weren't on our patch, only the borders of it. So this ain't personal. But we'll double up your watch tonight, just so you feel better. We still need to know who she was, and why she was there, though, so keep your ears to the ground.'

When Alysha's phone bleeped, she checked the caller ID, rolled her large brown eyes, then spoke carefully into the phone, before clicking off.

'That was feds again,' she said quietly to her lieutenants. 'I told them I'd meet them at the flat in fifteen minutes. We can't let too many eyes see them same feds coming in and out my gaff.'

'I'll stand guard on the stairs,' Panther told her. 'Give you the warning when they're on way up.'

'How much money have we got on us?' Stephanie said, not even bothering to check, this time, if the lift was working. Climbing thirteen flights of urine-smelling, graffitied concrete stairs, in the biting early evening wind, she knew, was preferable for Georgia than travelling in a coffin-sized, shit-ridden lift.

'I've got some cash,' Georgia told her. 'I can give her twenty and then I'll put a form in, and get it back, later.'

'Hope that's enough, she's getting very greedy.'

Georgia half-smiled. 'I told her we need this information,

pronto, which we do. So, we have to pay for the privilege. We need to know if Zana was involved with any local gangs before we can go any further with her murder investigation. DCI wants that info, and we have to deliver. With Grainger reporting everything we do back to him I feel like I've got a CCTV camera glued to my back.'

Stephanie puffed as she turned a corner. 'I need to get to gym, I'm not getting enough good sex, I'm out of condition,' she said, then catching the anxious look on Georgia's face, she said, 'I don't think we'll have Grainger with us for much longer, if you want my opinion. And fingers crossed Zana Ghaziani is connected to our investigation, because, for sure then the DCI will take Alison off the case. He won't put her on a fire victim for her first one back.'

'That's music to my ears,' Georgia said. 'It's not that I mind working with her, even with her nose on top her head, it's just that I really don't think she can hack it. Also, she's shagging the DCI.'

'Wish I was,' Stephanie puffed.

'I wish you were too,' Georgia said with a laugh. 'I bet you'd be a lot fitter.'

Alysha was back in her flat. Panther had tipped her off when the feds had entered the estate. She was racking her brains to think what she could tell them. Earlier this morning Harisha's girl had told her that the stash of SLR weapons was kept in a tunnel under the river. Alysha didn't want to tell the feds that yet, she might need the weapons for the ACs, or she might make more money selling them on to other gangs. Melek had given the ACs that info so they would stop torturing Burak … or had she? Alysha had sensed that Melek might secretly admire the ACs and might be talked into joining them. That would be big, getting all the SLR info. Alysha pulled her pink phone out. She had taken Melek's mobile number from her that morning before giving Melek her phone back. She called it. Melek might know something about the burnt girl, and if Alysha could trick her into saying something then Alysha would have something to sell the feds.

While she waited for Melek to answer, she stood in her hallway and looked out the window to watch. Thirteen flights and no lift – she reckoned she had ten minutes.

Melek picked up.

'How's you?' Alysha said coolly.

'Who's this?'

'Queen AC. Just checking you out. Was worried for you. How's the bastard that calls himself your man?'

'You've got a nerve. You murdered Burak.'

'Hey. This is a social call. No need for them accusations, girl. I just give him what he deserved, a thrashing. If he's dead, then it's cos he died, or someone else killed him.'

'You shanked him, and he died.'

'Listen, I rang you cos that girl got burnt up today, in between SLRs and my territory. Didn't want no harm coming to you. I'm looking out for you, see. Cos I know you'll come over to us, when you see the light. Do you know something about the burnt girl?'

Melek raised her voice in anger. 'You're a murdering whore. Zana Ghaziani was a sweet Muslim girl, nothing to do with SLR. Word is you killed her. I seen wiv my own eyes you torturing someone, so it's like your work. So fuck off phoning me, you hear? I ain't wiv you. Your days are numbered. SLR are gonna kill you all for what you done.

Alysha noticed Georgia Johnson and the fat fed walking along towards her flat. She hung up her phone, and smiled slyly. She had something. Melek had told her the burnt girl's name. She hadn't known that. Zana Ghaziani, she repeated to herself, a Muslim girl called Zana Ghaziani. Now she had something to sell to the feds.

She smiled again as the doorbell rang. Was Melek thinking she could scare her? That girl was a serious case of stupidity. How many of Harisha Celik's pussy-arsed Turks thought they could take her on? Not only was she a better fighter, she was also much smarter. She had killed before, and she would do it again, if it meant protecting what she believed in. Melek, sounding so nervous, had to mean she knew the Alley Cats were a force to be scared of. That made Alysha smile again, and she was still smiling when she opened the door to Georgia and the fat one. She had something to tell them, and she'd make sure she got corn for it.

'Got to be brief,' she said checking around for prying eyes outside, before bringing Georgia and Stephanie inside and stopping in the hallway. 'The burnt girl was Zana Ghaziani. Rumour is SLRs are responsible.'

'Why? Why burn her?' Georgia questioned.

Alysha shrugged, her brain turning fast. Why couldn't they just give her money and slow the questions down? 'Not hundred per cent sure of that, but for sure she had connections. My thoughts are that she was a girlfriend of one of them, and disobeyed gang rules. Harisha Celik is dangerous, cross him and he kills you.' She opened her hand, 'Which is why this is high-cost stuff. I'm in real danger here telling you all this stuff.'

'You've got my number,' Georgia said. 'You can ring me any time.'

Alysha kept her hand held out.

Stephanie looked at Georgia and then back to Alysha. 'Burak Kaya?' Stephanie offered. 'Was she perhaps his girl?'

Alysha nodded, not having a clue if the girl even knew Burak Kaya. 'Could be that's what got him killed, too. You know what Muslims are like over their daughters.'

'You mean it could be the girl's family, and not the SLR,' Georgia questioned.

Alysha nodded. 'S'pose, but SLRs are involved, that's what I heard,' she lied. 'Maybe the family paid SLRs to kill them both. Harisha would do anything for corn.' She rubbed her forefinger and thumb together, indicating it was time to get some paper payment herself.

Georgia handed her a twenty.

'Got to be worth more?' she said, snatching the note.

'We already have her handbag with her name and address on it, so we knew who she was.'

'You weren't sure though, or else you wouldn't have asked,'

72

Alysha said with a knowing smile. 'And now you are.'

'And now we are,' Georgia mimicked. She looked around, obviously waiting to be asked into the lounge, but Alysha stayed leaning against the wall in the hall, not offering the usual cup of tea.

'I need more on her,' Georgia said to her. 'If you want more money, ask around for me. Find out everything about her. Who she knew, who she hung out with, who she was definitely sleeping with. We'll be back.'

'I told you, I heard it was SLR responsibility,' Alysha reminded her.

'I need to know more,' Georgia pushed. 'I need to know who she was currently sleeping with, and hanging out with, and who she fell out with.' Georgia handed her the twenty pounds, and as she turned towards the door, she said, 'We'll be back.'

'I'm risking my arse for this,' Alysha said as the two feds headed out her door.

'You've got my number,' Georgia said turning back and pinning her eyes on her. 'Keep in touch.'

Stephanie waited until they reached the stairs to speak. 'I've had a text from PC Bevan, family liaison officer at the Ghazianis'. The parents have identified the shoe, and the remnants of material stuck to the body, as well as the hijab in the bag. That's three confirmations. Can't get surer than that. The corpse was Zana Ghaziani.'

'And we now know that she hung around with the SLR gang,' Georgia said with a nod.

'And, likely, Burak Kaya,' Stephanie nodded. 'Who was also murdered.'

'I think we can be sure that this is connected to our case,' Georgia agreed.

'And Alison Grainger's,' Stephanie added.

'And I think you're right, she isn't quite ready to work on a burns murder yet,' Georgia said with a raise of her well-groomed eyebrows.

'Shame,' Stephanie said. 'I'll phone the info to the DCI.

73

Shall we grab a takeaway?'

Georgia nodded. 'Good idea. First we'll pay a visit to Mr and Mrs Ghaziani.'

The Ghaziani family lived in an affluent part of Camberwell. The houses in the street were mainly Victorian, tall and elegant, and most were set back from the road behind well-tended front gardens. Georgia noticed the panda car parked outside the house as she and Stephanie reversed into a space a few yards down the road.

'At least we don't have to break the news,' Georgia said, speaking half to herself.

'Sympathy isn't a necessary qualification for being a good detective,' Stephanie told her. She was stabbing numbers into her mobile. She had a brief conversation and then clicked off.

'PC Bevan is in there,' she told Georgia. 'She says both the parents are there. '

'Good,' Georgia nodded.

As they made their way around the two cars in the driveway, Georgia put her hand on the bonnet of each to test for warmth. One was a black Volkswagen Golf, and the other a green Ford van. She shook her head. 'Neither has been driven too recently,' she said to Stephanie, who made a note.

Georgia then took in the house and large front garden. 'Doesn't look like finances are a problem here,' she said. 'Do we know what they do?'

'Bevan said they own the dry cleaners in the row of shops at the bottom of the hill.' As she rang the doorbell she said quietly, 'There's a brother, but no other daughters.'

Georgia had the sleeves on her black leather coat pulled up her arm and was rubbing disinfectant hand gel over her hands and in between her fingers. She slipped the tube back in her pocket just as the front door opened.

The mother was timid, but on her guard. Her greying dark hair was mostly hidden under a clay-coloured scarf edged with flowers. A coffee-coloured sarong adorned her body and hung loosely down to her sandaled feet. Georgia put her age down as mid-thirties, young to have two children that old, but she knew Muslim women sometimes married very young. The slight hunch in this woman's back implied she was older, but her hands and perfect skin told another story. The father stood behind his wife. He towered over her, had an angry face and a beak-like nose. Georgia was immediately reminded of a crow.

She and Stephanie held up their ID cards.

'I'm so sorry for your loss,' Stephanie said sincerely, 'but I'm afraid we need to ask you some questions.'

PC Bevan stood in the hall as they stepped into the house. Georgia caught her eye, and tilted her head to the side. Bevan immediately showed them into a room, excused herself, and left.

The room was large but cluttered. Cardboard boxes of clothes filled up one side of the room, and too many chair throws in various brightly coloured patterns were scattered across the furniture. Much to her relief the woman didn't offer them tea or coffee.

'Where was your daughter going today?' she asked the mother.

The father answered. 'To visit the library was what she told us. She was studying for exams. She was taking her A-levels. She had ideas on going to university.'

Stephanie took out her notebook and started taking notes.

'We knew she was seeing someone,' the father then added with a shake of his head. Before Georgia had the chance to ask how, he said, 'She didn't tell us, but we knew.'

'She was forbidden to have boyfriends,' the mother said. 'When the time came we would choose for her.' She looked at her husband, and then shook her head, 'She disobeyed our wishes and now she has been punished for it.'

The father put his hand up to hush his wife. She became silent.

'Do you have any idea who she was seeing?' Stephanie asked her.

The mother shook her head.

'But you know she was seeing someone. And that he wasn't

75

Muslim?' Stephanie pushed.

The woman turned to her husband.

'Mrs Ghaziani, we need your help to find your daughter's killer,' Georgia interrupted. She raised her voice and her tone hardened. 'We need to know who she was seeing.'

'We don't know,' the father raised his voice back. 'But we do know she was disobedient, she brought shame to her family, and has been punished.'

Stephanie ignored his tone. 'What about at school? Other kids in her class? Do you know who she hung around with? She must have been influenced by them.'

'Oh, she was,' the father said, at exactly the same time that the mother said, 'She has brought shame on this family. I am not sorry for her.'

'She was burnt alive,' Stephanie reminded her.

The mother shifted uncomfortably, but neither answered.

'Did you know her friends from school?' Georgia asked.

The father shook his head, then lowered his gaze, then his bird-like head.

'Well, outside school then?' Stephanie pushed. 'Who did she hang out with?'

'Her brother, Wajdi,' the mother said quickly. 'He is a year older. He looked after her. He would know more, but he isn't in, so I'm afraid ...'

'Where is he?' Georgia cut in.

'He has gone to pray.'

When will he be back?'

'I've no idea, but he will be back.' The mother was looking at her husband again. She looked back at Georgia and then, very cautiously, she said, 'There is a Turkish girl who she had been friendly with. They were at school together, but then this Melek left. We had forbidden Zana to see her.' She shook her head. 'She is a bad girl. She would have led Zana astray.'

'Melek? Do you know her last name?' Stephanie asked scribbling in her notebook.

The woman looked to her husband, who had turned his head away. She looked back to Georgia. 'Melek Yismaz. Detective, we must have our daughter's body back. We need to bury her. Enough disgrace has been brought to us, now we must bury her, and move on.'

Georgia stared at her. Even with her own incapacity to feel sympathy, this woman amazed her. This was a mother, a mother whose daughter had just suffered an agonising and terrible death, and the woman was only interested in guarding the family reputation.

'We will let you know when we can release the remains of your daughter,' she said studying the mother closely as she spoke. 'There has to be a post-mortem first, and a lot of tests.'

'Still …'

'This is a murder case,' Georgia raised her voice and cut her off, 'When the pathologist is satisfied he has finished his tests, we will release Zana for you, but I'm afraid until then, it won't be possible.'

The parents exchanged glances. 'When will that be?' the father asked.

Georgia turned from the fearful eyes of the mother to the hard, cold, piercing dark eyes of the father, 'As yet, I have no idea. When we know, then you will know.'

They both stared at her.

'I'm sure you will want us to find the person responsible for this,' Stephanie said to them. 'And we are relying on your full cooperation to help us.'

'She brought the family into disrepute,' the father said. 'She did it to herself, out of shame.'

'You think she set fire to herself?' Stephanie said.

'Yes.'

'How was she when you last saw her?' Georgia asked.

'Ashamed,' the mother answered. 'Her brother caught her without her hijab. She was wearing lipstick and high heels, standing on a corner talking to that whore Melek Yismaz.'

'Go on,' Georgia pushed.

'Wajdi was furious. He told her to wipe her mouth and to put her hijab back on and show respect. She said she was sorry, and was going to the library to work.'

'And he believed her?'

'Yes.'

'Dressed in high heels and lipstick?'

'She didn't leave home like that.' The father's tone was becoming angry again.

'We're going to wait here for your son to come back,' Georgia told them 'Meanwhile, I would like to take a look at Zana's laptop.'

The parents exchanged a look.

'I'm sure, as a student, she had a laptop,' Georgia pushed. 'I would like to see it, please.'

The anxiety etched across the mother's face didn't go unnoticed by either Georgia or Stephanie.

Alison Grainger was trying, unsuccessfully, to unscrew the top from a bottle of sparkling mineral water. She was sitting opposite DCI Banham, in his office.

Banham was watching her. He was considering how best to go about handling her. He knew not to offer to help with the bottle. She was a fiercely independent woman with a fiery temper, which he had too often been on the wrong end of. All the warning signs were there now. Her nose had started twitching as she tried and failed to loosen the top. She reminded him of a cross squirrel. When he had once told her that, only in fun, she had really gone off on one, told him he didn't have the first idea how to romance a girl. He had never said it again. Right now he could see that squirrel. Like she was trying, and failing, to get through the wire of a bird feeder, to get to the nuts.

Paul Banham had been in love with Alison Grainger for years, since they had worked closely together on so many jobs when he was a DI and she a sergeant. She had kept him at a distance; although they'd had a short fling, she had immediately regretted it, told him it was a mistake and to pretend it never happened. For him it had meant everything, but he accepted the rejection, and carried on as if it hadn't happened. Then, when a close colleague had been trapped in a fire and died, the affair had restarted. He felt she had turned to him for comfort, but he was happy to accept that. Then the affair intensified, and had now been going on for a couple of years. He wanted nothing more than to be with her at every given moment. After his young wife and their eleven-month-old baby had been murdered, fourteen years ago, Banham had believed that he could never be happy again. Being with Alison had changed all that, although he wouldn't dare tell her. She constantly told him to take things one day at a time, and he had learned from experience that one riled DI Alison Grainger at your own peril.

Right this minute, looking at her sitting opposite him, fighting with the bottle of water, he knew well enough that it was herself she was angry with, for fainting at the burned cadaver earlier.

As well as being her lover, he was also her superior officer, and it was his job to make reports on her progress to the powers that be, and, if necessary to recommend if she needed more time off, but he also knew doing that would be walking on eggshells.

He waited till she had won the battle with the lid of the water bottle.

'How do you feel?' he asked tenderly.

'A little better.' She swigged from the open bottle and put it down on the desk.

His concerned blue eyes pierced into her. 'You aren't the first officer to faint at a murder scene,' he told her gently. 'Fireman still do it, all the time, and I still throw up at post-mortems. People tease me about it behind my back, but I've got broad shoulders. My real concern is, how are you really feeling?'

'I told you, I'm fine, now.'

He didn't agree. He thought she looked pale and tired, but he didn't dare tell her that. 'You know I love you.'

'Is this about me fainting, or are you going to propose to me again? You know I'm not the marrying type.'

He shook his head. 'No, I won't propose again, but I care about you. That's allowed, isn't it?'

Tears suddenly filled her eyes and ran down her face like

out-of-control mice. She covered her face with her hands.

He immediately leaned across the desk and held her hands. 'It's all right,' he whispered. 'Did it all come flooding back this morning, with the fire?'

She shook her head, sniffed, and then lifted her face to look at him. 'No,' she said shaking her head. 'It's my hormones, they are all over the place. I'm pregnant.'

'What?'

'Don't ask me to repeat it.' She stared back at him. 'I didn't mean it to happen.'

He looked at her. 'It is mine, isn't it?'

'Yes, of course it's yours!'

'Why didn't you say?'

'Because I've only just found out. I did a test, last week, and I was waiting for the right time.'

He couldn't take his eyes off her. Slowly, it was sinking in. He was going to have a chance to be a father again. A lump was forming in his throat. He really hoped she wasn't going to say that she couldn't cope with it.

Like any other seventeen-year-old girl, Zana's bedroom was covered in pictures of boy bands, photos of herself with friends, and family photos. There were some of her wearing her hijab, and one of her without it. Georgia leaned in and studied that photo. Zana was eating an ice-cream and smiling, her long dark hair tumbled around her shoulders and down to her tiny waist. 'She was beautiful,' Georgia said turning to look at the mother.

There was no answer or reaction. Georgia moved to the next photo. It was Zana with another dark-haired girl. This girl had white streaks in the front of her hair.

'Who is she?' Georgia asked the mother.

'That is the Turkish girl,' the father answered in a clipped tone.

'Melek Yismaz,' his wife added quietly, as her eyes turned to watch Stephanie.

Stephanie was sitting behind a small desk in the corner of the room where Zana's laptop was. She had it open and turned on. 'Do you know her password?' She asked the mother.

'No.'

Georgia and Stephanie exchanged a look. 'We'll have to take it away for a bit, but we'll bring it back,' Stephanie told her.

Georgia was looking at the multitude of pictures of the group One Direction that surrounded the walls. 'Try *One Direction*, or a combination of,' she said to Stephanie.

Stephanie typed the letters. It wouldn't open. She tried it a few different ways, still having no luck. 'We'll take it with us,' she said. 'TIU will open it.'

Mr Ghaziani turned and walked out of the room.

'You don't happen to know the names of the boys in the band, do you?' Georgia asked Stephanie.

'I know that one's called Liam, and one's Harry,' she said. 'Lucy likes Liam.'

'Try them both,' Georgia suggested.

Liam sent the computer whirring into life.

Stephanie speedily scrolled through the icons, then clicked on documents, and scrolled through them.

'Would it be possible to get a glass of water?' Georgia asked the mother.

There was a moment's pause and then the woman said, 'Would you like tea?'

'Three sugars for me,' Stephanie said cheerfully. 'Many thanks, and no sugar, or milk, for my inspector.'

The mother glared at Georgia and then left the room.

Georgia closed the bedroom door behind her and moved quickly back to Stephanie, whose fingers were going nineteen to the dozen on the computer.

'Just school stuff and music files, so far,' she said, flicking through them, then closing them, then clicking on the Pictures icon. The photos screen whirred up, and Stephanie speedily opened each file. Family pictures at first, then another called 'G'. This was all pictures of Zana and Melek, dressed in high heels, modern clothes, and full make-up. The next picture was of Zana kissing a boy. 'This guy's familiar,' Stephanie said peering in closer.

Georgia moved to look. 'That's Burak Kaya,' she said. 'Our murdered gang boy. Alysha Achter's info is right as usual. Looks like Zana was very involved with South London Rulers.'

'And look at this,' Stephanie had clicked on the next file, it had been titled *War*. The first photo showed Zana with a swollen eye. The next one with blood running from her nose, and the next was a picture of her arm and upper back, where the skin was crinkled, bright red, and blistering, clearly having been burnt. The burn seemed to be in the shape of an iron.

There was a noise from down stairs and the sound of a male voice they didn't recognise. 'The brother's back,' Stephanie said.

'Take the computer,' Georgia said, pulling the lead from the wall.

The bedroom door opened at the same moment, and Wajdi Ghaziani put his head around the door. 'I was told you wanted to talk to me,' he said staring at the laptop in Stephanie's hands.

He must have taken the stairs five at a time, Georgia thought, proof enough that there were things on her laptop that they didn't want the police to see – the burn on Zana's body being one of them.

'Yes, come in and close the door, please,' she told him.

He obeyed, and walked over to sit on the edge of Zana's bed, his eyes still glued to the computer that Stephanie was holding.

'Do you ever use it?' Stephanie asked him.

He shook his head.

'So it's all Zana's documents?'

He shrugged and nodded.

'We will be taking it, for a bit. It may help us find out what happened to your sister,' Georgia told him, taking him in as she spoke. He too had very dark hair and dark features, was around eighteen years old, dressed in jeans, a dark sweat-shirt with a hood, expensive trainers, and carrying an iPhone in his hand, and, he looked nervous.

'I'm sorry for your loss,' Stephanie said to him.

82

'I was supposed to look after her, keep her out of trouble,' Wajdi said at the same time as the mother called out from the outside for the door to be opened. 'I failed,' he added. He stood up and opened the door for his mother who was carrying a large tray with a teapot and two china cups, a bowl of sugar, a jug of milk, and a plate of chocolate biscuits.

She placed the tray on the bed beside her son and glared at him as she started to pour the tea. Georgia put her hand over the tea strainer. 'Thank you,' she told the woman. 'We'll do that.'

The woman looked at her, then said, quietly, 'Very well.'

She settled on the bed beside her son.

Georgia was becoming impatient. 'Rather than ask your son to accompany us to the station, for everyone's sake, it will be easier to talk to him here,' she told her.

The woman nodded. 'Please,' she said.

'In private,' Stephanie snapped, not bothering to hide her irritation.

The woman nodded, looked at her son again, and then walked to the door. Just before she left the room, she turned back, 'I am respecting your wishes, so please you respect ours. We would like our daughter back, to bury her. I do not want to have to beg you.'

Stephanie nodded her head sympathetically. 'As soon as that is possible we will,' she told her, moving to close the door behind her.

'What do you know about your sister's friends?' Georgia asked Wajdi.

'I know I tried to keep her behaving, and she wouldn't.'

'How did you try to keep her behaving?' Stephanie asked.

'I used to tell her, if she hung around with people like Melek Yismaz, she would come to harm.'

'Tell us about Melek Yismaz,' Georgia asked him.

Stephanie had plugged the laptop back in and was now flicking through the picture file again.

'She's a skank who hangs around with the SLR gang. They're the biggest and most dangerous gang around Camberwell.'

'Does the name Burak Kaya mean anything to you?'

Wajdi nodded. 'He was one of them.'

'How well did she know him?'

He hesitated, before answering, 'Too well.'

'They were lovers?'

His voice became angry. 'In his dreams.'

'Did you hate him?'

'I hated him hanging around my sister. I told him to leave my sister alone.'

'But he didn't, did he? So what did you do then?'

Another silence. Then he shrugged.

'First of all you took it out on your sister, that's right isn't it?' Georgia pushed.

'That's not right, no,' he snapped at her.

'So do you know how she got these bruises?' Stephanie asked, turning the computer round so he could see the photos they had found of Zana's bruised face and burnt arm.

Another pause, then he said quietly, 'Ask Melek Yismaz.'

'Where will we find her?'

He raised his voice again. 'How would I know? If I knew I would find her myself. She led my sister astray, and now Zana is dead.' He buried his head in his hands.

'Your father seems more concerned about family reputation than your sister's welfare,' Georgia said.

He lifted his head. 'My sister was a skank.'

'Your point?'

'We are Muslims.'

'And?'

'You wouldn't understand.'

'Yes, I would, and I do,' Stephanie raised her voice. 'I understand your sister has suffered an agonising death. We intend to find out who did that to her. So what can you tell us about that, Wajdi?'

He glared at her, then he said quietly, 'I gave her the odd slap, to keep her in line. She needed it.'

'These are serious bruises.' She clicked another photo. 'And that is a burn?'

'I didn't do that to her.'

'Do you have any idea who did?'

A look of panic spread across his face. 'You think I killed her because she was a skank?'

'Did you?

'No.'

'You just said that you kept your eye on her,' Georgia pushed. 'So it must have made you very cross when she disobeyed you.'

He didn't answer.

Georgia stood up, leaving the untouched tray of tea on the bed. 'Don't go far,' she said, nodding to Stephanie to take the laptop. 'We will be back. In the meantime I want you to get me a list of all her friends, everyone she knew and hung around with.'

He was about to protest, but Georgia put her hand up to silence him. 'As you say, you watched out for her.' She held his gaze. 'So you will have followed her and you'll know who she hung out with. I want a list of them, all her schoolfriends, her enemies, everyone that knew her. I'd like the information by tomorrow at the latest.'

Wajdi turned his head and stared at the wall.

Seven

'I left my ceiling half done this morning,' Georgia said as she clicked her seat belt into place. 'That all seems so long ago.'

'It's been a long day,' Stephanie agreed. 'Fancy a pub supper and a few drinks, instead of takeaway?'

'Certainly do,' Georgia said turning to her friend. 'But just one vodka as I'm driving. Where do you fancy?'

'Friar's Arms?'

'No,' Georgia shook her head. 'Too near the station. Let's get completely away from work, just for one hour.'

'The Crown in Wandsworth, then, that's always quiet, and the food's good.'

Georgia nodded, and then pulled her mobile phone from it pouch. She was about to settle it into its hands-free holder in her car, but changed her mind. 'I'll just call Alysha Achter first. She might be able to get an address and phone number for this Melek Yismaz, and info on her. TIU might take a couple of days. I'll tell her it's worth a hundred quid.

'A hundred?' Stephanie argued. 'I reckon for that, she should catch the killer for us.'

'I worry about her.'

'I worry about you. If you weren't so adamant that you weren't the mothering kind, I'd say you were broody.'

Georgia flicked Stephanie a glance, but didn't answer.

Alysha picked up.

'We are also looking to trace a girl called Melek Yismaz,' Georgia told her. 'Have you heard of her?'

Alysha paused, giving no indication she'd heard the name. 'You are asking a lot of me,' she said after a second. 'I've been asking round 'bout Zana Ghaziani for you. People get wind of me asking all these questions, and then I'm in danger. You only gave me twenty in paper. Is that all my life's worth?'

Georgia had clicked the phone to speaker, so Stephanie could listen in.

Stephanie shook her head.

'I told you, I'm always just a phone call away,' Georgia assured her. 'Any hint of trouble and you call me. No matter when, I'll be there.'

Stephanie lowered her eyes and shook her head again.

'Yeah, yeah, all that,' Alysha said dismissively, 'What happens if someone gets to me before you do? Forgot all the kids around here that have died helping you, have you?'

Georgia flicked a glance at Stephanie.

'You don't know what it's like living round here, you truly don't,' Alysha continued.

'Then tell us,' Georgia interrupted.

Alysha said nothing.

'Alysha, you already said Harisha Celik was your worst nightmare. We need your help to put him away. Then he is out of your hair. For that I need to trace a girl called Melek Yismaz.'

Alysha became silent.

'If you don't know her, or haven't heard of her, we need you to ask around and track her whereabouts for us.

'How much will I get?'

Stephanie glanced to Georgia.

'Hundred pounds,' Georgia told her.

Stephanie shook her head and rolled her eyes.

'She hangs out with Harisha Celik,' Alysha said. 'So when do I get the corn?'

'Tomorrow. But I need her address,' Georgia said sharply.

'Ask Harisha Celik.'

'She's his girlfriend?'

'Yup. So, go ask him, if you can find him.' She paused and then added, 'What I heard is that he has a lock-up, somewhere at the edge of this estate. Reckon he keeps stuff in there.'

Georgia turned to Stephanie. 'What do you mean by stuff?' she asked Alysha.

'Weapons, maybe, but I can't say for sure. I just heard that, when I asked around about Zana Ghaziani.'

Georgia looked at Stephanie again. 'I need to know where this lock-up is.'

'No one knows exactly. I asked, but no one knew for sure. But what I heard was that it was near here, that's all I know.' There was another silent pause and then Alysha said, 'He'll have a key though, at his flat, no doubt. So, find that key, and you've got the lock-up. I heard there are machetes in there, too.'

'Who did you hear all this from?' Georgia asked still looking at Stephanie.

'Here and there. Can't tell you exactly, but you know from past experience, that what I hear is sound, and that what I hear I pass on to you.'

There was another thoughtful pause, during which Georgia held Stephanie's eyes. Both knew, if the information was correct, then the net was over Harisha Celik.

'I hope you can find that lock-up,' Alysha said after a second. 'Help us all out, that will. Another scum off our estate if you put him away; but I'm in real danger if anyone knows I passed all this on.' Again she paused, as if thinking before saying, 'So what's happening? You coming round again tomorrow with my corn? You be real careful. I don't want no people seeing you keep coming here, and getting wind I'm talking to feds.'

'I'll be careful,' Georgia assured her. 'I'll ring you tomorrow.'

As soon as Alysha clicked off from the call, she immediately turned to her three lieutenants who were sitting around her feet, on the floor of her thirteenth floor flat. Tink was painting Alysha's toenails in a shade of bright purple as she listened. Panther was drinking from a bottle of beer and stifling her laughter. 'You really doing this well, girl,' she told Alysha as she clicked off.

Lox had been taking everything down in a pink notebook.

'You def made sure the lock-up is clean? No sign of no

blood nowhere, or DNA, and there def ain't no weapons left in it?' Alysha asked Panther.

Panther nodded. 'It's done, we cleared it all, an' then checked and then double-checked after. There ain't nothing in there to say we been in it. All the weapons are in his tunnel.' She laughed, a big hoot of a laugh. 'Harisha Celik ain't 'alf gonna get a scare. He's gonna think there are ghosts at work. Not that he can get in there, with Lox's new lock.'

'He might be locked up before that,' Lox said. 'Wiv luck. Then, we can take possession of all the gear, plus what's down there. That lot gonna be worth a lot of paper, when we sell it.'

'And when Marcia nicked her dad's builder's van to drive you to the tunnel with all the gear, you made sure all the stuff got cleared from the van, and then you sprayed that van too?' Alysha checked again with Panther.

'Yup, Queen. It's clear,' Panther nodded. 'The machetes are safely inside that shit Harisha Celik's tunnel. Lox broke the lock, and she put our lock on it, so SLRs will have to break that lock to get into the tunnel.'

'Yeah,' Lox confirmed. 'We was hurrying, though, cos we thought SLR would have soldiers about, guarding the joint, but we never saw none.'

'Not till we got back here. They're all over the bloody shop, round here,' Tink said. 'They're on our case, looking to get us for what we done to Burak.'

'Not for long,' Alysha told them. 'We just gotta stay low in here, till the feds pick up Harisha. Which they will, cos I shopped him real good over the lock-up, and now we got his weapons in the tunnel, we got a backup, to get them all sent down.'

Tink looked up from dabbing the overlap of nail polish from the side of Alysha's toe. 'There was a lot of machetes and guns in that consignment,' she said. 'I went down and up a lot of times to get them in there.'

Panther nodded. 'She had to go down a lot of a few times, cause she could only carry so much at the one time.'

'It's one 'ell of a drop, even when you've got the rope round your waist, then you have to lower yourself into the tunnel,' Tink told her. 'So it's an armful at a time. The guns are in the empty crates down there, and the machetes are wrapped. They're all dead safe. Perfect timing for the feds to arrest Harisha.'

'There weren't no SLR crew nowhere,' Panther said shaking her head. 'We was prepared to knock the fuckers out, but never saw not one. Harisha has def sent them over 'ere, looking for us,' she told her. 'So it were a synch. Tink put the weapons in there, and I hauled her in and out.'

'The padlock weren't no problem, neither,' Lox told her, 'SLRs will get a shock when they can't get into it, 'less they break my lock, and they'll have a job doing that.'

'You've all done so good,' Alysha told them. 'That black fed is bringing me round a ton tomorrow, not a lot, but the funds are building.'

'The street girls are bringing in loads with the crack they're selling to their punters too, so we've got a big kitty from our cut of that,' Panther said, looking at Lox, who was the money holder, for confirmation.

Lox nodded.

'We're gonna start with the swings and slides in the playground,' Alysha said. 'We'll get a quote on that, and see if we can get it going for the summer, then the kids can play out.'

'We gotta sort the Wilkinses too, remember, we said we'd sort them,' Tink reminded Alysha.

'Yeah, that's happening,' Alysha told her lifting her two thumbs in the air. 'And plans are all in place.

'Great stuff,' Panther said, high-fiving the girls.

'And then, when Harisha's arrested and put away for Burak's murder, we let things die down, then we get the weapons back out,' Alysha told them, 'an' sell 'em, from there, on to the North London mob. Don't want them on South streets,' she added.

'There's other guns in the tunnel too,' Tink told her.

'More for us to sell,' Alysha smiled. 'That'll bring in a tidy profit.'

'And then I can 'ave my beauty parlour, an' we can build the play area back up?' Tink asked, child-like.

'That's exactly what will happen,' Alysha told, her rubbing the top of her pink hair. 'This time five years from now, this estate's gonna be a great place to live, not an old shit-hole like it is now.'

'We're like Robin Hood,' Lox said.

'Who's Robin Hood?' Tink asked.

Alysha, Panther, and Lox shook their heads.

'Don't matter,' Alysha said. 'You're great.'

Georgia turned off the main road and into the side road that led to the Crown. 'Bell the DCI,' she said to Stephanie. 'Give him the update on the lock-up info, and ask him if he can get us a warrant issued for first thing tomorrow. Tell him we believe the information is sound and there is a good chance a consignment of machetes is in that lock-up, possibly firearms too. We have reliable information that the key to the garage is in Harisha Celik's flat. Ask the DCI to get a search warrant so we can turn Celik's flat upside down first thing in the morning.'

Stephanie started to press his number into her phone. 'This is the best part of today, she said, 'He's such a dish.'

'He's spoken for,' Georgia reminded her. 'And don't fall out with Alison Grainger, she's giving us enough trouble already.'

'A girl can dream,' she said, just as Banham picked up.

Stephanie switched the phone on to speaker. She repeated what Georgia had said, and asked for the search warrant to be issued, adding that they now had information that the murder of Burak and the burning of Zana had some kind of a link. Banham asked her to tell him more. Georgia then spoke as she drove. She told him that their informant had told them about Melek Yismaz, that they had photos of Melek and Zana Ghaziani on Zana's computer, that Zana and Burak Kaya had been close.

'Coincidence?' Georgia said into the hands-free, 'I don't think so.' They were sending the computer over to TIU first thing in the morning, and would wait to see if that brought more to light. Georgia wanted to bring the parents in for questioning, she thought it highly possible that Zana's murder was an honour killing. However, Zana was definitely connected to Burak Kaya and therefore the SLR gang.

'A raid on the lock-up might lead to us solving both these murders, guv.' At the very least it would bring in a very good result for the Serious Crimes Unit; a consignment of arms would be off the streets of South London. She could then arrest Harisha Celik and question him about the murders.

Banham was delighted with their work. He would call by a friendly magistrate on his way home, he told her, and get a warrant tonight. They could then go straight to Celik's flat with a team of uniformed officers first thing in the morning. He would also arrange for the CO19 gun unit to be there for backup.

'DI Grainger will take the morning's meeting,' Banham said. 'The post-mortem on Burak Kaya is scheduled for tomorrow morning, but DI Grainger has already spoken to Forensics and the wounds on Burak Kaya's body were likely caused by a machete. If you can pull a consignment of them in, and prove Harisha Celik was involved, then we just need to match the weapon to the wound and Celik will be back behind bars where he belongs.'

He said PC Bevan would be with the Ghaziani family, 24/7 at present, she would be keeping track of their movements, and he would make sure that it stayed that way, while TIU had the laptop and they were waiting to see what else that turned up.

Stephanie asked if Banham wanted her to phone Alison to pass all this info to her. Banham said it wouldn't be necessary because DI Grainger was there, with him, at the station, listening to the call. They were on their way to the Friar's Arms to have supper, and perhaps Georgia and Stephanie could join them for a drink and an update.

Georgia looked at Stephanie, threw her eyes to heaven, and then indicated, and turned the car round, heading back the way they had come.

'So much for a quiet, home cooked supper in the Crown,'

she said, speeding back in the direction of the station's local, the Friar's Arms.

'I expect she's too embarrassed to come in tomorrow unless she meets us and sorts it,' Stephanie said.

'I don't think her a wimp for fainting but I do think she isn't ready to tackle a fire murder victim investigation, just yet,' Georgia said, sighing irritably.

'What irritates me more,' Stephanie added, 'Is the fact that she ignored our warning, strolled on to the murder scene, and messed it up.'

Georgia shook her head, although she kept her focus on the road. 'No, what really irritates you,' she teased her friend, 'is the fact that she's getting laid by the DCI. Now that *really* gets to you.'

'His loss,' Stephanie said cheerfully, reaching into her pocket for the remains of a large Mars Bar.

'You'd think she would want to be in on all this,' Georgia said, noticing Stephanie peel the chocolate wrapper down, stick her finger into the gooey caramel and then lick it from her finger.

Georgia became immediately irritated. 'Don't eat all of that or you'll spoil your dinner. And can you watch where you put the wrapper?'

'Now I *know* you are a frustrated mother,' Stephanie laughed, biting the end of the chocolate bar, and then wrapping the rest in its wrapper and pushing it into the pocket of her parka. She lifted her hands in surrender mode. 'All sorted,' she said. 'No need for panic.'

'I'm thinking of the car. I hoovered a multitude of crumbs from in here at the weekend.'

Stephanie put her hands in the air defensively again. 'There are no crumbs. Mars Bars don't make crumbs.'

'Yours do. You get chocolate everywhere. You can never eat chocolate, or anything for that matter, without half of it sticking to my car upholstery.'

'You do know that if you were a mother, your kids would leave home,' Stephanie laughed.

Georgia said nothing.

Alison was sitting on her own at a table in the Friar's. Georgia and Stephanie made their way across the pub to join her. Banham shouted across from the bar to ask what they wanted to drink: Georgia a vodka and tonic and Stephanie a pint of Guinness.

Georgia pulled a stool from under the table and sat beside Alison. Stephanie settled in a chair opposite and studied the menu.

'No problem about today,' Georgia said quietly to Alison, thinking how pale and tired she looked. 'It happens to us all from time to time, it certainly has to me.' It had been a long day, and two murders on her first day back was, understandably, taxing. Still Georgia had to agree with Stephanie, Alison wasn't ready, as yet, to lead a double murder investigation, and one that was, probably, gang related.

Before Alison had the chance to speak, Banham was back with the drinks. As he handed Alison a glass of orange juice, Georgia caught Stephanie's eye. This woman didn't even drink.

Banham clinked his glass of red wine against Alison's orange juice and winked at her.

Feeling a little uncomfortable, Georgia stood. 'I'm going to order food,' she said. Stephanie followed. Neither noticed as Banham got up and followed them.

'Christ, she even drinks fruit juice,' Stephanie said as she joined Georgia at the food board.

'Nothing wrong with that,' Banham answered, making them both jump in surprise and embarrassment. 'But actually, Alison does drink, just not at the moment, as she's not feeling very well.'

Georgia felt a rush of heat to her dark cheeks. 'Look, sir,' she said, 'It could have been any of us, this morning. That cadaver wasn't a pretty sight. So perhaps you could assure her we don't think any less of her, and, if she is still heading this investigation, there's a lot to get on with.'

Banham raised his eyebrows but didn't answer.

Stephanie flicked a warning glance to Georgia and then buried her head in the cardboard menu standing on the counter, listing the specials for the day.

'Without wishing to speak out of turn, Guv,' Georgia continued, ignoring the warning glance from Stephanie. 'She is supposed to be joint SIO on this investigation. We have made headway today, and she has a lot of catching up to do.' She noticed his angry glare but was determined to have her say. She rubbed her lips over each other, slightly nervously, and continued, 'What I am trying to say, Guv, is, in my opinion, and given that this second murder involves a woman burnt to death, and because of what happened to Alison's colleague ...'

'You think I should take her off the case?'

She was a little taken aback with the sharpness in his tone, but wasn't the kind to back down. 'Yes, guv, I do,' she said. She flicked a glance to Stephanie, who was still bent over, studying the menu, and wearing a pained frown across her forehead.

Banham stared at Georgia. 'When I last looked, DI Johnson, I was the senior officer in this station.'

'Guv.'

'So, I make the decisions.'

Steph's body sunk even lower over the menu, and Georgia would swear she saw a little warning shake of her head.

'Guv,' Georgia said again, but this time there was a hint of submissiveness in her tone.

'Alison is staying on the case,' he told Georgia. 'And, I will be working more closely on it. I'll keep my eye on Alison.' He stared straight at Georgia, 'So she won't be, as you might want to think, someone that needs carrying.'

Georgia took in breath, and then nodded, 'Guv,' she said quietly.

'Secondly, I would remind you that she is the more experienced of the two of you, therefore more senior. I decided to make you joint SIOs, as I believed the case would benefit from your experience with gang crime. Thirdly,' he moved closer to her. 'If I hear any more of your schoolgirl bleating about the capabilities of one of my senior officers, then it is you who will be off this case. Do I make myself clear?'

Georgia blinked. 'I'm sorry, sir, I just …'

'I invited you here to get an update, and to buy you a drink. I am up to speed with the case, the warrant will be here waiting for you when you arrive in the morning, and I have bought you a drink. There is another free table over there. I am going back to DI Grainger. I will see you in the morning. Enjoy your supper.'

As he walked away Stephanie turned to Georgia,

'I shouldn't have opened my mouth, I get it,' Georgia said.

'Well, I'm not opening mine, either, after that,' Stephanie said. 'Let's down our drinks and go back to Wandsworth for that quiet supper.'

'Do you still think he's a dish?' Georgia said as they got in the car and set off, for the second time in the direction of Wandsworth.

'Yes, but I also think he's blinded by his feelings for Alison Grainger. Listen, what you said was true and right, but my advice, as a mate, is keep your opinion to yourself.'

Next Morning

Stephanie was holding the warrant. CO19 were parked in the road adjacent to the Bugle Estate, where Harisha Celik lived with his older brother. Three patrol wagons heaving with uniformed officers turned into the Bugle Estate. They parked up, one behind the other, and the occupants started piling out onto the pavement.

Some of the estate residents had started to notice and word was going round that there was another police raid. Some half-dressed residents were running out their doors desperate to hide their small stashes of drugs. Other were frantically throwing covers over the cannabis plants they were growing in their back rooms, all anxious that it might be their flat that the feds were about to turn over.

'OK, let's do it,' Georgia shouted, slipping her arm into the sleeve of her black leather jacket as she slammed her own car door closed.

Dressed in a clean white T-shirt, a black lambswool cardigan, jeans, black boots, and her leather jacket, she headed for the steps at the side of Celik's block, closely followed by Stephanie, and a team of uniformed officers. The front three PCs carried the red battering ram between them. They had a warrant, and nothing would stop them going in. If necessary, they would to take the door down with the ram.

But before Georgia even had time to knock, the flat door opened, and Harisha Celik's face appeared, a look of contempt written across it.

'Looking for me?' he asked, raising his eyebrows, and eyeing Georgia with contempt.

She waved the paper in front of his face. 'Please stand aside, I have a warrant to search your premises. And while my officers are doing that, I'd like to ask you some questions.'

The uniformed officers made an attempt to go in, but Harisha blocked their entry with his foot. 'Nothing in there to find,' he said, 'but please feel free.' As they moved forward to enter, again he blocked their path with his foot and stretched out his hand. 'But show me the warrant first.'

He was playing for time. Stephanie wasn't having it. She all but waved it in his face, forcing him to take a step back. She used that step to enter the flat.

'Be my guest,' he said sarcastically with an exaggerated sweep of his arm gesture. The police trooped in. Georgia moved to the back allowing them all to file in before she followed. Celik again blocked her with his foot.

'If anyone breaks anything,' he said glaring at her. 'I'll make sure you pay for it.'

'Ditto,' she answered holding his eyes. 'If you have broken anything, like the law, I will make sure you pay for it.'

He dropped his gaze to her crotch and then lifted it back up to her breasts. In the background drawers and cupboards had started to be turned upside-down. He ignored the noise and kept his gaze on her breasts. 'Said you wanted to ask me a question,' he said with a sarcastic smirk, sucking in air as his eyes moved back to her crotch. 'The answer is, yes,' he said lifting his eyes back to stare into hers.

She resisted the urge to smack him hard in the face. 'I'd like you to accompany me to the station to answer some questions to do with the murder of Burak Kaya.'

Immediately his temper flared. 'You think I'd kill my own cousin?'

'I've no idea. Could you also tell me where your friend Melek Yismaz lives?'

'I've no idea.'

'But you know who she is?'

He shook his head. 'Should I?'

Georgia took a step in the flat and stayed facing him in his hallway. She was pleased, at that moment, that she had decided to wear her high-heeled black boots. As it stood, she was looking down at him.

'There are two ways we can do this,' she said holding back the anger that was starting to boil inside her. 'So here's the choice: You give me Melek's mobile number, now, and then you accompany us, of your own free will, down to the station, and you answer all our questions. If we are satisfied that you had no connection in the murder of Burak Kaya, then you will be free to go. However, if you tell me one lie, just one, like saying you don't know how to contact Melek Yismaz,' she raised her voice and sharpened her tone, 'I will lock you up, and charge you for obstructing a murder enquiry. Having been inside twice before, you know as well as I do that it'll carry a custodial sentence, in your case a heavy one. So I am warning and advising you. Either way, I will find the information that I want.'

She held his angry gaze.

'How are you doing inside? Stephanie shouted to the team as she stood in Celik's hallway watching the police turn each room upside down.

'Nothing yet, ma'am.'

'Just keep looking, we will find it.'

Harisha raised his hands defiantly. 'Find it? There's nothing to find.'

'Melek's phone number?' Georgia reminded him. 'Oh, and the keys to your lock-up.'

'I ain't got no lock-up,' he said, shaking his head and frowning. He pulled his phone from his pocket and clicked Melek's number up. The screen displayed a number, her photograph beside it.

'Someone's having a laugh with you,' he said showing Melek's picture and her number scrolled across the screen. 'I'm clean, no drugs, no lock-up. You ain't gonna find nothing in here. Whoever said you would is having a laugh on you, mate. Got a pen, have you, to take the number down? CVs, that's something you might find in there,' he smiled sarcastically. 'I'm looking for a job.'

She wrote Melek's number down. 'In the car,' she said, nodding to a uniformed officer to take Harisha to the waiting police van. 'And, I am definitely not your mate.'

She followed and watched the PC seat Harisha in the prisoner's chair at the back of the van, before slamming and locking the rear door. She was also worryingly aware of the van full of CO19 officers standing by. A half a dozen or so of them had surrounded the flat, and one officer stood on the roof with a gun. So far they had found nothing to link Celik to any firearms, she pushed the guilt from her mind, ignored the residents crowing around their windows watching the goings on, and went back into Celik's flat to help with the search.

When she was satisfied they had covered every inch of the flat, Georgia called Jim, the CO19 firearms team's sergeant.

'Finished,' she said flatly. 'No sign of firearms, no paperwork for a lock-up, and no key. So if you want to go, I'll call you if anything changes.'

She ended the call and looked at Stephanie.

'Now to phone that news in to the DCI,' she said.

Stephanie shook her head. 'Something's not right,' she

100

offered. 'He got wind of this, I'll lay money on it.' She stabbed Banham's number into her phone and handed it to Georgia. '

'Alysha Achter has never given us wrong information before,' Georgia said as she waited for Banham to pick up. 'You can go and find Melek Yismaz,' she told Stephanie handing her the phone number. 'We need to talk to her pronto, and I've heard nothing from Alysha, as yet. I'll have to stay here a bit longer and make sure the flat is put back and secured. He's going to really take us to task over this.' She drew an intake of breath. 'If Melek is his girlfriend, chances are she'll know where the lock-up is, so we need to talk to her, trick her into thinking we know.'

'Will do,' Stephanie nodded.

Banham picked up and Georgia gave him an update. She listened for a few minutes and then clicked the phone shut. 'Forget finding Melek Yismaz,' she told Stephanie. 'Alison Grainger has already tracked her down and gone to see her. Banham just informed me. Her details were on the police computer. She has a record, for possession of cannabis and shoplifting. We could have checked that last night.'

'Like we had time.' Stephanie looked sympathetically at Georgia. 'It's not your fault we haven't found the key,' she said. 'We took a chance, odds were in our favour, but it backfired.'

'OK. Let's call it a day,' Georgia said to the uniformed officer leading the search. 'Secure the flat and check for damage. We don't want to give him an excuse to sue us.' She turned back to Stephanie. 'I am going to have to really face the music for all the manpower I've used this morning.' She turned away, and said half to herself. 'And the DCI will really enjoy giving me a dressing down.'

'I could make a comment about that.'

'No don't.'

'No I won't. You left your sense of humour at home this morning.'

Melek Yismaz was cooperative and polite when she took the call from Alison Grainger. She said she had heard on the news

101

that a Muslim girl had been found killed and was concerned it might be Zana as she hadn't heard from her. Then Alison told her that they had taken Harisha Celik in for questioning, and Melek became quiet.

'We are concerned for your safety,' Alison told her.

'Oh my God. Why?'

'Can I meet you and talk to you,' Alison asked, then, 'Where are you now?'

Melek agreed to meet Alison but said it would have to be somewhere where no one would see them. Harisha, she said, was very strict about her talking to feds, and he wouldn't be pleased.

They arranged to meet in a Starbucks on the high street a little way from the Aviary Estate.

Melek was there when Alison arrived. Her dark eyes were outlined in long, sweeping strokes of thick black eyeliner. Her face looked quite pale against the black eye make-up, which she'd complemented with dark red shiny lipstick. The top of her hair was secured onto the crown of her head, like a 1960s beehive style, heavily back-combed, with cheap scented hairspray to hold it in place. She wasn't unlike Amy Winehouse, Alison thought, which brought to mind the many young, impressionable, and vulnerable girls that get lured on a downward spiral of drugs by ruthless men like Harisha Celik. Melek had bad skin, a sign of being a user, and a heavily concealed bruise on one side of her face. The girl was on a bad road, Alison felt sure, but with an animal like Celik for a boyfriend, what chance did any vulnerable girl have?

'Look, I'll get straight to the point,' Alison told her placing a syrupy, toffee-flavoured drink on the table in front of Melek. 'We have photos of Zana Ghaziani with you. Her parents have also told us that you hung about together.

'She was my best friend,' Melek told her as Alison settled into the plastic bench opposite. Alison was holding the bottle of fizzy water she had bought for herself. She started to struggle to get the top off.

'When did you last see her?' she asked.

Melek shrugged. 'Yesterday. We spoke every day though. I spoke to her yesterday, Sometimes it was difficult for her to get out, what with her parents and brother the way they were.'

'Did she mention she was going out, yesterday?'

'Yes,' Melek lifted her eyebrows and nodded. 'She said she was meeting someone, and she's tell me about it, after.' She paused and placed her drink back on the table, as if she no longer fancied it. 'When I heard a girl had been set on fire, I thought, but prayed, it wasn't her.'

'Who told you?'

She shrugged. 'Everyone's talking 'bout it. Word spreads quick round here.'

'How did you know her?'

'We were at school together. I knew her for years.' She reached her hand across to Alison, who was still struggling with the bottle. 'Do you want help with that top?' she said taking it and starting to loosen it. 'I left school a year early, to get work, but Zana stayed on.' She released the cap and handed it back to Alison.

Alison was grateful. The smell of the toffee syrup was making a merry-go-round spin in her stomach, and she was praying she wouldn't vomit and show herself up yet again. 'Go on,' she urged Melek.

'Zana wanted to take her exams and have a career, very against her parents' wishes, I would add. They wanted her to work in that bloody horrid dry cleaners of theirs, marry a nice Muslim boy.'

'So they're very strict?'

Melek nodded. 'They used to send Wajdi to follow us when we went out.' She hesitated. 'He's a pig. He beats her if he catches her with me, or not wearing her hijab. She's got … she had,' she took a breath, 'beautiful hair.' Melek shook her head and raised her thick eyebrows as she bit into her lip to stop herself crying. 'They resent me because I don't have a job, and I wear make-up and have a boyfriend.'

'Do you know her brother well?'

'Well enough to know he was bully, and she was scared of

him.'

Alison put the water on the plastic table. 'Have you witnessed him hurting her?'

'Yes. But I always thought it was just ...' She stopped speaking and looked at Alison. 'I shouldn't be doing this.'

'What?'

'Talking to you.'

'Why?'

'It won't bring her back, will it, and it might get me into serious trouble.'

'With who?'

'Harisha, who do you think?'

'Do you want to help us find Zana's killer?'

'Yes, very much.'

'I need to build up a picture of Zana's life, and you can help me.'

'We hung out a lot together, Wajdi followed us, we used to dodge him when we could. I think he only did it because the parents told him to.'

'You say Zana had a boyfriend?'

Melek looked nervous. 'Yes. She had a few. I think she liked Burak best.'

'Burak Kaya?'

She nodded. 'Yes.'

'Did her family know this?'

Again Melek looked nervous.

'Please Melek, for Zana, answer my questions. You said you want us to catch Zana's killer? '

Melek said nothing.

'She died a very painful death. If it was my friend, I would want to help.'

'Look, I do. I really do, but, it's very complicated.'

'Because of Harisha Celik?'

'Yes.'

'But he isn't here. No one knows you are here. So talk to me.'

'I could have been followed.' She stood up. 'And if he hears that I talked to you, he'll be angry. He's very possessive. But, yes, I want to help Zana. '

'OK. Then I'll drive you to the station, in my car. You can talk to me, and another detective, in private.'

Melek looked at Alison, but said nothing.

Alison stood up. 'Come on. Let's get out of here.'

Melek looked around her, then she stood up. She looked around again, then followed Alison. When they got into the street she kept looking around.

'This is just an ordinary car, not a police car,' Alison told her. 'No one will question you being in it.'

She opened the passenger door and Melek got in.

Eight

Harisha Celik sat in Interview Room C. Beside him was his solicitor, a small man named Simon Prezzioni who wore thick-rimmed glasses and sat with his head bent, reading Celik's notes, but paying no attention to his client, who was tapping his beautifully manicured fingers on the table with impatience.

Georgia and Stephanie were in the viewing room watching. Georgia had purposely left Celik for a full hour to let him cool his heels. She had nothing, as yet, to charge him with. She had to now hope she could trip him into incriminating himself, but knew she was treading very thin ice; Harisha was astute.

'We have to pull something out of this interview, after this morning's shambles,' she said turning to Stephanie.

'Don't be so hard on yourself. Just because we didn't find a key to a lock-up in his flat, doesn't mean there isn't one,' Stephanie assured her. 'You said yourself that Alysha Achter's a reliable informant. We know Celik imports drugs and weapons, and that there's a strong possibility he killed both Burak and Zana. You were right to turn his flat upside-down. '

'The DCI has got it in for me because I spoke my mind about Alison Grainger.'

'He won't hold that against you.' Stephanie told her. 'He's too professional.'

They both turned back to watch Harisha Celik, who was now laying into the solicitor. The solicitor was saying nothing.

Georgia picked up her notebook and headed for the door. 'Life was better when Celik was behind bars. Let's see if we can put him back there. We need him to incriminate himself, it's our best chance. We'll take it in turns, question him and lean heavily on everything he says.'

Stephanie saluted happily. 'Yes, ma'am.'

'Are you going to pay for the damage to my flat?' Harisha

Celik demanded as Georgia turned on the recorder.

She reminded him that the interview was also being videoed. Then she added, without looking at him, 'And yes, if anything was broken or damaged, it will be replaced, but I'm assured nothing was. So there's just a lot of tidying up for you.'

'I don't do tidying up.'

'You get your girlfriends to do that, do you?' Stephanie chuckled. 'Quite the little romantic, aren't you? How many girlfriends have you got?'

'Not counting Zana Ghaziani,' Georgia said in an icy tone, 'because she is dead. But then you knew that, didn't you?'

Georgia watched his dark eyes narrow. He reminded her of a cockerel. His black hair was combed away from his face and lacquered into a stiff quiff, obviously in an attempt to make himself look taller. His top lip protruded slightly. He wore his diamond earring in his left earlobe. He was well turned-out, especially considering she had called, unexpectedly, first thing that morning. His nails were beautifully manicured; he wore newly pressed jeans and an expensive black leather belt dominated by the large silver lion's head buckle. His shirt was grey silk, with a new black leather jacket over it.

'What do you know about the murder of Zana Ghaziani? Stephanie asked him.

'That she was burnt,' he said leaning back in his chair.

'Who told you?'

He shrugged. 'Everyone.'

'Everyone?' Georgia pushed. 'Who is "Everyone"?'

'It's been the talk of the streets since yesterday,' he said in a condescending tone. 'So, I can't remember who.' He raised his voice and glared at her. 'Everyone.'

She glared back.

'Don't look at me like that,' he told her. 'I didn't kill her.'

'Did you know her?'

He shrugged. 'Yeah.'

'How well?' Georgia pushed.

'Not like *that*,' he said, with a shake of his head and an added tut.

'So how, then? How did you know her?'

'She hung around a lot.' He shrugged and shook his head in a disinterested fashion. 'Some of my mates knew her well.'

'Which mates?'

'Not sure, guys around the streets. Can't remember names.'

'Convenient,' Georgia said holding his eyes.

'And her brother, do you know Wajdi Ghaziani?' Stephanie asked.

He shook his head. 'No.'

'Her parents?'

'No.' He raised his voice. 'I said I hardly knew her, let alone her family.'

'But you knew they were strict Muslims, and had forbidden her to go out with boys,' Georgia pushed.

'No. Look, why am I here? I told you, I don't know her well. I heard she was burnt, and that's a shame, but it's nothing to do with me.'

'What about Burak Kaya? That's to do with you,' Georgia pushed, holding his now angry eyes.

He raised his voice. 'You don't think I killed him? He's my cousin.'

'I heard your family row a lot,' Georgia said leaning back in her chair.

He stared angrily at her, then he looked at his solicitor and blew out air. 'That's an accusation. She can't do this. Why aren't you saying something?'

'Mr Celik has already told you he knows nothing about either of the murders you are asking about,' Prezzioni said, somewhat nervously. 'If that is why you have brought him in, then he has answered your questions, and said he cannot help you. If you have …'

'He hasn't answered all our questions,' Stephanie interrupted, flicking her glance to Celik. 'We need to check out your lock-up, so could you let us have your key, so we can just take a look around.'

He stared at her, and then blinked and shook his head.

'If you've nothing to hide,' she said in a friendly tone, 'that will get us off your back. Just let us have the key …' she paused then added, 'and the location, and then you can go.'

He threw his eyes northward and shook his head. 'Haven't got a clue what you are talking about. I don't have a lock-up. I keep my Porsche in the street. No one round here would dare touch my car.'

'They would be afraid of the repercussions,' Georgia nodded. 'What would you do to them, Harisha? What would you do if someone scratched your Porsche?'

'They aren't *afraid*. People like and respect me.'

'Oh, please.' She shook her head. 'Be honest, Harisha, you terrify everyone around the neighbourhood. Your previous record speaks volumes. Two lumps inside for grievous bodily harm. You're vicious.' She raised her voice. 'No one would touch your car, because they are afraid of the consequences. What do you terrify them with? Machetes, is it? Or guns, the guns and machetes that you are bringing into the country?'

Harisha turned to his solicitor. 'She's trying to set me up here. Can't you do something?'

'Mr Celik's previous record bears no connection to these current murders,' Prezzioni said, a little weakly. 'Mr Celik has paid the price for his crimes. They are in the past.'

Georgia ignored him. 'Where is your lock-up, Harisha? If you've nothing to hide, tell us and we'll be off your back.'

'Watch my lips,' he said making Georgia fight to control her temper. 'I ain't got no lock-up, and you have wasted your time, and mine, looking for one. I do *not* know what you're on about.'

She glared at him, her mind racing faster than a greyhound after a rabbit. What was she going to say to the DCI? Her information was proving not to be right.

Harisha then spoke again. 'If I had anything to worry about, or hide, I'd get myself a nice top of the range lawyer, now wouldn't I?' The diamond in his ear was twinkling in the light, sarcastically, Georgia thought. 'And I ain't. All I have is *him*.' He turned and looked at Prezzioni. 'Who don't know nothing, cos he's an idiot.' He leaned further across the desk. 'See, if I was guilty I'd have a proper representative. So you and I both know you are pissing in the wind. So can I go now?'

'Where did you get the money to buy your nice top of the range car?' Georgia asked, ignoring his remark. 'A black Porsche, with a personalised number plate, and tinted windows.' She shook her head and clicked her tongue against the roof of her mouth. 'That wouldn't be cheap. And that is a very expensive sound system that you have in your flat.'

'It's my brother's flat, not mine,' he answered, leaning back in his chair, confidently.

Georgia picked up the papers in front of her, and started reading. 'It says here, on your form.' She looked up and straight at him. 'The form that you filled in, and signed, that you are self-employed. What self-employment job pays enough for you to buy a Porsche, but live in a council-owned flat with your brother?'

He didn't flinch. 'I am a disc jockey.' The condescending tone had crept back into his voice. 'I do gigs abroad. I'm good at them, innit, so it pays well, and instead of cash they buy me sounds and motors, so I travel and do more gigs.'

'So you must have a garage then?' Stephanie said to him. 'For your music collection, as I didn't see a lot of music in the flat. Where do you keep your CDs, Harisha? Your records? A good disc jockey would need a lot of music.'

He shook his head. 'My music is with my friend, abroad. An' I told you, I ain't got no garage, or no lock-up. I don't need one. And no one round my way would touch my car.'

Stephanie shook her head.

'Too afraid of you, I'd say,' Georgia added.

Harisha leaned across the desk again and said, very casually, 'See, I think you have been talking to a sly, lying bitch called Alysha Achter.'

Georgia's face must have given her away.

'Yes,' he grinned, pointing his forefinger at her. 'Now why do I know that?' He burst out laughing and tilted his head sideways, keeping his finger wiggling in his irritating fashion. 'See, I know that, cos she tells all them porkies about everyone else around the estate. She fancies herself as a tough nut. She's way above her station.' He laughed, an irritating chuckle. 'Got that right, didn't I?'

Neither Georgia or Stephanie answered, both waited for him to say more.

'Did she mention that she's been importing machetes, over from Europe, in these conversations you had with her?' He glared at Georgia.

Georgia felt the chill down the back of her spine, but was careful to keep her face impartial.

'No I thought not.' He shook his head and his face became very serious. 'That's why you turned my place upside down, innit? She told you it was me bringing in weapons, didn't she.' He shook his head. 'No, see, it's her that's doing all of that, she is trying to confuse you.'

There was a few silent seconds while Georgia digested that, then she said, 'Who is Alysha Achter?'

His tone changed to angry. 'See, that proves I'm right and you're the lying bitch. Every fed in the country knows that little skank. She's got a record longer than her arsehole, or at least she should have, with the stuff she does. 'Cept she gets off all the time.' He leaned forward accusingly. 'An' I think that is because she informs for you. I am right' ain't I?'

Again Georgia fought to keep her face indifferent.

Harisha raised his voice. 'Trouble is ... she tells fucking great whoppers.' His voice dropped in volume and he leaned on one elbow, tilted his head onto his hand, and winked at Georgia. 'You've been had over, darling.'

Georgia was fuming, but fought not to show it. She held his eyes.

He leaned back in his chair. 'Now, if you were very, very nice to me, and I mean very, very nice, then I might tell you where *she* has a lock-up. Bet you didn't know that she has a lock-up, did you?'

Georgia didn't answer.

'No I thought not. And a crew, a gang of real,' he adopted a pretend, scary voice and indicated inverted brackets, with his two fingers, 'dangerous girls, call themselves Alley Cats?' He brought his hand to his mouth and tilted his chin enjoying the sudden power he was wielding as the two detectives pinned their eyes on him and gave him their full attention. He lifted his forefinger. 'No, see, I can tell you know nothing about that. Well, you wanna start looking at that bitch, cos,' he raised his voice and slammed his hand on the desk, 'she *has* been importing machetes, and she has been using the bastards to hurt people, and someone is gonna get her for it.'

'I need to remind you, you are being recorded,' Georgia said to him. 'Can you prove your accusations?

'Put it this way. There is a lock-up, edge of Lark and Sparrow block on the Aviary, and I have heard that those tarts go in and out there quite some bit.' He winked at her. 'Bit of a clue there for you.'

'Number?'

'Number what?'

'Number of the block?'

'Dunno. S'got a skull in green graffiti over the door handle, and peeling dark red paint on it. Can I go now?'

There was a silence during which Georgia thought of the cock-up she had made if all this proved to be true. Alysha Achter had never let her down before, and this low-life sitting in front of her was known for lying. She really hoped Alysha hadn't started down the wrong road, for all their sakes. Georgia knew she had to look into this. If there was a lock-up with enough machetes and firearms in it to cause havoc across the whole of South London, she had to find it and get the weapons off the streets, whoever was responsible. She also believed that would lead her to Burak Kaya's killer, and possibly to Zana Ghaziani's too. The thought that Alysha might be involved in any of it would be a real kick in the gut.

'So, can I go now?'

'Yes, you can go,' she said. 'But don't go far. We are watching you.'

'Fuck me, I'm pissing myself.'

'Am I supposed to have someone with me?' Melek Yismaz asked looking curiously as Banham followed Alison into interview room B, pulled out a chair and settled beside Alison, opposite Melek.

'You don't have to, as you are eighteen, but if you would feel more comfortable then I can get you a legal representative,' Alison offered helpfully. 'This is just for me to take a statement from you. I will record, and write down, all you tell me, and then you can sign the statement at the end. Are you OK with that?'

Melek frowned nervously, and then nodded. 'Yes.'

'You are not under arrest,' Banham assured her, in his usual calm and friendly tone. 'You are helping us with our enquiries into the death of your friend.'

Her eyes suddenly filled with fearful tears. 'Harisha would go mad if he found out. He mustn't know about this.'

'Well he won't, not from us,' Alison said with a reassuring smile.

'Why are you so afraid of him?' Banham asked her, in his gentle tone.

She shook her head.

Has Harisha hurt you before?' he pushed.

She shook her head and looked down at the table. 'No.'

'Well if he ever does, just pick up the phone and ring me,' Alison said, passing her a card with her mobile number on it.

She looked up. 'Might be a bit difficult, if I'm dead.'

'Has he threatened you?' Banham asked with concern.

Again she shook her head and looked back at the desk.

'So what is there to be afraid of?'

'He's possessive with me. Doesn't like me talking to the feds. He's nervous of them.'

'Has he reason to be?'

'No.'

'You said earlier that Zana and you hung out together,' Alison reminded her.

'Yes, we were good friends, very close, we have been … were since we started school.' She glanced nervously at

114

Banham. He gave her a reassuring smile.

'You told us too, that you had witnessed beatings that her brother and family had given her?'

Melek swallowed and nodded. 'Yes, I have. I took photos a few times, when Wajdi marked her face.'

'She told you her brother did it?'

Melek nodded. 'She had a burn on her back, too, from when her mother burned her with an iron because she caught her without her hijab.' She took an intake of breath to fight down her emotions. 'That was awful, poor Zana could hardly move with the pain.'

Banham and Alison made eye contact.

'You also told me she was friendly with Burak Kaya?'

'Yes.' She looked up, then squeezed her lips together, and then nodded her head. 'Yes, she was.'

'Were they lovers?'

She nodded again. 'Yes.'

'Had she had other lovers?' Banham asked.

'Oh yes, many.'

'That would have made her family angry,' Alison said. 'If they knew she had many lovers. Do you know if they knew specifically about Burak?'

She shook her head. 'I'm not a hundred per cent sure on that. They knew she wasn't a virgin, because they found a Durex in her bag and were always calling her a whore.' She blinked a tear, and then flicked it with the back of her hand, smudging her heavy eye-make-up and making the bruise on the side of her face more prominent.

Alison passed her a tissue. Melek took it, held it under her eye and then wiped, smudging the black make-up across her cheek, making it look even worse. Alison said nothing.

'Did you ever hear her parents threaten her?'

'I never spoke to her parents. I was banned from their house. They think I'm beneath them, I'm the reason Zana's a rebel.' She shook her head. 'It's them, they allowed her no freedom.'

'Do you know her brother Wajdi well?'

'Yes. He was always looking for her, and often found her

with me, and then he'd drag her home.'

'Did you ever hear him threaten her?'

'Yes, and me, he threatened me many times.'

'What did he say?' Banham asked.

'Things like, if I didn't stay away from his sister, I would get a lesson taught me, things like that.'

'Did he ever show any violence to you?'

She shook her head. 'He would know that Harisha is my boyfriend, and if anyone hurt me, Harisha would kill them.'

'Did Burak feel the same about Zana? Would he have killed anyone who hurt her, or who she slept with, perhaps?' Banham asked.

'I don't think so, but I don't know that for sure,' she said.

Alison looked up. 'Was Zana sleeping with anyone, other than Burak, currently?' she asked.

Melek shook her head. 'I don't know about anyone, and I think Zana would have confided in me if she was.'

'She confided in you about everything?'

'Most things.'

'Did she mention being afraid of anyone, apart from her family?'

Melek shook her head. 'She was afraid of her parents, for sure. She was always saying that. They were very strict.'

'Were they particularly angry with her currently, did she say?'

Melek shook her head. 'Not that I know of, but she was always in trouble.'

'Has Harisha been violent with anyone who frightened you?' Banham asked her.

'No, but he would, if anyone hurt me.'

They sat in silence, while Banham and Alison were taking all that in. A few seconds later Banham said, 'Have you had many lovers, Melek? He must have noticed the reaction on her face, as he quickly added, 'I'm sorry if this sounds personal, but I do think it is relevant.'

'No. I haven't,' she sounded a bit indignant. 'Harisha wasn't the first, but then I am eighteen.'

'But Harisha is your only current lover?'

'Yes, he is.'

'Where do you go to make love?' Banham asked her.

'Pardon?'

'You must have somewhere where you can be private together? He lives with his brother. Do you have a private place for just the two of you,' Banham pushed. 'His lock-up, for instance, do you go there to have privacy?'

She looked embarrassed. 'I didn't know he had a lock-up. He has a flat. I go there.'

'He shares his flat?' Alison said.

'With his brother, yes, but we get privacy.' She looked at Alison. 'Is this anything to do with anything? Is it relevant? I only agreed to come here to help you find who did that to my friend. I'm answering questions about my own sex life now. I am over sixteen, I can sleep with who I like, can't I?'

'Yes, of course you can, and yes, it is relevant,' Banham answered quickly. He smiled and held her gaze. 'I'm really sorry to ask you, because I agree, it is very personal. We are trying to find who murdered Zana, and her boyfriend Burak Kaya, and it is relevant.'

Melek looked down at the desk shaking her head. 'If Harisha finds out I've been talking like this, he will be furious, he'll …'

'He'll what?' Banham raised his voice.

She didn't answer, so Banham pushed, 'Is there something you aren't telling us, Melek? Is Harisha involved in some way and you are trying to protect him?'

'No,' she protested. 'No, no, he isn't.'

'If he is, then don't protect him, for your own sake, tell us what you know; withholding evidence is a criminal offence and could carry a custodial sentence.'

She was crying now. 'No, I don't think Harisha is involved at all. He wouldn't kill Zana, or his cousin. I've told you all that I know. Can I please go now?'

Banham nodded, 'Yes, of course you can. Please sign your witness statement, and I am so sorry that we upset you. You have very helpful.'

She nodded, hurriedly read the statement that Alison handed her, and then signed it.

'And don't forget you can call us at any time,' Alison said as she was signing. 'Or if there is anything else you think of that may help us.'

Alison accompanied her up the one floor, and towards the exit. As they approached the sergeant's desk on their way to the street door, Melek stopped in her tracks.

Harisha was standing at the sergeant's desk with DI Georgia Johnson. He was signing for the personal belongings that had been taken from him before they took him to be interviewed. When he turned and saw Melek, his face took on a look of thunder.

'What are you doing here?' he shouted down the corridor at her.

Melek was suddenly flustered. 'They brought me in to answer some questions. I've not …'

'Shut it. Tell me later.'

Immediately, she became silent.

Alison steered her towards the exit.

When they were out of his earshot, Alison said, 'You've not what? What were you going to say then, to Harisha? "I've not", you said, and then you stopped.'

'Nothing. I was just going to tell him I hadn't said anything about him, which I haven't.' The girl was clearly terrified, she was nearly stuttering as she spoke. 'Because there was no need, because he hasn't done anything wrong, as far as I know. If Wajdi has gone too far, then he deserves to be in trouble, that's all I've said, him or that evil mother of his, but I haven't said anything else.' She turned and hurried towards the street door.

Alison followed. 'I'll get someone to drop you home,' she told her.

'God, no, don't do that. If I turn up in a fed's car, someone else will kill me before he gets the chance.'

The girl was shaking. 'OK, no problem,' Alison said. 'I'll drop you off myself. I'll just get my keys. Wait here.'

On the way to get her car keys, Alison walked into the

station reception and over to Georgia, who was still with Harisha Celik.

'Hold Celik back for another half an hour before releasing him,' she said quietly to Georgia. 'That girl is terrified of him, and we don't want another murder.'

'Is she still here?'

'I'm dropping her home. I just need to get my keys.'

As Alison went back for her keys, Georgia hurried to the door where Melek was nervously waiting.

'Hello, I'm DI Johnson,' Georgia said offering her hand. Melek looked back at her but didn't take her hand. 'A friend of Alison Grainger. Do you know an Alysha Achter?'

Georgia could tell by the nervous look that came to Melek's face that she knew exactly who Alysha was. Melek took her time answering. 'Yes, everyone knows her. Why?'

'What do you know about her?'

'Not much,' Melek said, but not confidently enough for Georgia to believe her.

'Does she hang about in a gang?'

'Everyone does, it's the only way to survive around our way, but you wouldn't understand that.'

'Yes, I would, actually. What gang does she hang around with?'

Again, Melek took a thoughtful pause. 'I've no idea. I don't know her that well.'

Georgia held her gaze, lifting her eyebrows minutely to let Melek know she didn't believe her.

'Where's Alison Grainger?' Melek said quickly. 'I want to go now.'

'On her way,' Georgia told her handing her a card. 'That's my personal mobile,' she told her. 'If you can find out any more about Alysha Achter, I would be very grateful.'

Melek snatched the card nervously and pushed it in her bag.

The lunchtime meeting was in full swing when Alison got back from dropping Melek at the corner of her road. Georgia and Banham were at the front of the room by the whiteboard. A photo of the charred body of Zana had been newly attached to the board with the aid of Blu-Tac. There were pictures of the Ghaziani family on there, and their names in red marker pen under their pictures. Photos of the butchered Burak Kaya were at the top of the board on the left side, his name written underneath in large red marker pen. There were close-up photos of his wounds next to it: his leg, his shoulder, his forearm, his hands, and his chest. Underneath were photos of the gang members from SLR that were known to the police: Harisha at the top, and Melek, Bilaboo, and Trent.

'OK, so we're trying to piece together a picture of the current gang feuding around that area at the moment,' Georgia said, pointing to the various people and reminding the team of their relationships with each other. 'The blood pattern from Kaya takes us back to the side of the Aviary Estate. Harisha Celik's territory is two hundred yards further down the road, and we have good information,' she paused as she spoke, hoping that that was the case, 'that the territory of the Aviary is causing new gang rivalry, although which gangs are vying for it, we have yet to fathom. We need to find that out, so keep digging, interview possible gang members from a little further afield, see if you can get them to talk.'

'You said you thought Burak Kaya had tried his hand at taking the territory, and paid with his life,' Hank Peacock said.

'It's a possibility,' Georgia said cautiously.

'But by who?' Peacock asked.

'So, question is,' Banham interrupted, 'who is currently running the drug and street trade around the Aviary? We have information that the SLR are moving in. Burak Kaya was one of them, and if Celik had his cousin killed, it would mean there was rivalry within that gang. There's another possibility. So work on that, keep asking around. We're all very aware of the wall of silence around that estate towards the police, but DI Grainger,' he looked over at Alison and beamed as he spoke. 'has befriended Harisha Celik's girlfriend, Melek, who has given us a statement. Melek has said that Zana was terrified of her parents and, in particular, her brother.' He pointed to the picture of Wajdi Ghaziani pinned to the whiteboard. 'It's highly possible therefore that Zana's death was an honour killing, and we're waiting on more info from Zana's laptop which is with TIU as we speak. Meanwhile, there's a family liaison officer with the Ghazianis 24/7. There is also a link with the SLR, as Zana was the girlfriend of Burak Kaya. We need to work with that. We need you all on the streets talking to whoever will talk around that estate.'

Georgia butted in. 'Forensics have told us that the wounds on Burak Kaya match a machete. We know that a batch of them came in recently from Europe, and we've been told by Harisha Celik that they are being kept in a lock-up near the Aviary. We suspect Celik is behind this consignment, so his information may not be sound. But check it out. It could be the vital piece of the puzzle.'

Banham flicked a glance at Georgia. 'This morning our boys, along with a CO19 firearms team, turned Celik's flat upside down. We found nothing. No key, no contract, nothing on his phone connecting him to a garage, a lock-up, or a dealer in Europe. His solicitor is threatening us with harassment, so we need to be very sure from now on.'

Georgia felt her cheeks flush with embarrassment at the realization that Banham's remark was aimed at her. 'Celik has told us that one of our trusted informants is importing machetes, and is laying the blame at their door.' She watched heads turn to each other and then back to her. All the team had, in the past, made comments about the validity of Alysha Achter as an informant. 'Celik tells us he earns his money not from drugs but as a DJ on the continent. He says there is a lock-up near or on the Aviary, with some distinctive graffiti, a skull and cross in green on a red door with peeling paint, which is where the weapons are being stored. I've circulated the description to uniform and asked them to keep an eye out when patrolling the estate. Sergeant Green and I will be paying a visit to Alysha Achter tonight and we'll have a look for that lock-up. Should we find it, we'll call it in, request backup.'

'Do that,' Banham nodded his agreement. 'If you take

Sergeant Green with you, Alison and I will go,' he turned to Alison, checking she was up to it, and was met with a brusque nod, 'to talk to the Ghazianis.'

'Melek Yismaz told us the mother has previously burned Zana with an iron for not wearing her hijab,' Alison told the team. 'Melek took photos of the injury; again, we're waiting on TIU for all the photos on the laptop.'

'I've seen them,' Stephanie confirmed. 'They're being blown up as we speak.'

'We'll talk to them,' Banham said, 'but at this stage we'll only bring them in if it's absolutely necessary. The post-mortems on both victims have now been put back until tomorrow.' Banham looked around the room. 'Any volunteers?'

Georgia caught Stephanie's eye. Banham was well-known for throwing up at post-mortems, and after Alison fainting at the crime scene of a burns victim, there was no chance she would volunteer. It was Georgia's chance to climb back into the DCI's good books.

'Sergeant Green and I will go,' she said.

'Jolly good,' he said dismissively. She watched him beam at Alison, who was sitting at the front of the room, pale and looking as out of place.

Stephanie batted her eyelids at Georgia. Georgia grinned, and then looked up and noticed Banham was glaring at them.

Nine

Melek Yismaz had asked to be dropped a five-minute walk from her street. She said she fancied a walk, but Alison knew she was nervous of being seen in a car that belonged to a 'fed'.

Melek thanked Alison and started her walk home, taking the route around the side of the estate where the footbridge crossed a dried up stream and the parkland had become waste-land.

She had been walking for only a minute when she saw Bilaboo and Trent, Harisha's lieutenants, walking towards her from the other side of the pathway.

'Harisha wants you, innit,' Bilaboo told her as he approached. Bilaboo was another of Harisha's cousins; he was also over six and a half feet tall. He had come from the same part of Turkey as Harisha. The families had moved to England in the same year. The two boys had lived on the same estate in Bermondsey and grown up together, attending the same school, and bunking off lessons more frequently than attending them. They were selling drugs together from an early age, and both served time together in young offenders' centres, and then separately a few years later, in open adult prisons, for grievous bodily harm. Out of his seventy-strong gang, Harisha Celik trusted Bilaboo most of all, and Bilaboo, in his turn, worshipped Harisha Celik.

Melek felt threatened by their friendship. She knew Bilaboo would do anything for Harisha, and that he came before her in the pecking order of the gang. Normally Bilaboo was polite and kind to her. He took care of her when Harisha lost his temper and took it out on Melek. He would always walk her home to make sure she got there safely, but not say a word about the fact that Harisha had given her a slapping and then left her to fend for herself. To be Harisha's girlfriend, she'd had to be initiated into the gang, and pass a test, to prove loyalty to Harisha. The test involved having sex with a few of his chosen soldiers while

123

Harisha watched. Bilaboo and Trent were among the chosen eight. The gang-rape she was forced to endure was both demeaning and painful. She had been treated like a piece of meat, her hands had been tied, her knickers removed, and one by one each of the eight were told to enter her. They were not allowed to ejaculate, that was for Harisha alone. When they were near to ejaculation, they were to pull out and her job was to suck them off while Harisha watched. It was clear that Bilaboo hadn't wanted to partake, but he would never go against the word of Harisha. He was the last in the queue of eight. He had entered her only very briefly, and then kept his gaze averted to the garage wall while she performed the oral sex. All the while it went on, Harisha stood watching, telling them they were his brothers, his family and his blood, and he was happy to share with them.

After it was over Melek had become hysterical, and had shouted at Harisha that no family she knew had sex with each other, nor did they dish out that kind of pain if they cared for someone. That had earned her a hard slap across the mouth from Harisha. Her lip had stayed swollen for a week.

Walking towards her now, she was aware Bilaboo's large, dark eyes, with the over-long lashes, looked furious.

'Harisha wants you, innit,' he said again, gripping her arm and quickly turning her to walk in the opposite direction with him. Trent then moved in and gripped her other arm, walking close to her, as they started to frog-march her back to the street.

'Ow! You're hurting me,' she protested, attempting to pull away from them. 'What's going on?' I can walk on my own!'

They ignored her.

She raised her voice. 'I said, let go you're hurting me.'

Trent smacked her across the back of the head. 'Shut up.'

'You bastard.' Her tone was furious. She kicked him in the leg. That was the start, Bilaboo and Trent then both turned on her. Bilaboo grabbed her long black hair, twisting it round his hand until he reached her scalp, then tugging her head back and downwards, until she was bent backward and nearly dragged along the path. 'Heard you've been talking to the feds,' he said, still not looking at her. 'Against SLR rules, you know Harisha don't like none of us doing that.'

Trent landed a globule of spittle on her face. 'Fucking arsehole, fed sucker.'

Bilaboo's grip was now so tight on her hair that she was twisting her body to avoid her hair being tugged out. Her back was bouncing on the paving stones as she was dragged along the pathway towards the road.

From her upside-down position, body and head throbbing, she spotted the familiar black Porsche, with its tinted windows, speeding up the street. It pulled to a screaming halt by the pavement.

As they reached the car the back door opened, and she was thrown in, catching her shin as she fell, landing face down on Harisha's lap.

He was sat, bolt upright, wearing his dark glasses and staring straight ahead.

She struggled to get up, she was feeling dizzy and shocked. As she opened her mouth to protest his hand clamped over her lips. He removed his tinted glasses with his other hand and glared at her. 'You've said enough already.' His lizard-like eyes pierced into hers, and the scar on his neck seemed very prominent as his lip curled angrily.

He removed his hand from her face. 'We don't talk to the feds. You know that.'

'Harisha, I didn't, all I …' The hand clamped over her mouth again.

'You have broken SLR law and you will be punished.'

She bucked her head to free herself. He removed his hand, but held the cold glare.

'I had no choice,' she argued. 'I didn't tell them anything. They were asking about Zana. They knew she was my friend, and they dragged me in to tell them about her. I just told them that Wajdi was loose with his fists. That was all I said. Nothing about you.'

'What else they ask you?'

'Nothing. I swear I said nothing to them. It wasn't my idea, they made me come in, like they made you, to give them a statement. Harisha, two people have been murdered.'

'Don't tell me what I already know.' He curled his fist and landed a punch on her nose before she knew it was coming. Her hand flew to her nose as she tasted blood. She tried to sniff it back but it spilled through her fingers and ran over her hand.

'Not in my fucking car,' he shouted. 'Don't bleed in my fucking car.' He pressed the window button and shouted to Bilaboo and Trent, 'Get her out, she's fucking bleeding in my car.'

She had the back of her hand to her nose as the door opened and she was pulled out.

Bilaboo then dropped her on the pavement. Then she felt her feet being lifted, and Bilaboo was dragging her, her body bouncing again, across the stony ground beneath it, back over the path, out of sight of the road, then behind a tree on the wasteland, near the edge of the path, where again she was dropped.

Harisha was following, unzipping his jeans and as he strolled, checking around him to see no one was watching.

Bilaboo stood one side of him to mask any view as Harisha stood over Melek and pulled a knife from his ankle.

'No, please, Harisha, I haven't said anything.' Melek shrieked at him. Her jacket was already torn, and her face grazed and raw from being dragged, as well as the nosebleed she still endured. She started to sob loudly.

He ignored her plea. Bilaboo lifted her so her face was against the tree, then she felt the knife in the top of her jeans, by her spine. Her body shuddered as the knife moved, and she realised Harisha was tearing her jeans open. Next thing she felt the ice-cold wind on her bared buttocks. She tried to kick. Bilaboo and Trent stepped in and held her ankles and her wrists. Then she felt Harisha tickle her bare flesh with the sharp edge of the knife. She gasped. Next she knew, he had cut into her G-string, and she felt it fall from her, leaving her shivering buttocks bare and in full view.

She was frightened and angry and started to struggle.

126

Realising she was no match for Bilaboo and Trent, she then started to scream.

'Shut it.' Harisha quickly pulled the remains of her G-string from her bare bottom and in an instant had it tied around her mouth and face. Then she felt his penis against her, and next thing he had entered into her from behind, smashing her face brutally against the tree as he bounced ferociously against her.

Realising it was futile to fight, she buried her face into the tree and sobbed.

He was getting rougher as his excitement built. 'You're a cunt,' he shouted at her. 'Say it, what are you? Tell me? Tell me!'

She could only cry. Her G-string was bound around her mouth, as she whimpered and attempted to speak.

'Say it,' Harisha commanded, nearly out of breath from excitement, as he bounced speedily and brutally against her.

Bilaboo leaned over, took the knife from where Harisha had dropped it on the floor, and cut the G-string from her face so she could speak.

'A cunt,' she whispered through tears.

'And I am the boss.'

'And you're the boss,' she whimpered quietly.

The bouncing was increasing in frequency. The zip of his jeans was cutting into her bare bottom and thighs. He hadn't even bothered to take them down.' Say it again,' he panted, pushing hard in her.

'You are the boss.' she repeated.

The pain and pressure was becoming nearly unbearable. She was fighting with herself not to cry out. It suddenly came to an abrupt halt, and he leaned his weight against her against her for a couple of seconds, breathing heavily, before pulling himself out of her and zipping himself back into his jeans.

After telling her to call him when she was ready to apologise for what she had done, he turned and left.

Bilaboo and Trent followed him.

She clung to the tree, her face raw and throbbing, her nose still bleeding, and her bottom cold and raw.

When she heard the engine of the Porsche start up and the car roar off down the road she picked up her broken G-string, and attempted to cover her sore and throbbing body, then she stepped out of her jeans. They were muddy and filthy. She turned them back to front and stepped back in them, tying the torn material in a make-do knot to hold it together at the front, before pulling her large baggy T-shirt down to cover the damage.

She was five minutes away from her home, but did she dare go there now? She was filthy, and grazed, and bleeding. She had to pray that no fed would see her and pick her up again. The consequences of that were too terrifying to think about.

DCI Banham's eyes were fixed on Alison as she sat questioning Wajdi Ghaziani in the large front room of the Ghazianis' Victorian house.

Wajdi gave short, polite answers to her questions. He kept glaring at Alison, a look of contempt across his face, making it obvious he had no respect for women.

He admitted he had often smacked his sister, but that was reasonable, he told Alison and Banham, as Zana behaved badly and disrespected her family. When asked about the photos they had found on her computer of her swollen and beaten face, he became very defensive and said that was what he was protecting her against. Who was responsible for them, he didn't know, but he was on a mission to find out. In the end he looked after his sister, and how dare Alison even infer that he might be responsible for that damage. It was the gang she hung around with, he told her, they were violent bullies. He didn't know who they were, but he knew they were dangerous and trouble, and Wajdi, as all good brothers would, was trying hard to protect his sister.

Banham was taking in all Wajdi said, but he was becoming concerned about Alison. He thought she looked pale and tired. It had been a long, hard couple of days for her, and he intended to take great care of her from now on. She was carrying his baby, so however independent she wanted to be, it was his responsibility to make sure she was all right. His baby daughter, Elizabeth, had been brutally murdered, found lying in the arms of her murdered mother, fourteen years ago. Now he was being given a second chance to be a father, so he was taking that very seriously. He took a breath. Alison had only said she thought she was delighted at being pregnant. Alison was an independent woman and she would do what she wanted to do, but he really hoped it included him. Right now she needed some TLC. After interviewing the Ghazianis, he was going to drive her home, put her in a warm bath, and cook her supper. He felt the tingling of happiness that he had felt the night that Alison and him had first got together, a few years back, though that had been very short-lived. The next morning Alison had told him she didn't want it to get heavy, she wanted to keep the relationship casual. Shortly after that, when a fellow officer was killed, in the line of duty, Alison changed again, becoming very introverted, blaming herself for not preventing the death. She had become heavily depressed, said no longer wanted the relationship to continue and had taken compassionate leave.

Banham had visited her regularly during that time, in his role as DCI, building her confidence back up, telling her what a good detective she was, and how much they all missed her. Eventually she came back, but asked for a transfer to the Sapphire rape unit; she wanted to work with emotionally scarred women and track down their rapists. She started to find herself again during that time; she re-started their love affair, and then decided to come back to the murder division.

Now she was pregnant, and things might have to change again, although Banham knew her well enough to know she wasn't the kind to put her feet up and take nine months off.

'I've done nothing wrong,' Wajdi said again. 'It is my duty to stop my sister disrespecting my parents, and if that means a smack, then that is what happens.'

'Not in this country, it isn't,' Alison said sharply, handing him the photo of Zana with the iron mark burned on her back. 'What do you know about this?'

Wajdi shook his head. 'She didn't mean the iron to land,' he said. 'That was an accident. Zana had no right to photograph it. Mama was ironing and Papa was shouting at Zana. Zana walked into the iron. It was an accident. No one burned her on purpose.'

Alison stared at him.

'Don't look at me like that. It was an accident. She didn't report it because it was an accident.'

'But she did photograph it,' Alison reminded him. 'Perhaps she didn't report it because she was afraid. Of your parents? Or of you? Who was she afraid of, Wajdi? Alison pushed.

'No. She took no notice when I smacked her; she went with bad people and has gone and got herself killed.' He put his hands to his face, then took them away, and looked at Banham, ignoring Alison. 'Why don't you find who killed her, my family are grieving and you pick on us?'

'We intend to find who killed her,' Banham told him,' And they will be brought to justice.'

'He will not get away?' Wajdi asked.

'No, not a chance.'

'I am looking too, I will find …'

'Please do not try and take the law into your hands, or you will find yourself on the wrong side of it,' Banham said rising. 'Thank you for your time.'

Alison and Banham then spoke to Mrs Ghaziani, who related the story word for word about the iron burn. She showed Alison where she had stood, where Zana was and how she walked, backwards, into the iron. She said her bad friend, the Turkish girl, Melek, made her put it on Facebook.

Banham studied the small woman. She was polite, cold, with busy eyes on the move all the time.

The father had been asked to wait in another room with the family liaison officer while they questioned his wife. He was then called in, and he too, told the same story. Asked to demonstrate where everyone was, he pointed to the ironing board, and indicated exactly as the mother had done, where Zana walked in, and how she was half dressed, and the angle she was when she walked into the iron. It was identical, so much so, it could have been fabricated.

'Melek Yismaz was the influence that sent Zana down the wrong road,' the mother said as Banham and Alison thanked them for their time. 'But she is still our daughter,' she told Banham, 'and we need to bury her. You must understand. In our country we have a culture, it is the way.'

Banham glared at Mrs Ghaziani with his piercing blue eyes. 'In our country,' he told her, 'we have a law, and it is my job to see that is carried out.' He turned towards the door. 'We'll be in touch,' he put his arm protectively on Alison's back and headed back down the stairs.

The father followed them to the door. His heavy, high brow furrowed as he spoke. 'As soon as possible, we want our daughter,' he said again. 'This country has a lot to learn from Pakistan, about families and morals.'

'What do you think?' Alison asked Banham as they fastened their seat belts and he fired the engine.

'I think you look very tired,' Banham said tenderly. 'And I think nothing can be done until tomorrow. The post-mortem will tell us more. So that's it for us, until the morning.' He touched her hair and then stroked her pale cheek tenderly with the back of his fingers. He loved the feel of her face against his hands. 'I think I'll cook you supper and put you to bed.'

She lowered her eyes, and then threw them northward, letting out a loud sigh.

'What's wrong? Have I said the wrong thing again?'

'I'm not ill, quite the opposite. I'm in the early stages of pregnancy, and,' she turned to look at him, her eyes were intense. He knew that when those grey-green eyes were staring like that her temper was bubbling..

He just wasn't any good at saying the right things, but the truth was, he loved her to distraction.

He lifted both his hands defensively. 'And what?'

'And I am,' she smiled, 'delighted I am pregnant with your baby. But don't try and mother me, or I'll lose my enthusiasm.'

'I won't,' he shook his head. 'I promise I won't. I won't.'

Banham fired the ignition before she said anything else. He didn't speak another word until they got to the end of the road. 'I will take you home, though, and would cooking you dinner be too much?' he asked tentatively.

'Let's just pick up a takeaway,' she said.

'As long as it's not curry or Chinese, they can be quite spicy. Spicy food isn't good for mums-to-be, I read.'

'You're doing it again.'

'What?'

'Being all smothery-mothery.'

'Sorry.'

'Don't be sorry, just don't do it.'

'OK.' He drove for a little longer in silence and then he said, 'We are having fish and chips, I've decided. That's not mothering, that's the voice of your boss, being decisive; and stopping you eating the wrong things. Fish is very good for you.'

'That's fine,' she nodded.

They drove in silence for a few more minutes, then she said, 'I fancy three gherkins and a pickled onion.'

'Jesus!'

'I wouldn't mind a night of lust with the DCI,' Stephanie giggled to Georgia as they pulled into a parking spot a few roads away from the Aviary Estate.

'Dream on, he's all loved up with Grainger.'

'I bet I could change his mind if I could just get him in the sack,' Stephanie laughed. '

'If it's not food, it's sex with you,' Georgia said with a grin. 'Shall we talk about something else?'

'It's better than discussing the shade of paint you're redecorating your bachelorette pad with,' Stephanie teased.

'Not to me, it isn't.'

Stephanie lifted her bag across her neck so it was secure, then looked all around. Three squad cars were parked spasmodically along the road. She looked down the alleyway, as they made their way from one road to another and then into

132

the side road towards Sparrow block on the Aviary. Rain was spitting and the wind was blowing.

'There are garages all round here,' Georgia said walking past a row of lock-ups by Magpie and Lark blocks. 'The description has been circulated to all officers, but two more pairs of eyes can't hurt. Let's take a walk around all the other lock-ups.'

'Harisha Celik may well be lying.'

'I hope he is,' Georgia said turning to Stephanie. 'Otherwise it means Alysha Achter might be giving us duff information. She's never done it before, but ...'

'You'll feel let down,' Stephanie said finishing the sentence.

'Yes, I will feel let down. And I'll be furious, I have put my head on the block for her so many times, and if she is misinforming, then I will have her guts for garters.'

'Good, because sometimes I think ...'

Georgia stared at her,' Go on, what do you think?'

'I worry that you have an emotional attachment with her. She has no mother, and you have no children. Her mother came from the Caribbean, where your mother came from.'

'Observant of you,' Georgia said, looking around as they approached a row of garages. She dug in her pocket for a torch. 'Yes, I am fond of her. She's grown up on this crime-ridden estate without any parental guidance, and she's been badly abused. We have given character references to social and probation officers on her behalf, and kept her out of youth offenders' on account of her being an informant.'

She shone the torch, then switched it off, and looked back at Stephanie. 'Of course I feel a responsibility towards her. She's fifteen, not sixteen, you know it, I know it, but somehow she's managed to change all her official papers and become a year older. I also don't believe, for a second, that she even has a father. In the three years since we have known her, we've never seen him, not once.' She walked on and turned into another dark alleyway around the back of the estate. Two young black girls moved away from the corner of the alley as Georgia approached. 'So here she is, on this estate,' Georgia carried on, 'surrounded by hardened criminals. She swears she doesn't drink or take drugs and she survives by informing for us. Why wouldn't I believe her? Her past information has solved cases for us. So of course I don't want her to be playing us. Deep down, under that tough front, I think she's vulnerable, and I think she likes to know we are here if she needs us. I know of no other officer who has an informant on this estate, so she is like gold dust to our department.' Georgia shifted her shoulder bag across her body and pulled her torch out again.

They walked on, talking, and looking at the garages. Neither noticed, in the dark night light, that they were walking over dried spots of blood.

Then Stephanie spoke again. 'Given the choice between Alysha Achter and Harisha Celik, I'd believe her over him.'

Georgia nodded and smiled. 'You know, you are right, as usual. You're too clever for a sergeant. Alysha does bring out maternal instincts that I never thought I had.'

'Perhaps you should seduce the DCI.'

Georgia laughed. 'Oh, do stop.'

'The truth is, I think you'd probably rather paint all these run down garages than bed anyone. Look at the state of that one? She indicated to one that was hanging off its hinges, and covered in black gang graffiti.

'That's black paint, not red,' Georgia said looking closely, 'And all these garages are peeling and need painting. No sign of the one Celik says exists.

'It could be anywhere.'

'Maybe it doesn't exist.'

'Let's hope not.'

They turned the corner and headed to the stairs of Sparrow block.

Alysha had full make-up on and sported newly plaited cornrows that had been weaved with orange, red, and yellow beads entwined in the hair.

'People are gonna start talking if you keep coming round,' Alysha said as she opened the door. 'What you want now?'

'Have you got access to a lock-up?' Georgia asked walking straight into the flat and then the kitchen and looking around.

Alysha followed. She pulled out three mugs to make tea.

'Why would I want a lock-up?' She avoided looking at Georgia by busying herself opening a packet of tea bags and putting one in each cup.

Georgia's tone was hard. 'You tell me,' she said.

Alysha looked up. 'What is this? Are you accusing me of something, or something?'

'You've had your hair done,' Georgia said. 'Cornrows cost a lot to have done, don't they?'

Alysha stared at her. 'What's this about?'

'Alysha, we aren't stupid.' Stephanie told her. 'We know you're far from squeaky clean. We've got you off the hook for soliciting many times.'

'That was years back. I don't do none of that no more. You know I don't. I'm on probation. I don't want to go to prison, I don't want no more of any of that, I want to get it right now. Oh, and just for the record, Tink does my hair, for free. Should you want her services, I'll let her …'

'Cut the butter wouldn't melt in your mouth act,' Georgia snapped. 'This is me you are talking to. Do you have access to a lock-up?'

'No.' Alysha banged the mug down and turned angrily to face Georgia. 'Listen, I put my neck on the line and I help you, let you know what's going on around here. If I was found grassing up to feds, I'd be dead. You and I both know that.' She held Georgia's eyes. 'I don't do no soliciting. You told me to stop, and I did. I manage OK. I get a bit of money from you lot, and what I get from the social. Why'd you think I have a lock-up?' She looked at them, and then breathed a sarcastic sigh, and half-laughed. 'Oh I get it, you arrest Celik, the,' – she indicated with her long, vivid orange, nails the inverted comma signs – 'guilty as hell bastard who has a business going on with a stack of machetes and firearms that could kill half of South London, and he tells you it's me that's doing it. So, cos you can't prove its 'im, you come round to ask if I've got a lock-up. Are you 'avin a laugh? Is that what this about?'

'No, this isn't a laughing matter,' Stephanie said sternly.

'I don't know where he keeps them,' she raised her voice. 'I only know he deals them.'

'Then you need to find out exactly where this lock-up is, because without any proof, we don't have a case,' Georgia told her. 'What about Zana Ghaziani, and Burak Kaya, have you any more information for us, on them?'

'I'm asking around,' she said lowering her eyes. She then lifted her head and said,' You know I do all this, put my head on the block for you all the time, and do you even care that the council won't put no money into building up the kids' playground area down there. I mean, in the end it stops crime, don't it? Cos it keeps the kids occupied, an' then they don't go wrong as they grow up. Oh an' we need money to rebuild them youth clubs an' all that.'

'I'm sorry, Alysha, it isn't my job,' Georgia told her, although she secretly admired the girl for caring. 'I have asked you to ask around about Zana Ghaziani. What have you found out?'

'I've said, I'm on it, but as yet nothing more to report.'

'Well get on it more,' Georgia pushed. She then turned and walked out of the kitchen, into the untidy lounge room and started looking around.

Alysha followed. 'Why am I getting all this interrogation and grief? I ain't done nothing.'

'Where did you really get your hair done?' Georgia said without looking at her. 'Hair extensions aren't cheap, you said you were short of money.'

Alysha became angry. 'What you accusing me of, here? I ain't done nothing. My pal Tink, she's the real business at it. She does all this.' She looked at Georgia, both trying to read the other, 'If we 'ad enough money we'd open her a hair an' beauty shop round here.'

Georgia didn't answer. She turned and started looking around the room. There was a picture of Alysha with Tink, Lox, and Panther on the side. 'Is that Tink? The skinny one with the

136

pink hair?

Alysha looked a bit shocked. 'Yeah, that's her. You know her. She grew up round here. She's given up doing punters, she just wants to do hair and beauty, an' practices on me, that ain't no crime.'

When Georgia didn't answer Alysha started to get irritated. 'Listen, we are just trying to survive. We don't do no soliciting, and we don't take drugs no more, none of us. We all just hang out together, just girls havin' a laugh, that's all.'

Georgia turned to face her. 'Your gang, is it?'

Alysha was getting angry. 'Everyone's got a gang of mates, ain't no law says you can't have mates. We look after each other, an' we all want good stuff for the kids on the estate. We are working on it, too. I know I gotta stay clean and out of trouble, but I also gotta watch it down here. There's a lot would kill me soon as look at me if they knew I was snitching to you feds, so I need my mates.'

Georgia's tone softened. 'I am aware how vulnerable you are,' she said speaking kindly for the first time since she had entered the flat. 'And I told you, you can call me anytime, I am your friend, your very good friend, but if you break the law I will be your worst nightmare. Do you understand?'

'I ain't done nothing.'

'Good, because there's no getting round me if you have.' She looked Alysha in the eyes and Alysha looked at her back. 'So you need to tell me the truth. Are you pulling a girl gang together?'

Alysha frowned, then lifted her eyebrows and cocked her head to one side. 'I've got mates, girls, yeah, told you, we have to be in gangs round here, and I have mine, but we don't do nothing other than paint our nails and do girls' stuff, and try and help the kids to get their play area back.'

'Do your girl gang friends know you inform for me, because that could make you vulnerable?'

Before Alysha had time to answer, Georgia's phone rang. She checked the screen and put it to her ear.

'I'll be right there,' she said into the phone after listening to the caller.

'Sergeant Green, Steph,' she called urgently into the kitchen, 'cancel the tea. Something's come up.'

Ten

Just as Banham walked into the room, holding a plate of fish and chips, Alison's phone rang. He waited while she took the call, watched her take both gherkins from the plate and munch into them as she spoke. 'Uniform officers at the Aviary have located a lock-up that matches the description Celik gave us. I'll have to go.'

'I'll drive you. I'll put the fish and chips back in the paper and you can eat them in the car.'

'No,' she shook her head. 'We'll reheat them and eat them when we get back, that'll be better.'

He watched as she ate the gherkins. 'You want to be careful of indigestion,' he told her but his words trailed off as he realised she wasn't listening. Her teeth were holding the second gherkin in a vice-like grip while she used her hands to pull on her fur-lined parka and then covered her long hair with a woolly, bobbled cap.

'Just as well it's me and not Georgia Johnson driving,' he said as he grabbed his own thick sheepskin coat.

'Why?'

'She forbids strong-smelling food in her car, and if you leave dirt from your shoes, or empty sweet papers in there, you live to regret it.'

'I'll remember that,' she said, disappearing into the kitchen and reappearing with the pickled egg she'd persuaded Banham to get at the takeaway. It was wrapped in kitchen foil, which she slipped discreetly into her pocket. Banham held her eyes for a minute, then her said tenderly. 'You need to watch your intake of acid, your stomach –'

'You said you wouldn't nag me,' she interrupted.

'I suppose eating is out of the question,' Stephanie said feebly as they made their way from the bottom of the stairs on

139

Sparrow block across to the run-down garages by Crow block.

Georgia nodded. 'Yup, and sex,' she told her lightly. 'So get used to it, it's going to be a long night.'

Stephanie raised a woolly gloved hand in a mock gesture. 'As I had my mind set on the DCI, I accept no sex, as Grainger is back,' she said shaking her head. 'But going without supper, now that really is way past the call of duty.'

'With all the faeces around here and the stink of urine, I'm not sure I ever want to eat again,' Georgia said.

'As soon as we're finished, I'm buying us both a large Chinese takeaway,' Stephanie said.

'Time we've finished here, all we'll get will be a disgustingly greasy kebab,' Georgia told her. 'Served by an equally disgusting shop owner who is only open late because if anywhere else was open, then no one would buy his food. Oh, and I'll have to watch you don't get desperate enough to try and seduce him,' she teased. 'So, better idea – we go to a twenty-four hour garage and get you a curled-up sandwich, less likely to give you the runs.' She noticed the painful expression Stephanie had pulled. 'Or you could give up food just for today,' she suggested.

'I'd rather give up being a detective.'

About a dozen uniformed officers had surrounded the dark red garage. The paint was certainly peeling down the door which also displayed the skull and cross that Celik had described and there was a padlock securing it.

Georgia's heart hit her boots. If Harisha Celik was telling the truth, which now seemed likely, that also meant that Alysha Achter was lying to her. The arms and drugs that Georgia was confident lay the other side of this garage door would now lead back to Alysha. Harisha would never give up his own supply.

Georgia was up to her neck in it with the DCI as it was. An informant who gave duff information would only serve to lessen his confidence in her detective skills. The team had been giving her grief for months about Alysha. None of them, including Stephanie, fully trusted the girl. All frequently brought up Alysha's past record for under-age prostitution, selling class A drugs, and use of a firearm. Georgia always defended her, believing that the system had let her down. If it turned out that the girl was playing Georgia, then not only would Georgia look a fool, having allowed her, normally, sound judgement to be shaken, but it would stand in the way for her future promotion. In the short time she had been a DI, she had already made mistakes. She knew that Stephanie was the more experienced of the two of them, and had passed her DI exams, but had turned the post down because of her domestic responsibilities. Georgia needed to prove her worth, and as joint SIO on this case, she needed a good result if she was to win respect from the whole team.

As usual around this estate when anything went down, a crowd gathered. That was now happening, mainly kids, as young as six or seven, circling around with their goose-pimpled legs curled around the pedals of bicycles that were far too small for them. They were the 'youngers', the 'tinies', of the estate gangs, there to grab information and then cycle back and sell the information to the elders on the estate, so the elders were up to date with what was happening. These youngers could outrun any police officers, so were paid by the elders to hide drugs and guns when a police raid took place.

But who were the elders, or gang hierarchy around here? These youngers knew, but would be paid not to tell. Georgia hoped Alysha wasn't up to her neck in a girl gang, as Celik had suggested. She had a soft spot for Alysha, and she also admired the fact that Alysha cared and wanted to help these kids. It was obvious, just by looking around, that by rebuilding the recreation area and, as Alysha suggested, the community centre, that these youngsters would have more chance of avoiding a life of crime. Banham continually told Georgia that it wasn't her job to nag the council, she was a detective, not a social worker, but Georgia believed a good detective looked at all ways of stopping crime, and that Alysha's plan was a good one.

She looked up and saw Alison Grainger followed by Banham making their way across the estate grounds.

'Have you found out who the lock-up belongs to, yet?
Georgia asked the uniformed sergeant who was waiting with his team for further orders.

'Belongs to an Albert and Vera Wilkins, ma'am,' Sergeant Austin told her. 'They live on Magpie block, number 211.'

Georgia shouted across to Banham and Alison as they approached. 'Garage belongs to Albert and Vera Wilkins. They live round the corner.'

Alison glanced at Banham, then back to Georgia. 'Let's pay them a visit. See if they'll give us a key, before we take the door down,' she shouted back.

Georgia turned to Stephanie. 'You go and grab a bite to eat while I do that,' she told her with a grin. 'And then oversee the door to door. Show everyone the photos of Burak and Zana. If anyone shows even a faint recognition when they look at either of them, bring them in for questioning.'

'Will do, ma'am,' Stephanie nodded. 'Thanks, but, we won't hold our breath on that score.'

'You never know,' Georgia winked, 'Might be your lucky day. You didn't think you'd get a food break before midnight, and hey presto, the magic fairy obliged. So don't give up.'

There was an icy wind blowing. Georgia watched Banham pulling Alison's woolly hat further over her head and checking her scarf was warm against her neck.

'Don't fuss, I'm fine,' Alison told Banham, then looking to Georgia, she said. 'Let's go then.'

'If you don't get a key within the next ten minutes, this door's coming down, tell them,' Banham shouted as the women walked towards Magpie block.

On hearing that, the young kids on bicycles turned and rode off. They had info, and they needed to sell it before anyone else did. The bicycles all sped along the footpath, bells ringing loudly.

'Sergeant Green,' Georgia called out to Stephanie. 'See what direction those kids are heading.'

Stephanie lifted a thumb. 'Will do my best.' But she was too late. The kids cycled past her, knocking her over, and disappeared before she could even get back up.

Melek Yismaz was being very cautious as she crept around the back of the Aviary, heading for the Sparrow Block. She had been warned, by Alysha's girls, of the heavy police presence. They were everywhere, stopping people as they walked around the estate, and knocking on doors. If they spotted her, shaking and filthy, grazed and bruised, with a swollen face, thanks to that bastard Harisha and his boys, then, for sure, she would be picked up and brought in again, and that wasn't worth thinking about.

She was very familiar with the estate and knew all the nooks, crannies, and alleys that she could hide in if she saw a fed, and that gave her the upper-hand, just, as she crept, slowly and cautiously, towards Sparrow block.

She was angry as well as shaken, but there was no way he was getting away with what he had done, and this opportunity was perfect for her. Alysha had summoned Melek to the flat immediately when she'd rung and told Alysha what Harisha had done, and said she wanted to join the ACs. She hadn't dared go home first to change, so she had nipped into the Indian shop on the outskirts of the Aviary – the one that kept open all hours and sold all kinds of food and drink. There she had nicked the table cloth from under the display of freshly cooked chapattis, and now, to add insult to injury, as well as being cut and bruised, she stank of curry powder. But beggars couldn't be choosers, she told herself, covering her nudity was more important. And not just because the sharp wind was biting into her private parts – that in itself was a bastard – but more worrying was the feds seeing her; a half-dressed, injured girl would be stopped and questioned immediately.

There was no way she could have gone home. If her father saw her torn jeans and bare arse, she would get the beating of her life, or worse still be dragged to the feds again. Harisha had gone too far this time, her arse was raw and throbbing from the bastard's roughness. She was fighting the urge to cry – and that wasn't like her. Her journey to the thirteenth floor of Sparrow block was taking a very long time, but she was getting there. She and Alysha Achter had business to sort.

Vera Wilkins looked terrified as she opened the door of her flat to the sight of Georgia and Alison flashing their warrant cards. She quickly crooked her turkey neck to the left and then to the right. No one seemed to be watching her, so she opened the door and ushered them hurriedly inside.

The flat smelt musky and stale as they followed through into the sitting room.

The room was dark and old-fashioned, an over-crowded mess. The sideboard was dusty and cluttered with fading photographs in old frames, and little trinkets obviously collected over the years. Dusty imitation flowers stood in a long-stemmed green glass vase, a few odd glasses on a tray beside it. Georgia found the room depressing.

She thought Albert's clothes looked as though he had owned them since he was a boy. The grey flannel trousers and home-made knitted waistcoat looked exactly like the one child evacuees always wore in wartime photographs, the only difference being that Albert's trousers went to all the way to his ankles. Georgia was reminded of those frightened young boys, with short haircuts and gas masks in their tiny, terrified hands. She appreciated this old couple had seen many, many changes during the years they had lived on the estate.

'How long have you lived here?' she asked as she waved away the teapot of tea that Albert offered. She didn't want to think how long the tea might have been in the pot, or the state of the cup it would be served in. Alison also refused.

'We've been here since we married,' Albert answered looking over to his gentle-faced but highly nervous wife.

'We celebrated our golden anniversary two years ago,' Vera nodded, pushing a hair-clip that had slid from her fine, light grey bun at the back of her head, back into place.

'How long have you had your garage?' Alison asked.

The couple turned to each other, both looked terrified.

'You have a garage at the edge of the estate. 14b, is that

right? The red one with a skull and cross pinned to the door?' Alison persisted.

Albert shook his head, as Vera nodded hers.

'It's a straightforward question,' Alison said a little curtly.

When both became silent, Alison said, 'You need to know that we are investigating a murder enquiry, and this lock-up could have something to do with it. If you withhold vital information, or give us false information, that is a crime that could carry a custodial sentence.'

Georgia glared at Alison, as the old couple made eye contact.

'I'll tell them,' Vera said. Her hand had moved fearfully to her cheek, and Georgia noticed the large liver-coloured age spot above the woman's now trembling, lips. Georgia knew, that this couple had been warned off talking to the feds, threatened that the punishment from the ruling gang would be too terrifying to think about. Watching the behaviour of this vulnerable old couple made her more determined than ever to crack down on crime around the Aviary.

'We do have a garage,' Vera said, still looking at Albert for assurance.

Albert looked back at her, terrified. 'We had a car, you see,' she told them. 'A little Nissan Micra. I used to drive us in it as Albert's eyes aren't too good these days.' She frowned and hesitated, taking a second before saying, 'The car was stolen. We didn't get it back, nor could we claim the insurance money for it. The insurance company said the garage wasn't secure enough, so they wouldn't pay out. We couldn't afford to buy another car.' She shrugged. 'Anyway, next thing we knew, we'd lost the garage too.'

'How do you mean lost the garage?' Alison asked her.

Vera looked at Albert again. He was now sitting upright and nearly stiff with terror.

Vera shrugged and shook her head.

'Did you report any of this?' Georgia asked her.

She shook her head, still watching Albert. 'We didn't need a garage, as we didn't have a car anymore, so we didn't say anything. When we walked past it, it was occupied, and we were told to make ourselves scarce.'

'By who?'

'We couldn't say,' Albert butted in. 'Can't tell these days, they all look the same, hoods up, and masks over their faces.'

'Were they male or female?'

'Both, both, there were both,' he answered quickly nodding his head a little too many times. 'Look, we don't want to say any more. Will you go now? Please?'

'It isn't as easy as all that,' Georgia told him. 'If you didn't report the keys as stolen, then officially you're still responsible for it. If there is anything in there that shouldn't be, then you may be held responsible. Unless you can tell us who has taken it over?'

'And you need to give us the key,' Alison told him. 'Or we will break the door down.'

Albert's voice was breaking as he spoke. 'We haven't got a key, they changed the lock.'

'Jail would be preferable to being killed,' Vera said. Noticing the shock that registered on Alison and Georgia's faces, she explained, 'That's what happens round here if you talk.'

'We haven't anything to tell you, and we haven't got a key, so please will you go now,' Albert said, his voice now quiet and defeated.

Georgia stood up and headed for the door. Alison followed her.

'Don't go to bed just yet, you might not be sleeping here tonight,' Alison told them as she opened the door to let herself and Georgia out.

'What was the point in frightening them?' Georgia said angrily as they walked back down the one flight of steps at the side of Magpie block. 'They already live in terror on this estate. All the honest citizens do. And it's mostly our fault. We have failed them by not protecting them from the gangs and drug barons. Frightening them will make it worse. That man looks like a heart attack waiting to happen.'

146

'If there are weapons in that garage, then who do you think will carry the can, not the bullies,' Alison argued. 'That couple need to know that we are to be feared too if they get on our wrong side, otherwise our battle against gang warfare round here is lost. Right now we are in mid-fight.'

'Gang fighting has escalated nearly out of control in the past few years,' Georgia argued. 'You've been out of this for a while, and this estate is the worst in London. It's –'

'Oh do give it a rest,' Alison snapped back. 'I've been in the force a lot longer than you, and just because I took time out does not mean I took up knitting,'

Vera and Albert were standing at their window watching Alison and Georgia walking back to the garage.

'We should have said something, we should have told them,' Vera said to Albert.

'They can't prove nothing,' he argued. ''Sides, getting done for withholding evidence is a lot more preferable than seeing you beaten up again. That would be more than I can take.'

'Maybe if we had told them, then all this would go away.'

'It'll never go away.' He shook his head. 'It's like the last lot. They got them, finally, after all the hidings people took, and now it's starting all over again. It's never going to end, flower. I just wish we didn't know what we know and hadn't seen what we have seen.'

'But we do know, and we did see, so now we're involved.'

'Well, block it from your mind. Tell yourself we don't. We don't know nothing.'

The red enforcer crashed through the lock-up door, and Alison, Banham, and Georgia moved straight in. They stared around an empty garage that reeked of cleaning fluids.

'Someone's tipped someone off,' Alison said.

'Or Harisha Celik has lied to us,' Georgia suggested, feeling, secretly, a little relieved.

Banham shook his head. 'He wouldn't have had time to sort anything out,' he said, turning to take Alison's arm. 'Home,' he said to her. 'Come on, let's get you home, you look exhausted. And you need to eat.'

'It's been a tough day,' Georgia agreed, noticing Alison blush as Banham spoke to her as if she was a small child. But Banham wasn't even listening, he was heading out of the garage, in the direction of his car, holding Alison's arm as if it was a crystal glass.

Georgia watched them.

All she had to look forward to was a long hot bath.

When Melek finally got to the thirteenth floor flat, Alysha, Panther, Lox, and Tink were all there, waiting for her.

She sat down gingerly on the chair that was offered and started sobbing.

'Pack that up,' Panther told her sternly. 'If you want to join us, you'll have to be a warrior. We fight blokes, if we have to.' She looked round at the other girls, laughed, and added, 'Only difference is, we always win.'

When Melek quietened down, Alysha said, 'Anyway, we got Tink here. She can fix you up. She's brilliant at making you look fabulous, whatever the problem. She's gonna be a beautician and hairdresser soon.'

'It's only surface grazes,' Tink said, moving in to study Melek's messed up face. 'It won't scar. I'll clean it up for you, and make it look much better.'

'My arse is cut too, and my best fucking jeans are in shreds, and I'm wearing a tablecloth that stinks of chapattis, anything you can do about that?'

'Laugh at it,' Alysha told her, grinning at the other girls. 'We've all had a lot worse than that.' She gave Melek a few seconds to take that in, then she said, 'We don't get upset in the Alley Cat Crew. But we do get even.'

'We got each other, an' we work together and things get done,' Panther told her.

'Lox here got raped, regular, by her dad; started when she was about eight,' Alysha said with a matter-of-fact shrug. 'Panther was thrown on the fire, when she was nine, for not getting enough money on the streets to pay her uncle's dealer. Tink was locked in a room and not fed till she'd done thirty punters in a morning. She was eleven then. Oh, and I've had to kill someone to survive here. I know your Dad's loose with his fists, and Harisha's a cunt, and rapes you to keep you in your place, but now you've seen the light fings will get better for you. Well if you work well and we join you up, then they will, but you gotta prove yourself before you can be an Alley Cat. '

The other three verbalised their agreement, as Panther proudly showed her scars and missing teeth, and then Tink too lifted her skirt and showed the scar she got from a violent pimp.

'If you join us,' Alysha told her, 'then as well as yourself, you 'ave to 'elp the other lost kids round 'ere that are going through all the shit we went through, and help them get chances so they don't all end up as skanks or druggies.'

'What d'you mean?' Melek asked.

'We make money, but we use it to rebuild the estate and make things happen, like Tink's gonna learn hair and beauty properly and then teach it. Panther's doing self-defence, stuff like that. You're a looker, you could be a model if you wanted. As an Alley Cat we would help you, and then the money you make you'd invest back in our youngers an' stuff.'

'What, don't you buy nothing for you when you make money?' Melek asked them.

'Yeah, bits, but we don't do alcohol no more, an' we don't do drugs,' Tink told her. 'But we get money all ways we can.'

'Like I'm good at shoplifting, but then I sell the stuff I nick, or take it back to the shop for my money back, and we invest it into the estate,' Alysha explained. 'You still wanna be wiv us?'

'Yeah, I wanna be with you,' Melek said. 'Not SLR, no more.'

Alysha studied her, then nodded. 'Good. I'm glad you've seen the light wiv that cunt Harisha. An' you understand Burak deserved a punishment?'

'Yeah, I know,' Melek said. 'He was a lieutenant, they're all the same. He deserved what he got, no doubt.'

'But we never meant to kill 'im,' Alysha added quickly.

'That was an accident. SLRs done over a couple of our old residents, stole their car and their garage, an' wouldn't give them no corn for what they done. That stunk an 'e deserved a beating. They was pensioners an' he mugged them, hurt then, frightened them, stole from them, an' on our turf. We was never gonna let him get away wiv that, so we wanted to hurt him, but not kill him, but he died.' She shrugged. 'We never touched you, cos we don't hurt girls …'

'Unless they start on us, or cross us,' Panther jumped in.' 'Then we treat them same as blokes that cross us.'

Melek nodded. 'I hear you, and I'm not crossing you. I wanna be an Alley Cat.'

'Fair enough,' Alysha told her. 'Well you 'ave to go on trial first, you'll understand that.'

Melek nodded and wiped her nose with the back of her hand. 'I ain't afraid of a fight, even if I'm upset now.'

'You never grew up the way we all did, having to beg and whore for food,' Panther told her. You 'ad parents and things.' Her voice became threatening. 'So, you're on trial, we'll be watching you.

'I'll prove myself,' she said. 'You wanna get Harisha an' I know more about him that anyone.'

'That's true, she does,' Lox said, looking at Alysha. 'An' I never grew up on this estate neither, but you know I'd give my life for you.'

Alysha nodded warmly. 'Yeah, I know, an' me for you.' She turned back to Melek. 'You'll start as a soldier, but you can work your way up,' she told her. 'We are out to get money in our coffers, the more you get us, the better you'll do.'

'It's a bit like being Robin Hood, if you know who he is,' Tink said.

'Yeah, I do,' Melek nodded.

'That's good, cos I'm still not sure,' Tink told her. 'But Panther says he's really famous, and one day we might be.' Tink was now dabbing Melek's cuts and cleaning her face up. 'No one gets away wiv hurting an Alley Cat. If they do, the rest of us will kill them.'

'It's a lot better than them SLR,' Melek said quietly.

'Yeah, it is. But you have to pass a test,' Alysha told her.

'I'll get you inside info on Harisha an' stuff.'

'Good,' Alysha nodded. 'And you can get that cunt Harisha back for what he's done to you.'

'An we'll make sure he goes down, too,' Panther assured her. 'Then he'll be out of your way, and clear of our territory,'

'I told you about the tunnel under the river near Lambeth, didn't I?' Melek said. 'That's where he keeps all his gear; guns, drugs, and machetes too. I'd be dead if he knew I'd told you that.'

Alysha nodded. 'Yeah, you did, and we made good use of that information,' she grinned. 'So you wanna know what you gotta do?'

'What?' Melek asked, looking from one face to another.

'You are gonna get cuntface, Harisha, locked up on a rape charge,' Alysha told her.

Melek looked suddenly dry-eyed and sober. 'What, snitch to the feds?' she said looking baffled. 'I thought we deal with our own stuff.'

'We do,' Alysha agreed looking from one Alley Cat to another. 'But this is the plan. You are gonna talk to the feds,' Alysha told her, looking at Panther again. 'Because, she paused carefully weighing her words, 'we use the feds too.' She let that sink in. 'See that's how we do so well. It's called being cleverer. Feds think we are the victims, and we let them think that. An' so they help us, an' in return we can help our estate, an' rebuild our estate.'

Melek stared at Alysha. 'You're a grass?'

'No. We are victims,' Tink said sincerely.

''Cept we've learned that if you wanna survive you have to be smarter than everyone,' Lox said.

'The authorities have written us off as a waste of money and space,' Alysha said. 'No good to no one. So, we've turned the tables. '

'Together, we have a plan,' Panther added.

'And we will win,' Alysha assured her. 'Harisha is scum.

You said that yourself. You wanna get one up on 'im?'

'Yes, I do.'

'Then let's get 'im put away, and all like 'im. He's poisoning all the youngers for miles around, feeding them crack. He needs to be got rid of. Don't matter 'ow we do it, as long as it's done. And that's where you come in.'

Melek stared at her, but said nothing.

'Harisha will go down for a long time,' Lox assured her. 'So never again will he nor his bastard Turks bother you, after this. If they try, we'll fight together. We've already killed one.'

'We never meant to kill Burak,' Alysha said again.

Melek nodded slowly. 'OK. I'll do it,' she said.

'You won't regret it. We'll look after you,' Tink told her.

'But if you double-cross us,' Panther said looking at her with cold eyes. 'Then, we will kill you.'

'Cos Alley Cats are going forward,' Alysha said stretching out her hand to Melek. 'And we don't let nothing get in our way. So?'

Melek hesitated and then reached out and took Alysha's hand. 'Count me in,' she said. 'But could anyone lend me a skirt to wear, or a pair of jeans? I can't go home like this.'

Eleven

02:00 Thursday

Desk Sergeant Derek Spaniel disliked working the all-night shifts. When he was a young PC he'd set his mind on a CID job for the very purpose of avoiding the dawn choruses. In those early days of his police career he'd enjoyed working nights. It was the dragging himself out of bed at 3.30 in the morning that he couldn't abide. CID didn't have to do all that.

Then he got married, they had a baby, then another, and it just never seemed to be the right time to sit those CID exams. And now the years had gone by and here he was, looking forwards to his pension. He kept a photograph of his large family on his desk, and a brochure for Las Vegas. That was where he was taking them all when he retired next year, and he was counting the days.

He had just been to the canteen and got his supper, with some strong tea in the mug his youngest grandson had brought him last Christmas, when the internal phone rang. It was Valerie on the switchboard.

'There's a Mrs Wilkins on the line asking to speak to DI Johnson or DI Grainger. As neither are here,' Valerie told him, 'd'you want to talk to her? She sounds a bit all over the place.'

'Put her on,' he told Valerie, balancing his large oatcake on the counter and his full mug of tea on his paperwork.

'Sergeant Spaniel speaking, can I help you?'

'I was wanting to talk to Detective Johnson or Detective Grainger,' she said. Her voice was nervy and hesitant. 'Is that possible?'

'It isn't, I'm sorry, madam. I can pass a message to them for you. What was it concerning?'

'Er ... oh, er, I can't ... it's a bit worrying. Sorry, no, I need to talk to her ... Detective Johnson.'

153

'About what, madam?'

'It's about some …' The line was getting fainter, as if she was moving away from the phone.

'Sorry, I missed that, could you speak up, please, Mrs Wilkins? I'm having trouble hearing you. What is the message for DI Johnson? Hello? Can you give me your contact number and I'll pass it on to her, please. It's about, what?'

There was silence the other end.

'Mrs Wilkins, this is a bad line. What was it about?'

Her voice was very faint. 'Nothing, oh, er … nothing. I'll call again?'

'I can put you through to the investigation room. If no one's there you can leave a message, would that help?'

'Oh … er, yes, if you like.'

The new SLR lock-up reeked of engine oil. It had previously belonged to a car-mad retired businessman. The man had recently passed away, his cars sold, so when the SLR heard about it going empty they broke in, changed the lock, and took it over. It was their current meeting place.

The location was perfect, on the corner of some parkland and near the boundary of their territory and the Aviary. Every now and again the gang took over a new lock-up, and moved some of their stash of arms and drugs from the tunnel to their new garage, ready to be sold on the street. Moving their gear around kept the feds at bay. If any of them got a sniff that drugs were in a lock-up, by the time they came to investigate the gear had been moved on. Harisha was always one step ahead.

He was going to have to forfeit the weapons he had recently stashed in his acquired lock-up on the Aviary. He didn't mind, it was a cheap price to pay for grassing Alysha Achter. Her DNA, and her skanky Alley Cats', would be all over it after what Melek had told him they'd done to Burak in there. Now Alysha Achter would get her comeuppance. Her and those skanks would be arrested in no time for possession of weapons. The chief skank was already on probation, so she would get a long lump for possession of dangerous weapons and drugs with intent to sell. He smiled at the thought of her rotting in jail. He would take over the business on the Aviary and no one would dare stand in his way. There were good pickings; lots of youngers around to feed free drugs to, get them begging to buy crack in no time, and then they were his to use; build up his street girls, and make himself even riches.

The rest of his stash was under the river, in the locked tunnel. It was safe there. In the next few days he would send his inner circle of lieutenants over to move some of it to this new lock-up, ready to sell on the streets. By that time Alysha Achter would be out of his way and he'd move onto the Aviary.

Since his encounter with Melek he'd been home, changed, bathed, and eaten, then spent two hours on the phone wheeling and dealing drugs and firearms to his contacts. The power that made him feel always gave him a hard-on, so he had called in two of the gang girls and had sex with them. He was about to do it again when his mobile had rung, with news from Bilaboo and Trent that the feds were all over the Aviary and had broken into the lock-up as planned.

He told Bilaboo that he was delighted, things were going to plan. That was when Bilaboo broke the news that the feds had found nothing: the drugs, guns, and machetes that had been stored in that lock-up had disappeared, and the lock-up was empty.

Harisha immediately flew into a rage. 'Those filthy skanks must have been tipped off. They've stolen my gear, again,' he told Bilaboo. 'They think they can make us look like cunts. They must be found and punished. Call a meeting,' he barked. 'As many soldiers at the new lock-up as we can track, and asap. No one does the SLR down.' Then he added that Bilaboo should also pass the word that soldiers were to be careful if they were carrying weapons, as it was highly likely a stop and search patrol would be in place.

Harisha kicked the chair hard as he clicked his phone shut. Not only were those skanks trying to make him look like a cunt, but Melek hadn't phoned him yet to apologise for displeasing him earlier today. Normally, after he had beaten and raped her, she would be on the phone within the hour, crying and saying she was sorry, that she couldn't live without him. Now, hours had gone by and he had heard nothing.

By the time Harisha showered and got to the meeting, the soldiers had gathered. He walked to the front of the lock-up and stood on an old wooden box. He was a short man so he always stood on a box when addressing his gang, it made him feel more powerful.

Most of the soldiers had their hoods up and were carrying. They had been expecting friction because of the death of Burak, and then Zana, so all were tooled up in case anything went down: shanks, bats, cleavers, hammers, and a few guns. The Chinese boys had machetes inside large windbreaker sweaters, and were ready to do serious damage with them, but it seemed none had, as yet, even seen any of the top Alley Cat girls.

'You must be very careful what you are carrying,' Harisha told them. 'It's flooded with feds out there. You must carry indiscreet tools. Nothing that can link us back to the missing gear from the Aviary lock-up'

'Everyone is out an about looking for them Alley Cat skanks, an' we're heavily tooled, innit?' Odd, a Chinese boy, told him.

'Just be careful,' Harisha warned them. 'Anyone got anything to report on bout Zana or Burak? he asked.

'I heard Melek took photos of Zana when she was beat before,' Odd said. 'She's put them photos online too. There's one on Zana's Facebook, Wajdi shouting at her, and you're in it, Harisha, you're in the background, and it's on fucking Facebook.'

'How's I on it?'

'Zana must have been with Burak, hanging out an' all, and Wajdi turned up. You was just hanging in background, but it was you,' he said. 'Feds'll cop that one soon enough.'

Harisha looked furious. 'Melek's been mouthing off,' he told them. 'I sorted her earlier, but I ain't seen her since. When I see her, I'll tell her to take the picture down, but still, I could just be there, couldn't I? I didn't have to be involved just cos I was hanging out in the back of a picture someone took. Ain't no crime in that.'

Bilaboo shook his head. 'Melek ain't got sense,' he said.

'I saw her earlier,' Adder said.

Harisha's head turned in Adder's direction, ears pricked. 'How's that? Where d'you see her?'

'You sent me over to Aviary to watch the lock-up that the feds found and were breaking into. I saw her then. She's on Aviary territory.'

Harisha turned his angry eyes to Bilaboo, then he brought them back to Adder. 'Doing what?' he asked.

Adder shrugged. 'Dunno, she looked a bit roughed-up. She was at the back alley that leads to Sparrow block.'

Again Harisha turned to Bilaboo. The penny was beginning to drop. 'That's where them Alley Cat skanks live.' he said, his voice giving away his anger as he looked at his cousin Bilaboo.

'Find her. I want her brought in here,' Harisha shouted at them all.

'What, you think she's a turncoat?' Bilaboo asked shaking his head in disbelief.

Harisha raised his voice again. 'We need to find her. She knows way too much. So get out there and get looking. Just take weapons you can conceal, but take your phones in case you need backup or something. She'll fight you, if you try to get her.' He raised his voice and gave the word, 'Everyone get out there, and find that slut, and I want them Alley Cats.' He turned to Bilaboo. 'Phone Melek, tell her I want to see her, or arrange to meet her, and then bring her here, to me.'

'S'pose she don't wanna come?' Adder asked. 'I wouldn't want to hurt her if she's your girl, like.'

'Not a problem for me, bro,' Harisha assured him. 'Drag her if you have to, just get her here, and call me when you find her. No matter what time it is.' He looked at his lieutenants, his eyes flaring angrily. 'If Melek has gone over to Alley Cats, or is fed-telling, then what happened to Zana Ghaziani will feel like a piece of sweetcake compared to what we'll do to her. And get them skanky Alley Cats picked up. We'll bring 'em all in here,' he smiled, and then his eyes narrowed. 'And then we'll really hurt them.

07:00 Thursday

When Georgia had got home last night, she had lain in the bath for a full half an hour, with a note-book and her thoughts, and then she had slept for five hours without waking. She had needed the sleep. Today she and Stephanie would have to face the post-mortem of a burnt cadaver that, only a few days previously, had been the living, beautiful, and bright seventeen-year-old, Zana Ghaziani. Also on the mortuary table would be the butchered body of Burak Kaya, only eighteen himself.

Two young lives wasted, and for what?

Georgia was now standing next to Alison Grainger by the whiteboard at the front of the investigation room, heading the morning meeting. Banham had taken a place at one of the desks, about halfway back, where he sat listening, but never taking his eyes off Alison. Georgia was glad that Alison had all his attention, it kept it off her, but she also knew that everything she said and did was reported back to him.

The usual keen trainee detective, Hank Peacock, had worked late into the night last evening, and had been in early this morning to finish off. Being a whizz kid with computers, he had spent the evening going through all the files on Zana's laptop, her tweets and her Facebook page, as well as what remained of her mobile. With help from the boys in the TIU he had retrieved the SIM card from her melted phone, and had some of her texts and messages. They were printed out, along with the photos that been taken by Melek of Zana's burn, and a photo on Facebook of Zana's brother Wajdi, who looked as if he was threatening his sister. Zana had her hands held up defensively as Wajdi's finger pointed ominously at her. The photos backed up the texts he'd recovered. Zana had texted Melek that Wajdi was threatening her. She had then forwarded that same text to Burak Kaya, adding kisses at the bottom. There was a text to Zana from her brother, telling her that she was behaving like a whore, and he would knock that out of her, so she had better look out.

As Hank Peacock passed the texts and the photos around the team, Georgia immediately noticed Harisha Celik in the back of the photo with Wajdi.

'That's Celik in the background,' she said, holding the photo up so Banham could see. 'Could it be the family paid his gang blood money?' she suggested. 'The family are strong suspects, but they have alibis,' she carried on. 'Perhaps they paid the gang to set her on fire. No one would suspect them if the connection was made between the SLR and Zana; her boyfriend was Harisha's cousin. Suspicion would fall on a rival gang.'

'That's highly possible,' Banham nodded. 'Good thinking.' He then thanked Hank Peacock for his hard work, and told him how much that effort had now helped the case. Hank beamed proudly, just like his namesake, Georgia thought, flicking a side glance at Stephanie Green who, she noticed, was busy eyeing up Banham.

'Bring Wajdi Ghaziani in for further questioning,' Banham said to Alison and Georgia.'

'It's the post-mortems, this morning,' Georgia reminded him, 'of Burak Kaya and Zana Ghaziani. Someone needs to be there.'

'You go and bring in Wajdi,' Banham told Alison. 'Take Barry and Eric with you.' He turned to Georgia. 'Sergeant Green can attend the post-mortem with you,' he said nonchalantly.

Banham's reputation at post-mortems when the cadaver was female went before him. Zana Ghaziani's corpse was in a very bad condition, and Georgia was fully sympathetic that Banham wouldn't be attending. Banham had told her of discovering his wife and baby murdered, and Georgia knew, only too well, how damaging emotional scars were. As she caught the look of amusement that passed between Barry Mitchell and Eric Peters, she glared angrily at them. 'We'll all meet back here later,' she said. 'Is there anything else?

Hank Peacock had his hand in the air again. 'There was a

phone message, ma'am, from a Mrs Wilkins. It came in at 2 a.m. You might like to hear it.

'Most definitely,' she nodded.

He pressed the phone through to speaker. 'I don't like leaving messages,' the nervous cockney voice of Mrs Wilkins said. 'Don't know who's listening, do ya? I'll write it down and bring it to the station for you in the morning. We didn't tell you, tonight. We were afraid of what they'll do, see. It's about that boy that was killed …' The line then went dead.

Banham looked at Georgia.

'That's changed all plans,' she said picking up her bag. 'Stephanie you go to the post-mortem and take notes for me. I'm on my way to the Wilkins',' she looked over at Banham, 'if that's all right with you, sir,' she said.

'I'll go with you,' Banham said quickly.

'I'll go, if you like,' Alison said, 'and we'll pick up Wajdi after.'

'No,' Banham shook his head. 'The Aviary is very dangerous at the moment. It's not out of the question that someone would throw something from a high-up flat, and it could land on you, Alison. I won't have you in any danger.'

Georgia turned to see Alison's cheeks mottling into a dark blush. Georgia had been to the estate more times than she could even begin to count. It was their area, and part of their job. Alison was supposed to be heading a murder investigation, what was the DCI thinking, talking to her like that? She was only, very newly, back in the serious crimes department, and she'd already started tongues wagging by fainting at a murder scene. She needed to build the respect of the team and Banham was making her look like a wimp. Judging by Alison's reddening face, the woman was thinking the same.

But, as usual, Banham hadn't noticed. 'We'll talk to the old couple,' he told Georgia. 'Bring them in if they clam up. Alison, take Barry and Eric, and ask for three uniform cars for backup and bring in Wajdi Ghaziani. We'll hold him, until we get the results of the post-mortem, and then we'll re-interview him.'

'Guv,' Alison nodded obediently, but it wasn't hard to see that she was furious.

'OK, everyone knows what they are doing,' Banham said. 'Let's get going then.' Georgia lowered her eyes. Banham couldn't help himself, even after twelve years in CID, and with the constant memos circulating the office about racism and sexism, the man was just blind to his own chauvinism.

Alison caught up with Stephanie Green as she made her way to the car park. 'I'm coming to the post-mortem,' she told her.

'But DCI Banham …'

'Just click the lock before he comes out and sees me,' Alison said pressing the passenger door handle urgently. 'I won't be treated with kid gloves.'

Stephanie clicked the lock, slipped herself in the driver's seat, and said nothing. She watched Alison click her seatbelt closed and then fired the engine.

'People are saying I'm not up to the job, because I fainted over Zana Ghaziani's burnt body,' Alison said to her. 'But it's more complicated than that.'

'You don't have to justify yourself to me,' Stephanie said in her motherly tone, as she indicated to turn right out of the car park. 'I'll let you know if I see him, and you can duck.'

'I am up to the job,' Alison persisted. 'And if I go through with this post-mortem, the next one will be easier.'

Stephanie nodded. 'Fine by me. You're the boss. Just don't get me into trouble with the DCI, that's all. The next one is unlikely to be a burnt body, though, have you thought of that?'

'Exactly,' Alison said, hardly listening.

They drove in silence for a few minutes, and then Alison lowered the window. 'Have you got any peppermints?' she asked.

'In the glove compartment. Are you sure you'll be OK? I can easily drop you back if …'

'I'm fine,' she snapped. 'I need the peppermints now.' She looked at Stephanie, and then took a deep breath. 'OK. I'm going to tell you something, as you are a mother, but it isn't for common gossip. I'd rather the men in the department didn't know.'

Stephanie nodded, 'OK.'

'Or DI Johnson either.'

Stephanie was about to say that Georgia was her boss and her friend, and she didn't want split loyalties, but before she had the chance, Alison blurted out, 'I'm pregnant.'

Stephanie nodded, carried on driving, but made no comment. The thought then passed through her mind that the father had to be Banham, it couldn't be anyone else, so her own chances of getting him in the sack were now well up the Swanee. She eyed the Twix in the front compartment as Alison searched for peppermints. Chocolate always helped when sex wasn't on the cards.

'Aren't you going to say anything?' Alison asked her.

'Congratulations?' Stephanie grinned, then shook her head. 'And no worries, I'm not one for gossiping. Can you pass me that bar of Twix in there, I didn't have time for breakfast.'

Max Pettifer and the smell of disinfectant greeted them as they entered the post-mortem suite and were handed the green gowns to cover their clothes. Mr Unpopular, as Max was known to all who worked with him, had as much sensitivity as a brick. If Alison did faint again, in here, then a video of the deed would be on Max's mobile and over to Banham's before Alison could even breathe in smelling salts, Stephanie thought, and Stephanie would then get it in the neck for allowing Alison to join her.

Stephanie had a stomach like an ox, and had to admit to finding it amusing when those around her crashed, or puked, or hit the stone floor with a bang, and then woke up, apologetically, while Mr Unpopular carried on dissecting regardless. Georgia always made a point of crunching peppermints throughout post-mortem proceedings, to prevent any embarrassing or queasy moments. Poor DCI Banham always puked, no one could remember a time when he hadn't, and Max ridiculed him, mercilessly. Now Banham was a DCI he made a point of avoiding post-mortems suites.

Stephanie prayed that today, and for everyone's sake, Alison would get through the procedure.

The cadavers lay side by side on metal gurneys. Both had been incised with the usual T-cuts across their upper torsos. The next procedure was the removal and weighing of the organs. Stephanie looked at young Zana's grey and shrivelled skin and thought of Lucy, her own daughter. Stephanie was glad that she had passed her teenage phase and was away at university in Canterbury, with her mind set on a career in the force. At least she was safe from street gangs.

Max Pettifer removed Zana's heart and dropped it on a little metal tray to be weighed. As he began dictating verbal notes into his Dictaphone, Alison's mobile trilled loudly. He threw his eyes to heaven and flicked an angry glare in her direction. Alison ignored him. She pulled her phone from her pocket, checked the number on the screen, and then turned to Stephanie, mouthing that she needed to take the call. She then turned and made her way outside into the hospital corridor.

Stephanie had her own phone turned off, deciding she needed her full concentration to get the PM findings down accurately. Max Pettifer never repeated anything, no matter how many people requested it. DC Martin was also there, on exhibits. He had started photographing both the corpses, and was now doing close-ups on the wounds from the machete on Burak. Stephanie watched, knowing how vital these photos would be when it came to getting a conviction.

After close examination, Max informed them that the deep wounds were likely made by a machete, giving them the exact size of the instrument used.

'The cause of death wasn't any of these, though. That was done very nicely by a short knife severing the pulmonary artery.'

He stood back while DC Martin photographed the wound in question. A big surprise came when Max examined Zana's organs. In her the womb he discovered a foetus. He looked up, his long eyebrows reminding Stephanie of a rabbit's ears.

'This girl was pregnant, but only just,' he said, before turning back and muttering the same into his Dictaphone.

Stephanie looked at Martin. That was something none of the team had thought of, but raised the suspicion towards her family, Stephanie thought.

'How long before we can get DNA from the foetus?' she asked Max, feeling very relieved that Alison had left the room.

Max glared at her. 'I'll get on with it, and when it's done, I'll let you know. I'm a pathologist, not a magician.'

She was used to his rudeness. 'How long will that take?'

'How long is a piece of string?'

Stephanie hurried out after removing her gown, overalls and gloves. She spotted Alison standing by the shop doorway next to the entrance. 'I've got interesting finds,' she told her, quickly repeating the two new pieces of information that had come to light.

'Wow,' Alison said, taking it in. 'And that was Melek Yismaz on the phone, and in a sorry state,' she told Stephanie. 'She says Harisha beat and raped her yesterday, after she gave us a statement, and he is threatening her again. She wants me to meet her, see her injuries, and bring a charge against him.'

'The day is just getting better and better,' Stephanie smiled. 'Do you want me to come with you? We can send Barry and Eric to pick up the Ghazianis.'

Alison shook her head. 'No, Melek may clam up if there are two of us. You go with Barry and Eric and bring in Wajdi. If Zana was pregnant that makes the family even stronger suspects, so if the parents so much as open their mouths to protest, then arrest them both.' She took in air and looked at Stephanie. Her eyes filled with tears. 'God, I'm glad I didn't see him remove that foetus,' she said quietly.

'So am I,' Stephanie said gently, placing an arm on Alison's arm. 'It's OK, it's normal to feel tearful,' she told her. 'I cried all the time during my first pregnancy. I had no reason, but I still did. It's those female hormones, they get all shaken up, all over the bloody place, like a cocktail waiter's tools.'

Alison burst out laughing. 'What?'

'Just trying to make you smile, see it worked. By the way, I'm very sorry about your colleague who died in that fire, but

164

you have to know it wasn't your fault.'

'I do know,' Alison said unconvincingly. 'Can I nick one of the bars of chocolate in your car? I'll take the tube and meet you back at the Station. If Banham asks where I am, tell him I've gone to meet Melek Yismaz in McDonalds in Lambeth. I can grab a large double burger and fries for my lunch while I'm there.'

'Are you sure I can't go with you? Stephanie teased. 'I'm always up for a big one.'

'It's nice of you to offer to come with me,' Georgia said making polite conversation to Banham as she drove in the direction of the Aviary, 'but there was no need, I've been here many, many times before, and there are a fleet of uniform cars around today should I need backup.'

'I'd prefer none of my female officers went alone to this estate,' he told her.

Georgia said nothing. The man couldn't help it. He obviously had no idea that sexual equality existed in the force. How had he got to the position of DCI without being constantly reminded, she wondered. He must know that women in the Met had the same training as the men, and they know how to take care of themselves. All the female officers in the station moaned privately about his chauvinism, but it hadn't stopped him reaching DCI; perhaps because he meant well, or perhaps because the powers that be were currently men. She hoped that would change in the future. Anyway, she suspected the root of it was what had happened to his wife and baby. Irritating as he could be, she quite liked him, and believed him to be a compassionate man.

It amused her that Stephanie fancied a night of lust with him, but she was grateful that it wouldn't happen. Stephanie always described, in full graphic detail, the intimacies of her sexual conquests. Bedding Banham and then describing the moment to Georgia over morning coffee would have made Georgia uncomfortable around him. As it was, Stephanie had already bedded most of the men on the team, and Georgia knew more about all of them than she wanted to, but that was Sergeant Green, and Georgia accepted it. Georgia knew she too had irritating habits, although office gossip wasn't one of them.

She carried on driving, nodding politely every time Banham reminded her that a red light was approaching, or the road was clear to overtake. She refrained from shouting that she could see for herself. He was her boss, and she was ambitious, so she managed to keep buttoned; just.

'Alison and you drive the same car,' he said after a while.

'Yes, you said before.'

'She's a terrible driver. Have you ever been in a car with her?'

'No, no I haven't.'

'My advice is don't.'

'Right.' She decided it was time to change the subject. 'It's Magpie block. They live on the second floor.'

'Yes, Alison gave me the address.'

They walked into the estate, and through the grounds, past the lock-ups and onto the Magpie, on the other side.

As they turned towards the stairs, a pail of filthy liquid came hurtling down from one of the flats high up on Sparrow block. It was too far up to see which flat it had come from, or who threw it. It landed by Banham, stinking and soaking the bottom of his jeans and into his shoes.

Then the sound of tin saucepans banging against each other followed the water, as the residents over on Wren block, again too high up to see from which floor, chanted, 'Out, feds! Out, feds!'

Georgia pulled her mobile from her pocket, and speedily rang for uniform presence to be seen in force on the estate grounds. She didn't envy them their job.

'The residents are nervous,' Banham said to her. 'Two recent murders, they're afraid of being questioned by us. They all know the punishment for talking to the feds.'

'Nervous of who?' Georgia argued. 'No gang runs this estate at the moment. So who are they nervous of?'

'Zana was killed only a few hundred yards away,' he

reminded her. 'Police presence is unwanted, and the residents are very edgy.'

'My snout tells me the SLR are moving into this territory. That must be true, because they are very violent and these residents are certainly afraid.'

'Perhaps there's another gang on the estate, and this is gang warfare starting?'

'Either way, Harisha Celik is involved,' she argued. 'I only wish we could get him behind bars.'

The saucepan banging and the chanting stopped abruptly. The culprits had obviously been tipped off that the feds were on their way up the many flights of stairs, or they felt they had done enough.

'Word travels quickly,' Georgia said. 'It's like even the pigeons are spies, flying from flat to flat with news of what's happening on the other side of the estate.'

'That explains why Mrs Wilkins was nervous of leaving a message.'

'I doubt very much they'll even open their door now, not with eyes everywhere,' Georgia said. 'Perhaps we should ask them to meet us away from here. Shall I call them?'

Two hooded youths who were walking towards them must have noticed who – or what – they were; they both immediately ducked their heads, turned, and hurried in the opposite direction. Georgia clocked them, but then walked on and joined Banham.

'We are never going to stop policing this estate,' Banham said raising his normally calm voice. 'No gang will undermine our power. Every gang so far that has tried, we've rounded them up and put them away. No one is bigger than us, they will learn that.'

Georgia nodded her agreement and then walked ahead towards the steps. She forced herself to keep a straight face as the noise of Banham's shoes, squelching with water, followed her.

Predictably, Mr and Mrs Wilkins didn't open the door, so

Georgia phoned their number. The phone rang off the wall. She lifted the letter flap and peered through.

'They might be out shopping,' she said to Banham.

'Or they might be at the station delivering the letter she said she was going to write us,' Banham suggested.

Georgia moved over to the kitchen window to peer in as far as he could see. Breakfast crockery was laid on the table and there were two bowls awaiting filling. 'It doesn't look as if they've eaten breakfast yet,' she said turning around as a few hooded youths of various different races, with bandanas covering their faces, walked towards them from the corner of the walkway.

'Do you know the couple that live in here?' Banham asked them, flashing his ID card.

All stared at him. One shook his head before turning and hurrying back down the stairs. The others then followed.

Banham noticed a handle sticking out from one of the boy's pockets. 'He's carrying,' he said to Georgia.

Georgia called through to the uniformed sergeant covering the estate door to door and described the boy. 'Tell him to bring the enforcer up,' Banham said decisively.

'Guv.'

Within minutes three strong uniformed police were hurrying up the side stairs carrying the red enforcer. Banham gave the order and they slammed it into the front door of the Wilkins flat.

'Mrs Wilkins?' Georgia shouted as she walked in. The only response was of nearby front doors opening to see what was happening, and neighbours spilling onto the walkway to see what was going down.

'Keep everyone away, please,' Georgia told the uniformed police who were on the walkway with her.

She walked further into the Wilkins' flat. 'Mrs Wilkins,' she shouted again.

She looked down and noticed money scattered all the way down the hallway, twenty-pound notes, quite a lot of them, and she was aware of an unpleasant smell. She picked up the money.

'Christ, don't say someone has broken in and tried to make away with their life savings,' Banham said, opening a door which led to the kitchen.

Georgia walked a further down the hallway and opened another door. It was the bathroom. She walked in. All was tidy and still. 'They're out,' she shouted to Banham.

'All in order here,' Banham shouted from the kitchen.

'They will be terrified when they come back. Let's get their door fixed back on before we give them a heart attack,' Georgia shouted coming back out of the bathroom and carrying on down the hall. She pushed open another door at the end, it was a bedroom. The bed was neatly made with a threadbare blue and white candlewick bedspread covering it. A browned wedding photo, and one of Albert in 1950s army uniform, was in pride of place on the mantelpiece, and a few bits of cheap paste jewellery lay in a glass bowl beside it. Georgia was uncomfortably aware of a smell.

She walked back up the hallway and peered into the kitchen as Banham walked out and headed down the hall. Everything in the kitchen was neat and in place, but she noticed the smell wasn't as strong in here.

She came out of the kitchen and walked back down the hallway, checking the rooms again. Banham had gone into the bathroom.

At the end of the hallway was another door. She opened the door. There was a small single bed in the corner. It wasn't made-up, it displayed an old stained mattress covering the bed springs.

She closed the door behind her and breathed in the stale smell again. There was a cupboard at the end of the corridor, Georgia knew that from Alysha's flat, which followed the same layout. She walked over to the cupboard. The latch wasn't fully down. As she touched it the door swung quickly towards her, feeling heavy as it swung against her. As she took a step backwards, Mrs Wilkins' body fell on top of her. It was soaked in congealing blood.

'Guv,' Georgia shouted, as she leaned in further and saw the body of Mr Wilkins, a screwdriver in the artery at the side of his neck, covered in blood and face down on the cupboard floor.

The blood that had run down the inside of the cupboard door was only just congealing. The couple hadn't been dead very long. The ceiling and the walls too were splattered, as was the floor underneath them.

She checked for any signs of life. There was none. But they hadn't been dead long. The killer, or killers, couldn't have gone far, and were bound to be covered in blood.

Georgia had her phone to her ear. 'All units, Aviary Estate, Magpie block, requesting ambulance and urgent forensic team.'

Banham was standing the other end of the hall. 'I'm sorry,' he said. 'I can't, I really can't, I'm sorry.'

But Georgia wasn't listening. She was thinking about the two youths in hooded tops, who had run when they saw her approaching the flat.

Twelve

Banham went outside to try to talk to the neighbours while Georgia made the necessary emergency calls. Predictably, none of the neighbours admitted seeing anyone walking along the walkway earlier that morning, nor did they admit hearing anything, although all were keen to know what was going on.

Banham walked back in to the flat and joined Georgia in the lounge to wait for the forensic team and the doctor to arrive.

'Those two hooded youths that we saw as we came onto Magpie block earlier,' Georgia reminded Banham. 'They hurried past us, hands in their pockets. They had their heads down too. Can you remember what they were wearing?

'Dark grey hooded fleece tops and jeans,' Banham told her. 'I've instructed the uniform team with a description, they're scouring the estate now. Unfortunately I didn't get a look at the faces.'

Georgia shook her head. 'Nor did I, but one was much taller than the other.' Banham nodded his agreement.

'Both grey hoodies, but my recollection is one wore baggy khaki trousers.'

'The other dark blue jeans.' Banham said.

Georgia nodded. 'Yup, and both wore trainers.' She shook her head and frowned, 'Wait till the press hear about this, they'll have a field day.'

'So we have to get moving and find their killer. Have you spoken to Alison?'

She shook her head again. 'She's bringing the Ghazianis in.'

'But you spoke to Barry, didn't you?'

'Yes. He'll ring back when they've picked up the family, and then they are coming over here.'

'Good,' Banham nodded.

'I wish we could get the CCTV on this estate working again. It's been broken for two years now,' Georgia reminded him.

'Last council worker that tried to fix it got mugged, so it remains broken.' She shrugged. 'Means we can't see who came and went in the last few hours.'

'Good morning, again.' It was the bright voice of Max Pettifer and the forensic team arriving. Pettifer put his head round the door, took one look at Banham, and burst out laughing. 'Someone needs to make you a nice strong cup of tea,' he said chuckling and raising his rabbit ear eyebrows a few millimetres. He disappeared, chuckling to himself, as the uniformed officer showed him down the corridor to the old couple's bodies.

The outside of the flat had now been cordoned off and access to the first floor completely blocked. That would prove interesting, Georgia thought, at least the residents living on this level would now have to communicate with the police, even if it was to complain about having to walk around to the fire escape at the back of the building to get to their front door.

The youngers had also started arriving in the grounds below. They were shouting up, questioning the police, ever hoping for the first bit of info so they could cycle off and sell it to the elders and make enough to buy themselves a McDonalds meal. Older residents were also stopping and staring as they passed nearby, some hanging around for a few minutes before wandering off. Banham and Georgia left Max Pettifer and his team to do their work, and went to join the search for the two hooded youths they had seen earlier. Both knowing full well, that on an estate this size, and with the attitude that the residents held towards the police, the job was comparable to finding a needle in a haystack. However, it was a starting point. They discussed calling out Indie 999, the police helicopter, but Georgia pointed out the estate was riddled with youths hanging around, all wearing hoodies and trainers and looking similar from the air. A ground search was best. They agreed to split, each of them could take a group of uniformed officers and a couple of sniffer dogs.

Hooded youths seemed to be around every corner, some with peaked caps under the hoods, preventing anyone getting a good look at their faces. Why couldn't they ban the wearing of hoods, Georgia thought. Hoods wasted more manpower time, when searching for a person on CCTV cameras, than anything else.

Fortunately Georgia had a sharp memory. One youth was short and thin, wearing baggy khaki combat trousers; his mate was taller and broader and wore denim jeans with large leg pockets (for carrying weapons, Georgia thought, or blood-stained clothes perhaps; the killer would have blood on their clothes with an artery stabbing, that was for sure). Both youths wore grey hoodies, one a peaked cap too. They had seemingly vanished, or changed their clothes. Still, there were many youths standing around, in packs. No schools or jobs to go to, Georgia thought sadly, as she questioned blank and indifferent faces. 'I ain't heard, or seen, nothing,' was the answer each one gave her. No wonder so many of them turn to drugs and crime, Georgia mused, Alysha Achter was right, there was nothing around here for them to do. Her eyes scanned the broken-down, burnt-out community hall, and then the play area, with the remains of an old child's train lying broken in the dirt, beside the rusted slide covered in faeces; the place once called the kids' area.

Banham's words jumped into her head. '*If you start feeling sorry for them, then you should be a social worker, not a murder detective.*' She turned her attention away from the play area and focused, now she had four murders to solve, and no clue to hang her hat on; she needed to think. She could see those two youths, clearly, in her mind, the khaki combats, so low slung, hanging from thin bony hips, the crotch nearly even with his knees. She had also noticed his small feet. Thinking about his mate, taller and broader, she remembered, clearly, the large leg pockets of his denim jeans, but couldn't remember seeing anything in them. Both had their hands dug into their pockets, and both walked with their heads bent low. They could have come from anywhere, they might not even live on or around this estate, they might well not be the killers, or they might have done the deed, and were now safely back on home ground, maybe miles away.

A word with Alysha Achter was needed. Alysha knew, mostly, everyone on or around this estate. But with the strong police presence around, and now two more murders, the girl would be nervous, so Georgia would wait for an hour or so.

So why murder Mr and Mrs Wilkins? Georgia asked herself. The empty lock-up, she felt sure, was involved. There were still SOCO officers working at the garage, hopefully that would shed a light. Harisha Celik had accused Alysha of starting a dangerous gang, of trading drugs and weapons. Alysha was on probation; if she was found to be in any way involved with drugs and firearms, she'd find herself in youth offenders', and Georgia would lose her best snout. Georgia paid her well, so she knew she had enough money, and Alysha had told Georgia countless times that the prostitution, the drugs and handling of guns, was in her past. Georgia had no reason not to believe her, Alysha's information was always right, and Harisha *was* known to be involved in the firearms trade – only no one could prove it, as yet.

Her phone chirped. It was Stephanie.

'You've heard about the Wilkinses, then?' she said as she picked up.

'Yes, I'm on my way over to you. And we've arrested the Ghazianis, the mother and father.'

'And Wajdi?'

'He wasn't there. He's at the shop, according to the parents. Alison's gone to meet Barry and Eric there to pick him up.'

'Interesting. Business as usual when their daughter has just been burnt alive? Did the parents get aggressive?'

'Yup. They refused to answer any questions unless we released their daughter's body. I explained that we needed to keep it, to help find her killer. So Mrs Ghaziani threw a cup of tea at me, and Barry arrested her for assault.'

'She likes burning people then?'

'Yeah, like the iron burn was an accident, too. The father attacked Barry as he arrested her, so Eric arrested him. They are strong suspects, ma'am.'

'Yes they are, for Zana's murder, but they couldn't have murdered the Wilkinses. They hadn't been dead long when we found them.'

'Wajdi could have killed them. We don't know yet that he is at the shop.'

'The Wilkinses knew something,' Georgia said. 'And someone knew they were going to tell us what they knew. So what was it? And how did that someone know?

'Answer that and we are half way there.'

'It has to be to do with their lock-up.' Georgia pressed her phone to her ear with her shoulder and used her spare hand to flatten the wiry stray hairs that were blowing out of place at side of her carefully gelled ponytail. She pulled the clip from the side of her hair and re-clipped it tidily over the stray strands, and then ran her fingers, busily, through her pony-tail as a way of combing it. 'Alysha Achter tells us that Celik took the lock-up from them, to use for storage of arms and drugs, but it's empty. Alysha's info has always been right, so I reckon Celik was tipped off that the Wilkins were going to talk. He cleared the garage, and then silenced them.'

''Cept he doesn't do his own dirty work.'

'No, he doesn't. I'm looking for two youths I saw earlier near the Magpie Block. I think they may well have seen something.'

'I'm still on with the Ghazianis being involved,' Stephanie said. 'Honour killing, we know families who have had their kids killed just for looking at a bloke. You said yourself Harisha could be in the back of that photo because he was paid by the Ghazianis, to sort out Zana. And let's not forget Burak Kaya was killed within yards from the Wilkins' flat. So maybe there is a link.'

'You think Celik would really have Burak Kaya killed? He's his cousin.'

'Maybe he didn't,' Stephanie argued. 'Maybe this was a plan that went wrong. Maybe Wajdi killed Burak for going with his sister, and Harisha Celik killed Zana in revenge. Just food for thought.'

'What does Alison think? '

'I rang her. She was just leaving McDonalds in Lambeth, and on her way to meet Eric and Barry.'

'What was she doing at McDonalds in Lambeth?'

'Meeting Melek Yismaz.'

'She didn't tell me. When did she decide to meet Melek Yismaz?'

'Oh, sorry, guv, I thought she had. Melek rang her during the post-mortem. She said she has important information on Celik. It turns out she wants him charged with rape.'

'Hang on, Alison was at the post-mortem?'

'Yes.'

There was a pause. 'The DCI told her not to go.'

'She didn't like being told by Banham, personal reasons, so, she went.'

Georgia blew out air. 'And Melek is bringing a charge against Harisha for rape?'

'Yup. She's given Alison a statement.'

'Well that's terrific news. We can arrest Celik again. I'll let the DCI know, and when you get here, we'll go and get Celik.' She paused and then added. 'I won't mention Alison being at the post-mortem, though, I'll pretend I didn't hear that.'

'Did you know Zana was pregnant?'

'No.'

'Part of a burned foetus was found in her womb during the post-mortem,' Stephanie said quietly.

The hair on Georgia's back ran cold.

'Fortunately Alison wasn't in the room when Max Pettifer announced it. I'm not sure she would have coped if she had of been. She was quite traumatised when I told her.'

'I'm not surprised. A fire victim on your first day back isn't the best way to re-start your career in the murder department, and then a burned foetus, that's too much. We have to remember she took compassionate leave after losing a friend in a fire.'

'Yes, quite.'

'Banham was right, then, wasn't he? She shouldn't have

gone to the post-mortem. She isn't ready to fling herself in the deep end.'

'We'll have to keep our eyes on her.'

'We're investigating four murders,' Georgia said sharply. 'We've got enough to cope with, we are not nannies.'

'I'll remind you of that next time you mention Alysha Achter's welfare.'

'She my snout, I have a professional duty to be concerned for her welfare,' Georgia argued. She was walking towards the Sparrow estate now and had her eyes peeled all the while she was talking. 'Alison is a senior investigating officer. If she can't look after herself then she shouldn't be doing the job. A vulnerable old couple and two murdered teenagers are our priority right now.'

'Yes, but Alison is one of us.'

'Of course she is,' Georgia said softly, 'and, we'll keep our eyes on her.' Her tone then changed back to the professional one. 'The press will be on this like vultures very soon.' The thought of headlines, accusing the police of not being able to protect an elderly couple on a dangerous estate had jumped into her mind. 'We are against the clock here. And I agree there may be two killers out there, and there may be a link, and someone around here will have seen or heard something, but we need answers. We were fighting a wall of silence before, now with this murder, we'll never get witnesses to come forward. We have to work flat out to find evidence.'

'My money is still on the Ghazianis, especially now we know Zana was pregnant.'

'How long before we know who the father was?'

'Ask Max Pettifer. You know what he's like. She imitated his Scottish accent. '*The tests will take as long as they take, and if that involves more tests, then they will take as long as they take. There you have your answer*. Or not.'

'He's just arrived down here, now, on this crime scene,' Georgia told Stephanie. 'So it could be days.'

'Melek Yismaz told us told us Zana was in a relationship with Burak Kaya, but she also said she slept around. So another

177

scenario worth considering is that Burak found out it wasn't his baby. He was an SLR gang member. Perhaps he ordered her killing, and then someone got to hear of it, like Wajdi Ghaziani, and got to him first.'

'And the Wilkinses heard or saw something?'

'That could fit.'

Georgia noticed three girls standing together by the stairs to Sparrow block. One was Alysha Achter. She put her hand up and indicated that she wanted her to stay there.

'Talk of the devil. I've just spotted Alysha Achter,' she told Stephanie, 'I'll talk later. Get back to Alison, tell her as soon as they have picked up Wajdi, to get over here. When they do, you and I can go and get Harisha Celik.'

'Will do.'

'Let me know as soon as you arrive. '

'Will do.'

Alysha was leaning against the stairway at the corner of Sparrow block. She was with Panther and Lox. Panther's hair was typically wild. She wore a cream hooded sweatshirt under a sleeveless padded gold jacket. Her hand was against her chubby face and Georgia noticed the tattoo of a cat on her forefinger, and her long plastic nails which were painted black. Lox Georgia had known since the girl had worked the streets. She was also on probation. Pencil-thin, her face was pale but her skin clear. A sign, Georgia knew, that she had stayed off the drugs. She was very pretty, although nervous as a rabbit under her tough exterior. Today her long dark green-streaked hair was tied back in a tidy bun, and, in her neat red velour tracksuit, a hooker was the last thing she looked. Georgia liked her, she knew that Lox too was a victim of circumstance. She had come from a well-to-do home, been abused by her father, had run away, ended up in a horrific world of drugs and street prostitution. Without Alysha's help, Georgia was confident that Lox would have been found dead in an alleyway by now. Alysha was fifteen going on forty, and a very good influence on all the lost souls around the estate. How could Georgia not want to help Alysha? Alysha herself had had no help in life but wanted to help everyone else, and in doing so was helping the police clean up the estate.

'I need to talk to you,' Georgia said to her.

Alysha looked from Panther to Lox.

'Have you been hanging around the estate grounds all morning?' Georgia asked Alysha.

'Who's dead?' Panther asked.

'Shut up, Panther,' Lox said quickly.

'No, it's all right. I'm not on your case, Lox,' Georgia assured her. 'I am here to ask for help. I need to find two youths I saw earlier. Both were wearing grey hooded tops and trainers, one was in khaki combat trousers, the other denim jeans. Have any of you seen anyone who matches that description hanging around?'

'That sounds like everyone around here,' Alysha said flatly.

Georgia glared at her. 'The question was have you seen two youths, together, matching that description? The boy wearing denim was taller than ...'

'No.'

Georgia stared at Alysha and then turned to Lox. 'I'm glad you've given up working the streets.'

Lox looked blankly at her, and then flicked her eyes to Alysha.

'You look well, I'm very glad to see,' Georgia continued.

Again Lox turned to Alysha. It was obvious she relied on her. But would it be possible that there might be a morsel of truth in the fact these girls were starting a gang? They'd sworn to Georgia that they were going straight. If they formed a gang then they would have to start fighting over territories, and they might need weapons, sell drugs to make money ... Georgia really hoped that wasn't going to happen. She wanted them to stay away from crime and have better lives.

'So who's been killed today?' Panther asked again.

'Word travels fast around here,' Georgia said, holding her gaze.

'There's half a million feds around the estate, and Magpie's

179

been cordoned off,' Panther said screwing up her face in disbelief. 'It don't take a genius to work out someone's been murdered.'

'Two people, actually,' Georgia said. 'A retired couple, Mr and Mrs Wilkins, from Magpie block. Do you know them?'

Panther nodded solemnly. 'I think I know who you mean,' she said.

Georgia turned back to Alysha. 'Can I have a word?' she said. 'In private.'

Alysha rolled her eyes to Heaven and turned to the other two. 'Can you beat it for a bit? I'll bell you when I'm finished. It won't take long.' She turned back to Georgia. 'All I know is what them kids on the bikes have been shouting.'

'Which is?'

'That there's another murder over on the Magpie, and asking us to pay 'em to know who it is.'

Georgia thought about finding those kids, and asking if they had seen the two hooded youths hanging around the Magpie, but she knew they would just lie, waste valuable time. 'I'll meet you back at your flat in a few minutes,' she said to Alysha. 'I want to talk to you and it's safest there. No one will see us talking.

Alysha glared angrily. 'You don't live round 'ere, so you don't know what's safe or safest, or who'll see what.' Her dark eyes looked frightened as well as furious. 'What is it you want, now? You keep pushing me.'

Alysha was right, Georgia realised, and right now she was frightened and had reason to be. At this moment, everyone was watching everyone, noticing who talked to who, and where and when on this estate, and someone was killing because of it. Chances were the Wilkinses had been seen, or overheard, talking. It was Georgia's responsibility to protect her informants; she had failed the Wilkinses. She couldn't let anything happen to Alysha. Alysha was a teenage girl, who survived more or less alone on this crime-ridden estate, whose mother came from the same part of the Caribbean that Georgia's mother did, and who, if Georgia had of been lucky enough to have had a daughter of her own, would very likely, have looked exactly like Alysha.

'Sorry,' she said softly. 'I need to find two youths who earlier were wearing grey hooded tracksuit tops, one was shorter than the other. Any idea who I am looking for?'

'I haven't heard, or seen, anything.' Alysha said turning away. 'I'll bell you if I do. OK?' She turned and started to walk away.

Georgia raised her voice and her tone hardened. 'No, it isn't OK, Alysha.'

Alysha stopped and turned back. She looked confrontational now.

Georgia walked up to her, keeping her voice down. 'I have information that you are pulling a gang together. That you are setting up your own criminal empire. What do you say to that?'

Alysha looked down, then up, and then burst out laughing. 'Excuse me?'

'That you're pushing class A drugs,' Georgia continued straight-faced, 'making money from prostitution by training girls up for the streets, and importing dangerous weapons.'

Alysha looked down then up again, and then lifted her eyebrows as she turned to look sideways. She then turned back and looked at Georgia. 'Do you really think if I was, that I would have to put my own neck on the line to sell information to you?' she said quietly. 'Do you really think that?' She shook her head and sucked in air, 'I had you down as sharp.' Then she raised her voice, and her tone hardened. 'Who told you that shit? Harisha fucking Celik, was it? To get himself looking squeaky clean. I already told you, he's importing weapons, and he's killing people ...'

'That's a big accusation, Alysha. What have you got to back that up? How do I know it isn't you using that lock-up for storing arms?'

Alysha's eyes shifted upward and then sideways to check she wasn't being watched. 'I've given you good info before,' she said. 'That should be proof enough. And, I'm on probation. I want a better life, for myself and for the kids round 'ere. You want proof that Celik is storing arms around here. Ask anyone, and no one will answer you, cos they wouldn't dare say a word, cos they are shit scared of what he'd do to them if they did. That should be proof enough. Why are they shit scared of 'im? Cos he has guns that he'll use if he needs to. I'm risking my life bein' your snout, and you should pay me very well for it, because I'm doin' your job for you. An' I ain't earning money any other way. No way am I doin' tomming no more.'

Georgia studied her. 'I do pay you.'

'Not enough.' Alysha lowered her voice. 'I told you what Celik's about. An' I also told you I'm finished with all that whorin' and stuff. You know I'm on probation, why would I want to start some criminal empire? I got mates, ain't no harm in hanging out wiv your mates. You just saw my mate Lox. She ain't doing the streets no more, she's gonna start a girl band. She's got a great voice.' She screwed her mouth sideways and raised her eyebrows, 'And I ain't being funny, but you ain't thinking Panther is a tom, are you?' She squeezed her lips together and raised her eyebrows again. 'What bloke would pay for her to do him? If she laid on top of him, she'd squash him.' She batted her eyelashes, 'An' she looks like a bloke.'

Georgia had to agree there.

'We hang out, an' we stay out of trouble, and we've got plans. Tink is gonna open a beauty and hair shop, make an honest living, an' we are gonna keep on at the council till they make our estate good again. See, what you gotta look at is the long picture, if you raise the next generation right, then all this guns and drugs and killings could stop. But someone's gotta help the kids. You could help us.'

'That's not my job,' Georgia said, though she knew what Alysha said made sense. Alysha had made many mistakes, but, like Lox and Panther, she had been a victim of the real criminals, and was now trying to make something of herself. Serious Crime department knew that Harisha Celik was a drug baron who imported weapons, they just couldn't prove it. Alysha had given them good information in the past, helping to put criminals away, so why would Georgia believe Celik and not Alysha?'

'I am risking my ass talking to you now, big time.' Alysha said. 'For my own good, I should just walk away.'

Georgia shook her head. 'We're doing stops and searches all over the estate at the moment. I'll search you, to make it believable. Turn round and put your hands against the wall.'

An anxious look crept over Alysha's face.

Georgia noticed. 'Please don't tell me I'll find anything?'

Alysha threw her eyes northward and clicked her teeth with her tongue. 'There you go again. Not trusting me. No, course I ain't carrying.'

'OK. Turn around and put your hands against the wall, you can talk to me while I search you.'

'Jeee-sus!' Alysha said as she obeyed.

'OK, what do you know about Mr and Mrs Wilkins?' Georgia asked, patting Alysha's body up and down.

'They was well-liked. They minded their own business, never said nothing to no one, and never made trouble.' She paused and then said 'Did they inform for you too? Cos now I'm very scared if they did.'

'You've no need to be,' Georgia just stopped herself putting a reassuring arm on Alysha's shoulder. 'You've got my number. Ring me anytime, and I promise I'll come to you. As far as I know they weren't informants, not in my squad, but I'll check that out, and let you know for sure.' She patted her on the back, as if finishing off the body search. 'I want you to ask around, and then ask some more. I need to find those two youths, and I need information on the Wilkinses, all their comings and goings, who they talked to, especially who they have talked to recently. I am going to find out who killed them, and I am going to make this estate a safe place for you all to live on.'

'It'll be over the lock-up. They had a car, kept it in a garage. Harisha stole the car. It was the talk of the estate. No one minded him nicking the car, but then the insurance wouldn't pay the Wilkinses, cause the car keys was gone with the car. Harisha nicked the keys a day earlier. He had got one of his bastard henchmen to mug the old lady and steal her handbag as she came home from getting her pension. Her keys wsa in her bag. He let himself into her flat, took the car keys, and drove the car away, then threatened to hurt her if she told the insurance the truth, so she didn't and the Wilkinses never got no insurance payout. They couldn't buy a replacement car, they ain't got the money, so that prick Harisha took the garage over. That's the one your lot are sniffing round now. Harisha uses it.'

'Why didn't you tell me all this before?'

'People was in earshot.'

'You mean he's threatened the Wilkinses before?'

She shrugged. 'That's what he's like, never even gave them no money for stealing their garage from them. I bet them machetes he imported from Europe was in there at some time, but they'll be somewhere else by now. He moves things about all the time.'

'What have you found out about Melek Yismaz, Harisha's girlfriend?'

Alysha cast a glance to the ground, and then looked up again. 'I'd say she's with him cos she's too scared not to be. He threatens, bullies, and sexually abuses his women.'

Georgia thought that sounded right. 'Did you find anything out about Zana Ghaziani?'

'She don't live on this estate. She hung out with Burak Kaya, so she would be involved with them SLRs. She was burned though.' Alysha shook her head and said almost to herself, 'SLRs are cutters. They cut you in bits.' Her head turned back from the wall to look at Georgia. 'That's why it's weird she was burned.'

'Keep your mobile open,' Georgia told her, 'the new one, with the new number that I bought you, I'll be ringing you in a couple of hours. I need information on who went near the Wilkins flat earlier today, and who has visited or spoken to them recently. Especially, I want to know who those two youths were who were leaving the Magpie earlier.'

'And I want money,' Alysha said very strongly. 'I'm risking my neck here for you, big time. You have gotta make it worth 'my while.'

'I'll get you some money,' she said to her.

'I've just given you some really good info there,' Alysha said, looking Georgia in the eye. 'I would like a very big wad for that.'

'Find out who those hooded youths were that I asked you about, and I'll give you a bonus.'

'Enough to buy a new slide for the kids' playground,' Alysha persisted. 'Or you speak to the council again about the state of our kids' play area.'

Georgia shook her head. 'I've tried talking to the council for you. I'll get you some money,' she said sincerely.

She walked on. Her mind turning over what Alysha had told her. If Harisha Celik didn't give the Wilkinses money, then where did the wad of cash on the hall floor in their flat come from? The Wilkins were pensioners. Was that their life savings, and did their killers intend stealing it from them, and were, then, disturbed? If so, by who? Her and Banham, possibly? The hooded youths, she saw earlier would then be prime suspects, but finding them was like a needle in a haystack. She'd have to hope Alysha came up with something. Alysha was right about the estate needing so much doing to it. Top priority should be the CCTV.

Her phone trilled. She checked the screen. It was Banham.

'Is Alison on her way over?' he asked as she picked up.

'After she's picked up Wajdi Ghaziani, he's working at his shop. I spoke to Sergeant Green, Melek Yismaz wants Harisha Celik charged with rape. Alison has her statement, so we can arrest Celik and bring him in again.'

'Alison was at the post-mortem this morning, and left halfway through, what do you know about that?' Banham asked her.

Georgia threw her eyes to heaven. Not all this again. She wasn't interested in Banham and Alison's private life, they could sort it out themselves. 'I wasn't at the post-mortem, so how would I know if Alison was there, sir.' She took a deep breath. 'Sir, with respect, DI Grainger is the senior investigating officer on this enquiry, so it isn't my place to tell her what not to do.'

'She's not answering her phone.'

'Have you tried ringing Barry or Eric, they were meeting her?'

'Meet me at the edge of the Magpie. We are going to the Ghazianis' shop.'

She took another intake of breath. 'Sir, again with respect, I'm looking for two youths who probably have vital information on the Wilkins murders.'

'Well, you're not having much luck finding them.' His voice had risen in volume. 'So put Sergeant Green on that, and come with me.'

'I want to pick up Harisha Celik up again. I'd like to lock him in a cell so he can't go missing. I strongly suspect he's involved somewhere in these murders. We have an accusation of rape against him, so we can arrest him.'

'Well done to Alison for that, then,' Banham said. 'OK, take Sergeant Green and uniform backup with you. I'll go over to the shop.'

'Will do, sir. I also need to have a chat with the SOCOs at the lock-up down here. Our informant insists that Harisha Celik has, at some time, kept firearms and drugs in there and the dogs are making a lot of noise, so I'm on my way round to check that out first.'

'I'll meet you there. Why do you think Alison isn't picking up her phone?'

Georgia wanted to say, because Banham was getting on her nerves, as much as he was on hers, but she didn't.

'She's probably got no signal,' she said instead.

Thirteen

There were only two SOCO officers still working at the lock-up as Georgia walked up the alley. Georgia immediately recognised one of them: his name was Tony James, an officer originally from Ghana. Georgia had had a brief fling with him when she was a young DC. Tony seemed pleased to see her. His white teeth gleamed against his skin as he smiled and his brown eyes twinkled.

'Good to see you,' Georgia said, noticing he was holding a see-through evidence bag between his thumb and forefinger, which looked to contain a piece of silver foil.

'A little find that might make you want to buy me a drink by way of a thank you,' he said grinning as he handed Georgia the see-through bag. 'And we've found traces of firearms and cocaine having been in here.'

It wasn't silver foil, Georgia realised, as she slipped see-through gloves over her hands to examine the contents inside the evidence bag, it was a silver letter S, part of a broken charm or pendant. The design was identical to the tattoo on Burak Kaya's forearm.

She ignored the hint of a drink invitation, he was always trying, but the affair was history for her, she had no care to rekindle it. 'Well done,' was all she said as she turned to see Banham hurrying up the path. The estate kids were also still hovering at the edge of the path, on their bicycles, trying to listen in, so she waited till Banham was directly beside her before discreetly showing him the silver S.

'Found inside the lock-up,' she told him, 'Along with traces of cocaine, and firearms residue. As I'm pretty sure the S doesn't stand for Saint something or other, my next guess is South London Rulers. I'm going to enjoy questioning Harisha Celik again,' she said.

'He'll deny it, and it is only circumstantial,' Banham warned

187

her. 'Charge and hold him for rape. We have the written statement that Alison has taken from Melek Yismaz, but we'll need more than a broken silver charm to pin a murder on him.'

'I'm convinced he's guilty as hell,' she said.

Banham nodded. 'So hold him on a rape allegation while we test his clothes, and you can re-search his flat. He won't expect that, his defences will be down, and we may find something. Get a warrant though. Is Stephanie on her way over?'

'As we speak.'

'Good. I'm going to the Ghazianis' shop. You and Stephanie take a team of uniforms with you when you pick up Celik. Get your request in for the warrant first, and make sure that there is a strong police presence left down here. The press are going to be everywhere on this and we need to be seen to be doing something. So keep up the door to door, however futile you believe it to be. I'll meet Alison and we'll head back to the station, and I'll interview Celik with you.'

'Sir.'

He handed the silver S in its evidence bag back to Tony. 'Well done,' he told him, 'Get it in for DNA testing asap.' He then hurried off towards his car.

'He's like a clingy child,' Georgia said to Stephanie as they climbed into Georgia's car and clicked their seat belts in. 'He doesn't seem to want Alison out of his sight. I couldn't stand it.'

Stephanie shook her head and threw her eyes to heaven. 'I don't blame her for avoiding his calls.' She pulled a bag of prawn cocktail flavoured crisps from her pocket and as she pulled on the bag to open it, some of them went flying onto the floor of Georgia's car

Georgia sighed loudly, but said nothing. She had more important things on her mind. 'You spoke to Alison, though?' she asked her.

'Yup, about an hour ago,' Stephanie now had her mouth full of crisps and sprayed as she spoke. 'She was leaving McDonalds, and on her way to Battersea to pick up Wajdi.

188

That's when she told me Melek was making an official statement against Harisha for rape, and she wants him charged.

'That is music to my ears,' Georgia said, indicating and turning into the main road. 'So where is Melek now, if Alison has gone to pick up Wajdi?'

'Waiting in the McDonalds. Alison will go back and get her after Wajdi has been picked up, and then bring her to the station to take an official statement.' She tipped the last of the packet into her mouth and then crushed the empty bag in her hand sending a few crumbs over herself, which she unconsciously brushed off and onto the floor of Georgia's car. 'So we can hold Celik, officially while we test his clothing, that could take up to thirty-six hours, giving us time for forensic testing on the silver charm, and more time to find something at the Wilkins flat to charge him with murder.'

'And pigs might fly,' Georgia said sarcastically. 'He wouldn't have murdered them himself. He'd have ordered their killing.'

'My money is on the Ghazianis being right in the middle of this, and they're also at the station. Once we've got Wajdi, we can try and find how it all fits.'

Georgia nodded her agreement. 'The day is getting better,' she said, then unable to ignore the crisp packet that Stephanie had scrunched into a ball in her hand, she added, 'Put the crisp bag in the plastic bag in the glove compartment would you, and take it into the station and bin it, I don't want the smell of stale prawn cocktail over my car.'

'I'll leave it in Harisha Celik's bed,' Stephanie grinned.

Celik answered his door dressed in dirty jeans and a shirt that looked like he'd worn it rolling in mud. He paused momentarily when he saw the two detectives, giving Georgia the moment to lodge her foot in the door so he couldn't close it.

'Now what the fuck?' he shouted at her. 'I'm bored with all this shit.'

'Where have you been in last few hours?' Georgia asked him.

'In bed, sleeping.'

'Dressed like that?'

'Is it any of your fucking business what I sleep in, or are you making a pass at me?'

'We want you to come to the station and answer a few questions.' Stephanie told him.

'I did that yesterday.'

'Different questions,' Georgia snapped. 'There have been developments.'

He threw his eyes northward and glared with a bored expression across his unshaven face. 'Such as?'

'Two people have been murdered on the Aviary, this morning,' Stephanie told him. 'Do you know an old couple called Mr and Mrs Wilkins?'

'No, why should I? I don't live there.'

'Think carefully, Mr Celik,' Georgia's voice was cold. 'Accusations have been made against you, and lying in a murder investigation carries a custodial; as I told you before, with your previous record, a heavy custodial.'

'I've just said.'

'We would like you to come and answer some questions,' Stephanie said again.

'So either you come of your own accord, or we arrest you?' Georgia asked. 'My patience is running thin.'

He rolled his eyes. 'I'll get changed.'

'No, as you are,' Georgia said grabbing his arm.

He resisted, pulling out of her hold. 'Take your fucking hands off me …'

'Harisha Celik, I am arresting you in connection with the murders of Albert and Vera Wilkins,' Georgia said, reading him his rights.

Stephanie was patting his pockets. 'Have you got your door keys?'

Before he had time to answer, she'd found them. Georgia pulled his two hands behind his back and clipped handcuffs on him. Two uniformed police moved in to flank them as Georgia and Stephanie walked him down the path and Stephanie turned him towards Georgia's car.

'Not in my car,' Georgia said nodding to the uniformed PCs, who guided him towards the police wagon.

Harisha had clocked Georgia's car. He turned to her as he climbed into the back of the police wagon. 'Nice car,' he said. 'Hope it don't get nicked.' He made it obvious he was clocking the numberplate, then looked back at her. 'I'd hate to think what would happen if joyriders borrowed your nice car for an hour or so. People do all sorts of things in nicked cars.'

'Shut your mouth,' Stephanie raised her voice at him. 'My guv'nor's not in a good mood, and nor am I.'

'You think I'm in a good mood?' he snapped back. 'After what you did to my flat yesterday, and what did you find, sweet fuck A, and now you arrest me again for something I know nothing about.'

'You will,' Georgia said as the uniformed PC started to close the door on him.

'We'll soon prove exactly what you know,' Stephanie added.

He pushed to hold the door with his foot. 'You'll plant something, you mean, cos you are too fucking thick to realise I'm innocent, man, and this is harassment.'

The PC moved his foot and shut the van door.

Georgia's phone chirped and took her attention. She was glad. Celik was winding her up, and knowing he had raped Melek Yismaz earlier, it had taken a lot of control to stop herself landing him a hard smack in the mouth.

The call was from was Banham.

'The shop's closed,' he said. 'No sign of Wajdi Ghaziani. Barry and Eric are here, but no sign of Alison either, and she still isn't answering her phone. Have you heard from her?'

'No, sir, I haven't.' Georgia looked at Stephanie. Stephanie shook her head. 'Have you checked with the neighbouring shopkeepers?' Georgia suggested.

'A couple said say they saw Wajdi arrive earlier, but they didn't see him leave. They said he rarely leaves before closing time. All said they had seen him talking to women, but all described the woman they saw him with differently.'

'I'll make a call, and get back to you,' Georgia said.

She clicked off and tried Alison's number. It went to voicemail.

She dialled Alysha's number.

'Have you got a mobile number for Melek Yismaz? She asked as soon as Alysha picked up.'

'No, I haven't.'

'Well get me one, and phone me straight back, it's urgent.'

'Oh, just like that,' Alysha said sarcastically. 'I'll try, but no promises and you know you owe me.'

'Have you got any information on the Wilkinses?'

'I'm working on it.'

'Then I don't owe you, until you deliver information. First, I need to contact Melek. It's urgent, so I need her mobile number, like this minute. Call me back with it.'

'Suppose …'

Georgia clicked her phone to end the call.

'What's up?' Panther said as Alysha threw her phone down on the bowed brown sofa, and looked across at Panther, who had been curled up on a bean bag opposite.

'Melek.'

Tink was sitting on a stool in front of the old wooden sideboard which stood adjacent to the door. She had been pulling a hot and steaming straightening iron down her long pink hair with speed and efficiency. She stopped what she was doing and turned back to Alysha. 'What 'bout Melek?'

Lox looked up from the floor where she was lying on her stomach, pink plastic calculator in her hand, adding up figures. In front of her were three tins, each with a tidy pile of notes in them, labelled *children's playground*, *community centre*, and *projects*.

'That was the black fed again,' Alysha told them. 'She's asking for Melek's phone number.'

Panther put the can of Pepsi she was drinking on the table in front of her. She sat up. 'Melek's instructions were to ring the other fed, Alison Grainger, and tell her Celik had raped her,' she said looking from Alysha to Tink and Lox. 'She's got the clothes on, to prove it, and the cuts and bruises. Celik should be behind bars by now. So what's happening? Why the other fed want Melek's number? Something wrong or something?'

'That black fed sounded worried,' Alysha told them. 'And Melek's not rung us yet, neither.' She clicked a number on her mobile and lifted it so the others could hear it ringing. No one picked up. 'She ain't answering the Alley Cat mobile we given her, neither,' Alysha said. She started texting a message. 'I only 'ope she ain't in trouble again, with the SLRs?'

'Yeah, she should be answering her Alley Cat phone,' Tink said, frowning. 'Now she's worrying me.'

'She better not be fucking crossing us,' Lox said angrily. 'Or I'll do her myself, and ain't that the truth,'

'Has she answered that text?' Tink asked Alysha.

Alysha pushed her tongue into her cheek and shook her head. 'Not yet.'

'D'you think she's in trouble?'

'I dunno,' Alysha said. 'But I ain't giving that fed the Alley Cat mobile Melek's on, cos their tech people could trace her, and that would put them one step ahead of us. We need to know what's happening.'

'She won't answer if she's still with that Alison Grainger. It may be taking longer than we fink. She might 'ave to go to the station an do it?' Tink said.

'Didn't she say she would ask to meet her in McDonalds in Lambeth, and then bell us after?' Lox said. ''S a while away anyway.'

'I got an idea,' Panther said shuffling her mighty weight forward and leaving a dent in the bean bag where she had been sitting. 'You got Melek's old mobile there?'

Alysha picked it up from the table. 'Yeah, it's here.'

'Send it a text from you. Say to get in touch with feds, that it's real urgent, like. Say that they are looking for her, and everyone's worried about her. Keep it simple though. Then, I'll go and dump the phone near Harisha Celik's flat. I'll ring and tell you when it's dumped, then you ring the black fed and give her that number. She'll get them fed techs to trace it, and they'll find it near that prick's flat. He'll be in the loop again, and he'll be hot-collared for wherever she is.'

Lox and Tink nodded. 'Yeah, that's good, Lox said. 'Want me to come wiv ya?'

'Yeah. Good thinking,' Tink agreed.

Alysha picked up the phone and started to text, her over-long finger nails working ten to the dozen. 'I hope she ain't doing us over, and still being his girl,' she said looking up. 'That would screw everything up, and we'd really have to think hard to get us out of that big mess. Don't forget Melek knows what we done to Burak.'

'I'll just kill her if she is,' Panther said. 'That'll fix her. I'll pump 'er till she ain't got no more blood to come out of her twisted fuck of a head.'

'We all will,' Tink agreed.

Alysha pressed *Send* and looked up. 'Suppose SLRs have seen her wiv us, and they took her. They gonna give her another beating. And if they think she's come over to us? Alysha looked around at the girl's thoughtful faces. 'That could be what has happened, cos one fing's for sure, she should 'ave belled us by now. We've told her she's on trial to be an Alley Cat, an' if that's put 'er in danger, then we need to look out for her.' She looked to Panther. 'What you fink, Panth, you reckon we should go check this out?'

Panther shook her head. 'Not yet. Give me the phone, I'll go dump it near Harisha's, while I'm there, I'll check out what's going down.'

'Where d'you reckon we'd start looking for her, if SLRs have taken her again? Lox asked.

'Try all his lock-ups. 'E's got a new one from what I hear, over near the open parkland.'

'I'm coming wiv you, Panth,' Lox told her. 'You ain't going alone, case it's dangerous.'

'We'll bell you as soon as we've dropped this mobile round Harisha's, an' then you bell the black fed wiv the number,' Panther told Alysha.

'I'm on it,' Alysha nodded.

'An we'll put the word out while we're out. An' if she's in trouble, we'll round up,' Panther said. 'No fucker gets one up on the ACs.'

The girls all high-fived each other.

Stephanie organised two female PCs to take a patrol car over to McDonalds in Lambeth. They had the description of Melek, their instructions were to pick her up and bring her back to the station.

Georgia had left word that under no circumstance was Harisha allowed to know Melek was anywhere in the station, and to make sure this time there was no possibility he could bump into her. She had made a rape allegation against him and it was their responsibility to protect her.

As soon as Georgia arrived back at the station she rang the station sergeant to check that Harisha Celik had been stripped and his clothes had been sent to Forensics for testing. She was told that was in hand. She then rang the lab herself and begged for the earliest possible result on the DNA from the foetus that was found in Zana's post-mortem. She was told they were doing their best. She thanked them, as politely as she could muster, having heard the phrase a million times before during a murder enquiry, and asked them again to make it top priority, along with Harisha's clothing.

Then Banham rang with an update. He had spoken to all the neighbouring shopkeepers, but no one had actually spoken to Wajdi this morning, although some say they saw him earlier, most said they had seen a woman, or maybe even two, go into Wajdi's shop, but none could accurately describe Alison.

'Customers would go in and out,' Georgia told him. 'That just confirms that Wajdi was there at some time this morning, but it doesn't confirm at what time, so doesn't put him in the clear for the Wilkins' murders.'

'I'm keen to find Alison,' Banham said.

'Of course,' Georgia said as politely as she could muster. 'And I'm keen to find out who murdered four people.' He was beginning to irritate her. The press were swarming around the station asking about the latest murders. She had three prisoners locked in cells, all needing interviews, she was expecting a rape victim to arrive, and half a dozen forensic tests needed chasing.

'She isn't answering my calls,' Banham said.

'I've asked my snout to get me Melek's mobile number,' Georgia told him. 'As soon as I get it, I'll call her. Uniform are on their way to pick her up anyway and bring her in. Alison put in a request for that, apparently, as she was leaving McDonalds. And I'll get Wajdi's description circulated to all patrol cars in the area.'

'She should answer her phone?'

'She may still be with Melek at McDonalds,' Georgia said. 'And I think McDonalds at Lambeth has a basement, so she may not have signal. Or she could have gone, and left her phone behind.'

'Can you phone TIU to put a trace on her number and get back to me,' he said.

'Shall we wait until uniform pick up Melek, they'll be back with her in about fifteen minutes. Also I am waiting on getting Melek's mobile. I'll try that when I get it, we can then ask her ...'

'No. Do it now,' Banham barked. 'TIU will tell us if she's turned her phone off, or if she's out of range, if not they'll tell us exactly where she is.'

Georgia took a breath in. 'Listen, guv, as a friend,' she said softly. 'She just might need you to back off a bit. I'm more than sure she'll be in touch soon.'

He raised his voice. She could hear panic in his tone as well as anger. 'I told her to keep in close touch. I am her boss as well as her boyfriend, and that was an official order. She has only just returned to murder investigations. I need to keep my eye on her.'

'You also told her not to go to the post-mortem,' Georgia reminded him, 'And she did.' Georgia immediately bit her tongue. She knew shouldn't have said that. 'Sir, I know she's newly back in this department, but she is a very experienced

196

detective, and she can look after herself.'

There was a pause and then Banham shouted, 'She's pregnant.'

It took a few seconds for Georgia to take that in. 'Oh,' was all she could think of to say. She just wasn't good in emotional situations.

'She's carrying my child. I want to know where she is.'

Georgia looked across at Stephanie and signalled for her to pick up the phone and listen in, although Stephanie could probably hear from where she was, as Banham was shouting loudly enough for the whole station to hear.

'Stephanie and I are going to interview the Ghazianis now,' Georgia said, unsure what else to say. 'I'll get onto TIU first, and then back to you as soon as I hear from her.'

'I'm on my way in,' he told her. 'I'll interview Harisha Celik with you while I'm waiting on TIU. If I don't hear from Alison in the next fifteen minutes, I'm calling Indie 999, to get the 'copter out.'

Stephanie and Georgia looked at each other. 'Just hold fire, Guv, see what TIU can find out,' Georgia said realising she had to keep him calm. She fully understood, because of the murder of his first wife and baby, why he was panicking. However, she also knew that any moment Alison could ring, or stroll in to the station, and the DCI would look a complete fool, especially if he had called out the 999 police helicopter search. 'I'll talk to you when you get here, sir,' she added.

As soon as she clicked off she turned to Stephanie, 'What's your ex in TIU called, is it Greg?'

'Er,' Stephanie had to think for a moment. 'I've got two in that department, Greg was one, yes, and the other is Ralph Stenet.'

'Blimey, who'd have thought you'd have a fling with Ralph Stenet!' Georgia said, trying to contain her giggles. 'He's only about four feet tall!'

'He's cute! Well, he was at the time. I think.'

'Whatever. Just get on to one of them, and get a trace them to put a trace on Alison's phone, tell them Alison must never know. That'll keep the DCI calm for a bit. Four bloody murders, and the DCI's decided to have an emotional wobbly.'

'It is understandable. She's pregnant.'

'Did you know?'

'Yes, she told me.'

'You didn't tell me?'

Stephanie shook her head. 'It wasn't affecting her work.'

'It is now.'

'And now you know.'

'Guv.' It was Hank Peacock. He was hurrying from the outside doors down the corridor towards her. 'The reception area is full of press, what shall I do?'

'Ignore them,' Georgia shouted at him, her patience beginning to crack. She turned her back on the young trainee detective, who was blushing like a Belisha beacon because she had shouted at him. She immediately wished she hadn't.

As Georgia made her way to Interview Room B, Stephanie turned to Hank. 'It's getting very tense,' she said quietly. 'Don't take it personally.'

'I can't ignore them,' he said. 'They're following me. I just went out for a milkshake, and they followed me, they were all firing questions at me.'

'You'll have to get used to that,' Stephanie said in her motherly tone. 'Tell them we'll call a press conference later.' She turned her back and hurried after Georgia.

Mrs Ghaziani had calmed down. She sat opposite the two detectives, wringing her hands together.

'I have never been locked up before,' she said. 'Is my husband also locked in a cell?'

'A first for everything,' Georgia told her. 'Did you say no to legal representation?'

'Yes, I have done nothing wrong. It is my right to request my daughter's body back to bury it. All I have said is that I must bury her, in my religion ...'

'Yes, you said,' Georgia interrupted. 'And we explained that

198

it wasn't possible. This is a murder investigation, and if you don't want to be charged with disrupting it, then you must allow us to do our job.'

'When can I –'

'How long is a piece of string?'

'Pardon?'

'Where do you think Wajdi has gone?'

'I have no idea.'

'He isn't answering his phone.'

'He will have his reasons.'

'Might avoiding police questioning be one of them?'

'My son has done nothing wrong.'

'Then why doesn't he answer his phone?'

'I cannot give you an answer to that. How would I know? I am locked up and can do nothing, not even bury my daughter.'

'Mrs Ghaziani, I have photos of your daughter, from her own computer; pictures of her with bruises and a beaten face. There is one with an iron burn on her shoulder and back.' She watched Mrs Ghaziani's forehead furrow as she continued speaking. 'I also have a statement from someone who claims she was told, by Zana, that you are responsible.'

'They are lying.'

Georgia stared at her. 'Or are you?'

'It is that Turkish girl, isn't it?

Neither Georgia nor Stephanie answered.

'Melek is the one should be locked up. My daughter was a good girl. She hung around with that tart, and things happened.' She leaned forward. The woman's eyes were the colour of steel. 'I have lost my daughter and you accuse my son? You are a disgrace.'

'Did you burn your daughter, Mrs Ghaziani, with an iron, because she was seen out without her hijab?' Georgia asked holding her eyes.

The woman's hands flew to her face. 'No.' Her eyes looked everywhere but back at Georgia.

'I have a witness says you did.'

She fixed her steel-grey eyes on Georgia. 'Why would a

mother harm her daughter?'

'Because she disgraced her family.'

The eyes hardened and she raised her voice and body. 'How dare you?'

'Sit down, Mrs Ghaziani,' Stephanie raised her voice back.

Mrs Ghaziani obeyed.

'Your daughter was pregnant, did you know that?' Georgia said to her.

The woman bowed her head, and then shook it, and then mumbled a prayer. After she had finished she looked up. 'I will say nothing more,' she said, raising her hands by way of confirmation.

Mr Ghaziani's interview was nearly identical. He was asked the same questions, and he gave the same answers.

As Georgia and Stephanie walked back down the corridor, Stephanie said, 'It was as if they had planned their answers in advance.'

'Keep them both locked up,' Georgia said. 'If Wajdi hears his parents are in police cells, he may crawl out of his hole. Meanwhile, try TIU again, see what news they have. Banham will be back any second.'

As Stephanie turned her phone back on to make the call, her answer phone bleeped, alerting her to a waiting message. She checked the message and turned to Georgia. 'The PCs that were sent to pick up Melek Yismaz in McDonalds said there was no sign of her when they got there. They asked the staff, but no one could recall her clearly.' She frowned, shook her head and looked at Georgia. 'I guess loads of people go in and out, so it is possible they wouldn't notice everyone, if they are busy.' She shrugged. 'Lunchtime, yes that makes sense.'

'Get on to TIU, tell them it's becoming urgent,' Georgia said at exactly the same moment as her mobile burst into 'Onward, Christian Soldiers'.

'The guv'nor, again,' she said.

Fourteen

His voice sounded anxious. 'I'm on my way in. Any news?'

'Melek Yismaz wasn't at McDonalds when the patrol car went to pick her up,' Georgia told him. 'And we haven't, as yet, got an official statement to charge Celik. He's in custody and his clothes are with Forensics.'

'I'm on my way in.'

'Oh, well you may want to come in via the back fire escape entrance,' Georgia suggested. 'The front of the station is swarming with journalists.'

'I'm driving into the underground car park now,' he told her. 'So, I'll do that.'

'The last time anyone spoke to Alison she was in McDonalds with Melek Yismaz? Is that right?'

'Yes, according to Stephanie, Alison left with the strict instruction that Melek was to wait for a patrol car to take her to the station.'

'Alison was on her way to the Ghazianis'. And I've just come from there. No one remembers seeing Alison either. I'm concerned, very concerned.'

'I'm waiting on a call from my informant,' Georgia told him. 'She is getting Melek's mobile number for us. TIU will put an immediate trace on it. I mean perhaps she has lost her nerve about charging Celik with rape ...' She stopped in mid conversation, as Stephanie walked up to her, her phone in her hand, and said, 'TIU say Alison's phone is switched off.'

Georgia repeated the information to Banham.

The desperate sigh that he let out the other end of the line worried her.

'She can't talk wherever she is,' Georgia assured him. 'She's just left the Sapphire rape division before she came back to major incidents. She knows how to handle rape victims.'

'I told her to keep in touch with me,' Banham barked.

'Sir, I'm not getting involved in your personal life, but she is an experienced officer, your beef seems personal, not professional. We need to focus. There are press everywhere around the station …'

'I can see them,' he said. 'I'm walking round the back with my head down.' She heard the sound of the door peep. 'I've just entered the building. I'll meet you at the interview suite.' He clicked off.

Georgia shook her head and let out a heavy sigh.

'Problem, ma'am? Stephanie asked, raising her eyebrows.

'Guv'nor seems to have taken his eye off the ball,' she said quietly. 'There are four bodies in the mortuary, and a reception full of hungry press all awaiting answers as to why a vulnerable old couple have just been murdered in cold blood on an estate where the police presence was high.' She shook her head. 'Alison isn't answering his calls, so he's not interested in anything else.' She shook her head. 'She went to the post-mortem when he told her not to, and she probably isn't ready for the earful he'll give her. She's busy and I think he is emotionally suffocating her.'

'She's not returned our calls either,' Stephanie reminded her.

Georgia shrugged 'I think Melek has got cold feet about bringing an allegation against Celik.'

'You're the senior investigating officer around here,' Stephanie said to her, 'which means you carry the can.' Stephanie lowered her voice 'Alison should keep in touch with us, as well.'

Georgia took that in. 'What do you think?'

'I think the DCI is right to be concerned about one of his officers,' Stephanie told her. 'I'm a little edgy about Alison myself. I'm surprised she hasn't phoned you, or even me.'

'Well, please don't say that in front of Banham,' Georgia advised her. 'I'm on my way to interview Celik with him, without a statement from Melek Yismaz. I only hope she isn't going to retract her allegation. Let me know if you hear anything. I'll catch you later.'

As she hurried through main reception on her way to the interviewing suite, she passed Stan Gayle, the front-of-house sergeant. Before he could ask her what to do about the press she waved her hand dismissively.

'Tell them we've nothing to say, at the moment.'

'They need to be told something, ma'am.'

'Tell them to follow the yellow brick road,' Georgia said, slamming the door behind her and hurrying down to the interview suite.

Harisha Celik had been stripped of his clothes and was dressed in a white forensic suit with white plastic shoes. He sat, a look of thunder written across his face.

'I ain't talking to you without my brief,' he said. 'I've rung him, and he's on his way. This is harassment, I ain't done nothing.'

'Jolly good,' Banham told him evenly. 'Then you'll be out of here soon.' He looked down to the recorder, which was switched off, and then back up to Celik. 'The CD isn't running, so this is all off the record. I thought you might want to talk about your girlfriend.'

'Which one?'

'My, my, you are a one,' Banham said with a small, forced smile. 'The gorgeous Melek Yismaz of course, that's what she's known as, isn't she? Gorgeous Melek? I would have thought she'd be enough for you.'

Celik folded his arms and leaned back in his chair. His dark eyes looked bored as they stared back at Banham and then flicked a condescending glance in Georgia's direction. She felt a strong urge to hit him.

'So where is Melek now?' Banham asked him.

'How the fuck do I know?' He started walking his fingers on the desk and dropped his gaze to watch, like a bored three-year-old.

Banham glanced at Georgia.

Georgia took the hint and stood up. 'I'll check if your brief is around,' she said quickly leaving the room to give Banham time alone with Celik, and her the chance to take a deep breath. The urge to smack him hard across the head, for what she knew he had done to Melek, was becoming very strong.

Outside a uniformed PC was leaning against the wall. The woman was yawning. Georgia didn't want her overhearing what went on inside the interview suite, just in case Banham lost his temper. 'Can you get me Mr Celik's file?' Georgia asked her.

As the PC made her way back into the reception area, Georgia followed her.

'I'll need to tell the press something,' Sergeant Gayle said to her as soon as she walked through the door.

She took a deep breath in. The day was getting to her. 'Tell them we'll call a press conference later,' she said, then lowering her voice she said, 'I need Harisha Celik's personals.'

Sergeant Gayle turned his back, opened a filing cabinet and pulled out a large envelope that was tied and bound with string. It was labelled *Harisha Celik*, underneath the name was a list of everything that was inside it. He handed the envelope to Georgia. She tipped the contents onto the desk and took the mobile phone, then she put everything back and handed the large brown envelope back. 'I'm borrowing this,' she told him keeping her voice low. 'Off the record.'

He pretended not to hear.

'Let me know as soon as his brief arrives,' she added.

She made her way back down the corridor, scrolling the phone's address book as she walked. As soon as she reached Melek's name, she pulled her own phone from her pocket and stabbed the numbers in, pressing the call button. The phone went straight to voicemail. She put Celik's phone back on Gayle's counter.

'Think this slipped from the evidence bag, Stan.'

Georgia walked a few steps back down the corridor and phoned Alysha.

Tink was twisting red strands of nylon hair in between Alysha's plaits as the phone that Georgia had given Alysha started to ring. Alysha glanced down at it, then turned her head as far as she could in Tink's direction.

'That's the fed's phone. She'll want a number for Melek,' she told Tink. 'Ring Panther from your phone and ask if they've dumped Melek's mobile yet.'

Tink stopped the plaiting, picked up her phone, and pressed a key. She was nodding within seconds. 'Just done it,' she told Alysha. 'The phone is outside Harisha's gaff, she threw it in his dustbin.'

Alysha rang Georgia straight back but the line was engaged.

Georgia was on the phone to TIU. TIU told her Alison's phone was still turned off. Georgia gave them the number she had just taken from Celik's phone for Melek, and told them to put a trace on that, as a matter of urgency. She checked Celik's address list again. There was no number for Wajdi Ghaziani listed. Wajdi must have a mobile number; Mrs Ghaziani was insistent that she didn't know it. A clear lie, Georgia thought, what mother doesn't know her son's mobile number? Especially a son that works, closely, with his parents in their family business. Even if she didn't know it off by heart, surely it would be in her phone? Then she realised that Zana would definitely have had it, so she rang TIU back to ask if there was any chance of retrieving it from Zana's SIM card. They said they would keep trying, and get back to her. She told them she owed them all a large drink, and hung up.

She noticed Alysha's number on her screen as having tried to ring her. She was about to re-ring Alysha when Sergeant Gayle appeared beside her.

'Mr Celik's legal adviser has just arrived.'

'I'll be there in two minutes,' she said, deciding to give Banham more time with Harisha. If Banham had landed Celik one, then Georgia would be delighted. Celik was a rapist, rules and protocol could go to hell.

She walked back through the incident room, stopping by Hank Peacock's desk. He was still fiddling with Zana's laptop and downloading pictures. There was the blown-up photo of Zana in Peacock's in-tray, a clear outline of an iron burn on her back and a face that was swollen, bruised, and bleeding.

'You've been a lot of help, Hank. Would you mind taking that laptop back up to the TIU, ask them to retrieve every email and Facebook message on it, deleted ones, everything.'

Banham had kept his gaze fixed on Celik. 'Off the record,' he said to him. 'I think you know Melek is bringing a charge of rape against you.'

'I ain't raped no one, what do I need to rape someone for?' Harisha raised his voice. 'I got girls begging for it with me.'

'Is that right?'

Celik nodded.

'Then you won't mind giving me Melek's mobile phone number, off the record. I can talk to her, tell her it's a serious offence to lie, blacken a character.'

'I ain't raped no one.'

'No? Give me her phone number and I can speak to her, tell her not to waste police time, as you say she is lying. And, that's one charge less for your brief to have to argue.'

'Ain't no charge for me to argue, cos I ain't done nothing. You're the cunt that's breaking the law. See, you're talking to me without my brief present, I already said I'd say nothing without him.'

'You also said you've done nothing wrong.'

'I ain't.'

Banham shrugged. 'I'm trying to make life easier all round, get you out of here, if you're innocent.' He leaned back in his chair and folded his arms, but he was finding it hard to stay calm. Where the hell could Alison be? It wasn't like her to be unprofessional, even if he had been overprotective as Georgia Johnson was insinuating. Alison had a duty to keep her senior officer informed of her movements and she hadn't done that.

'We'll wait then,' he said, keeping as focused as he could. 'For your brief.' he paused and added, 'And for the forensic results on your clothes.'

'Listen, mate, that won't tell you nothing, cos even if her DNA is on my gear, that ain't says nothing, 'cept I fucked her. And why wouldn't I? I have, many times, but I ain't, *no way*, raped her.'

'So give me her phone number, and I can talk to her and stop wasting all our time.'

Banham noticed Harisha narrow his eyes, then he lifted his forefinger and his thin mouth spread into a small, nasty smile, and then a chuckle. He pointed his finger at Banham as the penny dropped. 'You don't know where she is, do you?'

'Do you?'

His smile widened. 'She's done a runner, mate, cos she's been telling big fucking porkies.'

'Maybe she's frightened you'll do it again.'

'I ain't done nothing.' He crossed his arms.

'Then give me her phone number.'

'I ain't got it.'

'You don't expect me to believe that.'

'She just got a new mobile, and I ain't got the number.' Harisha stretched his legs forward and pushed the chair back. He folded his arms. 'Now, I ain't saying nothing else without me brief.'

Banham took a deep breath. He wasn't giving up. He needed to contact Melek, Alison may well be with her. 'She's brought a charge against you for rape, and now she's gone missing,' he said. 'So where do you think she'd go?'

'To the bottom of a river, with a bit of luck.'

As Georgia walked back into the waiting room she immediately recognised Celik's brief. 'We meet again,' she said sarcastically. At the same moment her mobile rang. 'I'll get someone to bring you through in just one minute,' she said turning her back on him, and picking up her call.

'I need a few minutes, alone, with my client,' Simon Prezzioni told her.

'Wait there,' she said flicking her hand, not looking in his direction as she spoke. Alysha's name was on her phone screen. She walked through the pass door and took the call.

'Tell me it's good news.'

'I've got the number for you,' Alysha told Georgia, reeling

off the same mobile phone number that Georgia had just taken from Harisha's phone.

Georgia thanked her, and was about to click off when Alysha shouted that thanking wasn't enough. She wanted to be paid for the information, she told Georgia. Getting the number had taken a lot of favour-pulling, so she expected either a very big wad of paper in return, or a firm promise from Georgia to lean on the council to get the play area cleaned up.

'I know you can do it, yeah?'

Georgia told her she'd get back to her. She walked back to reception and dropped Celik's phone back to Sergeant Gayle to put back in Celik's envelope, then hurried down to the interviewing suite, where she called Banham out.

Once outside, she told him her informant had given her a number for Melek Yismaz's, she had also found the same number on Celik's mobile. She told him she was handing the number over to TIU to put on immediate trace, if Alison was with Melek, she added, then problem solved. 'However, she felt they needed to step up the search now for Wajdi, as no one could find a mobile contact for him. He was a strong suspect and Alison's last known location was at his shop before Barry arrived.

'Have all area units been alerted with descriptions?' he said.

'Yes, sir.' She quickly added, 'I'm confident Alison knows what she is doing, sir. And I'm sure she'll be in touch with one of us any moment.' She was embarrassed and wasn't good at sympathy. 'Celik's solicitor's arrived, wants a few words alone with his client, shall I bring him through? It's Simon Prezzioni again, so expect a load of bullshit.'

She noticed that the pretty PC, who earlier had been standing outside the interviewing room, was back, and smiling in Banham's direction. Georgia bit her tongue, she felt like reminding her that this was the serious crimes department not a dating agency. Instead she told her to show Mr Prezzioni through to Interview Room C.

'I'm giving it another thirty minutes and then I'm calling Indie

999,' Banham said to Georgia as they waited for Prezzioni to have his few moments with Harisha. 'It isn't like Alison not to be completely professional.'

Georgia nodded. She was irritated by Alison. The woman had been nothing but trouble since she came back. She had ignored the advice to stay clear of the charred cadaver, and messed up a crime-scene by being pig-headed, then she had ignored Banham and gone to the post-mortem, and now she was ignoring all of them, seemingly thinking she could work alone. She should know by now this was about team-work. The woman was sapping the DCI's energy. Girlfriend or no girlfriend, Georgia would be letting her feelings be known when she wrote up her report on the case.

Simon Prezzioni scowled at Georgia as she followed Banham into the interviewing room. He had told her on many occasions in the past that he didn't like her and he didn't think women should be in the force. Well, Georgia liked him even less, and at this moment in time she wasn't in the mood to take any of his shit.

Banham pulled out the chair for Georgia to sit on. 'This is DI Johnson,' Banham told Prezzioni, knowing full well the man knew who she was. He paused, held Prezzioni's gaze, and then added, 'She's heading this investigation.'

Prezzioni and Georgia locked eyes. Prezzioni reeked of Turkish cigarettes, his yellowing fingers further confirmation of his habit. He also had ill-fitting false teeth which rattled when he was irritated, making it impossible for him to control his spittle. Georgia rolled a tissue into a ball in her hand, ready for the onslaught as she turned the CD to 'on'.

'When did you last see Melek Yismaz?' Banham asked Harisha immediately.

Harisha threw his eyes to heaven. 'Already told you, yesterday.'

'When, yesterday?' This was Georgia.

'After I left here?'

'Did you have sex with her?'

209

'Yes. She was gagging for it.'

Georgia glared at him, but managed to refrain from commenting.

'Do you have a written allegation that my client raped her?' Prezzioni interrupted.

'We have an allegation, yes,' Georgia answered.

'A written one?' Prezzioni pressed.

Georgia hesitated. 'We will have.'

'She don't seem too keen to make one,' Celik said to Prezzioni, then indicating Banham with his head and smiling widely, he added, 'He told me they can't find 'er.'

'There are witnesses to the rape,' Georgia said quickly.

'Oh, that'll be them toms then, them big fucking liars that call themselves Alley Cats,' Celik told Prezzioni. 'Trying to frame me, see.' He leaned towards Georgia. 'They've already wasted your time, and mine, with accusations about me having machetes in lock-up garages. You didn't find no weapons though, did you?' When neither Georgia nor Banham answered, he continued. 'No, cos there ain't any. And you turned my flat upside down looking. Thought you'd have got the message, them Alley Cat liars are the ones should be sitting here, not me.' He indicated to his head with his finger. 'You've got this all wrong, as fucking usual.'

'Clean as a whistle, are you?' Georgia said.

'You have nothing that says different,' Prezzioni argued, staring with his cold black eyes.

'Three previous convictions for carrying, a custodial for GBH, and another for dealing,' Georgia answered, staring into his condescending face and squeezing the tissue in her fist.

'He's paid his dues for those,' Prezzioni retorted.

Georgia looked at Celik. 'Where were you this morning before we came round?' she asked him.

'In bed.'

'How do you know Mr and Mrs Wilkins from the Aviary Estate?' she pushed.

'Never heard of them.'

'I think you have,' she argued. 'They own the garage, the

garage that you told me is being used for illegal weapons that this so-called Alley Cat gang are apparently bringing into the country.'

Prezzioni turned to look at Celik. That was obviously the first he had heard of this.

'I told you what I knew,' Harisha said, raising his voice. 'Them Alley Cat girls had a lock-up on the Aviary.' He turned to Prezzioni. 'I don't know nothing about who the lock-up belongs to, except I do know that it ain't me.'

Georgia took out the evidence bag containing the letter S that she was sending to Forensics, and placed it on the table in front of them. Harisha's reaction told her that he recognised it.

'Recognise it?'

'No.'

'An S, very much like the S tattooed on Burak's arm. For South London Rulers, is it? It may even be yours. It was found in the same lock-up.'

Harisha shook his head. 'I've never seen it before. You're jumping to conclusions.'

'But you also have a tattoo like this on your arm,' she pushed. 'An S with an L and an R. For South London Rulers, that's the name of your gang, isn't it?'

'No. It's the initials of this tart I used to hang out with.'

Georgia blew out air. 'Oh please. And I suppose Burak used to *hang out* with the same *tart*, did he?'

'That charm doesn't prove anything,' Prezzioni said coldly. 'Except you've found a charm in the shape of a letter S. It could belong to anyone. What that has to do with a fabricated rape charge?'

'We'll see what Forensics tells us,' she said, realising she wasn't getting very far.

'You have nothing to hold my client on,' Prezzioni said, pinning his cold gaze on her.

'We have an allegation of rape which we are taking seriously,' she argued. 'Your client's clothes are with Forensics, and until those reports come back, I'm afraid we will be holding him.'

'How can she allege anything if you can't find her?' Harisha argued.

'Do you know a Wajdi Ghaziani?' Banham interrupted.

Georgia noticed Harisha pause before he answered, 'No, should I?'

'Are you sure?'

Prezzioni raised his voice. 'My client has just said he doesn't know him.'

'And I asked him if he was sure,' Banham argued.

Georgia squeezed the tissue, she was expecting the spittle any minute now.

'But you knew Zana Ghaziani?' Banham asked.

'Who?'

'Burak Kaya was your cousin. Zana Ghaziani was his girlfriend.'

Harisha shrugged irritably. 'He had lots of girls. I don't know one from another.'

Georgia put her elbows on the table and interlocked her fingers. The urge to slap him was getting stronger.

'This is bordering on ridiculous,' Prezzioni said. 'My client is arrested because a jealous girl accuses him of raping her and then doesn't come in to make a statement.'

'That allegation was made to a senior officer, and we will be detaining your client until we have our DNA test results,' Georgia said raising her voice and speaking a little more heatedly than she wanted.

Harisha raised his voice. 'Why would I rape her? She gives it freely, not only to me but to everyone.'

Georgia *so* wanted to slap him.

Celik noticed her steely, angry, glare and carried on. 'OK. She's pregnant, or so she says. I'm not that interested, because she's a slag and a liar. An' I've told her that. If she has told you I raped her, then it's because she's mad at me. I haven't raped nobody.'

Banham sat up 'When did she tell you she was pregnant?'

He shrugged. 'I don't remember. I was hardly listening. Could be anyone's, but it ain't mine. You want me to give you

212

names of some guys who I know have had her recently?'

'No.' Georgia shook her head and told the recorder that the interview was terminated.

'I'll tell you something off the record,' Celik said, ignoring the fact that Prezzioni was shaking his head fervently for him to keep quiet. 'She texted me earlier.' He put his hand up. 'I have deleted it, before you ask, so no, I don't have her number. She said she's going to kill herself if I don't accept the fact she's pregnant with my child.'

Banham stood up. 'Why didn't you say any of this before?'

'Because she won't. She is a pathological liar. She's probably not up the fucking duff, either. And ... *I didn't rape her.*'

As soon as they left the interview suite, Banham told Georgia to ring TIU to see if there was any news on Alison's phone being back on.

As she dialled the number Banham walked on ahead and asked Sergeant Gayle if anything had turned up on the CCTV that they had taken from the area around the Ghazianis' shop. It hadn't.

'As soon as anything shows, we'll be onto you, sir,' Stan told him.

Georgia meanwhile was smiling. She lifted her thumb high in the air to let Banham know they had something. Banham hurried back to her.

'They've got a lead on Melek's phone. She's is in the vicinity of Celik's flat.

'Alison's phone?' he asked almost pathetically.

'Is still switched off,' she said gently. 'Maybe Melek *is* suicidal, and Alison is talking her down. Makes sense why she turned her phone off,' she added.

'She should have called it in for backup if that's the case.' He shook his head. 'That's not like her. But if she's with Melek at Celik's flat, then she might be in danger.' He was back with Stan at the desk within seconds, instructing all free patrol cars to get over to the area of Celik's flat and trace Melek and

Alison's whereabouts. He then rang Indie 999 and put a helicopter on standby, telling them one of his officers was missing, and she was pregnant.

Georgia went to Harisha's cell and asked permission to take the keys to his flat from his personals. She told him they had traced Melek to that area.

He told her to take the keys, better than having the feds break down the door, he said. But if Melek was in his flat then she had broken and entered, because he hadn't invited her and she hadn't been there for ages.

When Georgia reminded him that he had admitted having sex with her yesterday, he told her he did it in his car. 'If she hadn't wanted it,' he added with a wide grin, 'then she wouldn't have got in the motor in the first place.' His grinned widened yet again. 'Truth is, Melek finds me irresistible. Most women do.'

'Shame castration has gone out of fashion,' Georgia said as she turned to leave the room.

Georgia and Banham followed the police sirens and were inside Celik's flat, looking for Melek and Alison, within the half hour.

Georgia kept her own phone to her ear, talking to Ralph in the Technical Investigation Unit all the while. All he could tell her now was that the phone was near a signal box.

'Melek's not in the flat?' Banham confirmed.

'But she's not far away,' Georgia said. Then she looked at Banham. Both were thinking the same thing.

'Unless Harisha has had her taken hostage,' Banham said.

'So she could be nowhere near here, but her phone might.'

It was only a few more minutes before one of the PCs searching outside in the area around the flat called out. He had found the phone. It was in the black dustbin marked 'number eighteen' in large letters. Number eighteen was the flat where Harisha Celik lived with his brother.

Georgia looked at Banham. 'She had her phone with her this morning,' she said as she flicked through the recent call history. 'She used this phone to arrange to meet Alison this morning.'

She noticed the colour had completely gone from Banham's face.

'Where is Alison?' he said. 'Her last contact was with Stephanie, when she was leaving McDonalds and on her way to pick up Wajdi Ghaziani.'

'And no one can find Wajdi Ghaziani either,' Georgia said.

Fifteen

Georgia knew Banham was thinking the worst.

'If the SLR gang have taken Melek hostage,' she said in an assuring tone, 'and were stupid enough to take Alison with them, then as soon as Alison showed her ID they'd let her go.' She shook her head. 'They wouldn't dare. They know the consequences for kidnapping an officer.'

'It isn't like Alison not to phone in. This doesn't feel right,' he said. 'Jesus, I hope Wajdi Ghaziani hasn't done anything to her. If he's murdered four people he wouldn't have anything to lose.'

Georgia thought about telling him that it was only a couple of hours since Alison had phoned in and spoken to Stephanie, but she didn't feel she should suggest that he was overreacting. Wajdi Ghaziani was missing, and even Georgia now felt nervous for Alison's safety. She pulled her phone from her pocket. 'I'm ringing my snout,' she said to him. 'She knows everyone and everywhere around these parts.'

Banham nodded his approval. 'I'll go back to the station ...' he started to say but before he could finish the sentence, his phone rang. He checked the caller ID and pressed the speaker button so Georgia could hear. 'Yes, Sergeant Green,' he said pointing his finger to the phone and looking at Georgia to get her attention as Stephanie spoke.

'Sir, Barry and Eric have been back to the Ghazianis' and ...' Stephanie cleared her throat. 'They, accidentally on purpose, broke the back door so it opened. The lock was loose, or something.'

'Fine,' Banham said ignoring the fact that Stephanie was admitting to entering a property without a warrant. 'And?'

'They've found a screwdriver behind the counter, with blood on it.'

Banham looked at Georgia. 'Were both the old couple

definitely killed with screwdrivers?'

Georgia shrugged, unsure how to keep him calm. 'We'll have to run that by Max Pettifer, sir. But it looks that way.'

'Any signs of Alison having been at the shop?' he asked Stephanie, the anguish on his face returning.

'No, sorry, sir, absolutely none,' Stephanie told him. 'All patrol cars have been put on high alert. I've every possible unit on it, now. And there's a patrol car waiting at the Ghazianis' house. He'll have to go home some time.'

'Check the hospitals, too,' he told her.

He clicked his phone and looked at Georgia. 'Take backup with you if you're going to talk to your informant,' he said to her. 'I don't want you on the Aviary alone. I'm going back to the station to re-interview Harisha Celik, and then Mr and Mrs Ghaziani. Keep in close touch, but don't be on your own.' He turned and hurried towards his car.

Tink wiped a tissue across Panther's long brown toes to remove the hard skin cream she'd been rubbing around her friend's feet. She looked up and listened as Alysha picked up the call from Georgia.

Alysha clicked off. 'All going to plan,' she told her lieutenants. 'They've found Melek's phone. Now the black fed's on her way over here, and needs us to ask around if anyone has seen that Alison Grainger and Melek in the last hour. And she wants to know where Wajdi Ghaziani might be hanging out.'

'Cool,' Tink said, lifting a bottle of green nail varnish from her manicure box. 'We're on course then. What we telling her?'

'I don't want that colour,' Panther interrupted, pointing at the green nail polish and shaking her head. 'It makes me think of dead people.'

'Whass up wiv you?' Lox said to Panther, 'You keep talking like that. You've seen dead people before.'

'I got the willies over them Wilkinses,' Panther said swallowing down and pulling a pained expression. 'D'you think they've gone green yet?'

218

'Nah,' Tink shook her head quickly, and then smiled. 'Takes weeks for that to 'appen.' She flicked a look of concern to the other girls as she wiggled a purple nail polish bottle in front of Panther's face. 'This one, then.'

'You alright?' Alysha asked Panther, 'Cos that black fed's on 'er way over, and we need to square up. We got a chance here to make a killing, so we gonna get in there. You know do the scratch our backs if we scratch hers bit.'

Panther nodded her head at the mauve nail polish. 'Yeah, that one's nice,' she told Tink.

Tink turned the lid and pulled the brush.

'They was an all right old couple, I liked them,' Panther said quietly.

'They was a bit stupid, but they never wanted no trouble,' Alysha agreed, catching Tink's eye and mirroring her concerned look.

'An' they never called us dirty names when we was working the streets,' Lox put in. 'They just turned their heads away, and never judged no one,' she paused and said quietly. 'I 'ate this fucking estate,' she said.

'Don't let them Wilkinses get to yous all,' Alysha told them. 'Ain't no wars ever won without killings. We are changing things round 'ere. It's gonna get better.' She rubbed Panther's large shoulder. 'We don't want our kids 'avin to suck cocks or hide rock in their mouths so they can eat every day. That's the only choices we 'ad. Kids need chances, and we're gonna give 'em some.'

Panther shrugged.

'Come on, think of them tinies out there,' Tink said to her. 'We were them once, and we never 'ad no one to give us nothing. Right now they ain't got nothing neither, 'cept cold bones and empty tummies.'

'We know what it feels like to be abused and not wanted,' Alysha said. 'But look at us now?' She looked at Tink and Lox, and then back to Panther. 'If we want to 'ave kids, we 'ave to make sure they get better than we did. We know how hard it's been to stay alive.'

Panther nodded, but kept her head down.

'We've done bad things,' Alysha said to her, 'but we 'ad no choice. We're doing all this for the future of this estate, and if that includes people being killed, then that 'as to be, Panth. You 'ave to 'ave casualties in war, don't ya?'

'She's right,' Tink said.

'I'm not 'avin a good day today,' Panther said. 'The brother I never really knew was shot two years ago today, and now them old couple.'

'Then make it a reason to fight harder,' Lox said gravely.

'Yeah,' Alysha agreed. 'If we don't change this estate, no one else will, cos no one else cares, and it'll get worse. Them feds don't understand nothing, not who we are, and not what we 'ave had to do.'

'Panther, we're your family,' Lox said. 'We're here for you, an' we won't let you down.'

'Right on,' Tink nodded.

'We can't replace your brother,' Lox said sincerely, 'but we are your sisters, OK?'

'OK,' Panther perked up. 'So what we gonna say to feds, cause I tell you I'm thinking now that Melek is a worry, she should have phoned us by now, shouldn't she, and I 'ope she's all right. We could give them the number for the Alley Cat phone we gave her, we ain't getting no answer from it but the feds could trace it and find her, and know where she is.'

'Not a bad idea,' Lox said looking from Alysha to Tink.

Alysha nodded. 'We'll think on that a few minutes,' she said.

Lox opened her leopard-print bag and pulled out her pink calculator. She started pushing buttons. 'Business,' she said. 'If that black fed wants more info, then we want the play area sorted. If she won't pay us enough to do that, then we gotta get a written promise from her to lean on the council out to do it, or we say we won't help her.' she looked over to Alysha. 'Do the feds think Wajdi Ghaziani killed his sister?' she asked.

Alysha shrugged. 'Dunno.'

'He's an arse-hole anyway,' Tink said. 'All that family are.

Zana was all right, an' she was Melek's mate, so we ain't worried 'bout dropping him in it.'

'He beat up his sister enough times,' Lox added.

'Where will he be, d'you think?' Alysha asked looking at Tink for an answer.

'He'll be in the mosque, praying for Zana's soul, I'd say for sure,' Tink told her. 'They do all that, an' specially cos the feds ain't given up what's left of 'er body for burial.'

'That'll be worth a lot,' Lox said. 'We can't let 'er think that info comes cheap.'

Alysha looked at Panther. 'When yous two dressed up as blokes this morning and went an' put the usual cash in the Wilkins' door, for the lock-up, didn't you notice no one around?'

'No, we never saw no one,' Lox told her.

'Cos, that's what's odd, see that black fed said the Wilkins hadn't been dead long when the feds found 'em.' Alysha shifted on the sofa and sat up. 'So, I reckoned they was done in by someone who came on the estate, like early this morning. And it's unlikely that any South London Rulers could have got on the estate and none of our street girls seen 'em, cos they would have reported it back to us.'

'You thinking SLRs have got soldiers on our estate and we don't know about them?' Lox said looking at the other two.

'I think it's possible.'

'You mean, you think we can't trust all our street girls, and the lookouts?' Lox said. 'One could be double-doing us cos SLRs are givin' better drugs an' stuff.'

'Yeah, that's a poss,' Alysha said. 'SLRs are gonna try and get our girls to go over to them. They want this patch, they've moved on it already, or they're fucking trying to, ain't they?'

'So I gotta look out for a turncoat,' Panther said.

'Yeah, you 'ave,' Alysha said.

'What we think 'bout Melek, do we trust her?' Panther asked,

Alysha shook her head. 'Dunno. She should have made a statement by now to the feds, accusing Harisha of raping her, and then she was told to phone us to say done it.'

'Means Harisha won't stay locked up if she ain't?' Tink said.

'I 'ope Harisha ain't using her as a scape-goat to double cross us,' Panther said.

'Well if she ain't answering,' Alysha said scratching the roots of her hair extensions, and looking from one to another, means either she's still with that fed Grainger, or she's in trouble, or she's working for SLRs.'

'I'll kill her first,' Panther said.

'What did the fed say about her?' Tink asked.

'Said Alison went to meet her, and they can't contact either of them, an she said she needs us to help find Wajdi Ghaziani, cos they think he's involved.'

'Let's get 'im for her, then,' Tink said. 'I've always hated him. He hurt his sister a lot, an' we don't care if he gets done for murder.'

'Yeah, fine by me.' Alysha shrugged, then shook her head, thoughtfully. 'I don't reckon Melek's bright enough to double cross us,' she said.

'She is in love with Harisha, it makes you do mad things,' Tink said. 'She'll do what he tells her to, an' 'e's a clever, cruel bastard.'

'We gotta give the feds solid information?' Lox said. 'Cos we want that playground sorted. An if we can set Harisha Celik up for a long stretch too, then that would be two plans accomplished.'

'What about giving them the whereabouts of the SLR machetes and weapons, the ones we took from the lock-up to the tunnel?' Tink suggested. 'A location and a big load of weapons,' she looked at Lox, 'that's gotta be worth a lot.'

'If we give up them, we'll lose loads of dosh from selling them on to other gangs,' Lox said.

'But we can ask for a big reward instead, an' they'll give it for weapons,' Tink argued. 'And Harisha will, most definitely, go down for handling of all that shit. That tunnel's got loads of his stuff in it. He'll never wriggle out of that.'

'But we cleaned them till they shone, so they didn't have none of our DNA on them, an' that means none of his either, so nothing to prove they are his,' Lox argued. 'And, we'll make so much more selling them on to North London gangs.'

Alysha put her hand up. 'Tink got a good point, there, Lox. We're all on probation,' she reminded her. 'If we go for a reward, then we stay clean. But if we sell them on, and we get caught, then we'll all go down, and then the estate won't get no better. The kids'll never get a new play area or a youth centre and we'll never change this estate to a good place to live on.'

'We won't have no kids to do it for, if we're in prison,' Lox said. 'You don't get sex in prison.'

'Exactly,' Alysha nodded her head and laughed. 'No sex in prison! I'd rather give the weapons up, and stay clean. We'll get the reward for the weapons. Even if sellin' them on would make more, it's a much better bet, but we'll hold back on that, an' give her Wajdi and find the other detective for her first, Who agrees?'

'I agree,' Tink said. 'And Melek will send Harisha down for rape, that'll be about seven he'll get for that, and we can get some of the street girls to say he threatened them with machetes and that, and he'll get another lump for handling and dealing, make about twenty. He'll be off our back, and we'll stay squeaky clean.'

'So we're giving the new mobile number we gave Melek to them, are we? Lox asked. 'They can trace Melek from it. She's with Grainger, ain't she? The other detective.'

Alysha looked at Panther and Tink. 'What you think?'

'She should have phoned by now,' Panther said, raising her voice. 'Why ain't she answering? I never wanted her in the gang with us, you know that?'

'She's a soldier, that's all she is. Every gang has to have soldiers in it,' Alysha told her. 'You are the lieutenants, I'm the queen, and the others are our soldiers.' She turned her young face to look at Panther, sensing her friend's insecurity. 'Listen, mate, we're sisters, right?'

Panther nodded. 'Right.'

'Each other's family. We'd die for each other, we all know we would. We trust us, but we need more than just us if we're seriously gonna rebuild this estate as a good place. We'll 'ave to take on the other gangs, and fight, hard and dirty, till we get the respect.' She turned to Tink. 'Other gangs will turn up when we stitch up Harisha, we know that, and we'll have to fight them too, and protect our territory, and keep it clean. To do that we need corn, and we need soldiers to fight wiv us. South London Rulers are massive. We need Melek right now to help us send Harisha down, and we *will* get him, I promise, mate. But then someone else will take his place and we 'ave to stay on top of all of the shit if we turn this estate round. We know it ain't gonna be easy, so we need lots of soldiers and the street girls running with us.'

'She's right,' Tink assured Panther.

'The street girls are making dough, it's their choice, an' they're 'appy to do dealin', when it's needed. And right now on this territory we need to keep selling, to users, no one else, but only for a bit longer, cos in five years this is gonna be a totally clean estate, and a good place to live and grow up on, not the shithole that it is now, where the only way to make corn is cocksucking or drugs. An' them changes will be down to us Alley Cats. An' we will do it.' She smiled at her friend. 'We're blood, us four, family, an together we are gonna make fings better.'

'She's right,' Tink said looking up with the mauve nail varnish brush in her hand. 'We're gonna win this postcode war, and when we do, an' all the kids are 'appy cos we've built youth clubs an' fings for them, then I think they'll probably get our statues carved and put at the front of the estate grounds, like they did for that bloke that won the other war for us.'

'What bloke? Panther asked her.

'The fat bugger, wiv the cigar.'

'What fat bugger?'

'Winston Churchill,' Lox told her.

'How d'you know 'bout that?' Panther asked Lox.

'I done him at school before I ran away.'

'What, really done 'im? Tink asked. 'Like slept wiv 'im?'

'No,' Lox laughed. 'He's long dead. 'Sides, he was a fat bastard. I don't do fat bastards – well, not any more.'

'So we know what we're agreein' then,' Alysha said, giggling at Lox. 'Let's hold off on the weapons in the tunnel for now, we'll get Wajdi Ghaziani first. Panth, get one of the street girls on it to check out the mosque, see if he's there. If not, we're on the case. Let's find him.'

'Will do,' Panther said stabbing a number into her mobile.

'I think we should give that fed Melek's Alley Cat number and let them trace her,' Tink said. 'Johnson will pay good for that cos she's looking for Alison. An we'll know where Melek is, an if she's in trouble, we can 'elp her.'

'Yeah,' Panther agreed. 'And if she isn't …'

'She's in big T,' Lox nodded. 'But don't give the weapons up, not yet,' she added.

'I'll go wiv that,' Alysha said to Tink.

The girls all looked at each other, nodded, and high-fived in agreement.

Banham pulled out the chair out without taking his eyes off Harisha Celik. Stephanie turned the CD on, but kept her finger hovering near the switch. She wanted to be ready to click it quickly to off, if Banham lost his temper.

Banham didn't waste a second. 'I haven't got time to fuck with you,' he said as soon as she announced the CD was running and over her introducing the people present at the interview. He looked from Harisha to the duty solicitor who was sitting in, as Prezzioni had left the building.

The duty solicitor pushed his glasses back up the bridge of his nose, and looked up nervously.

'Where is Melek Yismaz?' Banham asked Harisha.

'Don't know what you're on about.'

'We know you do.' Stephanie said, hoping Banham would keep his temper.

Celik scratched his neck, shook his head, and looked at Banham. 'Whatever she's said, she's lying. I don't know nothing.'

'She hasn't said anything,' Banham retorted quickly, 'reason being, she is now missing, as is one of my detectives, who was last seen going to meet her. Melek's mobile has now been found, in the dustbin outside your flat, which tells me you know a lot about her whereabouts.' He raised his voice and his words became clipped. Stephanie sensed he was fighting not to let his personal anxiety show. 'Abduction and kidnap is very serious and carries a heavy custodial sentence, heavier when it involves a police officer. Do you want me to tell you what kind of a sentence you are looking at, or do you want to start talking to me?'

Harisha looked at the duty solicitor and shook his head. The solicitor leaned forward and cleared his throat. 'My client has already told …'

'Your client is lying,' Banham told him. He turned back to Harisha and raised his voice. 'When was the last time you spoke to Melek?'

Harisha slowly leaned back in his chair, and folded his arms. 'I'm saying nothing.'

'Help us, and you help yourself,' Stephanie said making a quick decision to play good cop, bad cop.

'You're accusing me of kidnap. I ain't done nothing.'

She decided to change tactics. 'Where can we find Wajdi Ghaziani? She asked him.

'Oh, *now* you've got it right,' he said, his thin mouth curling at one side. 'He's just killed his sister, right?'

'Where will we find him?' Stephanie pushed.

'I ain't a grass, an' you're accusing me of rape and kidnap, so if you're so fucking clever, which I can assure you, you ain't, then you fucking find him yourself.'

Banham stood up suddenly, pushing his chair away with such force that it hit the wall behind him. 'Lock him up,' he barked to Stephanie.

'Temper, temper,' Harisha laughed.

Banham swung back immediately and raised his voice at the same time as Stephanie hurriedly told the tape that the interview was terminated.

'If anything happens to my officer and I prove you were in any way responsible, which I will,' Banham barked at him. 'You will be charged not only with rape and kidnap, but with cold-blooded murder. Because whatever it takes, Mr Celik, I will find those women.' He leaned down and into Harisha. 'And I am looking forward to putting you away for a very, very long time. He paused and held Celik's cold – though now slightly nervous – look.

Celik held Banham's eyes for a mere second longer and then turned to the brief. 'Fuck's 'e on about. I don't know nothing, and I didn't rape no one.'

'Let me know when your memory comes back,' Banham said as he marched out of the room, slamming the door hard just as Stephanie had got up to follow.

Five minutes later Stephanie settled into the chair beside Banham, who was still red-faced with anger, opposite Mrs Ghaziani in Interview Room B.

'I'll come straight to the point,' he said, again barely giving Stephanie the time to switch the recorder on, let alone announce who was present and the time of interview. 'Your son seems to have disappeared and we need to talk to him, urgently, in connection with your daughter's murder. We now have reason to believe he could have been involved in the murder of an old couple earlier today. One of our officers arrived to pay him a visit at his shop, and she, too, is missing. We are not charging your son with anything, yet, but it would be a lot better for him if we could find him and eliminate him from all our enquiries, so you need to help us.'

Mrs Ghaziani's eyes pierced into Banham, but she didn't speak.

Banham lowered his gaze and took a deep breath. 'I'll make myself very clear, Mrs Ghaziani,' his now a little louder. 'I suspect you know your son's whereabouts and ...'

'Why would ...'

'And, if I find out that you do,' he said speaking over the

woman, 'and have chosen to withhold the information from me, I will charge you with conspiracy and withholding vital information, which carries a heavy custodial sentence.' He gave her less than a second to digest that before asking, 'Now, where can I find your son?'

'I do not know where he is. He is his own person,' she said, lowering her gaze. She then brought them up again and looked straight at Banham. 'I want, and demand, my daughter back so we may bury her, as is right and decent, but you care nothing for my request, so I care nothing for yours.'

'We are doing everything to find your daughter's killer,' Stephanie told her. 'And if you didn't kill her then you will want to help us.'

'One of my officers is missing,' Banham said, clearly at the end of his tether. 'The last sighting of her was with your son. Now you need to tell me where you think he might be.'

Mrs Ghaziani put her hands to her ears.

Stephanie leaned over and pulled them away gently. 'Mrs Ghaziani?' she asked in a tone more calm than she felt. 'Where might he be? Who are his friends? Where does he go socially?'

Mrs Ghaziani shook her head. She looked very frightened. 'He works, and then he comes home. He is a good boy, unlike his sister.'

'He must have close friends?' Banham pushed.

'Only his family.'

'I've got a picture of your son with Harisha Celik, a known criminal and drug baron, so stop lying,' Banham told her, his voice was loud and authoritative.

Mrs Ghaziani folded her arms and became silent again.

Banham glared at her.

'Mrs Ghaziani, help us find your daughter's killer, please,' Stephanie tried.

'I will say nothing,' Mrs Ghaziani said and then turned and looked away.

After a few seconds, Banham turned to Stephanie. Before he had time to say anything, she leaned in and told the tape: 'Interview terminated.'

The interview with Mr Ghaziani went even worse. He sat staring at the wall, with his hands on his ears. Again Stephanie turned the tape off just before Banham, very understandably, lost his cool.

Once outside the interview suite, Stephanie put her hand on Banham's arm.

'Off the record, sir,' she said. 'I completely understand your concerns, but Alison's only been out of range for a few hours. Let's not panic or jump to conclusions.'

He shook his head. 'I know her. She wouldn't do that.'

Stephanie thought different, but decided not to tell him. 'I've got every available uniform trawling through CCTV in the area around the Ghazianis' shop,' she assured him. 'We'll find both of them soon, I am confident of that.'

'Try Forensics again,' he said to her. 'See if there's any news on the blood on the screwdriver.'

It had been hard work for Georgia getting Alysha to give her information. Alysha had reminded her how much she'd done for her in the past twenty-four hours, and how little she had got for it. Georgia then reminded Alysha of the three times she had stood as a character witness in the past three years, which had kept her out of youth offenders. That hadn't washed, Alysha had shrugged it off by arguing Georgia had only done it to keep Alysha on the estate as she needed a police snout, which was putting Alysha's life in constant danger. She went on to say Georgia didn't have a clue what living around here was like, that she took all the information Alysha and her friends got her for granted and paid them too little.

'There's gonna be less crime on this estate if kids grow up wiv somethin' to do, yeah? Which means less work for you an' better lives for us. You need to keep on at that council, get us the money to fix everythin' up.'

Deep down Georgia agreed and admired her thinking, but she kept professional and asked Alysha for the information she had asked her for.

'Right, yeah, look … it was a *lot* of trouble to get this, but we got that Melek's number for you.' Georgia was delighted and listened as Alysha told her that Lox, Tink, and Panther had been of great help acquiring the number, so they all needed paying for their time and trouble.

'Look, Alysha, I just don't have wads of money to give you. You'll have to wait a bit.'

'OK, yeah, that's fine, then you're gonna have to wait for a bit to get Melek's mobile number.'

When Georgia told them that she needed the number urgently, Alysha told her that they would accept a written guarantee, written out there and then, that she, personally, would go to the council and fight their case for a new play area for their kids on the estate. Alysha then added that they also could tell her where she could pick up Wajdi Ghaziani, providing she acted quickly.

'Do that and we can tell you where you can pick up Wajdi Ghaziani. If you work fast, innit.'

Georgia had no choice. She agreed to Alysha's terms.

Lox handed her a written agreement to sign, agreeing to help them fight the council. Georgia knew if she said she'd rather pay for the information from the account that the Met kept for paying their informants, then she might lose Wajdi Ghaziani. She needed the information and very urgently, so she signed their agreement. Georgia thought they should all be on *Dragon's Den*. She also agreed, after hard negotiation with Lox, to also give them a cash bonus if their info led to finding both Melek and Alison, on the condition the money would be used for the girls' expenses, to train as hairdressers or nail technicians.

As she left the flat Georgia was unsure if any of the things that she had promised were within her power, but she didn't have time to think about it right now. She was on the phone to Stephanie to get her to ring TIU to put an immediate trace on the new number.

'And find Andrew Ubdali, get him to take uniform backup over to the mosque and arrest Wajdi Ghaziani.'

She hurriedly called Banham's number.

Sixteen

Harisha Celik was livid. He was back in his cell, pacing up and down. The food that had been offered to him in a polystyrene cup and plate he wouldn't feed to the rats round his block of flats.

Prezzioni had assured him he was doing all he could to get him out, but as Harisha had been accused of rape there was no way he could get him released until the forensic tests were complete, which could be another twenty hours, or even more.

Harisha had really lost it then.

'Do your fucking job and get me out of this shithole *now*, or you can find another mug to feed your little coke habit.' He reminded the now trembling solicitor what a powerful man he was, how he was held in high esteem out on the streets, and that if Prezzioni didn't get him out then soon he would find himself out of a job.

'An' some stroppy female fed gave me this cup of cold tea and a slice of cold fucking toast on a plastic plate. How fucking insulting is that? So, when I get out of this hole,' he said, 'I am gonna track down that same mouthy female fed and squeeze her fucking throat until her face goes blue, unless you get him out of this khazi fucking sharpish!'

Prezzioni assured him he would do all he could, and then hurriedly disappeared. It was another couple of hours before he returned, bringing the news that Wajdi Ghaziani was the chief suspect for the murder of his sister, and now also the old couple on the Aviary.

'No one can find Ghaziani, so if you know where he is that's your ticket out of this cell.'

Harisha looked at him confused.

'Melek Yismaz has gone missing. There's talk that you had her kidnapped along with a detective named Alison Grainger.

231

Now I understand your thinking, Harisha, and she deserved a good slapping, getting herself up the spout like that. Word is she was even sleeping with your cousin … anyway, look, you know that kidnapping a police officer is a serious offence, and one that'll be hard to talk our way out of.'

Harisha immediately flew into another rage, denying knowledge of any of it. 'That's a load of shit! No way would Burak bounce on any of my women, uninvited, and I didn't give the word. That skank Melek is lying, as usual. Ain't it clear she's a liar? Accusing me of raping 'er. Like I needed to! Doubt that little skank is even up the duff anyway.'

Prezzioni smiled his crooked smile, displaying his yellowing teeth. He nodded agreement. 'But could you think again? Do you know where the detective and Melek might have been taken? I will personally assure Melek is punished. Just like Burak was.'

Harisha looked him in the eye and shook his head. 'I don't know nothing about it. Now, fuck off!'

Prezzioni hurriedly obeyed.

Harisha paced his cell for five full minutes before banging his fists hard on the door.

'Get me one of them detectives,' he shouted. 'I've got information that will interest them, and I'm gonna make a deal.'

Stephanie was on the phone to Ralph, a fat little ex-lover of hers who worked in the TIU. She was telling him that if he dropped everything that he was doing and put a trace on this latest number she was giving him for Melek Yismaz then she would make it up to him any way he wanted. She looked up and blushed the colour of a postbox when she noticed Banham standing by her desk. He couldn't have avoided hearing the filthy suggestions she offered as payment, nor the raucous laugh that echoed from the other end of the phone after she made the offer.

She held the phone to her ear while Ralph told her he was on it. She then thanked him, replaced the receiver, and still blushing, turned her attention to Banham.

Before Banham had time to speak Stephanie told him that three uniform cars were at the mosque, where Wajdi Ghaziani's presence was confirmed. 'They're surrounding all entrances, waiting on DI Johnson's arrival and instruction, sir. I've already alerted DC Abdali, he's on his way over to the mosque and will make the arrest on Ghaziani.

'Grab your coat,' Banham told Stephanie, pulling his car keys from his pocket and turning in the direction of the car park. 'Let's join them.'

As they made their way to the exit, Stan Gayle hurried after them.

'Harisha Celik has information on Wajdi Ghaziani's whereabouts,' he shouted as Banham was about to disappear through the door. 'Shall I put him back in an interview room, sir?'

'No, tell him to go to hell,' came the reply.

'Would you like me to drive?' Stephanie asked, aware how pent-up Banham was, and catching her breath as she hurried down the fire exit stairs to keep up with him.

'You know I don't like women drivers,' he told her politely. He was obviously totally unaware of the chauvinism in his remark. She watched him aiming his key at his car door and wondered what he would say if she offered him a blowjob.

Stephanie quickly made her way into the passenger seat, silently telling herself to keep her dirty thoughts to herself.

'Let me know as soon as you get a reply from TIU on that new mobile number Georgia found,' he said firing the ignition after checking that Stephanie was strapped in.

'They are making it a priority, guv,' she told him.

'So I heard,' he said lifting his eyebrows and curling the side of his mouth into the hint of a smile, which disappeared as he asked, 'Did they mention any update on Alison's phone?'

She shook her head. 'Still switched off,' she told him gently.

'I'm worried sick,' he said.

Her heart went out to him. The vulnerability in his voice was pitiful, and fully understandable.

'She's pregnant with our baby. If anything happens to

her ...'

'Let's get Wajdi Ghaziani in,' Stephanie said, butting in to help him hold it together. 'That may give us a lead. Personally I think ...'

'Indie 999 are on stand-by,' he interrupted.

Stephanie nodded, 'Yes, guv, I know. She looked him square in the face. 'Look, sir, off the record, Alison is pregnant and has just witnessed another burns murder, yes?'

'Yes, and?' His tone sharpened.

Stephanie chose her words carefully. 'She left the murder department after she saw a colleague burned in a fire before.'

'Yes.'

'So it is possible it's had an effect again and she's gone off to get herself together.'

Banham shook his head, 'No, that's not Alison,' he snapped. 'I know her, you don't.' He pulled the gear into reverse, then pushed hard on the accelerator, reversing the car with so much force that Stephanie nearly shot back through to the passenger seat. She just stopped herself telling him he was the last person who should be criticizing women drivers.

He turned the car and roared off towards the barrier. Stephanie held her breath; for that one second she thought he was going to drive straight through it, but he hit the brakes just in time for the barrier to open. The car shot up the ramp and out into the road.

He paused at the top and opened the window, then pulled a siren from under the car seat. He placed it on to his roof, set it to on. It immediately screamed its urgency.

'Let's get Wajdi Ghaziani,' he said.

Alison opened her eyes but couldn't see. The pain in her head felt as if she'd been hit by an express train. Panic raced through her. Where was she? Was she blind? There was a smell she couldn't quite make out: a mixture of mould, dirt, damp, and grime. She could hear water running, very faintly. She was sitting leaning against something. She patted around her. Damp and something uneven like stones. As she took her hand away

234

she could feel slime clinging to her hand. She lifted her hand. Something was immediately above her. So. A box, or a tunnel. That would account for the darkness, but as well as a pounding head, her eyes stung. Then she realised what it was – she had been sprayed with CS gas. She'd experienced that before, when it first came in and police officers were allowed to carry the spray. She'd gone on a training course to learn how to use it safely. Fortunately she had enough experience of the substance to know the blindness that it causes wears off of its own accord, as does the headache, given a little time. She had seen people react strongly, panicking when they couldn't see, screaming that their eyes were on fire, but their sight always came back, though slowly, and the criminals in question had never been permanently affected.

She started to turn her head but the sharp throbbing pain at her temple halted her. She lifted her right arm, her coordination was way off too, but carefully she managed to get her right hand to the right side of her head to touch her temple. It was sticky and there was a round bump. She brought her hand to her nose and sniffed. It was blood. So she had been knocked on the side of her head and sprayed with CS gas, but by who? And how long ago? She remembered nothing. Then her head shot upright and her hand instinctively went to her stomach as she remembered she was pregnant. Had her baby been harmed? Hot tears suddenly sprung out of her blinded eyes. She bit hard into her lip to stop herself, she knew the stinging increased with tears. She gave her belly a reassuring rub. Her hormones were all over the place, she needed to get a grip and work out where the hell she was. Did Banham know she was here, wherever it was, she wondered? She couldn't bear to think of the panic he would be in if he did. She had to sort this and get out of wherever she was. She tapped her body, but she couldn't feel her phone anywhere about her.

She sat still, trying to piece everything together. She had taken a phone call from the Turkish girl to whom she'd given her mobile number. Melek had called her in a highly distressed state, saying she had been raped again by Harisha Celik, was pregnant and bleeding. The girl said she was afraid to go to the station to make a formal statement, because the last time she had Harisha had seen her and beaten and then raped her. Now she was scared for her life. Alison had said she would meet her and escort her to a secure rape unit in the area to give her statement. They had arranged to meet in a McDonalds, near Lambeth. Alison would first talk to her, take her statement, and then take her to the rape unit.

She remembered being in the McDonalds with Melek. Then she remembered she had taken the call from Melek while she was attending the post-mortem with Sergeant Stephanie Green, so she had told Stephanie Green where she was going. Good, that would be a help. It was all coming back now. In the McDonalds, Melek had dropped the bombshell that Harisha Celik had had Zana killed, that he had also threatened to kill Melek too, to stop her talking, but he knew she was pregnant with his child, so he had raped her, Melek thought to bring on a miscarriage.

Melek made a statement confirming that she had been beaten and raped by Celik, and she was also going to give a statement saying he had discussed the killing of Zana in front of her. She told Alison that although she wanted to make this official statement, she was afraid of what Harisha would do to her. He was a powerful man, he had contacts everywhere and she knew the feds couldn't protect her twenty-four hours a day.

Alison had been sympathetic, and in the interest of gaining the girl's confidence, she had confided to her about her own pregnancy, and the two had got on like a house on fire. Melek had then agreed to go with Alison to the rape unit, after making a statement alleging rape.

Alison could remember the look of relief on Melek's pretty face when she assured her that Celik would go down for a very long time if Melek could prove that he had murdered Zana. Melek then dropped the bombshell that not only could she prove that he had murdered Zana, but also Burak, his cousin. She said she thought it was because Zana's brother Wajdi had something to do with it. Then Melek dropped another bombshell, telling Alison that Harisha took over un-used garages around the area to use for storing the weapons he imported. When he thought the feds might be on to him, he moved his gear on, and took over another garage in order to stay one step ahead of the feds.

Harisha, she said, had stolen a car from the old couple on Magpie block, a Mr and Mrs Wilkins, and then taken possession of their garage. The Wilkins had then, accidentally, discovered the weapons in the garage, and because they were afraid of the consequences, and had no idea how powerful Harisha Celik was, they had told Harisha that if he didn't remove the weapons they would inform the police – so Harisha had killed them. His weapons were now moved to another hiding place, under a river. Alison felt a shiver run through her veins as she realised that this was where she was at this very minute – under the river.

She also remembered asking Melek for the exact location of this hiding place under the river. Melek had told her it was difficult to describe, she didn't know the exact name of the streets, it was near Lambeth, but she knew where it was and she would take her there.

Alison had told her that she would need to phone for backup, in case any of his gang were around, and they had weapons, she couldn't take chances, or put Melek in danger. Melek had asked Alison not to phone till they were in the car, telling Alison she was afraid someone might hear. Harisha had over a hundred soldiers and they were all over the area.

They left the restaurant and got in the car. As Alison got her phone out to call for backup Melek had pulled a gun, a small pistol, and told Alison she couldn't let her call for backup, it was too dangerous for both of them. She had taken Alison's phone, made a call, and thrown it out of the car window, then had made Alison drive on with a gun in her side.

Alison's brain was hurting from the blow to the side of her head, she was racking her brains and thought she remembered driving for only a few roads, left or right, she couldn't remember, but obviously in the direction of the river. That was definitely where she was now, she could clearly hear water. Then she remembered that Melek made her park. So her car was on the street right now, she thought. That would be a great help if they were looking for her, they would have circulated her registration number, so a local patrol car would be bound to pick it up within hours.

More was coming back. She had tried wrestling Melek to get the gun out of the girl's hand when they got out of the car. That was when the gas was sprayed. Then she remembered the noise of a lock and the clank of a chain and she thought she heard something like a manhole being lifted. She had been made to kneel down on a cold wet pavement. It was falling into place now. Jesus!. She was in a hole, or a tunnel, She half-remembered Melek trying to get her to tie a rope around her, and going down a rope ladder, when she couldn't see.

She remembered going mad at her, screaming about her baby, and that was when it all stopped. So either Melek knocked her out with the butt of the gun, or she fell, blindly in the dark, and knocked her head.

Panic ran through her again. She could have harmed her baby! She felt a great urge to cry out, but managed to get a grip. She had to keep it together if she was going to save herself, and Banham's baby. And she was, that much she was determined. Banham had already lost a child many years ago. She wouldn't let anything happen to their baby, she just wouldn't.

She fought back the fear that nearly over-powered her. OK, so this was, more than likely, where consignments of weapons were being stored. No wonder no one, in the two years that it had been happening, could get a clue as to their location. Not sniffer dogs, not anyone, had come close to finding all these highly dangerous weapons that were being filtered onto the South London streets. But now she knew where they were, that was the first good thing about this, or was it? Panic again felt like electricity through her veins. If no one had found the weapons that were hidden down here, where she was, then how in heaven's name was anyone going to find her? Melek had thrown her phone out of the car window, not that a phone would work under here. Or would it? Phones could be amazing. She remembered a case where someone's phone rang from a grave where they were buried alive, and saved the victim's life because of it. But she didn't have a phone, so she would have to use the time it took to get her sight back to make another plan, because she was going to get out of here, for her and her baby.

'Oh, so you're not dead? I was a little worried.' It was Melek's voice.

She sat up. Melek was in here with her. Melek, she knew, had her phone on her in the car. She had seen it with her own eyes. So here was her plan. Melek hadn't tied her hands, they were free, so once she got her sight and her balance back, and she had enough experience of CS gas and head blows to know that wouldn't be too long, then she would have to overpower the girl and get the gun and phone, and this time she would make sure she succeeded. Meanwhile she was going to play friendly with the enemy.

'Christ, Melek, what's all this about? I'm your friend. I came out to help you. You've hurt and blinded me.'

No answer.

'What is this about, Melek? Tell me? I thought you wanted to put Celik behind bars for what he did to you and Zana.'

Still no answer.

Alison started to shuffle to try to get up, but it was slippery where she was, and she lost her balance and fell against the stone behind her. That unnerved her, she became still again.

She sat thinking. She was confident Melek had a phone on her, but not that there would be any signal under here. She had to stay calm. She thought of Banham.

Did he even know she was missing?

Seventeen

'Keep still.' Tink grabbed the can of quick-dry spray, aimed it at Panther's toenails, and sprayed hard.

'Blimey, mate,' Panther said flapping the air. 'That's fucking strong.'

'Well you won't keep still while they dry so I 'ave to,' Tink told her, leaning back and admiring the colour on Panther's toenails. 'Don't wanna smudge them.'

Alysha was watching from her position curled up on the floor next to Lox who was busily going through figures on her calculator and writing them down on a piece of paper. 'What's wrong? Alysha asked Panther, 'You're like you've got a spider in your G-string.'

'I'm all stewed up waiting for news about that Turkish bitch,' Panther said lifting her hands in exasperation. 'She's been gone ages, an' it don't feel right to me. The feds were gonna ring us back and tell us where she is an' we ain't 'eard not'in.' She shook her head. 'I'm thinking she's double-dealing on us, making bargains with the feds an all that. We give her a gun if you remember?' She looked around at the three girls, who were giving her their full attention, and carried on talking, 'I love that we're together an 'ave got plans to make the estate a good place an 'elp the kids to 'ave a chance wiv life.' Then she raised her voice. 'If she fucks this up, or tells the feds we give her a gun, we'll all be back in youth offenders.'

'She won't,' Alysha said shaking her newly plaited head of cornrows. 'Don't worry on that score, mate. We got far too much on 'er, an' it's 'er word 'gainst ours. Sides, Georgia Johnson said there's no word from Alison either, so it means she's still wiv 'er. They'll be giving it all this bunnying.' She lifted her hand and bounced her fingers against her thumb to demonstrate the point, then smiled sympathetically. 'Try and chill, Panth.'

'What d'you think of the colour?' Tink asked, nodding to Panther's painted toenails, in an attempt to distract her.

'I fink they're great, an' I reckon you'll earn really well doing nails and hair already,' Panther told her. 'You've really got the talent, an' it's all the rage at the mo.'

'Certainly beats sucking cocks and selling brown,' Tink laughed. 'An' I like making people look pretty an' things.' She smiled a childlike smile. 'It's what I always wanted to do. So it'll be great, an' when I've done college an' I can teach the kids that wanna learn, an we'll have done somefing good, if our kids don't get used like we did.' She shrugged, 'But it's like you said, Queen, we never 'ad no chances, we 'ad to earn a living.'

Alysha nodded. 'Yeah, well, DI Georgia Johnson better be good for her word, and come up with the corn, and we'll lean on her till she goes to the council for us. Once that's done an' the kid's playground fixed, then we're in business.'

'I'll make sure she does,' Lox said 'She more than owes us. We're doing all the detective work for her, so she 'as to pay up.'

Alysha nodded. 'I've been finking bout that gun that Melek's got. We just deny it if she tries to pin it on us, but it's got me finking bout the weapons that we moved to that tunnel, I said I'd fink on what to do with them.'

'And?' Lox asked.

'What I fink is, that it's best to do things legal now, when we can, and bleed the feds for everything we need cornwise.'

Lox held Alysha's eyes. 'If you say so, then that goes. But we are talking losing serious money if we do that. The North London gangs would pay good for them machetes, an they'd be off our patch,' she offered.

'I know.' Alysha nodded with the authority of someone three times her age. 'But when other gangs know we stole 'em, an' they will know, then they'll fink they have the right to steal 'em too, from us. There's a lot out there would kill us for that stash. The WC4s have got over a hundred soldiers to call on, that's double the SLRs and quads on us, an' our street girls as we stand.'

'She's right,' Tink said quickly. 'We only got a reliable dozen or so for backup, at mo. If we took on the WC4s on, or the KFADs, we'd get slaughtered, an' that's what we can't let 'appen.'

'We wanna lead a good example if we wanna help the tinies around 'ere,' Alysha added. 'So, I think we should offer 'em to the feds, get 'em off the streets, but insist we want a big reward. What you fink, Panth?'

'I'm thinking we should be worrying about Melek not phoning an telling us she's done what we told 'er to do,' Panther said again. 'The feds might 'ave traced her whereabouts by now, and not bothered to tell us, an' we need to know what she's up to.'

The other three looked at each other.

'She's had too long,' Panther pushed. 'Let's do something?'

Alysha shook her head. 'Patience,' she said. 'Harisha's still at the nick, and Melek will be with that Alison Grainger. It'll just be taking longer than we figured.'

'He ain't gonna be staying at the nick,' Panther argued. 'Not if Melek don't make them that allegation. What's to fucking wait for? She was told to meet Alison whatsit, make the allegation, an' then call us, an' she ain't done that. Without that allegation they ain't got nothing to hold him for.'

'They've found her old phone though, outside his flat,' Tink reminded her. 'An' while they are looking for her, they'll still hold him, on suspect of kidnap.'

Panther turned to look at Alysha and then back to Tink. 'The phone being outside his flat don't prove he kidnapped, or hurt her,' she said shaking her head. 'Can't hold him for that.'

Alysha had started scratching at the roots of the new cornrows that Tink had put in her hair. She lifted a small mirror and looked at them from all angles. 'You know what, Tink, these are fuckin' good. I reckon we'll start hiring you out for beauty stuff before we even send you to college cos I reckon you could make big dough for us doing this already.'

Tink smiled a wide satisfied smile.

'You do know that if she is double-crossing us, and playing us then she's gonna have told them SLRs that we moved the weapons to their tunnel,' Lox interrupted. 'Then the SLRs will steal 'em back, an' move 'em somewhere else, an' then we'll have lost them and we'll get nothing, cos they won't be where we tell the feds they are. So now I'm getting worried.'

'An if they let Harisha out,' Panther nodded. 'Then 'e's gonna come after us, big-time.'

Alysha let go of her cornrows and took a big intake of breath. 'Question is,' she said narrowing her eyes thoughtfully, 'is she still doing what we told 'er to, an' is it taking longer than we reckoned on? Or is she a turncoat?'

'Or is she in trouble,' Tink said, throwing a concerned look at the other three. 'She's an Alley Cat now. Makes her family, so I reckon we should find out.'

'You know I ain't never liked the bitch,' Panther said, voice raised.

'So where do we look?' Lox asked, looking from Panther back to Alysha.

Alysha slid one of her long, maroon-painted nail extensions in between her two bottom teeth and lifted out a piece of fried chicken. 'SLRs can't get the weapons, Lox, cos they can't get in the tunnel. No one 'cept us can,' she reminded them. 'Cos you broke their padlock and put ours on it, and yous got the key, Panth?'

Panther nodded. 'Yeah, it's right here in my bag.' She opened her bag and shuffled through the muddle of personal belongings. Then she frowned and rummaged again before looking up, and then down again, her hands working frantically through the contents. Then she tipped the bag upside down, threw everything on the floor, and again rummaged frantically amongst the contents. She flicked a desperate look at Alysha. 'It ain't here. The fucking key ain't here. I put it here. You saw me, din't you, Lox?'

'Yeah,' Lox nodded. 'You put it in the inside pocket.'

'And it ain't there,' Panther said, the colour draining from her brown face as she turned back to face Alysha again. 'I was so careful wiv it, Queen, and it ain't here.'

'Try the lining?' Tink suggested.

Panther pulled at the lining. She lifted the faux fur clutch bag in the air and shook it again. She shook her head again.

'Is anything else gone?' Lox asked quickly.

Panther shook her head again. 'Not that I can see.'

Alysha was now bolt upright. 'Did you leave your bag anywhere? Like, out of your sight, even for a second?' she asked her.

Panther shook her head. 'It's been in 'ere all the time.'

'Melek was in here,' Lox said loudly and quickly. 'Did we leave her alone, in this room, at any time?'

'Yeah, we left her when I went in the kitchen to get her Alley Cat mobile and the gun with you, Lysh, remember?' Panther said.

Alysha nodded. 'S'right, we did.'

'When I was getting the fried chicken?' Lox said.

'An' Tink was in the loo,' Alysha added, throwing her hands in the air. 'Fuck, Panth, I 'ope you ain't right, I 'ope she ain't pulled the key, cos then Lox is right, if she's turncoated on us with them SLRs we could lose everything.'

Tink jumped up. 'OK. So what'll we do?'

'We check the tunnel, first,' Lox said, pulling the zip up on her silver puffa jacket, and pushing her phone in her pocket. 'Let's get going.'

'No.' Tink put her hand in the air. 'If she's tipped off SLRs, they'll have gone to the tunnel, and that's what they'll expect us to do. We'll be walking into an ambush.'

'Ring round the soldiers for backup,' Panther said. 'We're gonna have about twenty or so of them to take on, at the least, so we need our soldiers. If they want a fight let's give them one they won't forget.' She turned to the others. 'Get your shanks.'

'No.' Alysha shouted and shook her head. 'That's what they'll expect us to do. We'll get the feds. That'll foil 'em. They won't expect the feds, but Tink's right, they'll expect us to turn-up with backup from the street girls.'

'Is that a good idea?' Lox asked her. 'To get the feds?'

Yeah,' Alysha told her. 'It's def a good idea. I ring DI Georgia Johnson, tell her we have info on the whereabouts of them machetes and weapons, and we think lots of SLRs will be there to defend them. She'll round up a load of feds with guns an' dogs an' stuff, and if Melek is there with them SLRs, they'll all go down together, an' we'll get the reward. Agreed?'

'Good thinking,' Panther said. 'Let's do it.' She smacked her palm against Alysha's.

'Yes, by me, too,' Lox said placing her hand on top of Panther and Alysha's as they high-fived each other.

Tink stood there, deep in thought.

Alysha turned to her. 'Tink?'

'Supposing Melek has been taken hostage by them SLRs, and is in trouble. She's one of us now, we need to help her.'

'Then we will help her,' Alysha said. 'We'll have the feds to back us, an' it'll be a hell of a lot easier than takin' on them SLRs ourselves. That's if she is in trouble, but she's nicked the padlock key so I'd say it looks more likely she's a two-timing cunt.'

'I can't see that she'd go back wiv the SLRs, or Harisha,' Tink argued. 'They killed Zana, her best friend, burnt her alive.'

'We don't know that for sure,' Panther said. 'That could have been Wajdi done that.'

'Either way, we need answers, 'Alysha said, grabbing her black puffa jacket and taking charge. 'Let's go an' get 'em.' She grabbed her cerise plastic bag, jingling the collection of keyrings attached to its zip as she threw it over her shoulder. 'We go to the river tunnel, on our own, first. We go very careful and we split two-two, look out for SLR soldiers. If we have trouble, or see any of them SLR pricks guarding the tunnel, that'll tell us, for sure, they know the weapons 'ave been moved there, and we'll know that's down to Melek. Call me, and I get straight on to Georgia Johnson. She'll get a round-up of feds, dogs an' all, an' they'll hot-foot it down there and catch 'em red-handed.' She smiled at Lox. 'An' we'll ask for a big reward. It'll be worth it to them.'

246

'Shame Harisha won't be there,' Tink said.

'He might, who knows,' Panther said. 'He mighta got himself released.'

'Let's go,' Alysha said. 'Don't look like time is on our side.'

The girls headed for the door. When they got outside, Alysha paused before locking the door. She told them to hang on another second. She ran in quickly and within seconds was back out and holding four heavy cricket balls. She handed one to each girl.

'We don't use them, or our shanks, unless we're attacked first,' she told them. 'And watch each other's back. Remember the feds will be with us. We can call them any time, and they will give us strong back up. Better that, than a fight. But, if we don't have a choice, use the balls and go straight for the jaw. Them cricket balls'll break a jaw in a second. And a jaw's better than a nose. They'll go down if you break their jaw, an if they don't, then use your shank.'

16:10

Sarah Petts often took the long walk home, passing the large McDonalds on the outskirts of town. The burger bar held memories of when her daughter was a student, and McDonalds had just become the place for teenagers to eat. She was going slowly today, her knees weren't what they used to be, and she was walking with care; just in case there was anything on the pavement that needed avoiding; there was always something these days that was easy to slip on. Sarah had recently tripped over a burger box and pulled a ligament, which still hadn't healed properly. She walked slowly with her eyes peeled.

As soon as she spotted the phone lying on the pavement, Sarah was immediately anxious that a youngster had lost it and their parents might be desperately trying to contact their child, so she bent down and retrieved it. At first, she was going to hand it in at the McDonalds – she felt sure whoever had lost it had been in there – but then she decided that the police station would be a better bet. The police could trace it quickly to its rightful owner.

The police station wasn't very far from where she lived. A short bus ride, but she had her pass, and she could see a bus coming up the road. She hailed it and climbed aboard.

Stan Gayle was at the front desk when Sarah Petts handed the phone in. He knew Alison Grainger's phone was a Blackberry Smart, just as this was. Growing excited, he thanked the woman, scribbled her details in the book, then pressed the intercom button through to the incident room.

'Where was it found?' Hank Peacock asked him.

'Outside McDonalds, near Lambeth.'

No sooner were the words out that Peacock was up and out of his chair and shouting to DCI Banham. Banham shot out of his office door, down the stairs and through the pass door in record time. He all but snatched the phone from Les as he recognised it immediately. Alison's. It had a fair few scratches, cracks, and dents from wherever and however it had landed, but it was the crack on the side of the screen that confirmed it. Banham had been with her when she did that one. She had got out of her car in one hell of a temper, they'd been rowing about him criticising her reversing. She'd got hold of the car door, still shouting, and slammed it hard, catching the side of her hand which held her mobile in it. And then she had screamed that that was his fault too. He'd offered to buy her a new phone but she'd refused, the crack didn't interfere with it working.

Banham stood, staring at that same crack, and found himself swallowing the lump that had risen in his throat. This confirmed his worst fears. If she wasn't in trouble, she would have rung to say she'd lost her phone.

He thanked Les, and hurried back to the incident room.

Georgia and Stephanie looked up as he stood, white as a ghost, holding the phone.

'This is Alison's phone,' he said to Stephanie. 'Get onto your friend in TIU, I need the SIM card, recent call history and texts, everything he can get.'

Stephanie took the phone.

'Now!'

'Yes, guv.' Stephanie quickly made the call and relayed the message. Her face then lit up as she listened to Ralph speaking on the other end and turning to Banham she said, 'Hold on, he's right here.' She passed the phone to Banham. 'There's good news,' she told him.

'I've got a trace on the other phone, sir, the number that you phoned through a little while ago,' Ralph was telling Banham.

'Melek Yismaz's phone,' Banham said looking across at Georgia who had been perched on the side of a desk going through images from Zana's computer prior to interviewing Wajdi Ghaziani, who was currently locked in a cell refusing to speak.

Banham put his hand over the phone. 'There's a signal on the phone number you got from your informant,' he told Georgia.

'Melek Yismaz's second phone,' Georgia repeated. 'That's great. Where is it?'

'At the moment they can only say somewhere in the Lambeth area,' Banham relayed. 'But he'll stay on it. First priority is this one.' He turned to Peacock. 'Get this over to TIU, and run all the way,' he told him passing him Alison's phone.

'The McDonalds is in Lambeth,' Stephanie said, 'Shall I send Barry and Eric over there again?'

'Yes, right away. Any sightings of Alison's car?' Banham asked Stephanie.

'Nothing reported, sir. All area cars are on it.'

Banham turned to everyone in the incident room. 'Listen up everyone, and leave what you are doing. Alison was last known to be on her way to McDonalds in Lambeth. Everything is on hold until we find her. We are all on this. I want every inch from Lambeth to here covered.' He turned back to Stephanie. 'Except you, you stay here. Give the location and Alison's car registration to Indie 999. Tell them it's on. They may be able to spot her car from the air. Keep in touch with TIU and keep me informed too.'

'Sir.'

As soon as Banham had disappeared into his office to grab his sheepskin jacket, Georgia looked at Stephanie. 'Jesus, I sort of hope she really is missing now,' she said. 'Imagine if she's having a quiet few hours in a park meditating on her future.'

'Don't,' Stephanie said shaking her head.

'Georgia,' Banham yelled as a man might to a disobedient dog. 'Now.'

Georgia and Stephanie caught each other's eye.

'Yes, sir,' Georgia said, rushing to follow him to the car park.

It was only a few more minutes before Stephanie had more information from TIU on both phones. She called immediately to Banham and Georgia, as they sped across London to Lambeth.

'The SIM card in Alison's phone,' she told him. 'I've got the call history, and traced the numbers.'

'Go on.'

'I'll print it out sir, and leave it on your desk.'

'Have you got it there, in front of you?'

'Yes.'

'Read it out to me.'

'No, sir, it's private and I don't think ...'

'We haven't got time for you to think or not,' he shouted. 'Just read it out.'

'There was a call to my number, but it cut off before it came through.'

'And, what else?'

She paused. 'There was a call to a clinic, earlier this morning.'

'What clinic?' Now his voice was nervous.

'The clinic of St Celia.'

'Did you phone it?'

'Yes,'

'And?' The nerves were back in his tone.

'It is a clinic for ladies' problems,' she said quietly.

250

Georgia turned and looked out the window.

'What does it do?' he asked innocently.

'Birth control and unwanted pregnancies, sir,' Stephanie said quietly.

There was a long silent pause and then he said, 'Anything else?'

'TIU have more on the other phone, the second number we have for Melek Yismaz. It is about two miles north of the McDonalds, nearer to Lambeth bridge.

'Keep on that, and keep me in touch,' Banham said, his voice flat.

'Yes, sir, oh, and Indie 999 are on their way to that area,' Stephanie told him, 'and the dog team are on standby.'

'Good.'

Georgia had her own phone pressed against her ear. She was talking to Stan, the desk sergeant, telling him to ask Wajdi Ghaziani if he wanted a solicitor. She said if he did, to leave a message with the duty solicitor that she would be back when she could. She also told him, on no account, and no matter what Harisha Celik's solicitor said, or what the DNA showed, was Celik to be released without her say so. She was frighteningly aware that she was running an investigation into four murders, and although a missing officer, and a missing rape victim, quite rightly, were taking priority, the murder investigation was still ongoing, and with the press on her back, and possibly her career on the line, she had to be seen to be doing her job, and the clock was ticking against the twenty-four hours she had to get a conviction on Harisha Celik.

'OK, everyone, please listen carefully,' Banham shouted into the police radio. 'Keep your eyes open and your wits about you. This is an emergency.' He turned to look at Georgia and his voice faltered slightly. 'A pregnant officer and Melek Yismaz, a young Turkish girl are missing, and we need to find them, they could both be in grave danger.' His voice cracked as he added, 'It's Alison Grainger. She is pregnant with my baby. Please, help me find them.'

Georgia squeezed her lips together. She'd surprised herself.

She rarely felt emotion at times like this, but the reference to *them* had really got to her.

'Why are you rubbing your stomach?' Melek asked Alison. 'It's not a baby, yet. And you don't want it, you said so.'

Alison stopped rubbing and listened. Melek's speech was slurry, but she also detected a slight echo. The echo confirmed they were quite far underground; less likely that Melek's phone would work, then, she thought. She knew she still had to bide time until her sight returned, but she didn't have a clue how long that would be, as much as she didn't have a clue how long she had been unconscious.

'I didn't say that,' she said politely. She had no idea who else was down there or what kind of a state Melek was in, so she played it carefully. 'I said I'm nervous of what lies ahead. I said that like you, I haven't been pregnant before and I'm not sure about the responsibility it brings.' She needed to keep her talking. Something wasn't right with her speech which was slow and slurry. She needed to know what she was facing down here. She couldn't see, she could only listen. 'Isn't that how you feel, about having a baby, Melek?'

'No. I don't want the bastard, simple as that.' By her slurred tone either she'd been drinking or had taken something.

'Anyway, it's alright, cos, we're getting out of it.'

Those words made Alison immediately sit up. As she did she banged her head on what felt like a stone wall behind her. She sucked air between her teeth to take the edge off the pain. Her head was already throbbing. 'What do you mean? Melek, what are you saying?'

'I've dealt with it.'

'How? Melek, are …'

'I've taken pills, I'm out of here.'

'What kind of pills?'

Melek didn't answer.

'Melek talk to me.'

'I don't know, but loads of them. I'll be dead soon, with a bit of luck. I've got some more if you want them.'

Panic hit home like a hot branding iron. 'Jesus, Melek. Tell me you're kidding.'

'Do you want me to feed some to you?'

'No.' Alison raised her voice. 'Stop this.' She was suddenly terrified, but she controlled it and continued talking. 'You're behaving irrationally. That's natural. You really don't mean this, Melek. It's your pregnancy hormones.' She started to get up, and banged her head again. 'Jesus!' There was definitely a brick or concrete ceiling immediately above her head, and yet she was sitting down. It must be a tiny tunnel. So how did they get down here? More to the point, how would she get out?

'Melek, what is this place?'

No answer.

'Melek, I need to get you help.' She raised her voice. 'Melek, you said you trusted me.' Her mind was now focused on her own baby. She wasn't going to let this woman take it from her. If Melek cared nothing for herself, or for the tiny life inside her, then she wasn't taking Alison's baby down with her. Alison would fight tooth and nail to save it.

'I don't trust no one. I don't want a baby. I want to die.'

'No, you don't. You have your life ahead of you.'

'I don't want this baby.'

'OK,' Alison managed to sound calm. 'You can get a termination, that won't be a problem. You don't have to go through with the pregnancy. Harisha will go to prison and you can start your life again.' Her eyes were itching now, that was a good sign she knew. She resisted rubbing them. She was het up, but she had to keep calm, all would be OK when the CS wore off, she could do something positive to get out of this cave. Christ, how long had she been unconscious? And how long since this girl took those pills? Alison just had no idea.

'Melek, does your phone work?'

'I don't know.'

'Is there a signal on it? Can you look for me?'

'Shut up.'

'Please, Melek, I want to help you.'

No answer.

253

'Jesus!' She nearly exploded with frustration. 'It's your hormones. It's not surprising, you've been raped and you're pregnant. You can't kill yourself because of that animal. Melek, let me get you to hospital. I will speak for you, and I will help you.'

Melek suddenly started to sob. 'I deserve to die. I did it. I killed her.'

Alison felt a shuddering chill through her whole being. 'Who?'

Silence.

'Melek, who's her? Melek, who did you kill?'

'Zana. I burnt her. I wanted to see her suffer.'

Alison became silent. She hadn't expected that. If this was true, and if she was admitting it to Alison, then she clearly didn't expect Alison to live and repeat it. Did Melek intend for Alison and her tiny baby to perish down here too? She had a fight on her hands. Alison would use every breath in her body to ensure that didn't happen.

She kept her voice even as she spoke. 'You asked to meet me because Harisha raped you, and murdered Zana. Surely you're not trying to protect Harisha now?'

'I lied. I was going to dump it on him. But I want to get it off my conscience before I die. I burnt her.'

Alison became silent again. She needed to think. Her brain was already racing.

A couple of minutes later Melek broke the silence. 'I killed Burak too.'

Another chill ran through Alison's blood. 'Now I don't believe you, Melek. Come on, let's get out of here. We can have a coffee and talk about hormones.' She was talking to her in a calm tone, and feeling anything but. 'I won't charge you with kidnapping me, and of course I won't repeat what you've just told me, because we know it's not true.'

'We'll never get out of here. I pulled the manhole cover down as we came in, and put the bolt on from the inside, so we can die in peace. No one can get in, even if they did find us, which they won't.'

Now Alison started to panic. 'Where are we, Melek?'

'Under the river, in an old tunnel. Harisha has made it so you can get in and out. There's a few rats around but no one else. He hides his weapons here. Water drips in, too. So if we don't die from the pills, we'll drown. Eventually.'

'Melek, listen to me …'

'Leave me alone, I've admitted to murder. Now I'm tired and I want to die in peace.'

'Melek, do not go to sleep. Melek. *Melek*!'

Alysha and Tink were on one side of the road, Panther and Lox on the other. They had been walking carefully down all the side roads and alleys from their estate to Lambeth, and were now approaching the road that led to the tunnel. So far there had been no sign of SLR soldiers. Alysha turned to Tink and shook her head.

'Not a soul around. Somefing ain't right,' she said to her.

'Yeah, just what I was finking,' Tink said looking over to Panther and Lox on the other side of the street.

As they turned the corner into Keepers Street, the road that led to the tunnel, Alysha pressed Panther's number into her phone. 'I'm gonna run ahead,' she told her. 'We reckon somefing's wrong. Watch my back, I'm goin' right up as far as I can to the manhole an' check the padlock.' With that she sprinted up the road at the speed of an athlete.

A helicopter appeared overhead, then dropped lower and began circling the area.

'Fed 'copter,' Panther shouted to Alysha, who was now by the entrance to the tunnel. Alysha got a good look at the manhole cover before turning and running back and joining the other three girls who had dived out of sight behind a few large recycling bins that stood on the pavement at the end of the short road. They flattened their bodies and slid to the side of the bins as the helicopter dipped and took in the area. It then heightened its flight and moved on.

'Someone's down there,' Alysha said to the others. 'Lock's been opened and tunnel's bolted from the inside.'

'Ain't no sign of no SLRs,' Panther said. 'And that was a fed helicopter, that was Indie 999.'

'There's trouble going on, I'll put corn on it,' Alysha said. 'An' I'll bet that 'copter's looking for Alison Grainger.'

'Who was wiv Melek?' Tink added.

'If the padlock ain't been broken, then it's been opened wiv the key, an' the only person could have that new key is Melek. So, she has to be down there wiv that Alison Grainger, but why, what the fuck's she playing at?'

'That's what we'd all like to know,' Alysha agreed pulling her phone from her pocket. 'What the fuck's she playing at.' She shook her head. 'Cos I ain't got a clue.'

'Our weapons are down there,' Lox said. 'If that fed is down there, she'll know that.'

'Maybe that's it,' Panther said. 'Melek has taken her to the weapons, so she can get the reward corn.'

'And we've lost out,' Lox said.

'Not yet we ain't,' Alysha said, reassuring her. 'Not if we phone Georgia Johnson now, an' say we was out looking for Melek and we reckon we've stumbled across a hiding place for them weapons, and someone is down there, possibly 'er missing detective.'

'Do it,' Lox said, as Panther and Tink nodded their agreement.

'If she's turncoated us,' Panther said, 'can I kill 'er?'

'Depends whether you wanna go back to prison or make the estate a good place to live,' Alysha said, turning to hold each girl's gaze, and then grinning as she pressed a number in her phone.

The sound of police sirens in the distance made them all turn again.

Georgia was in the car with Banham. They were driving around the streets near McDonalds when her phone bleeped. It was Alysha, giving her the address of a street near the bridge at Lambeth where, she told Georgia, they had discovered an old tunnel which might be the South London Rulers' weapons stash. She also said it was possible people were down there, trapped.

Banham was listening and immediately reeled off Alison's registration number and told Georgia to ask her snout if there was a green Golf anywhere around with that registration.

Within minutes Alysha could confirm the car and the registration number, telling them it was parked in Keepers Street. She even described its broken wing mirror.

Georgia turned to Banham. 'It's a yes,' she told him. 'And, remember, TIU said Melek's phone was near water. Alison and Melek …'

Before Georgia could finish speaking, Banham had swung the car round in the middle of the busy street and turned the siren on. 'On way,' he interrupted Georgia. 'Check on the dog unit and call a CO19 gun unit to standby, as well as all available backup.'

Eighteen

Stephanie picked up the call. It was Tony James from the forensic lab in Lambeth.

'Good news on the set of fingerprints from the cupboard door at the Wilkins flat. I ran the prints in the database, just on the off-chance, and it's come up with a match.'

'I won't need three guesses there,' Stephanie answered. 'Harisha Celik?'

'No. The name given is Melek Yismaz. She was arrested last year for shoplifting and dealing, so she's on the database.'

Stephanie nearly shot out of her chair. 'Thank you,' she managed to say, her mind racing. As Tony gave her the other forensic result, Stephanie's mind was on Alison. Alison was with Melek Yismaz at this moment, and Tony was telling her that Melek had either herself killed, or at least been there when two innocent pensioners had screwdrivers driven into their necks.

Alison was in serious danger.

She called Georgia's number and, before Georgia had time to say hello, relayed the news.

Georgia flicked a glance at Banham. He was driving down the middle of the busy Brixton High Road at eighty miles an hour, with the pool siren screaming its urgency. Behind them, four patrol cars, sirens screeching, struggled to keep up.

'There's more,' Stephanie told her as she heard Georgia's intake of breath. 'The long dark hair that Forensics took from the post at the edge of the alleyway where Zana was killed doesn't match her DNA – it's a match to Melek Yismaz.'

'Right,' Georgia said quickly deciding that now wasn't the time to relay this to Banham. He couldn't drive any faster, the speedometer was going off the dial as it was. If she told him, he might lose complete control.

'Can I come over and join you? Stephanie asked. 'I want to

help her.'

'Quick as you can.' Georgia told her.

'What news?' Banham asked as Georgia clicked her phone shut.

'It can wait,' Georgia said gingerly.

Three minutes later Banham roared into Keepers Street, closely followed by four patrol cars. He pulled up at the edge of the tunnel, where Alysha, Tink, Panther, and Lox were waiting.

Banham jumped out and ran over to Alison's car and felt the bonnet. 'It's still warm, she's been here recently,' he shouted over to Georgia

'The tunnel starts there,' Alysha told Georgia pointing to the manhole at the side of the road. 'I reckon she's down there. It's been locked from the inside so no one can follow them in. I fink it's where SLRs keep their firearms. So I reckon they've taken her hostage.'

'S'gonna be impossible to get in there, like that,' Panther added, shaking her head.

Banham had hurried back to the manhole and was now down on his knees over the large grille. He cupped his hands around his mouth. 'Alison. Alison. Can you hear me?' he shouted. 'Are you down there? Alison?'

Two fire engines, their sirens screeching, sped into the road and pulled up by the tunnel. Two firefighters jumped out and joined Banham, who was still kneeling over the vent, shouting into the grille.

Firefighter Joe Miller walked along the edge of the pavement from the manhole, looking for another way in, but shook his head in disappointment as he came back. 'Is the dog unit on its way?' he asked.

'As we speak,' Georgia nodded.

'How long to get this bolt off?' Banham asked, pointing to the bolt and chain that held the large grille in place from the inside.

'It's an emergency,' Georgia added, deciding now was the time to break the news, 'We think DI Alison Grainger is down there with a woman who has committed three murders.'

Banham stared at her. 'What?'

'Stephanie's call,' she told him. 'It was forensic confirmation of a match with Melek Yismaz's DNA at two of the murder scenes.'

Banham turned the colour of milk.

'Got the saw?' Joe said to his colleague

Georgia leaned in to Banham. 'Sir, why don't you go and sit in the car for a bit.'

'No,' Banham glared at her.

'These should do it,' Joe told Banham as fire-man Peter handed him a large pair of cutters. 'The chain's pretty thick though, sir, so it'll take a bit of doing. Why don't you go and sit in the car.'

'I'm staying here,' Banham told him, clearly trying not to shout with the frustration he was feeling.

The arrival of the dog unit took everyone's attention. Martin Jones, the handler, looked grim as he jumped quickly down from the van holding two Alsatians on short leashes. He led them over to the manhole. He was friends with Alison and Georgia knew from his face that he was desperate to find her.

'I need something of Alison's,' he said to Banham.

Banham rushed to her car and rattled the door. He lifted his foot and was about to kick a window in when Alysha hurried over and handed him her cricket ball. 'This'll break anything,' she said.

Banham was momentarily taken aback but swung it hard at the rear passenger window. It broke the window immediately. Banham reached in and took Alison's cardigan from the back seat. His eyes were brimming as he hurried back and handed it to Martin. 'She wears it a lot,' he told him. 'She feels the cold.'

Martin held it out so the dogs could take in the scent. One of them turned around in circles for a few seconds, then ran to the manhole and started barking. 'She's down there,' Martin shouted. 'Sadie's picked up a scent.'

The firefighters now had the drill up and running and had started sawing the manhole. The look of sheer desperation written across Banham's face was getting to Georgia. She felt responsible. Why had she been so dismissive of the danger Alison could be in? If she had done more it might not have got to this.

'Sadie is my best dog,' Martin said putting his hand on Banham's shoulder. 'If she says Alison's down there, then guaranteed, she is, and we'll get her out. So you just hang on, mate.'

'She's alive though? Banham asked piteously.

'She's alive, mate,' Martin nodded. 'Sadie wouldn't react with excitement if she wasn't. And Dougal isn't shouting. He's the corpse dog. So as long as Sadie is active, and Dougal isn't, then we're OK.'

Alison blinked several times, her vision was a little clearer, still blurred but better than ten minutes ago. Her sight would be back to normal soon, then she could start to do something about getting out of here.

Water was dripping, very slowly, behind her back. It was irritating, but it was the least of her problems right now. She blinked hard again, peering around, and noticed a large crate to her right. As soon as her vision cleared completely, she would investigate it, but from what she could make out, it looked likely to be weapons piled high from it. This looked to be the hiding place for Harisha Celik's weapon consignments, something else to deal with, but first she had to sort out Melek.

The girl hadn't spoken for a good few minutes. Alison could now see her lying curled up by the weapons. First thing Alison would do, when her sight fully returned, would be to get Melek's phone. It was a one in a million chance that it had a signal down here, but there was a chance. No one was going to just find them down here, how would they? And where were they? Alison only knew they were underground in some sort of tunnel. Her head was throbbing, and her side stung like a whole hive of bees had gone for her. Her ripped clothes proved she'd been dragged along unconscious. Then she remembered a gun. Melek had pointed a gun at her, in her car, and taken her phone.

262

No wonder she couldn't find it. Melek had rung a number on it, had spoken to someone, and then thrown the phone out of the car window. Everything was coming back now. They had been outside McDonalds. It was an abortion clinic, Melek had rung and made an appointment on Alison's phone, in Alison's name, for an abortion, and then thrown the phone out the window. Alison tipped her head back and sighed loudly. When the phone was found they would trace the call history and Banham would be told that she had booked an appointment at an abortion clinic. Not only would that break his heart, it would guarantee that no one would come looking for her. She wanted to smack Melek, there and then. Alison would never hurt Banham, she loved him and she wanted their baby. Yes, it had been a shock at first, but now she was sure that she wanted it more than anything else in the world.

She shuffled impatiently; she had to get out of here, there was no way she was going to perish in this disgusting hole and let Banham think she had done that.

She breathed back the urge to shout at Melek, and stayed calm as she spoke. 'Melek, why are we here? I'm feeling claustrophobic and …'

Melek's voice had changed, it was slurred and quiet, but Alison still heard what she said. Her words shook Alison's whole being. 'It'll be over soon. No one will find us here. I killed Zana, I burnt her, and I killed Burak. I've taken pills now.'

Alison took more than a second to register what she had heard. Then her anger started to build. So that was it? Melek had taken Alison as a hostage, so she could protect herself long enough to take her own life. Alison had told Melek earlier that she was pregnant, she also said she wasn't sure she wanted to be, but she only said it to make the girl feel more at ease, so she would pursue the allegation against Harisha. And if Melek had killed Zana and Burak, then why would she care if Alison perished too? This girl was obviously unstable. Alison had to do something, and quickly, before Melek fell unconscious. She couldn't let her commit suicide, and if she couldn't stop her then how would she get out of here? Melek intended that they wouldn't, that they would die down there together. Melek was very still, from the little that Alison could see of her, but she could hear her voice and it was very slurred, that didn't bode well.

'Melek, you have to stay awake. I am going to get us help. Which way is the exit?'

'I loved him. He two-timed me … with …' Her voice was so quiet and with the dripping water behind her, Alison had to strain to hear. 'With Zana.'

Alison turned to crawl over to Melek but immediately banged her head on the low ceiling. 'Shit.' Her head was already pounding and there was dried blood on the side of her temple. Her head spun and she felt dizzy. She knew she had to stay conscious. 'You killed Zana and Burak Kaya?' she said as she reached out and touched Melek.

Melek didn't stir.

'Melek what have you taken?'

'Burak was mine, she slept with him. So I killed them both.' Melek slurred.

'I thought you were Harisha's girlfriend.'

'Burak and I were going to be together. Zana took him from me. I've told you all. Let me die …'

'No. Sit up.' Alison tried to lift her but then stopped, remembering she was pregnant and had already taken a few knocks. 'Melek, I'm going to get help, which way to get out? Melek, speak to me. Sit up and keep talking.'

Melek didn't answer.

'Melek, you have a baby to think of. Don't do this. Is the exit in front of us or behind?' she asked desperately.

'Mr and Mrs Wilkins saw me …' Melek's voice was now barely audible, Alison had to strain to hear her. 'They saw me kill Burak. It was me, not that gang. I stabbed him.'

'OK. ' Alison took a deep breath as she took that in. If Melek had killed Zana and Burak, and Mr and Mrs Wilkins, another life would mean nothing to her. 'Melek, we can sort this, please think of your baby.'

Melek wasn't listening. 'I stabbed … the … screw … drivers thro … ugh their necks.'

Working in the Sapphire Rape Unit before coming back to murder had given Alison a lot of experience with traumatised girls, and she knew this wasn't a cry for help, Melek wanted to die. Alison was on all fours, with blurred vision, but she knew she had to do something if she was to save them all. She leaned over Melek, willing her own eyes to function, and fumbled for Melek's mouth. When she found it she forced it open and stuck her own fingers down Melek's throat. Nothing happened, so she tried again. Melek's head jerked, the girl gulped and threw up, but minimally, then she flopped her head down on the ground again and turned her mouth to the ground. Alison wiped her fingers on her jeans. Her whole body was stinging and her head pounded like a cement mixer. Desperation was setting in, but she had to hold herself together and get them both out.

Staying on all fours, and barely able to see, she started to crawl. She had no idea which way to go, it was a fifty-fifty gamble. She turned to her left, praying as she did, because time wasn't on her side.

She crawled, barely able to see in front over her, over the uneven and damp concrete, then her hand hit something. She made her eyes focus. It was another crate. She put her hand inside, but pulled it back quickly, as something sharp pricked her and a trickle of blood ran down her fingers. 'Shit and sod it,' she cried out, putting her hand to her mouth and sucking at the bleeding wound. She needed her hands to crawl, and now she only had one. She wanted to cry with frustration. She carefully put her hand inside the crate again to confirm her guess. She was right, it was machetes. Well, Serious Crime and the drug and arms team would be delighted with her, if she ever got out of here. Not only had she got a confession from Melek for four murders, but now she had found the weapons imported by Harisha Celik. Celik was going down for a long time because of this find. And no one could be angry with her for all the manpower that was being used up looking for her … then she realised that there wouldn't be any. If someone had found her phone, Banham would think she was in an abortion clinic. She felt another surge of anger, and then she forced herself to get a grip, self-pity wouldn't save her.

Joe Miller was kneeling down by the manhole sawing laboriously at the bolt and chain. 'It's quite hard going,' he said wiping his brow with the top of his arm and looking up at Banham. 'So bear with me, sir. We will get there. I promise.'

Sadie and Dougal were resting on their forepaws behind the firemen. Sadie's ears were pointed upwards as she listened, every now and again she sat up and barked her confirmation that the officers were at the right place.

Alison sat back and took stock of her situation. Her hand was still bleeding, so crawling onward was now painful and laboriously slow. She felt dizzy from the throbbing in her head, and her whole body felt raw from being dragged. Her shoulder too, was stiff and aching, she suspected it had been displaced, and she could barely see. Before she realised it she had opened her mouth and let out a desperate wail, 'Help, please, someone … HELP ME!'

The sound of the busy saw at work prevented her cry from being heard by any of the team at the edge of the manhole, but it wasn't missed by the sharp ears of the German Shepherd. Sadie jumped up and began barking. Then she ran fifty feet along the ground, and stood still, but carried on barking to let them know Alison was alive and directly under where she now stood.

'She's picked up on Alison's scent!' Martin, the dog handler, announced to everyone. 'I'm 99.99% sure that Alison is under that spot, sir. When they get the bolt and the chain free, they need to drop down into the ground, and turn immediately right, about fifty foot along,' he added. 'This dog is a genius, I have never known her wrong, sir.'

Banham knelt down on the ground beside Joe and tapped his arm to stop him sawing. Joe stopped.

Banham cupped his hand and all but screamed into the tunnel. 'Alison. Alison! Alison, can you hear me?'

Mostly all the officers, who were standing waiting to go in and help, looked pityingly at each other. All were fully aware that Banham's first wife and baby had been murdered, and all were praying Alison would be found, unharmed, and brought to safety.

Georgia was feeling ashamed of herself. How could she be such a mean-minded human being. All day she had dismissed any signs that Alison could be in trouble, merely thinking the woman just wanted space, or worse still, attention. Now she lowered her eyes and said a quiet prayer.

Alison blinked hard. Did she just hear Banham's voice? And from the direction she was heading? Was it even possible that he could have traced her, to this tunnel, under the sodding river! Or was she starting to hallucinate?

She jumped, forgetting the ceiling just above her head, and once again, banged her head. 'HELP! HELP! HELP!' She held her breath and waited. Nothing.

'HELP!' she screamed again.

Nothing.

She had to get to the exit. Just the thought that Banham might have found her spurred her on. She hunched her shoulders up, and bent her body over, like an old man, so the top of the tunnel just skimmed her back. This way she could move, very slowly, but she was on her way to the exit.

She didn't see the next crate. Her shin hit it first and she lost her balance and landed on top of it. As soon as she scrambled half-up, she peered down and looked inside the crate: Mac 10s, Machine guns that could shoot a hundred rounds in a minute. She just prayed that the dripping water hadn't dissolved all Harisha Celik's DNA from them, and they had enough proof to put him away. There was so much depending on her. She had to save Melek's life, no matter what the girl had confessed to. Serious crime squad needed Alison to help put away Harisha Celik, and the families of the victims that had been shot down by Mac 10s, or cut to pieces with Celik's imported machetes needed her to get him off the streets, away from the danger of hurting anyone else, but most importantly Paul Banham, and the baby inside her needed her to get to the exit. And she wasn't going to let any of them down.

She took a deep breath and stood up, and carried on at the pace of a snail. Then a knife-like pain shot through her abdomen, and fear shook her whole being. 'No. No. *God, please, please don't let me lose my baby.*' Within seconds the pain had subsided, but the thought of what might have been had completely bowled her over.

She opened her mouth and bellowed, 'HELP ...' and then the pain was back in her stomach and she fell forward onto her knees.

Sadie heard Alison's cry and immediately jumped up, barking hysterically and turning on the spot to signify that her target was in danger and distress.

'She's down there all right,' Martin said, watching Sadie barking and turning on the spot above Alison. 'I think she may be in trouble, we need to get to her.'

'How much longer with the saw?' Banham was getting frantic.

Joe shook his head. 'It's a bastard to get through. Few minutes, three, four, five at most. I'm going as fast as I can, mate.'

'Alison,' Banham yelled over Joe's shoulder. 'We're on our way. Hang on, darl ...' but his voice faltered, and Georgia watched his shoulders start to heave. DCI Banham had broken down in tears in front of most of the Metropolitan police unit.

Alison heard the dog barking, and then she heard Banham's voice again.

She laughed with relief. 'Hang on, nearly there,' she told her tiny bump as she sucked in painful air and fought back tears. 'Hang on, you just hang on, little one, d'you hear me? I'm down here, Banny,' she cried out, but her voice had become weak with the pain and was barely audible. She was about to walk on when she felt something on her foot. She looked down and saw it was a rat. She didn't know whether to laugh because she could see it, which meant her vision was fully back, or to cry because it was a rat.

She imagined Georgia Johnson's reaction. The intransient and stoic Georgia Johnson, who everyone knew had severe OCD, how would she cope, trapped in this dirty, rat-infested hole?

Things were getting better. She could see, she was going the right way out of the tunnel that she was in, and she could hear Banham, at least she thought she could. She hunched herself over again and moved onwards, with one hand on her stomach. Banham, and probably half the Met, were at the end of the tunnel, waiting for her. A moment later, she heard something that sounded like a drill. Was it a drill? Had Banham instructed someone to dig the road up?

Alysha, Panther, Lox, and Tink had been instructed to move back. They were back on the other side of the road, leaning against the bins, watching. Alysha turned her head as another ambulance, wailing its siren, turned into the road and screeched to a halt, allowing the police helicopter, that had been descending, to park and block access up the street.

'I've always wanted to go up in one of them,' Tink said pointing at Indie 999, 'D'you think they'll offer me a ride, if I ask nicely. I'd even offer my body for it.'

'We don't do no honking no more,' Alysha reminded her, smiling and shaking her head. 'You said you 'ated doing all that, an' you'd do it again just for a helicopter ride. You ain't 'alf fickle.'

'I'd want the 'copter an' all,' Tink joked back. 'Imagine us all, flying over the Aviary, and checking out our street girls in one of them.'

'We'll buy one, one day,' Alysha told her.

'Oh, dream on,' Lox laughed, then she became serious. 'I don't get this, you know. Why would Melek do this? She's double-crossed SLRs and given them up, and now she's double-crossed us, an' handed over the weapons instead of getting Harisha banged up like we told her.'

'Must be for the reward,' Panther said, shaking her head.

'Yeah, well we're getting that,' Lox said. 'I'll kill 'er if she tries to take that.'

'More to it than that,' Alysha said. 'Melek ain't that stupid, she'd know that SLRs, as well as us, would be after her, and she'll know she ain't got no one to watch her back.'

'Hey, do you think she's a grass? Panther said.

'Bloody 'ope not,' Alysha said. 'Deny everything, if she tries that on us.'

'We gave her a pistol,' Lox suddenly said.

'She can't prove that,' Alysha told her. 'Her word 'gainst four of ours.'

'They're like a big gang, them feds,' Panther said watching as the helicopter door opened and Sergeant Stephanie Green stepped out of it, helped by one of the officers. 'They all stick together.'

'So do we,' Tink said. 'Let's just 'ope we ain't going to prison over all this.'

'You know what, I'm gonna kill Melek anyway,' Panther said. 'I never did like her, and she's really fucked us over this.'

'We don't know for def that she's even in there, yet,' Alysha reminded them. 'Them dogs are pretty sure that Alison Grainger is, but no one's mentioned Melek.'

'If Melek ain't in there, we'll still get the reward, won't we? Lox said. 'Cos otherwise we've lost a hell of a lot of corn, we could have sold all them Mac 10s and machetes, made a right killing.'

Alysha turned to her. 'Keep your voice down, will ya? If we lose the weapons there is a good side to it. You gotta look to the future. This def is gonna put Harisha Celik away for a long stretch, right, and that leaves his territory clear for us.' She turned and pulled her mouth into a wide smile. 'We are gonna move onto his patch. We'll take over his girls, and use the money to rebuild the Aviary community centre and our shops.

We'll tell his street girls they only work if they want to, and we'll supply them with whatever stuff they want, the ones that need supplying, that is. If they don't wanna work, and want 'elp to get off the drugs, then we'll give it. We'll 'elp 'em and they can join the ACs. We'll need to build up our gang, the bigger we get, the more we can move in on other territories. We'll clean the whole of London up eventually, make loads of corn, and the feds won't know what's hit them.'

'But our estate and our kids'll come first,' Tink argued.

'Always,' Alysha said. 'No one on our patch will have to put up wiv what we have,' she said. 'Not so long as we rule the Aviary. An' rule we will, whatever the price, and whoever we 'ave to fight to keep it that way. And then we'll expand to other territories.'

'But we four run the AC's,' Panther said. 'No one else.'

'No, course no one else. But we 'ave to take on soldiers, cos they'll be others trying to muscle in on us all the time, and we'll need muscle to keep on top of all that, so we'll keep taking on working and fighting soldiers, and keep cleaning up more estates, and stopping the big dealers muscling in on kids, and we'll be looking to give all kids chances like we never 'ad.'

'We're family, though,' Tink said.

Alysha reached out and took her hand. 'Yeah, we are, an' always will be, mate.'

'It's nice to 'ave a family, I ain't never 'ad one before.'

'You wait till you have kids, an' we've built playgrounds and youth centres for them, and the estate's a great place to grow up on. You'll have a massive family then.'

Georgia stared in disbelief as Stephanie made her way over from the helicopter. 'How come you arrived in Indie 999?'

'You said quick as you can.' Stephanie grinned. 'I know Perry well.' She turned her head and winked at the skipper. 'He was in radio contact with us all, he heard you say, "Quick as you can," so he told me to wait outside the nick and he picked me up. Nice of him, wasn't it?'

Georgia was shaking her head in astonishment. 'Where did

he park, when he picked you up?'

'In the middle of the street.'

Georgia stared at her.

'I wanted to get here asap,' Stephanie told her. 'We all want to help Alison, so Perry helped me out. I've put him on a promise.' She looked at the tunnel and became serious again. 'Is she definitely down there?'

'We think so?'

'And alive?'

'That, we hope.'

Alysha and her girls were now walking up the road. Georgia signalled to them to join her.

'How's it going?' Alysha asked, watching Joe Miller still sawing madly at the chain that held the bolt in place.

'Nearly there,' Georgia told her. 'And this is all down to you. We are very grateful to you all.'

Banham was listening as Georgia was speaking to them.

'Yes, it is, and I personally thank you,' he said to the four of them. 'You may well have saved an officer's life. That's a big, big deal. We owe you, big time.'

The girls all made eye contact, and Alysha winked at them.

He pointed to where Sadie the Alsatian was sitting. 'We think she's under here,' he told them.

'Clever dog,' Panther said. 'Is Melek in there too?'

'That we don't know,' Georgia told them. 'The dogs have only got DI Grainger's coat.'

'How well do you know the tunnel?' Banham asked them.

None of them answered.

'Do you know what exactly lies beneath this padlocked grille? How we get into the space that's underneath?'

'Have any of you ever been down there?' Georgia questioned them.

Alysha flicked a glance at Panther and then back. 'I went down there, once, a long time ago,' she said. 'It's one long fucker of a drop, after you get the grille and padlock off. There was a rope on a hook, 'bout a foot down on the inside of the hole. You have to tie it round your waist and drop down. I remember there was steps too, made of thinnish metal stuff, on the side of the drain, but they didn't really look very safe, so you just have to use the rope and drop. It's like jumping off a wall. Someone has to wait here for you, to help bring you back up. If no one is here, you wouldn't be able to get out.'

Georgia noticed the look of horror that spread across Banham's face.

'It's off, guv.'

They looked around to see Joe Miller holding up the chain and one half of the bolt that he had managed to saw through.

His colleague Peter Hayes immediately moved in and surveyed the hole.

Georgia, Stephanie, and Banham hurried the few yards to the edge of the hole, closely followed by Alysha and Tink, Panther, and Lox, who were immediately told to stand back, by the uniformed police.

Georgia and Banham both knelt down by Joe and Peter, while Stephanie peered over their shoulder.

'There's the rope,' Georgia said.

Peter leaned in and, held onto by Joe, lowered his body, trying to reach the rope.

'Jesus, I wouldn't fancy going down there,' Stephanie said from behind Georgia.

'Don't worry, we wouldn't let you!' Georgia said, stifling the urge to laugh. The manhole was barely wide enough for a normal-sized person and Stephanie Green was fourteen stone.

'Got it,' Peter, suddenly said. He was leaning back from the entrance to the tunnel, and holding the long rope. After checking that it was secure, he started to tie the other end around himself.

Banham leaned into the hole. 'Ali-sooon! Can you hear us?'

They all held their breath. And then a faint cry came from the tunnel, 'Banny, I'm here. Help!'

As Georgia turned to Stephanie, Banham jumped up and snatched the rope from Peter's grip. 'I'll go first,' he told him.

'No, sir, sorry, I can't allow it,' Peter answered, pulling back on the rope. 'This is our job, and it may not be safe.'

'I'll take full responsibility,' Banham told him, pulling again to get the rope away from the fireman, which Peter resisted giving him.

'No, sorry, sir, I have to say no.'

'Give me the rope,' Banham half shouted, tugging and beginning to get the better of the fireman.

Georgia quickly intervened. 'Sir, get a bloody grip. It's not safe, and it's not your job, so stand away and let Peter get on with it.'

Banham attempted to push her out of the way, but she held her ground. 'I am Senior Investigating Officer on this enquiry,' she told him. 'And I am ordering you to stand back.'

Uniformed officers had now edged nearer, as had the other six firemen, and the Alsatian was barking furiously.

'Sir, I really don't think …' one of the officers said.

'Just get out of the way,' Banham shouted, grabbing at the rope.

'I'm sorry, sir, but no, and you're now wasting time.'

Georgia had had enough. She again raised her voice. 'DCI Paul Banham, I am arresting you for obstruction, you do not have to say anything …'

Nineteen

Georgia turned to Stephanie and told her to handcuff Banham.

'If you do,' Banham said threateningly to Georgia, 'you will be back in uniform for the rest of your career, and that's a promise. Now get out of my way.'

Georgia lowered her voice. 'Sir, I beg you,' she said changing her tactic. 'Let the firefighters go first. You're not thinking straight and you don't …'

'Let go of me. Now!'

Peter had meanwhile got another rope. He'd secured one end to the fire engine and was wrapping the other end round his waist. He picked up the rope attached to the tunnel wall. 'Let's tie this, and let's get in there,' he said to Banham, giving Georgia a reassuring nod as he wrapped the rope around Banham's waist, then double-checking it was secure.

Georgia was furious. If anything happened to either Alison or Banham, she would have to carry the can.

'I'll be right behind you,' Peter told Banham as he double-checked his own rope, and you'll do everything I tell you, have you got that?'

'Got it.'

'Good, then …'

'I'm not happy about this …' Georgia butted in, but stopped as she caught the warning shake of Peter's head.

'I'll take full responsibility,' Banham said, stepping carefully into the wide manhole, and slowly disappearing as his feet descended the thin iron steps that Alysha had described at the side of the tunnel wall.

'I'll be right behind him,' Peter said nodding assurance to Georgia.

Alison was trying not to panic. The pain in her abdomen wasn't consistent, it came and it went, but when it came it felt like she was being stabbed with a sharp knife. She made herself count her plusses. Her sight was as clear as it could be in the darkness of the tunnel, and that was a bonus. She also knew she was going towards the exit, but how far away that was, she had no idea.

Banham's voice seemed to just come out of nowhere. 'Alison! Alison, can you hear me?' and it sounded so close she thought she had to be imagining it.

'Paul, Paul,' she shrieked like some delirious evacuee. 'Paul, I can hear you.'

No answer. She lowered her eyes and let out a heartfelt sigh. She was imagining it. When she opened her eyes, he came into view. He was on all fours, crawling and speeding along the dirty tunnel like a manic over-wound toy.

She couldn't contain her tears.

They hurriedly scrambled the few feet to each other, and reached out and fell into each other's arms, both clinging and both trying to speak.

'I thought I'd …'

'Are you all right?'

Then he planted kisses all over her head.

Peter's voice came from behind Banham, 'I'm still here,' he said. 'So don't get too carried away. How are you, Alison? It would be good to get back to daylight.'

'You're bleeding,' Banham said, suddenly aware she had blood on the side of her head. 'She's bleeding,' he turned to tell Peter.

'I'm OK,' she assured him. 'I've cut my hand, that's all. And my head took a smack, but I'm all right, but Melek Yismaz isn't. She's further down the tunnel, she's unconscious and pregnant. She has admitted committing the four murders to me. She needs an emergency ambulance. And there's a large consignment of weapons and drugs that we need for evidence. She told me they belong to Harisha Celik.'

Banham turned back to Peter. 'Can you shout for two ambulances to stand by?'

'On way.'

'We'll get you out of here, and checked out first.' He was bent over and had started moving sideways still holding her hand. 'Are you sure you are OK?'

'I've got stomach pains, I'm getting anxious about them.'

She heard his sigh, but he made no comment.

'Did you find my phone?' she asked him.

'Yes.'

'And check the call history?'

'Yes.'

'Paul, that was her. That little cow phoned an abortion clinic while pointing a gun at me. So when you found my phone, and checked my call history, you'd think I was there, doing that, and wouldn't go looking for me.'

He stopped and turned to her, his voice breaking as he asked, 'So you didn't …'

Her tears matched his. 'I'd never do that. I love you and want this ba …'

'Ambulance standing by,' Peter yelled as he scrambled back towards them.

'We'll talk later,' Banham told Alison.

'How far is the entrance?'

'Not far. There are officers waiting, with ropes.'

'Ropes? For what?'

'We have to lift you out. I'll make sure they are careful. The paramedics are there, ready to help. How did you get yourself in here?'

'I don't remember everything about it. I couldn't see properly and Melek was physically moving me when I couldn't do what she wanted. And I'd hurt my head'

'How come?' His voice was now full of concern.

'A smack with something sharp, but don't worry, I'm OK now. Just tell our baby to hold tight.'

Light appeared, and she looked up to where the ground level and pavement were. 'The exit is coming up,' he told her.

She said a silent prayer as Banham tied the rope under her arms.

'Passing you over to Peter, now,' he whispered, kissing her

tenderly on the forehead.

She looked up and saw Georgia and Stephanie looking over the hole, both had their arms outstretched to her.

'Ambulance waiting for you,' Georgia shouted down.

'And I've got sherbet lemons,' Stephanie added, making her smile.

'We are going to hoist you up the side of a wall,' Peter said as he double-checked her rope was secure around her waist. 'I'm sorry, it'll be over in seconds, but this is the only way out.'

The pain in Alison's abdomen had struck again. She squeezed her lips together to help quell it. Peter noticed. He rubbed her shoulder. 'I'm gonna be right underneath you. You can't fall. You're in good hands,' he assured her pointing to the two fireman crouched down on the pavement beside Georgia, ready to lift her as soon as she came near enough.

'It's the only way,' Peter told her clocking the anxious look on her face. 'The ladder isn't low enough.'

'Be very careful,' Banham said in a tone a lot calmer than Alison knew he was feeling.

'Very careful,' Peter echoed. 'And I'll feel a lot happier when you are both out of here.'

'When Alison's safely out, I'm going back to get Melek,' Banham told him.

'We'll do that,' Peter told him. 'I'd like you out now, sir.'

'No point in bringing anyone else down, seeing as I'm here. She's not far along. Just be very careful of this one,' he said as Peter scooped Alison up in his arms.

'You can stop worrying about our baby,' Alison assured him. 'With our genes, it'll be a tough little survivor.'

'Gently as you go.'

He stayed as Peter talked her through the thirty-foot wall that they were going to have to hoist her up. She was to make tiny steps against it, as if climbing, and the rope would do the work. After so many feet there would be a ladder, and then a lot of helping hands to get her onto street level.

Her stomach pains were back but she kept that to herself. She didn't want Banham there if she started to miscarry on the way up. 'Paul, we need to move with Melek, she's pregnant too, so there's another little baby deserves a chance.'

'I couldn't have stood it down there,' Georgia said quietly to Stephanie as they knelt waiting by the hole. 'I'll bet it's infested by rats.'

'Try not to think about it,' Stephanie said pulling the bag of sherbet lemons from her pocket and checking there were lots in it. Just as she popped one into her mouth, Alison's face came into view. Within seconds Alison was lifted up and was sitting lying on the pavement beside them, being greeted by thunderous applause and cheers.

Two paramedics rushed in, one wrapped her in a foil blanket, the other pulled an oxygen mask over her face. Two more paramedics rushed in with a stretcher.

As they lifted her onto the stretcher, Georgia was studying the nasty gash on the side of Alison's head.

'Gently, she's pregnant,' Stephanie told the paramedics as they clipped a belt over the blanket on the stretcher to keep Alison secure.

'How are you feeling?' Stephanie asked her.

Alison pushed the oxygen from her face. 'I've got pains in my stomach,' she said, panic clear in her voice. She turned to Georgia. 'And, in case I don't make it, Melek Yismaz has admitted all four murders, and there are crates of weapons down there which she said were illegally imported by Harisha Celik.'

'We're gonna have you in hospital, and checked out within minutes,' a small female paramedic assured her. 'Of course you're gonna make it.'

'I've got stomach cramps,' Alison said, trying not to panic.

The two male paramedics immediately lifted the stretcher and carried her the few feet to the back of the ambulance. The male paramedic climbed in first and started to clean Alison's hand. Alison flinched with pain.

'Does that hurt?' the paramedic asked.

'No, it's my stomach. Where's Paul?' she asked looking out anxiously.

'He's just coming out,' Stephanie said, although she could see no sign of him. She turned back to Alison. 'You get going. Don't waste any more time. You've got a little-un in there, needs an eye keeping on.'

'I want Paul with me,' Alison said fretfully.

Stephanie turned back and looked towards the tunnel. Three more firemen were roping up and about to lower themselves down, but no sign of Banham.

'You get going,' Stephanie told Alison again, 'He'll follow you in a few minutes.'

'Where's Paul?'

'Come on,' Stephanie said in her usual motherly tone, as she climbed aboard and made the vehicle rock sideways in the process. 'I've done this pregnancy lark, your hormones play up and embarrass you no end. Paul'll be along in a minute, meanwhile you've got me and a bag of sherbet lemons to keep you company.' She handed the sweets to Alison then yelled to Georgia to let her know what she was doing. 'Let's go,' she shouted to the paramedic sitting in the driving seat.

As the ambulance sped off Stephanie lifted the oxygen mask from Alison's face and popped a sherbet lemon in her mouth. 'That'll keep you calm,' she said, smiling.

Alison reached for Stephanie's hand. 'Thanks.'

Georgia stood watching the ambulance speed out of sight. She was wishing she had a few more grains of compassion in her own make-up, but the trauma of her rape, and then the strong police training, had left her unable to sympathise with anyone no matter what the circumstance. She envied Stephanie.

Banham and Peter had reached Melek. Peter leaned over Banham's shoulder with the torch while Banham felt for a pulse.

'Very faint,' Banham said lifting her up. 'Let's make it snappy.'

Peter lifted her from Banham. 'Take her legs,' he said. 'I'll go first, and be careful over the boxes. Jim'll get them when we get her out.'

'No, leave the crates of weapons,' Banham told him. 'I'll get the tunnel secured, and a round-the-clock guard on it. We won't take any chances until bomb and firearm experts have taken a look.'

'Georgia will be pleased,' Peter said as he bent himself forward and slowly edged backwards to the exit.

'This girl is responsible for four murders,' Banham said. 'And she's pregnant.'

It wasn't easy, but they eased Melek to the exit between them. Peter lifted her on his shoulder and very slowly climbed the wall with a rope attached to himself and Melek, all the while reaching with his feet for the thin steel steps to get them up to the top of the hole.

Alysha, Panther, Lox, and Tink had moved near the tunnel again and were watching Georgia, who was standing alone, waiting. Alysha gave the three girls the nod and they walked over to join her.

'What luck that we stumbled across all this,' Alysha said to Georgia.

'It most certainly was,' Georgia told her.

'It was just a shot in the dark, really,' Alysha said, 'but looks as if our find has saved a couple of lives. We heard that the SLRs used it sometimes, and when we passed it and saw it all padlocked we got suspicious. Then, when you gave us your detective's car registration, and the car was there, it sort of fell into place. Very lucky though. Do you think they're gonna be OK?'

'I don't know the answer to that, I'm afraid,' Georgia said, smiling at her. 'But it would have been a lot worse without your help. DI Grainger is pregnant, and you may have saved her baby's life.' She looked around to each of them. 'I'm very, very grateful to you all. You've all helped this enquiry enormously.'

'That was fate, that was,' Panther said slyly. 'But glad we helped such a big amount.'

Before Georgia had the chance to answer Lox butted in. 'An' you don't have to be grateful to us for it,' she said. 'But you do have to keep your promise about sorting the council, and you do have to make sure we get a fat reward.'

'I'll do my best,' Georgia told them.

'You promised,' Lox said in a determined tone. 'If we've saved 'er kid, then you 'ave to help save all ours. Our kids' park ain't healthy. And you promised to talk to the council.'

'I said I would do my best.'

'What about Melek?' Panther interrupted. 'What'll happen to her?'

'She's being charged with four murders.'

Alysha, Tink, Lox, and Panther turned to look at each other. 'Holy shit,' Alysha said. 'Did you say four murders?'

Georgia nodded. 'We have proof, and she's admitted killing the Wilkinses, Burak Kaya, and Zana Ghaziani.'

Alysha and the girls looked totally stunned. Alysha was about to ask more questions but the cheer that went up as Peter appeared from the manhole carrying with the unconscious Melek took Georgia's attention. Paramedics immediately moved in and lifted Melek onto a stretcher and into an ambulance. Then Banham's face appeared, and with help from the firefighters he climbed onto the pavement.

Georgia went over to him. 'Are you OK, sir?' she asked him.

'Yes. Has Alison gone to hospital?'

'Yes, guv. Sergeant Green went with her.'

'I'm on my way,' he said, starting to hurry over to his car. 'Can you arrange for uniformed officers to go to the hospital and sit with Melek Yismaz until she wakes up. We'll need her statement as soon as she does. She has admitted all four murders, to Alison, I want round-the-clock surveillance on her until she wakes.'

'Sir,' she said.

He stopped, turned, and looked straight at Georgia. 'Then I want you to go back to the station, please. As soon as I get back from the hospital I want you in my office.' His tone was enough to tell her that, yet again, she was in trouble. Her concern for his safety had overridden any hierarchy, and he wasn't going to turn a blind eye to it. She had overstepped the mark and was in for a big bollocking.

'Sir,' she nodded, before turning to pass the instructions to the uniformed sergeant.

Alysha, Panther, Tink, and Lox had walked back over to the bins and were leaning against them, out of hearing distance of any police.

'So, what the fuck …' Tink said.

'… is Melek up to?' Lox finished.

Alysha and Panther shook their heads. 'Don't know,' Alysha said. 'But she ain't one of us, that's for sure. I'd have killed her myself if I'd known she done them old Wilkinses. They was a lovely couple, they never hurt no one, and we gave them our word that we'd look out for them.'

'She was still running with Harisha, and using us,' Tink said.

'Sure looks like it.' Alysha nodded. 'Fucking bitch.'

'If she comes round, I'll kill her,' Panther said.

'We'll all help you,' Alysha told her.

'From now on, we're more careful when we take new Alley Cats in,' Lox said to them.

'Yeah, agreed, but we still need more soldiers,' Alysha told them. 'I know you hate us having new girls, but it's gonna take more than just us four to hold on to what we got now. We are onto something here. Now the feds think we're the business. We've led them to here, and given up that stash of weapons. Other gangs will know that. They'll either think we're the shit, not to be played wiv, or they'll fink we're turncoats, and they'll try and take us on.'

'We're both though, ain't we? Tink laughed.

'S'right,' Alysha nodded. 'And other gangs are gonna wanna be challenging us, so we need to be ready. We gotta protect ourselves, and we gotta protect our estate. We swore we would, an' we're gonna hold strong to that. So, we need more soldiers. Feds 'll give us money for grassing up Harisha. He'll go down for a long stretch, and we've got his contacts and all his territory. But, we 'ave to protect it and ourselves. We don't let no one blow us off it. We'll turn that estate good too. If we want chances, outside of crime and prison, for the estate kids, then the fight ain't over, I'll tell you, Cats, it's only just begun.'

Tink nodded. 'She's right. 'We are gonna do that, an' be famous, and get respect with a capital R.'

Yup,' Alysha nodded and grinned. 'Everyone on our estate, and for miles around it, had all better watch out, cos anyone who disrespects us, or tries to muscle on our turf, or dirty it with drugs and weapons, will have us to face. We are gonna hold our estate together and make it clean.' She looked at each of the girls. 'So we are gonna need to get more girls fighting the fight. Agreed?'

They all high-fived each other. 'Agreed,' they shouted in unison.

'I'll be happier when the feds pay up,' Lox said.

'Yeah, won't we all,' Tink said. Then she lifted both her thumbs in the air, 'Cos I'm going to teach all the young girls, so they can do nails an' that an' don't have to go on the game.'

'An' Georgia Johnson is gonna get the council to re-do our kids' play area for the rest,' Lox said.

'We 'ope,' Alysha said. 'Our fight's only just begun.' She turned to them and became very serious. 'We have *so* gotta watch each other's backs now.'

Twenty

One month later

Georgia and Stephanie had been told to finish the paperwork and put the case to bed. Neither Banham nor Alison Grainger had been back in the office in the last four weeks. Banham had been with Alison, in hospital, during the long forty-eight hours when the doctors had tried, and failed, to save her pregnancy. The murder department had all signed a card and sent flowers, and Superintendent Beir had told them both to take at least a month off.

Georgia and Stephanie had just finished the final press conference and were awaiting forensic DNA results before closing the file on the case.

'Do you think, if you had got there sooner, you would have prevented the death of a pregnant eighteen-year-old girl?' one insensitive journalist had asked Georgia at the conference.

Georgia had hesitated, so Stephanie had answered. 'No, definitely not,' she said, glaring furiously at the man. 'We arrived at the scene very shortly after Melek Yismaz had kidnapped one of our detectives. She gave no prior indication that she was a danger to herself or to our officers, nor was it foreseeable that she would be armed, and despite all procedures being followed she was unfortunately able to incapacitate our officer and imprison her in the tunnel – a place to which there was no easy access. While inside the tunnel Yismaz committed suicide by swallowing a cocktail of pills, also trying to force the same death upon our officer. We could not have prevented Melek Yismaz's death.' She let that sink in, and then continued. 'The force, together with the other emergency services, did everything it could to save Melek Yismaz. Four firefighters and DCI Banham risked their lives in the tunnel to get her out. Sadly, she didn't regain consciousness.'

'How did you find the tunnel? It was well hidden, and no one can find any information on its existence.'

'By doing our job,' Georgia answered quickly. 'We are detectives.'

'Did you get a tip-off, or did you stumble across it?'

'As I said, by good detective work,' Georgia said, glaring at the pushy reporter.

'There were some local girls hanging around, talking to some of your officers when you brought the DI out. Did they help you find the tunnel?' another journalist asked.

For a second neither Stephanie or Georgia spoke, then Georgia answered. 'I didn't see anyone talking to my officers at the time. I was assisting in the rescue attempt of the women trapped in the tunnel.'

'There are always bystanders, as you know, when a police operation is being carried out,' Stephanie added. 'Normally they're asking questions, not answering them.'

'What can you tell us about ...' another journalist asked, bending her head and checking her notes, 'about DI Alison Grainger, the detective that lost her baby?'

'I have no comment to make on that,' Georgia snapped at her. 'That has nothing to do with this case.' 'She stood up. 'If you'll excuse us, ladies and gentlemen,' she said, 'unless there is anything else relevant to the case, I would like to bring this conference to a close.'

'You said that Melek Yismaz admitted to the murder of four victims before she died, do you have proof to back that up?'

'Yes we do.'

'What about the Ghazianis, and their son, who you originally arrested?'

'Released without charge.'

'Didn't you find blood on a weapon at their shop?'

'Yes, we found blood,' Georgia said, 'but not on a weapon. It's a dry cleaners and cobblers' and one of their screwdrivers was found to have blood residue. But it was a match to Wajdi Ghaziani. He cut himself while working. There is no charge against them.'

'And Harisha Celik? What is he charged with?'

Again Stephanie spoke. 'We have charged Mr Celik with the illegal importation of firearms and other weapons, and with the possession and distribution of Class A drugs.'

'And does the rape charge still stand?'

'Yes, it does,' Stephanie said, aware of Georgia's hesitation.

'Thank you for your time, ladies and gentlemen,' Georgia said, bringing the conference to an end in case she was cornered into admitting that everything wasn't yet water-tight.

They were now sitting in Georgia's office eating lunch. Stephanie had a large McDonalds strawberry milkshake which she sucked noisily through a straw. She put the sticky cup down on Georgia's desk and Georgia immediately moved the case papers out of harm's way.

As Stephanie bit into her double cheeseburger and fries she must have read Georgia's mind because she picked up her napkin just in time to catch some slippery green pickle as it slid from the burger. Normally Georgia forbade strong-smelling food in her office, but right now she was glad of Stephanie's company. No matter what Georgia did, or how many mistakes she seemed to make, Stephanie always stood by her and kept her spirits up. Stephanie was a true friend, as well as a first-class detective who was over-qualified for the position of DS.

Unlike Georgia, Stephanie wasn't ambitious, so she had been the only one in the team to say Georgia was right in threatening to cuff Banham to stop him going into the tunnel, saying that just because Banham was DCI, it didn't always make him right. And Georgia appreciated it.

She shook her head politely as Stephanie offered the paper envelope of French fries to her. She just stopped herself saying she would rather eat the paper. Georgia was edgy, she was worried about the consequences of her actions at the tunnel, and very concerned it would affect her next promotion. Stephanie must have read her mind.

'With everything that's gone on, I'm sure he'll have forgotten what he said about reporting to his office as soon as he gets here,' she told Georgia. Then, in her motherly tone, she added, 'It's been four weeks. He's had time to think about it and he'll realise you were doing your job.'

'I bet he won't,' Georgia said. 'And that's my recommendation for promotion down the Swanee if he makes it formal.'

'Won't come to that,' Stephanie said shaking her head. 'You won't be the first detective to be bollocked, and you won't be the last. If he does bollock you, it'll just be his male pride, nothing more. He's a chauvinist through and through, let's face it.' She put her burger down and looked Georgia in the face. 'If you want my advice, take it on the chin, say "Sorry, sir." And that'll be the end of it. He's got too many other things on his mind. He won't take it any further.'

Georgia gave her a grateful smile.

'You bollock me sometimes,' Stephanie reminded her.

Georgia squeezed her lips together to try to stop herself laughing. Stephanie had blobs of tomato sauce around her cheeks.

'And I don't take it personally. It goes with policing,' Stephanie carried on talking but her eyebrows moved towards each other. 'Why are you laughing?'

Georgia handed her a napkin and pointed to Stephanie's cheek. Stephanie wiped as she carried on talking. 'There was a lot of tension by that tunnel,' she reminded Georgia. 'We had a fellow officer,' she raised her voice, 'a pregnant fellow officer, trapped underground in a hole that none of us knew the layout of. We were all concerned. You were SIO, so it was your responsibility, and Banham was wrong.' She lifted her ungroomed eyebrows and looked sympathetically at Georgia. 'He's not above the rules.'

'I still shouldn't have shouted at him, or arrested him in front of everyone. I don't know what came over me.'

'Common sense, that's what came over you! And anyway, you did it in the heat of the moment, so tell him that. He's angry with himself, not you, because he thinks he should have got there sooner.' She paused and said quietly. 'Remember, he found his first wife and baby murdered all those years ago. That's what it was really about.' She frowned, then smiled sadly. 'And it's heartbreaking because of that,'

Georgia nodded. 'Thanks.'

'Anyway, you're in the borough commander's good books,' Stephanie reminded her. 'He's very happy. Four murders solved, weapons off the streets, and Harisha Celik behind bars. He's more than happy with the team you led.

Georgia nodded. 'Melek Yismaz died, though. I just wonder if the press were right. Could we have saved her?'

'We aren't Wonder Women. We did what we could. She nearly killed Alison, and was responsible for the loss of her baby.'

Georgia broke a piece of her crispbread in two, and stared at the Miso soup she had bought at the Japanese deli around the corner. She should try and eat, she knew, but she didn't have an appetite.

The phone rang and saved her the bother.

She checked the caller ID and then pressed the speaker button so Stephanie could hear. Stephanie picked up a pen and pulled some paper away from under her cup to write notes.

Mary in Forensics told them that they had completed the tests on Melek's unborn baby. The DNA proved, without a doubt, that the father was Burak Kaya and not Harisha Celik – exactly the same as Zana's baby.

'Thanks,' Georgia said, looking at Stephanie. 'Confirms the motive for Melek killing Burak and Zana. He two-timed her. Any idea which foetus was the oldest?'

'No, couldn't say on that one, but I have got another piece of information I think will interest you.'

The testing on Harisha Celik's clothing had produced Melek's pubic hair. Backed up by the dried semen found during Melek's post-mortem that tested positive to Celik, it was clear that intercourse had indeed taken place between them prior to her death. Crucially, though, the lab had found evidence of bruising and tissue damage consistent with Melek's account of her rape. Together with Melek's signed statement to Alison, which had been left in Alison's car when Melek kidnapped her, it was the evidence they needed for the CPS to agree to go to court with the rape charge. Georgia lifted her thumb up.

'Any DNA match from the weapons in the tunnel to link them to Celik?' she asked.

'No, it wasn't possible to get any DNA from any of the weapons,' Mary told her. 'It was like someone had wiped every one of them clean before storing them down there. No trace of anything.'

Georgia did have the silver S charm from the lock-up, but she feared that wasn't enough to link Harisha Celik to any firearms. Celik had, very predictably, denied all knowledge of the silver charm and the weapons. Still, Georgia had stuck her neck out and charged him with the offences, requesting that the judge did not allow him bail. If he got bail, both Georgia and Stephanie were aware he would go missing, and possibly harm Alysha Achter or her friends, who he would know had led the police to the tunnel. Georgia wasn't taking that chance. Those girls were like gold dust to the serious crime department, they were, without doubt the best snouts they'd ever had.

The judge had agreed to her request for bail to be denied, and she had been holding her breath waiting on the DNA tests. If there was no DNA on any of the weapons in the tunnel, Georgia would have no concrete evidence to back up Alison's statement, that Melek had assured her Harisha had imported them. Georgia's heart momentarily sank, but then Mary added that there was an unexpected bit of good luck. Whilst testing Celik's clothes, they had found traces of firearms residue, which proved he had been handling them recently. That would be enough, together with the statement from Alison, for the CPS to prosecute him. Georgia was now confident Harisha Celik was going to prison for a long time. This was turning out to be very, very good news.

The fact that the superintendent was delighted with Georgia's team was great, it kept their morale up. However, Georgia knew the real truth was that without Alysha Achter and her friends, they may not have found Alison until it was far too late. So Georgia had kept her promise and had pressured the council's parks and leisure department to again consider rebuilding the play area on the Aviary. The department agreed to reconsider. Deciding that wasn't enough, Georgia had requested help from the borough commissioner, explaining that she believed it was an essential part of helping to lower crime figures. He had been happy to oblige and was told it was agreed. Beir then pushed for them the council to rebuild the community hall at the edge of the estate. This too the council agreed to. It hadn't yet been started, but Georgia told Alysha to be a little patient.

'These things take time, Alysha.'

'Yeah, an' if finding Alison Grainger had taken time, then she'd be dead.'

Georgia accepted the point. She was keeping up the pressure on the council.

The Metropolitan Police had also paid out the weapons reward money to Alysha and her friends. Georgia was delighted when she heard that Tink was using some of it for her hair and beauty plans. The girls were restoring the derelict shop at the edge of the estate that they had now bought from the council. When Tink qualified, the plan was to turn the shop into a hairdressing salon, using the back to give classes on nail sculpture and hair dressing.

When Georgia relayed the news back to the borough commissioner, he agreed it would, ultimately, help to lower crime figures around the area, something neither the police, nor the council or local residents, had managed so far. Yet four teenage girls had made a start.

The day got even better when later that afternoon TIU finally retrieved a deleted message from Zana Ghaziani's computer, sent the day she was killed. The message was from Melek. In it she said that Wajdi had found out that Zana was pregnant, and was planning revenge. She said Zana was to come to the alleyway that day at 2 p.m., Melek had Burak's green cigarette lighter and she wanted to give it to Zana, so it was crucial Wajdi didn't find out where she was going or follow her. There was a PS saying that she was to delete the message from her inbox immediately after reading it, and then delete it again from her machine, so there could never be a trace of it. Somehow Zana had almost managed to do this, another reason it had taken the TIU so long to retrieve it.

'The lighter found at the murder scene was green,' Georgia reminded the team at the closing meeting on the case.

'It was even a little scorched from the blaze, and it had Melek's finger and thumb prints on it,' Stephanie added. With Melek's confession to Alison, that was evidence enough to close that case.

'And the forensic evidence on Burak Kaya and Mrs and Mrs Wilkins is sound,' Georgia told them, lifting a piece of A4 paper, which despite her quick thinking Steph had still managed to stain with a large ring of strawberry milkshake. 'The blood-stained screwdriver found in Melek's handbag matched the stab wounds in Mrs Wilkins' neck,' Georgia told them, 'And the blood-stained screwdriver found at the Ghazianis' shop matched Wajdi's blood only.'

'What a horrible way to murder that defenceless old couple,' said Grahame.

'At least they died quickly,' Stephanie said.

Georgia nodded. 'And a bloodstained knife found in Melek's underwear drawer was a match to Burak's blood. The shape of the blade was a perfect match for the wound to his heart. We know he bled to death from that wound, and we now know for certain it was inflicted with her knife. We also have the confession.'

Stephanie shook her head. 'She obviously tortured him too. His body was covered in machete cuts, and there were cigarette burns over his hands too. All those would have caused a hell of a lot of pain.'

'Jealous attack, no doubting that,' Georgia nodded. 'Melek was sleeping with him as well as Harisha, and that was all right for her, but when she found out he was sleeping with her best friend, she went mad, attacked him with a machete, and then she stabbed him in the heart to finish him off. She knew what she was doing. It was calculated and cold-blooded. She then killed a vulnerable old couple because they saw her kill Burak. And she set her best friend on fire.'

Stephanie looked up at Georgia, 'And she would have let Alison die if it wasn't for those four estate girls finding the tunnel while they were looking for Melek, worried for her safety.'

'Yes, we are very lucky to have those estate girls as snouts, there's no doubting that,' Georgia said. 'And they are turning out to be such good citizens. After all they have been through, all the abuse, and forced prostitution when they were under-age and vulnerable, they are making something of themselves, and fighting to clean the estate up. I'm so proud of them'

'You sound like a surrogate mother,' Stephanie teased.

Alysha, Lox, Panther, and Tink were, once again. gathered in Alysha's flat on the thirteenth floor, all holding paper cups filled with champagne. There was a half-empty bottle of on the table.

'Glad we kept this when we emptied Harisha's stuff out of the lock-up,' Panther said. 'If we'd put it in the tunnel with the weapons, the feds would be drinking it now and not us.'

'Yeah,' Lox agreed. 'But this is a one-off. We don't waste money on booze or drugs no more.'

Alysha tapped the twinkling stud that Tink had pierced into the side of her nose. 'This is a celebration. Tink's going to college, and Harisha is going to jail. We wiped all his DNA and prints from the weapons when we carried them into the tunnel cos we had to wipe our own off, but now the feds have got other DNA of his, linking him to the firearms, that is what I call real good luck.'

'And worth drinking to,' Panther said looking up from studying the gold toenail extensions that Tink had just given her. 'You know, Tink, I reckon I'll never wear shoes again. I love my toenails like this.'

'You need to sit still for 'bout twenty minutes,' Tink told her, 'while the glue on them dries.'

'And you have to make sure you are up and out of the 'ouse, by eight o'clock sharp, every morning,' Alysha told Tink, a proud mother hen. 'School starts at nine, and you ain't missing one bloody second of it.'

'We'll be your models, an' we'll look like popstars all the time, all shiny lips an' great toenails,' Panther said. 'And I'm gonna have permanently straightened hair.' She fingered her bright orange afro, and grinned her wide gappy grin. She had lost a side tooth in a fight but it had never bothered her.

'I don't think I can do miracles,' Tink laughed. 'But I reckon it'll look fabulous with dark red streaks in it.'

'You know, the council reckon they are gonna start on the play area within a couple of months,' Lox said. 'So I've ordered leaflets asking everyone to keep it clean.'

'I'll kick the shit out of anyone who graffities it,' Panther told her.

'The street girls are gonna keep watch on it, the ones that ain't too addicted,' Lox told them. 'I've said they'll get paid a bit for doing that. We're still making good corn from our cut of the money they make on our streets. We're gonna keep that side up, ain't we?'

'As long as the girls that work the streets want to,' Alysha said. 'They gotta be Alley Cat crew though, and fight with us when we need them, cause we will need them,' She flicked her eyes around her lieutenants and became serious.

'People are noticing that we're making changes round 'ere,' she said. 'Gangs are coming after us, so we gotta be ready.'

'What you mean, Queen, are you saying we got trouble brewing?' Tink asked her.

'Yeah, we 'ave got trouble brewing,' Alysha nodded. 'See, I did warn us that it ain't gonna be plain sailing. Well it ain't.'

'But Harisha's definitely going down, ain't he? Lox questioned. 'I mean that fed Georgia promised that he ain't gonna be seeing daylight for years.'

'We ain't gotta worry 'bout Harisha,' Alysha told her. 'We've stitched him up like he well deserved, and 'e's going down for it, but 'e ain't dead, you know.'

'What you saying, Queen?' Panther pushed.

'I'm saying,' she took a breath, 'I ran into Boss and Beat, Harisha's cousins, when I went over to talk to the SLRs street girls yesterday. Them girls are gonna join us, by the way.'

'Great,' Lox said. 'See, we got about seventy in our Alley Cat Gang now. And?'

'And Boss and Beat tried to frighten me. Like I gave a shit, but they did say that all the East Is Best gang had joined them. Said they weren't happy that they'd lost their weapons. Said they had more machetes coming over from Europe, and then they're coming after us.'

The girls looked at each other.

'What you say?' Panther asked her.

'I said, "Yeah, yeah", and like they should try.'

'Well they ain't scarin' us,' Panther said. 'Shall I beat the shit out of Yin, he runs the Chinese lot? The others'll back down if I give 'im a kicking.'

Alysha shook her head. 'I've got a better idea. Boss and Beat have been over this estate selling, did you know that?'

Panther jumped up, and one of her false toenails went flying across the carpet. 'How they fucking dare?'

'Careful,' Tink told her. 'I told you, you gotta stay calm till them nails are cool to go.'

Alysha lifted her hand. 'Cos we are gonna let 'em, that's how they can fucking dare,' she said. 'For now, we are gonna let 'em. They'll think they're cool, an' are taking over this territory. We'll let them, but we'll watch 'em closely, and when they've been doin' it for a bit, we'll have sussed where they keep their stash. We'll sell that info to Georgia Johnson, and get them stuffed up in clink with Harisha. We'll do that wiv the next lot that try it too, an' think they can stink up our estate, and we'll make corn out of it and invest that corn in our tinies and the new youth centre. Eventually no one will mess with us and we'll get a nice youth centre by then.'

'What about the Chinese?' Lox said. 'Cos if they mess up the start of the new youth centre ...'

'We'll run 'em a warning,' Alysha said. 'We'll set fire to a couple of their family takeaways down the East End, and if they don't back off after that, then we'll go after this consignment that's coming over, we'll nick it and we'll hurt them wiv their own weapons, and then we'll turn them in to the feds too. By then we'll have an 'undred girls, and we'll keep building on that, and getting this gang stronger and bigger, an' then we can always guard it, an' we'll 'ave a safe and clean estate.'

'Yeah,' Lox agreed, 'We'll play as dirty as we 'ave to.'

'But only with the bad guys,' Tink said.

'Yeah,' Alysha agreed, 'Eventually there won't be no weapons, and no drugs around 'ere to tempt the tinies with, and they'll have other choices too.'

'I'll get more girls then,' Panther said.

Alysha nodded. 'Yeah, and your job is to teach 'em how to fight strong, hard, and dirty. No one is better than you at it.'

'No one is gonna take this estate,' Lox said. 'I want kids, and I want them to be safe. What about old Robert, the blind man on the Wren block? He got robbed again the other day. They took his radio, evil bastards.'

'We'll find 'em and get it back,' Tink said. 'No one ever is gonna suffer like them Wilkinses did, not ever again.'

'An' we've been clever, mate,' Alysha reminded them. 'Remember, we got the feds up our sleeve. We don't 'ave to be afraid, cause the feds'll always back us, they need us now. And we'll kill, if we 'ave to, if it means protecting the young and old on this estate.'

'We thought we'd killed Burak Kaya,' Lox said. 'Turns out it was Melek done him in.'

'Yeah, but we would if we 'ad to, if it meant protecting our estate,' Alysha said.

'Why don't we call our gang Alley Cat Killers?' Panther said suddenly.

'I like it,' Tink said looking to Alysha for her approval.

'Yeah,' Alysha nodded and put her thumb in the air. 'I like it a lot.'

'Alley Cat Killers it is,' Lox said, high-fiving Alysha and spilling the champagne from the paper cups they both held.

'Let's finish Harisha's booze,' Panther said. 'And drink to Alley Cat Killers.'

Alysha lifted the bottle in the air like an Oscar, 'Alley Cat Killers,' she said, shaking it and sending some of the contents flying in the air like an exploding cork.

'Alley Cat Killers,' Tink said, holding a paper cup under the leaking bottle, then passing it on to Panther.

Panther filled her cup and raised it. 'To the end of them Chinese bastards around here,' she said.

'To the end of any bastards that try to dirty our estate or taint our kids,' Lox said, lifting her cup.

'Alley Cat Killers,' the girls said in unison as they high-fived their cardboard cups to each other.

Stephanie had told Georgia she was taking her to the pub for a very large vodka. All the casework had been put to bed, and normally the squad would go to the pub for a celebration, but they had decided not to out of respect for Banham and Alison's tragic loss.

'You deserve a drink,' Stephanie told Georgia quietly, 'And so do I, so let's down a few together.'

Georgia agreed wholeheartedly.

Just as Stephanie was clearing her desk and putting everything away, and Georgia was putting her coat on, Banham and Alison walked into the investigation room.

'My office, now,' Banham barked at Georgia by way of a greeting.

Georgia flicked a glance in Stephanie's direction and just as Stephanie was about to wink, to wish Georgia luck, Banham turned to her, 'You too, Sergeant Green.'

Surely Stephanie wasn't going to get it in the neck for going to the hospital with Alison without asking for permission from him, Georgia thought. It was an emergency, for heaven's sake. How insensitive could the man get?

Once inside the office Georgia and Stephanie stood facing him. Alison was next to Banham on one side of his desk, and

Stephanie and Georgia on the other.

Georgia thought how pale and ill Alison looked, and hoped she wasn't intending coming back to work immediately.

Banham pulled his chair out and gently helped Alison to sit in it. Then he turned back and looked first to Georgia, and then to Stephanie. It seemed a long few seconds before he spoke.

'There is a certain amount of respect that is expected from officers of your experience and positions,' he said to them, his blue eyes burning into Georgia. 'Telling your superior officer that he is "losing the plot and to get a grip" isn't what I would call respect.' He turned to Stephanie. 'And being told, via a message, that you, Sergeant Green, had taken it upon yourself to go to the hospital with my DI, and "would deal with it," is at the least, insubordinate.' He looked from one to the other. 'Your behaviour towards your senior officers, in front of an army of other officers and civilians, is totally unacceptable.'

Alison turned and looked away.

'I'm very sorry, sir,' Georgia said.

'Well I'm bloody well not,' Stephanie said defiantly, and holding Banham's fixed stare.

Georgia turned to look at Stephanie. Less than an hour ago Stephanie had told Georgia to take it on the chin and apologise to Banham, even though she wasn't in the wrong, and here she was doing just the opposite.

Stephanie opened her mouth to say more but Alison butted in. 'Stop it, Paul!' she said to Banham. Then she shook her head and said to the girls, 'He's winding you up.'

Banham's mouth then spread into a wide smile. 'Sorry. I couldn't help it,' he said. 'It was a way of breaking the ice. Actually, you were both right, and it is I who should be apologising to you.' He looked straight at Georgia. 'I was in the wrong, and I'm very sorry I embarrassed you.' He then turned to Stephanie. 'And I want to offer you my sincere thanks for going in the ambulance with Alison.' There was a pause before he added, 'And for the sherbet lemons.'

Before either Georgia or Stephanie could answer, he spoke again. 'So, by means of making amends, I wanted you to be the first to know that Alison and I are getting married.'

Georgia turned to Stephanie, both looked delighted and bemused as Banham carried on.

'It'll be a small, very small do, but we would both be honoured if you would join our celebrations.'

Stephanie sighed loudly. Georgia turned her head to look at Stephanie. She could read her thoughts. Banham was one of the few officers in the squad that Stephanie hadn't bedded, and she knew, by her friend's large sigh, that Stephanie acknowledged she had now missed her chance.

'I'd love to,' Georgia said smiling at Alison. 'And congratulations.'

Stephanie turned to Alison. 'He's a good catch,' she said. 'Bit of a chauvinist though,' she winked at her. 'Are you sure you're doing the right thing?'

'Watch it, Sergeant Green. I could take that invitation back,' Banham teased, lifting a bottle of champagne out from under his desk and holding it in the air.

Stephanie laughed. 'OK. I'll do anything for a glass of champagne.'

Crime Fiction by Accent Press

Katherine John
The Defeated Aristocrat

James Green
Bad Catholics

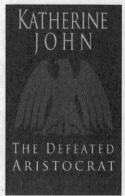
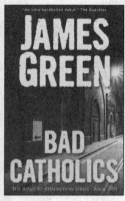

For more information about **Linda Regan**
and other **Accent Press** titles
please visit

www.accentpress.co.uk